Netherworld

by Ari Ryder

Netherworld

by Ari Ryder

Text copyright @ 2014 by Ari Ryder
Illustration by Ashley M. Pringle copyright @ 2022 Poison Apple Publishing.
Interior Design by Ashley M. Pringle.
NETHERWORLD & all related characters and elements are
TM of and @ Poison Apple Publishing.
NETHERWORLD Publishing Rights @ Ari Ryder
All rights Reserved. Published by Poison Apple Publishing.

Library of Congress Cataloging-in-Publication Data is available upon request.

ISBN: 978-0-578-38336-1

Printed in the U.S.A.

To anyone who needs a little hope.

Ari Ryden

Table of Contents

The Miller

A STICK CRACKING IN AN OTHERWISE-SILENT FOREST WAS never a good sound.

Casper Renolds froze, crossbow at the ready, listening. Caution tainted his brown eyes. It could just as easily be a deer as it could a bear, and Casper wasn't keen on meeting the second. The rapaxion bears in this part of the wild were vicious and territorial, not at all like the gentler brown bears to the east. His finger tensed on the trigger. He heard no further warning sound until . . .

"HA!" a voice exclaimed as someone tackled him.

Casper went sailing to the ground, his crossbow firing a bolt into the nearest tree. He was about to throw his attacker off when he realized *she* was laughing. His brow furrowed. When he looked over, he saw his sister shaking with mirth, clutching a stitch in her side. He shoved her off of him, prompting a shriek that trailed into more laughter.

"You should have seen your face!" she wailed.

"Kaelyn!" he growled, tossing a handful of dirt in her direction.

She dodged the bits of earth, grinning all the more.

"I told you to help Gran put the pot on," Casper chastised, attempting to be stern. It didn't work well under her joyous gaze, and he soon found himself smiling.

"I did," Kaelyn replied with a grin. "Which is precisely why I'm here. Supper's nearly ready, and Gran sent me to fetch you."

Casper sighed in defeat. He supposed he couldn't be upset with her for listening to Gran. The would-be hunter rose to his feet and offered his sister a hand. She took it, beaming. "Find anything worth hunting?" Kaelyn asked, almost teasing.

"Well, if I had, you've scared it away," he joked. He yanked the bolt from its poor, undeserving target. "You're lucky I didn't shoot you."

"You would have bloody missed anyway."

He scowled at her.

"Kidding," she amended.

"Aye. You'd better be."

Together they started back down the path, Kaelyn looping her arm through her brother's. They both had the same fair hair, but where Casper's eyes were brown, hers were a glittering blue. At twenty, he was the elder by two years, though it often felt so much more than that. After their parents died many years prior, Casper had become the sole owner of the gristmill and, by law, the male guardian of his younger sister. It was a heavy responsibility, but one he bore with pride.

The journey through the woods wasn't far. Soon they stood at the edge of the tree line overlooking a large wheat field that grew in the space between the forest and the well-worn dirt path to the city. A small stone cottage with a thatched roof stood not far from the giant windmill turning with the breeze. Forest hemmed the gristmill in on all sides, creating a square of natural walls that cut the Renolds family off from the rest of

Wayland. It was a classical and picturesque scene in the fading light of day. The siblings steadily made their way around the crop, ambling as if they had all the time in the world. Kaelyn chattered on about Market Day gossip, but Casper was hardly listening. His mind was instead preoccupied with the coming winter and how they would make ends meet before the first snow settled in. It was a five-mile journey for supplies, and Casper had sold their horse and cart to pay the taxes, forcing him to take flour into the city every Market Day by wheelbarrow. It meant selling less flour, which only got them farther behind.

Kaelyn seemed to sense his distress as they crossed the road, and she cast him an apologetic smile. "Everything will be all right, brother," she assured him, guessing at his thoughts. "You'll see."

He smiled in earnest, his trance broken, and pulled her into an appreciative side hug. He kissed the side of her golden-blonde head. "Aye, it will be," he agreed. It would have to be. He wouldn't let any other outcome be an option.

They'd reached the door by now, and Casper held it open for his sister. Once she'd passed through, he followed her inside and pulled the door shut. The room beyond was small and open with a gnarled wooden floor and stone walls. A perfectly made cot sat in one corner where their gran slept every evening. Stacked on a tiny stool beside it was a meager collection of books, the titles of which had long since been worn down on the spines by continual reading. The center of the cozy room housed a long wooden table with benches on either side where the Renolds family ate their meals, played games, or folded the wash on Leisure Day. Rows of iron pots and pans hung from pegs on one of the ceiling girders, and a handcrafted pine cabinet housed simple tin plates and cheap utensils. A ladder disappeared through a square hole in the ceiling, leading to the second floor, where Casper and Kaelyn shared a room. Near the fireplace, stirring the contents of a large cauldron over the flames, stood Gran. At first appearance, she looked frail and old with a wiry frame, but one look into her piercing blue eyes showed all the strength of a much younger woman. She wore a simple blue dress with a food-stained apron tied around her middle. Her gray hair was piled in an elegant updo, speaking of the neatness and care with which she performed every task. The blazing fire filled the room with warmth, and the smell of fresh stew made Casper's stomach ache with hunger.

"Empty-handed again?" Gran asked, her aged voice full of compassion.

"All the game must have headed north," he replied, leaning his crossbow against the wall near the door. "I could barely find any tracks."

Kaelyn gathered tin plates and set them on the long wooden table, then returned to the cabinet to fetch some goblets and utensils. Casper sat at the table with a heavy sigh, folding his arms over the tabletop. Hunting was almost a fool's errand of late. Casper managed to scare up a few squirrels or a bird now and then, but all the big game was scarce. It only furthered Casper's constant worry. Buying meat in town was far too expensive, and they were near penniless. Flour wasn't selling like it used to despite its necessity. Competing mills had sprung up at the other side of Wayland, and Casper simply couldn't keep up with them on his own. Lord Harlen was threatening to put them out of business if they didn't pay their rent soon, and with the local sheriff in his pocket and a distracted mayor, there was nothing to stop him.

"Never you worry, Casper," Gran spoke in a gentle voice. "Things will turn around. They always do."

She cast him a reassuring smile. He returned it half-heartedly. Gran gestured to the empty plates, speaking to Kaelyn. "Bring me those, would you, dear?"

Kaelyn beamed. "Of course."

As she moved to fetch them, Casper watched his family with a tired gaze, reminded of what he worked so hard for. There were similarities between Kaelyn and Gran when they stood side by side. The same dimpled smile and blue eyes. The same profile. The same gentility that masked a fierceness hidden underneath. He could hardly put a finger on the moment Kaelyn had grown from a girl into a woman, but she was a woman now. Casper wasn't the only one to notice. On the rare occasion when she joined him for Market Day, the eyes of many gentlemen lingered longer than they should, none longer or more uncomfortably than their landlord, Charles Harlen. Casper often kept these tidbits of information from his sister. She was a carefree and jovial spirit. He didn't wish to worry her unnecessarily, but Harlen had already approached Casper more than once, asking for Kaelyn's hand. He wasn't sure how much longer he could keep refusing without repercussion, or how much longer he could keep it from them. They seemed so happy and unburdened as Gran loaded plates with stew, Kaelyn bringing each to the table once Gran had filled it. The less he worried them, the better.

The last plate of stew was set in front of Casper, the aroma of which made Casper's stomach growl. There was no real recipe. The stew was made of whatever they could find and throw together, but somehow it always tasted wonderful. Casper credited this to his grandmother's skill as a cook—a skill she'd been carefully trying to pass on to Kaelyn.

His sister sat beside him. Gran set a wine jug in the center of the table, then sat across from them.

"Would you bless it, dear?" Gran asked of Casper.

"Of course," he agreed.

They each bowed their head respectfully, and Casper offered up a prayer to the Maker, thanking him for the food on their table, the roof over their head, and all that he provided them. It was a well-worn prayer, but nonetheless earnest, even if Casper felt like his prayers bounced off the ceiling lately. When he'd finished, Kaelyn reached for the wine and poured some in each of their goblets. He thanked her quietly, realizing he'd been in his head too much this evening. Not wanting to burden them with his thoughts, he picked a topic of conversation before either of them could ask him why he seemed troubled.

"Have you heard anything of your friend?" Casper asked Gran.

Gran sighed, looking vexed. "It's a bad business," she replied. "The burns were far too severe. There is no hope of her return from the Netherworld."

Casper's heart sank. The Netherworld and all its temptations offered the dead a second chance at life, but a soul needed a body to return to. If the legends were true, then Gran's friend would be trapped in a world between worlds, erased for all eternity. The thought chilled Casper to the bone.

"I'm so sorry, Gran," Kaelyn sympathized, reaching across the table to take Gran's hand.

Gran smiled gently and gave Kaelyn's hand a squeeze. "Thank you, my dear, but I think we all knew it was hopeless. Most who enter the Netherworld never make it out again."

"Some of them do," Casper said without thinking.

Both women turned their gaze on him, Kaelyn's almost a glare. He cleared his throat and attempted to amend his statement. "I mean . . . there's Bash . . . and Harlen."

"*Lord* Harlen, Cas," Gran corrected him. "Just because he's a vile man doesn't mean we should disrespect his title."

Casper resisted the urge to roll his eyes. "Lord Harlen," he repeated quickly, the name leaving acid in his mouth. "Anyway, it's happened before. That's all I meant."

He quickly shoved stew in his mouth to give himself space to think. He'd often had nightmares about the Netherworld—a dark and horrible place with changing landscapes and impassable tests. Gran was right. Hardly anyone survived who chose to fight, but stories were told of some who'd been granted second and even third lives. It made Casper nervous. One day, he too would have to face that cursed place. He'd face the Keeper, and he'd have to make a choice: to fight for his life at the risk of his soul or move on. *I'm definitely moving on,* he thought to himself. *It's not worth the risk.*

He wondered what had made it worth the risk to Gran's friend. Who would risk the peace of the Afterlife to come back to this horrible place?

"Did they find out what caused the fire?" Casper asked.

"No," said Gran. "But I have my suspicions it was no accident."

Kaelyn paused midway through bringing her goblet to her lips. "What do you mean?"

"The fire was far too convenient," Gran explained. "Mary had only just passed her first trial. If you ask me, someone didn't want her to return as a Netherworlder."

"Again with the conspiracy theories," Casper sighed, smiling slightly. "Honestly, Gran."

"They could be true," Gran defended herself, though she didn't seem upset by his jab in the slightest.

"There is no secret order pulling the strings," he assured her. "That's poppycock and tavern talk."

"Why not?" Kaelyn chimed in. "The city is vast. The Outer Edge more so. Who's to say there isn't a vile group of individuals plotting to control things?"

"I say," Casper countered. "What would be the point of that? People like us are already in our place, and people like *Lord* Harlen," he emphasized for Gran, "are already in command of our every move."

Kaelyn cast him a look of stubborn indignance, and he knew an argument would follow. She had a mind of her own, which Casper was actually glad of, but they often rowed about topics like this. He was content to keep his head down and get through another day. Kaelyn was the sort who would rock the boat if only she had the voice and platform to do so.

"People like us could change the world if we wanted to," she retorted. "You just don't want to."

A spark of flame lit in Casper's gaze. He wasn't usually confrontational, but Kaelyn was adept at winding him up. He opened his mouth to fire back, but Gran interrupted.

"That's enough, the both of you. Eat your stew and hop to bed. Lots to do tomorrow."

Casper bit his tongue out of respect for Gran, but he sorely wanted to retaliate. It wasn't that he didn't want things to change; he simply had no way to change them. His responsibility was keeping food on the table and protecting his family. Couldn't Kaelyn see that? But then, he supposed, he didn't want her to see that. He never complained of his worry or struggles. Never told her how many vile and relentless suitors he'd kept at bay since she'd come of age, Harlen the worst of them. He didn't want Kaelyn to know how dark and sinister the world could truly be. This line of thought cooled his temper, and by the time supper was through, he helped his sister clear the table with a stream of laughter and well-timed jokes. After a quick game of cards, they readied for bed.

Casper lay in his bed, staring at the slanted ceiling of the cottage in contemplation. His mind returned to the multitude of worries he couldn't seem to shake that day. He wondered, briefly, if he shouldn't let Kaelyn take more on. She was intelligent and capable. She could keep the books far better than he. It was an idea, at least. Casper set the thought aside for morning, drifting off to sleep, never imagining the thorn he was in a particular man's side or how instrumental he would be in said man's coming scheme.

NEAR THE HEART OF WAYLAND SAT PRIOR STREET, A LONG row of rich estates where Wayland's elite lived in manors made of the finest masonry. At the very end of the row towered a beautiful white marble home with columns at the front and a fine garden in the rear. An iron gate surrounded it, guarded by highly skilled men. This was the home of Lord Charles Harlen, one of Wayland's richest and most devious tyrants. He was by no means in charge of anything, but he had the money and resources to do whatever he pleased, thanks in part to a deal he'd once struck with Death. He owned more than half of the city and its surrounding area, including the mill where Casper tried and failed to make a living.

Harlen was more than just a shrewd businessman. Vile and villainous to the core, he was not easily trifled with. The Netherworld had changed him, made him stronger and more callous. No ordinary man could stand against him. Those who tried were silenced with nary a shred of evidence pointing back to the culprit. The rest were bought off with obscene amounts of coin. If they couldn't be bought, they were threatened with terrors unimaginable, and Harlen never failed to carry them out. In his right hand, he held the sheriff, giving him access to poison the Watch with his own thugs. In his left, Harlen held Wayland's darkest secrets gleaned from a network of loyal (and terrified) informants. The madman had but one goal: to rule the world. Death had given him power, and now Harlen was hungry with it.

Deep in the midst of Harlen Manor, Lord Harlen paced his ornate study, boots hardly making a sound on the expensive handwoven rug. A blazing fire from the hearth was the only light, casting his sharp features in eerie shadow. The man was nearing forty with dark hair to his shoulders, greasy and slicked behind his ears. He'd been handsome once, but age and a dark heart marred his appearance now. Something sinister lurked behind his cold, gray eyes. His white silk shirt was as perfectly pressed as the fitted black vest he wore over it, the solid gold buttons of which gleamed in the firelight every time he took a step. He was in a true rage tonight, barely containing his temper. Despite how powerful Lord Harlen was, Casper Renolds seemed to say no to him far too easily. He didn't understand it. Couldn't comprehend it. Casper was weak, insignificant—a poor, pathetic miller whose future Harlen held in his hands with a choking hold, and yet Casper did not yield. Not when the taxes on his land went up. Not when Harlen threatened every patron to buy from his competitors. No matter how tightly Harlen squeezed, Casper would not give him what he desired most, and time was running out to obtain her. Harlen had been hoping to do this the easy way, but Casper Renolds had stood in his way for far too long. It was time to remove him from the equation. It was for this reason he'd summoned the sheriff, who now lounged in one of the expensive leather armchairs, watching Harlen pace back and forth with apprehension.

Sebastian Carrow, most often called Bash, was different from Harlen in almost every way. Where Harlen seemed refined, Bash was rough around the edges. Broad shoulders and thick muscles were barely contained by the faded brown Watchmen's longcoat, and his boots were caked with mud and something that looked suspiciously like blood. A scar ran over his right eye, shallow enough that the dark-brown pupil was undamaged. His head was shaved bald rather than dealing with the patch where hair refused to grow—he'd been bludgeoned to death on his first trip to the Netherworld. Even his speech lacked the polished accent of a high-born Waylander. The only thing these two men had in common was the Netherworld triad tattooed on their wrists—the mark of those who'd survived the trials. It was in the Netherworld that they'd first met and formed an alliance. An alliance that had continued long after their return to the land of the living. Bash owed Harlen a debt he could never repay, and so he did as Harlen asked, usually without question. A native of the Slums, his moral compass had never pointed due north. Despite this, Harlen's request of murder made Bash uneasy. Killing the miller seemed like too obvious a play to him.

"Are you sure this plan of yours is wise, mate?" he voiced his concern. "I mean, killing the Renolds lad . . . it's a bit much."

Harlen whirled, fire in his eyes. "Have you lost your nerve, man?" he spat.

"No, I just thought—"

"Well, don't!" Harlen snapped. "We both know what happens when you start to *think*."

Bash bristled silently at the offense. It was true, he tended to be more brawn than brains, but he wasn't entirely unintelligent. He had a knack for strategy, which came in handy as the sheriff of Wayland's Watch. Normally Harlen valued that skill, but tonight reason had given way to passion—never a good thing for a Netherworlder. Unchecked rage could do unspeakable damage. Bash tried again, still tiptoeing on the proverbial broken glass.

"Do we even *need* the Netherstone to work?" Bash sighed, doing his level best to keep annoyance out of his tone. "The mayor is still hiding behind closed doors since you killed his daughter. You own most of the city. You may as well be the bloody king."

The corner of Harlen's mouth twitched in a dangerous half-smile, the one he always gave right before he lost his temper. "Have you forgotten our aims, Bash? Why we survived?"

Bash remained silent, knowing Harlen didn't require an answer.

"We must overthrow the Maker," he continued, circling the chair in which Bash sat. "To do that we need to be stronger, Bash. More powerful than a god."

"You mean *you* need to *be* a god," Bash uttered.

Harlen chortled, clapping a hand on the sheriff's shoulder. "Yes, well . . . I'm the leader and you're the lackey for very good reason."

Bash rolled his eyes, but he'd long since learned when to keep his trap shut. Harlen's temper was, after all, how Bash had obtained his dashing scar. "What do you want me to do?"

Harlen moved to the fireplace once more, cold eyes staring into the glowing embers. "Do you still have a contact in the Assassins Guild?"

"Aye," Bash replied.

"Send them a message," he ordered. "Tell them I'll pay any price for it to look like an accident."

"And the girl?"

"She's to remain untouched," Harlen said sternly. "Not a scratch. We need her."

Bash pushed himself to his feet with a resolute sigh. "Very well then. Consider it done."

Harlen didn't say another word. He simply stared like a madman into the flames. Bash took the lord's silence as his dismissal and departed out the study door, shaking his head in disapproval. Harlen didn't care one jot for Bash's opinions. Even if anyone suspected Harlen to be responsible, they wouldn't be able to stop him. Soon no one would be able to stop him. Not even the council. The thought brought a sinister smile to Harlen's lips. The murder of Casper Renolds would change everything.

Murder in the Dark

NIGHT CHOKED WAYLAND'S COUNTRYSIDE IN DARKNESS. Even the moon hid behind the clouds as if it knew something atrocious was about to happen. It was all the better for the nameless assassin standing on the edge of the Renoldses' wheat field. A light hooded tunic of deep ebony covered his torso, cinched with a sash of blood red. Black trousers, leather gloves, and sturdy boots completed the ensemble, all engineered for easy movement and blending into the shadows. A skeletal mask obscured his face with tunic hood drawn—a personal signature. On the rare occasion he let himself be seen, he enjoyed striking terror into the hearts of his victims. Only his eyes were visible, emotionless and cold.

He'd been told very little about his target, only that Lord Harlen wanted him dead and needed it to look accidental. Normally the assassin preferred time to watch his target and assess habit patterns so he could take advantage of them, but Harlen had paid handsomely for the deed to be done tonight. He'd been given enough to know the layout of the cottage and where Casper would now lie sleeping, dreaming of a better tomorrow that would never come. This murder would be simple—too simple in the assassin's opinion. But who was he to complain about the fifteen thousand that would line his pockets, all in gold coin? Certain that all in the household were now fast asleep, he crept through the wheat, barely making a sound save for the rustle and crunch of stalks being pushed aside and crushed underfoot.

He moved across the road and around the cottage, knowing his target well enough to know where Casper ate and slept. The lad would be soundly dreaming in the loft, to which there was an upstairs window. On a warm night like tonight, the window would be propped open to let a breeze into the room. Sure enough, when the assassin rounded the corner, the shutters for the loft window were open, as was the glass pane. Taking a running start, the assassin jumped, launched off the nearby hay cart, kicked off the chinked stonework of the cottage, and grabbed the ledge of the window. From there, it was all too easy for the lithe man to pull himself up and over the sill.

The loft room beyond was simple. Hardwood covered the floor and ceiling, while the walls were the same stone as the exterior of the home. Two pine beds were in the room. Kaelyn slept soundly in the one on the far wall, a dressing table and candle near the headboard. Casper was in the other, nearest the window. The assassin took in the room, studying the floor and every place it might creak if he stepped there. With catlike reflexes, he slunk across the space to Casper's bed.

Casper's mouth hung slightly ajar as he slumbered. That would make the assassin's job easier. He slid a small bottle of clear liquid from a pouch on his belt: a deadly poison containing ingredients found only in the Netherworld, making it nearly undetectable should doctors perform an autopsy. The bottle made only the slightest sound as the assassin pulled out the cork. He was just about to pour the contents between Casper's parted lips when Kaelyn stirred in the other bed.

The assassin ducked behind the curtain that covered the alcove with the wash basin. Kaelyn sighed and rolled over, falling back into her dreams. Once certain she was sound asleep, the assassin slipped from his hiding place and cautiously approached Casper. This time he didn't hesitate before he poured the clear liquid into the young miller's mouth. Casper swallowed automatically at the tickle in his throat, coughing a little.

Time moved at a snail's pace, but the assassin remained unmoving to watch his handiwork. Slowly, Casper's body began to show signs of slowing down. His breathing became labored and the pulse in his neck weakened. Soon the lad struggled to breathe at all. That was when his eyes snapped open, his body attempting to shock itself awake and fight back. It didn't last long. The assassin watched with pride as the light left Casper's eyes, his soul bound for the Netherworld. If the miller passed on, he'd be out of Harlen's hair. If he chose to fight, he'd never make it through the trials. He'd be erased from all existence.

As silently as he'd come, the assassin slipped back through the window, leaving Casper for his family to find.

A HORRIFIED SCREAM RIPPED THROUGH THE RENOLDSES' home the next morning. Gran was startled awake, her aged body moving as fast as it was able. The wooden ladder creaked as she climbed, careful not to catch her foot in the skirt of her nightdress. Her heart clenched when she reached the loft above. Kaelyn was sobbing over Casper's bed, trying in vain to shake him awake. His brown eyes were open, staring blankly, and his skin was a ghostly white.

"Maker, help us," Gran uttered, holding a hand to her mouth as she rushed to Kaelyn's side.

She searched her grandson's eyes, felt for a pulse—nothing. Shock hit her like a stone, nearly crippling her. "He's gone," she whispered.

"No," Kaelyn sobbed, shaking her head in disbelief. "He can't be gone. He can't be."

It didn't make any sense. Casper had been fine the day before. There was no wound. No sign of trauma or illness. Kaelyn didn't understand.

Gran placed her hands consolingly on Kaelyn's trembling shoulders. "He is young and strong," she murmured, "and he loves you so. If he chooses to fight, he may yet return to us."

Kaelyn felt a surge of hope, but she quickly shoved it down, recalling their conversation at the supper table as she turned her watery eyes up to Gran. "You and I both know the chances of that. You said so yourself. Few who enter the Netherworld ever return. It's not designed to be winnable. His soul is doomed if he fights."

Gran opened her mouth as if to negate her granddaughter, but her eyes seemed to agree. She took a breath instead and patted Kaelyn's shoulder. "We will watch him through the day."

Nothing more could be said or done. If Casper chose to fight for his right to live, the empty circle of the Netherworld triad would appear on his wrist, and he'd need a body to return to. All they could do was protect the one he had until he made a decision. Kaelyn looked tenderly on her brother's pale form and respectfully closed his staring eyes. She knew his views on the Netherworld. Knew that it was probably better for him to pass on and find peace with their parents. But there was a stubborn part of Kaelyn that refused to let this be the end. She couldn't stand to lose anyone else.

Casper was also all that stood between her and Lord Harlen. Despite his attempts to keep it from her, she'd caught Harlen's salacious glances. If there was any chance of Casper's returning, she wanted him to know he had her support. He could change his mind. She bent over him, hoping he could hear her wherever he was.

"Fight well, brother," she spoke softly near his ear. "Fight well and come home to me."

AT FIRST, CASPER HAD BEEN DREAMING. HE WAS NEAR THE stream in the woods, the first light of day painting the world with its glow. A doe stood on the opposite bank. It drank carefully from the trickling water, never noting his presence. A twig snapped, deafening in the quiet space. The doe's head snapped up. She spotted Casper, transfixed by his presence, then bolted in the other direction.

He turned, seeing what had truly frightened her. A massive bear ambled up behind him. Casper's eyes grew wide as the beast stood on its hind legs, easily ten feet tall. It made to strike. Casper threw his arms up. The beast's mighty paw threw him into a tree, knocking the breath from his lungs—a breath he never got back. Casper clutched his throat, struggling for air. His body tried to jolt him awake, but his eyes had barely snapped open before the world went black.

Casper crumpled in a heap in a strange darkness, gasping for air. Though he finally inhaled, it felt strange, as if it filled his lungs but no longer fueled his lungs. What sort of nightmare was this? Panic-stricken, he looked about. There was no sunlight, no breeze. Up and down seemed irrelevant. He pushed himself to his feet.

"Hullo?" he called out. His voice echoed in the void.

Where was he? Surely he was still dreaming. He called out again with no immediate reply. As the seconds ticked by, he thought perhaps he would never get an answer. Then, a voice spoke, deep, echoing, and ethereal. It seemed to come from nowhere and somewhere all at once.

"Welcome, Casper Renolds."

Casper whirled. Behind him stood a portly man dressed in brown robes. His head was bald and his eyes black, lacking any real depth. Though he appeared humanoid, Casper had a feeling he was far more than he seemed.

"Who are you?" Casper demanded, taking a step back. "How do you know my name?"

"I am the Keeper," he replied.

The figure said nothing further. He didn't have to. There wasn't a man, woman, or child in Wayland who didn't know of the Keeper: guardian of the Netherworld. Casper's heart fell into his stomach, and he shook his head in disbelief.

"No," he uttered, voice barely there. "I was asleep . . . I was just dreaming. Nothing could have happened."

"And yet you are here," the Keeper replied calmly. He'd seen all this before. The doubt. The bargaining. The inability to understand.

Casper felt like he couldn't breathe. He was scarcely twenty. How could this happen?

"How?" he demanded of the figure. "Surely you must know how!"

The Keeper expected this question. His tone remained patient. "Alas, I do not. I stand outside of time, but I do not have the ability to view all time as does the Maker. I only know what he chooses to tell me."

Casper's head was spinning. The conversation at dinner returned like a gavel against a sound block. He remembered wondering why Gran's friend would fight when it wasn't worth the risk. Perhaps the conversation had planted ideas in his head. Perhaps this was merely another nightmare. And yet, he felt strangely self-aware in a way he'd never been before. He held his hands up, examining them, looking for inconsistencies. They were just as rough and well-worked as before, lacking the absence of detail that usually occurred in dreams.

The Keeper interrupted his thoughts. "You must choose."

"What?" Casper replied, flustered.

"You must choose," the Keeper repeated patiently. "Will you continue on your way, or will you fight?"

This couldn't be happening. Casper knew he'd have to face this day eventually, but he'd been hoping it'd come when he was far into his old age. He knew the stories about the Netherworld—the horrors and the anguish. They were told every Holy Day in church, whispered about in taverns and ale houses, and woven into fables for children. The tale of Nex and Lumen, Death and the Maker, was common knowledge to all in Wayland, even to those who chose not to believe. He could almost hear Gran's voice reciting it to them now, called up from childhood memories hidden at the back of his mind.

"The Maker wanted to test the brave and true, to reward them with long life for facing his tests. But Death was jealous of the praise we gave the Maker while he was spurned, so he tainted the Netherworld and twisted it into a game only the dark-hearted would win. As punishment for his crimes, the Maker sealed Death away in the Netherworld, never to walk the mortal realm again. And he's still there." Gran paused for dramatic effect. *"Making deals, gathering followers, and trying to find a way to escape. We must beware temptation, and when the Keeper comes knocking, we mustn't give in. We must pass on and trust that the Maker has a plan for us."*

The memory stirred fear in Casper. The Netherworld was twisted to test someone in ways that went beyond torture. Sanity and sense of self were lost along the way. Those who survived were never the same. Gran had told him how to avoid this. So had the priests on Holy Day when he'd gone as a child. But something made him pause. A feeling that he couldn't explain. It seemed to prompt him to do the opposite. He knew that was madness. Was it the presence of the Keeper?

"Choose," the Keeper pressed gently.

Casper thought on it further. It would be easier to go on. His parents would be waiting on the other side to embrace him. So would Calvin, whose death was a continual source of private guilt for Casper. He could ask for forgiveness. He wouldn't be alone. He was about to verbally make a decision when another voice filled the void—Kaelyn's voice.

"Fight well, brother. Fight well and come home to me."

Kaelyn. Without Casper there was nothing to stop Lord Harlen from having his way with her. He'd been making advances ever since she'd come of age. By the laws of the land, Harlen could only marry Kaelyn with the consent of her male guardian. Since his father was dead, that duty fell to Casper. And now Casper was conveniently out of the way. Almost too conveniently. Fear held Casper's heart in an iron grip. Even if he chose to fight, he wasn't guaranteed to succeed. If he didn't fight at all, Kaelyn and Gran would be left unprotected. Were these words permission to do the opposite of what he'd been taught? Could there be honor in facing the Netherworld trials if his reasoning were noble? Gran had always said passing on was best, but she didn't judge her friend for trying. Perhaps there were certain circumstances where it was acceptable. He had wondered what had made the risk worth it to Gran's friend. Now, faced with the choice himself, he understood the full weight of the decision. Kaelyn needed him. Gran needed him. His family was more important than his self-preservation.

"Choose," the Keeper pressed again.

"Fight," Casper said quickly. He felt like he'd just eaten sand. He swallowed hard, hoping to alleviate his suddenly dry throat. It did nothing. "I will fight."

The Keeper smiled. "Very well." He bowed. "You will be tested, Casper Renolds. There will be three trials. Pass each, and you may live. Fail even once, and you are erased."

Casper's heart hammered madly in his chest. "What kind of trials?"

"Even I do not know the answer to that. Everything in the Netherworld is a test. It is up to you to decipher which are trials and which are trifles." The Keeper bowed. "Good fortune to you."

"Wait!" Casper shouted as the Keeper started to fade.

Soon the Keeper was gone, and Casper was left alone.

The lad sighed, looking about the void. There was still nothing there. He tilted his head to the side, brow knitting together. Maybe he simply thought nothing was there. He was standing on *something*, so there couldn't be *nothing*. Casper wandered forward, stretching his hands out around him. He didn't run into anything. It was pitch-black, yet still he could see. How was that possible?

He felt as if he'd been wandering for an eternity. He was tempted to sit down and give up, but the Keeper's words echoed in his mind. *"Fail even once, and you are erased."*

There was nothing for it. He had to keep going for his family's sake if not his own.

Suddenly something jagged and rough pressed against the palm of his hand. His brow furrowed. Had he imagined it? He pressed his hand more firmly against it, squinting through the looming darkness. He couldn't truly see it, but the more he ran his hands along it, the more his mind's eye could make it out—a stone wall!

Casper walked on, a hand constantly on the rocky surface to guide his way. He seemed to be in some sort of tunnel. Had it been there all this time? Or had his imagination conjured it? Either way, it was there now and growing more defined with each passing moment.

Soon a light emanated from somewhere up ahead. He could finally see the black, rocky confines of the passage. He continued forward, heart racing hopefully. He broke into a run, grinning when he finally burst into daylight. He found himself on a cliff overlooking a vast desert. His first trial had begun.

The First Trial

WHEN SOMEONE DIES, THERE ARE MEASURES TO BE TAKEN. The body must be embalmed to protect it while the soul is absent. It must be placed in a safe location and kept out of harm's way lest the soul have no body to return to. These were the steps that concerned Gran and Kaelyn once an empty black circle tattooed itself on Casper's forearm—he'd chosen to fight.

The doctor had been at a loss when he'd checked over the body. It seemed all the lad's systems had shut down one by one, but there was no cause that the physician could find. Gran thought nothing of it, but Kaelyn was suspicious. Casper had been young and fit. He'd shown no signs of ailment the night before. It was almost as if someone had nudged his passing on, and Kaelyn could think of only one person who might benefit from her brother's death—Charles Harlen. She lamented that she hadn't been forthcoming with her brother about Harlen's subtler advances. Perhaps if they'd both been honest with one another, they could have avoided all this. But what could they have possibly done? She had no proof of murder and no one who would listen even if she did. It wouldn't be long before Lord Harlen paid her a visit, of that she was certain. Sure enough, he showed by midday.

Gran was hanging the wash on the line when the sound of horse hooves met her sharp ears. The old woman looked up to see Lord Harlen riding up on his black steed. He wore a dark-gray longcoat over his black fineries. He dismounted, taking the reins of his horse in hand, and approached Gran.

"Afternoon, Ms. Renolds," he greeted out of formality.

"Lord Harlen," she replied, dipping her head. Her eyes betrayed her dislike for the man.

"I've just heard the terrible news. I came to pay my respects." He spoke gently, a tone that usually got him whatever he wanted.

Gran nodded toward the cottage. "Pay your respects all you like, but we won't be singin' a funeral dirge any time soon."

Harlen's brow creased. "What do you mean?"

"He has chosen to fight," Gran said pointedly, walking closer, "and if I know my grandson, I know he won't let death take him so easily. Lust after Kaelyn all you want, my lord, but don't make the mistake of thinking her within easy reach. The laws of our land are binding, even for you."

Harlen gave a tight-lipped smile. "Of course, madam."

Nothing more was said. Lord Harlen entered the house. Gran couldn't have stopped him if she wanted. He'd greeted her cordially, and she'd returned it. By the customs of Wayland, he was now a welcome guest on their property. Gran may have been old, but with age came wisdom. To turn Lord Harlen away now would only ignite his rage. There was naught he could do but look at Kaelyn unless she invited him to touch her, something Gran knew Kaelyn had no intention of doing. Even Harlen wasn't fool enough to break the rudimentary laws of Wayland.

The fuming lord looked about the small cottage. When he didn't find Kaelyn in the main room, he made his way up the ladder. He found her in the upstairs loft she shared with her brother. Casper's limp body was laid comfortably on his bed, arms at his sides and eyes closed. His blond tresses seemed to blend in to the pale white of his skin. Harlen wondered what manner of poison the hired killer had used, but he figured he was safer not knowing.

Tall candelabras had been placed around Casper's bed, a symbol of sanctity and mourning. Kaelyn knelt before the bed in silent prayer. Harlen approached carefully.

"Such a tragedy," he said gently.

Kaelyn gasped, head twisting in his direction. Her cerulean eyes looked him over in fear and contempt. With Casper all but dead before her, there was no one to force Lord Harlen away.

"Indeed," she said, turning back to her brother. She couldn't stand to look at Harlen, silently hoping he'd leave. His very presence made her skin crawl.

"How did it happen?" the lord pressed, moving nearer. When he stood just behind her, he looked down on Casper as if he truly cared.

"I'm not sure," she replied. There was a pause. "But I'll find out."

Her words hung in the air like a dare, filling her with determination. If she wasn't sure of Harlen's guilt before, she was certain of it now.

The corner of Harlen's mouth twitched, a half-smile there and gone. "I'm sure you will."

He should have told the assassin to burn the body, but then he supposed it wouldn't have appeared an accident. He needed that facade for his plan to succeed. Lord Harlen's eyes roamed Kaelyn's form, memorizing her curves and wishing desperately to touch her. Even he couldn't escape the punishment for that.

"Is there anything I can do to help?" he offered, hoping to gain her trust.

Kaelyn internally cringed at the offer, but she maintained composure. "Not at present, my lord, but should I need it, you will be the first to know."

"You know where to find me," he said, bowing. "I will leave you to grieve."

"Thank you for your kindness," she uttered. It was more a formality than a sincere statement.

"You will always have it," he replied.

Harlen's smile was as charming as a cobra's. He took his leave then, and Kaelyn finally allowed herself to breathe. Her eyes roamed over her brother's placid face and the stillness of his chest. She dared to hope he'd return to her. It'd only been a day, but already it felt like weeks since his absence. What darkness did he face? What pain did he feel? She sorely wished she could spare him all of it. Guilt gnawed at her insides. This was her fault. He'd been killed for her. She couldn't prove it, but in the depths of her soul she knew it. If she hadn't been an object of intense desire for the filthiest man in the realm, her brother would still be alive. The worst part was there was nothing she could do about it. She did not want or need Harlen's advances: They came without invitation. Why did he want her so? She had no title, no dowry. Nothing but her beauty. Even then, there were plenty of other girls more beautiful than she. Why couldn't the vile man just leave her be?

Kaelyn knew Lord Harlen's advances would only grow worse the longer Casper was gone. She feared she couldn't keep him at bay for long. The very notion made her blood boil. Frustrated and overwhelmed, she descended the ladder and began scrubbing the dishes in the wash tub furiously. Gran entered the cottage, her expression the epitome of concern.

"What did he want?" the aged woman wondered.

"To offer his aid," Kaelyn replied, her anger mounting. She scrubbed one of the tin plates so violently she almost scratched it.

Gran approached and set a hand on Kaelyn's arm to stop her. Without the distraction to channel her fear and rage, Kaelyn crumbled. Sobs wracked her petite frame, and salty tears mixed with the dishwater. Gran didn't say a word. She simply wrapped her arms around Kaelyn and let the girl cry.

FROM HIS PERCH ATOP THE CLIFFS, CASPER COULD SEE A river in the distance. It was difficult to make out through the haze of desert heat, but if he had to guess, Casper would say it was a few hours' journey. Finding water would be his first priority. He made mental markers in the canyon below to keep himself traveling in the right direction, then began the laborious process of descending the cliff face. The canyon wall here was perfectly grooved for climbing. *Almost too perfectly,* he thought to himself. But Casper couldn't dwell on that now. He needed to find water; then he could find shelter from the sun and devise a better plan.

It wouldn't be as easy as all that, Casper soon realized. The moment he reached the canyon floor, all his markers seemed to have vanished. He looked in both directions, finding the path ahead obscured by a flickering heat shimmer. *No matter,* he thought. He remembered seeing the river to the right, so he set off in that direction. Pebbles and loose sand crunched beneath Casper's boots. A few beads of sweat inched down his brow, curling the ends of his fair hair. He rolled up the sleeves of his white tunic shirt, and the farther he walked, the more he was tempted to throw off his umber vest. He settled for unbuttoning it at first, but time, sweat, and the unbearable weight of the fabric presently had Casper shucking the vest off and dropping it to the desert floor. He left it where it fell and continued on.

Buzzards circled overhead, a constant reminder of his need for water. If he died in the Netherworld, he'd fail and he'd never get back to Kaelyn or Gran. On and on he walked. How much time had passed? It felt as if the sun never moved. It simply stayed at the highest point in the sky, beating down on him with reckless abandon. He passed cacti and dry brush, even a few tumbleweeds. It was a landscape he'd read about in stories but never seen. How anyone could live in such a place was beyond his understanding.

After hours of aimless wandering, Casper finally sat on a flat rock to think. The sun remained directly overhead, stuck in a perpetual midday. Due to an unforgiving heat shimmer, the desert seemed to stretch on endlessly in every direction, interrupted only by the jagged canyon walls and few hills that hemmed him in. He had no idea if he was even heading toward the river anymore. If the sun never moved, night would never come. There would be no relief from the endless heat. Casper could feel his skin starting to burn beneath the harsh rays. With no shade anywhere in sight, he was doomed. The buzzards seemed to think so too, circling ever closer, waiting for him to drop. He pursed his lips. He wouldn't give them the satisfaction.

Casper pushed himself to his feet. Sitting had been a mistake. He felt weaker, dizzier. His muscles didn't want to obey, but he forced them forward. That was the point of this, wasn't it? To test his limits?

A chilling howl echoed through the desert canyon. Casper's head whipped in its direction. It sounded akin to a coyote, but something inside him had a bad feeling it was far worse. Fear propelled him forward in what he hoped was the right direction. The mysterious howl sounded again. It seemed to be moving away from him. *Good,* he thought. He had no weapons, nothing to defend himself with but his fists.

Another hour passed, or what he thought was an hour. Casper stopped in his tracks, eyes alighting on a rock in confusion. A sense of déjà vu hit him, followed by a surge of anger. It was the same rock he'd sat on before. Furiously, he kicked up a chunk of dirt. He was going in circles. But how could that be? He'd been walking in a straight line.

Casper turned toward a nearby hill overlooking the dry, cracking valley. It was tall and steep, probably difficult to climb. The thought didn't deter the thirsty Waylander. He needed water, and soon. He made a beeline for the hill, never taking his eyes from it lest it disappear. Dry brush littered the hillside, giving him handholds to navigate the steep incline.

Casper began the climb. The buzzards continued to circle, following his every move, a constant reminder time was running out. The embankment was steep, nearly vertical. His hands quickly became irritated from the plants he used to pull himself up. At first he thought it was simply because they were rough, but soon his hands began to blister and sting. He groaned at the pain. He wanted to let go and fall back down the steep embankment, but Kaelyn's voice echoed in his mind. And then, strangely, it echoed from above.

"Keep going, Cas," it encouraged. His gaze turned toward her intonation. Kaelyn was standing at the top of the hill dressed all in white. Her blonde hair fell in a curtain around her face, blowing in the warm breeze. *"You can do it, Casper. Fight."*

At first, Casper panicked, thinking she might be dead too. But a careful squint revealed her to be made of heat shimmer. She was a mirage of his own making. Casper felt his strength renewed. He reached for the next plant with determination, hoisting himself up another few feet.

"That's it," Kaelyn's visage spoke gently. *"Don't give up, brother. Fight."*

Casper grabbed another deeply rooted plant and another. He cried out at the vicious burning in his hands. Poison ivy was an annoyance, but this . . . this was agonizing. His foot slipped on a rock in the loose soil, and he fell flat against the sharp slope. His grip on the brush was the only thing keeping him on the hill. If he let go, he'd fall back to the desert below.

"Climb," Kaelyn's voice whispered in the wind.

He gritted his teeth, every instinct in his body telling him to let go. It was like holding his hands on hot coals.

"Climb," Kaelyn said again, voice ethereal as if it were the wind itself.

Casper cried out, pulling himself up farther. He dug his boots into the dirt and rocks, gripping each plant like a rung on a ladder. He was halfway up. Three-fourths. Nearly there. Finally, he hoisted himself atop the hill and collapsed on the flatter terrain. Kaelyn's mirage smiled and dissipated. Casper groaned and looked over his burning hands, red as a rose and covered in blisters and cuts. He wanted to lie there and catch his breath, but the buzzards' never-ending circles pressed him to keep moving.

Casper stood on shaky feet and surveyed the terrain. His heart gripped in despair. The river he thought he'd been heading for was gone, and the seemingly endless desert actually went on for miles in one big, canyon-encased ring.

LORD HARLEN SAT AT HIS ORNATE MAHOGANY DESK,

writing in a leather journal. His maid, Anna-Rose, cleaned the fireplace with well-worked hands. Though she was dirty from her day's work, she was no less beautiful. Chestnut hair was piled on her head, matched with equally striking brown eyes. As she worked, she could feel the burn of Lord Harlen's gaze turn on her now and then, raking over her body like a starving child might eye a piece of tempting food. Anna-Rose kept to her work, praying silently to the Maker. Though Lord Harlen followed the laws where Kaelyn was concerned, Anna-Rose knew well and good he'd raped more than one girl who'd caught his eye. They were either killed to keep their mouths shut or lost in the Slums to the whorehouses.

A knock on the study door interrupted the awkward scene.

"Enter," Harlen said, his tone one of boredom.

When the door creaked open, Bash stepped inside. "You wanted to see me, my lord."

"Ah, yes." Harlen smiled, charming as a cobra. "Leave us, Anna-Rose."

The maid silently thanked the Maker for answering her prayers. She stood and dipped her head, making haste for the door. Once they were alone, Harlen set aside his quill and closed the book he'd been writing in. On its dark leather cover was affixed a skull atop the three spirals of the Netherworld triad—the mark of Death.

"Have a seat," Harlen offered, indicating one of the armchairs.

Bash nodded and sank gratefully into one of the chairs. The sheriff didn't have a pleased expression on his face.

"You look nervous, Sebastian," Harlen noted as he stood. He glided to a small cart with crystal bottles and glasses. "Drink?" he offered, gesturing to the libations.

"No . . . thank you," Bash uttered.

Harlen shrugged as if it was no matter to him. The vile man picked up one of the half-empty bottles and poured the aged liquor into a glass for himself.

"A toast," he said, holding the drink aloft. "To your success and our sure victory, my friend."

Bash said nothing as the lord drank.

Harlen rolled his eyes and set the drink on his desk. "Out with it, man. You're making me nervous with your silence."

"I've heard from the council," Bash finally spoke.

Harlen scoffed.

"They aren't happy, my lord."

"The council is never happy," Harlen mused, sitting at his desk once more. "What is it this time?"

Bash shifted uncomfortably in his seat.

"Out with it!"

Bash jumped. He ran his fingers over his bald head. "They believe you are . . . overstepping your bounds," he said.

"Is this news to you?"

The sheriff didn't answer, a wise decision on his part.

"The council consists of old hags," Harlen spat. "They have no vision. No drive. They won't do what needs to be done to achieve our aims. Death chose *me*." Harlen's gray eyes clouded in madness. "*I* was given the stone. *I* was told how to unlock its secrets. The council is obsolete."

Bash still said nothing.

"I do hope you're not getting cold feet, Sebastian. I can replace you with a snap of my fingers."

"No, my lord," Bash muttered.

"Good."

Silence ensued, heavy and chilling as a tomb. Harlen used it to finish his drink and seethe internally. The council was a pack of dogs as far as he was concerned. They were all about tradition and order. Harlen sought to overthrow all of that. For almost a century, the Order of Nex had operated in secret. Most who chose to fight in the Netherworld never made it back out, and those who did tended to side with Death by the time things were said and done. It kept the public out of their affairs and so far allowed the Order to work unopposed. But what had they done in all that time? Death was still a prisoner in the Netherworld, and all this pomp and circumstance got them nowhere.

Lord Harlen stood. "I need to know I can count on you, Sebastian," he said as he strode across the room to the bookcase on the far wall, taking the leather journal with him. He signaled for Bash to follow. The sheriff reluctantly rose from his seat.

"Of course you can, my lord," he answered. Sometimes Bash questioned why he worked for Harlen, but then he thought better of it.

Harlen grabbed the spine of a book entitled *Netherworld History*, pulled it out, and pushed it back in. A metallic click and whirring filled the room. The bookcase sunk into the wall, revealing a narrow hall beyond. The two men disappeared inside of it. Harlen struck a match and lit a candelabra sitting in a niche on the wall. The bookcase slowly creaked back into place, once more obscuring the secret chamber.

The air was damp and cool. Candlelight bathed the dark space in a warm glow, but the way the light danced in Harlen's eyes was sinister. Bash tagged along behind him as Lord Harlen took up the silver candelabra and moved ahead. The sheriff was the only other person Harlen allowed in the passage. He trusted Bash with his life. Bonds formed in death had that effect.

The path soon turned sharply left, opening into a small circular room with a high ceiling. Bookshelves lined the walls with volumes the local clergy might burn at a bonfire: *A Guide to Necromancy, How to Tame Netherbeasts,* and *100 Ways to Get Away with Murder* among them.

Another desk sat at the center of the room, this one far less ornate and more practical. Harlen set the glowing candelabra atop the chipped wooden surface and pulled a key from a hidden chain around his neck. Bash watched the lord unlock the bottommost drawer of the desk and place the leather book inside it. The Order's secrets were not for the prying eyes of the staff to find. He locked the drawer and hid the key beneath his shirt once more.

Bash patiently waited to be noticed. Harlen had called him there for a reason, after all, and it was clearly one he didn't want to risk an eavesdropping servant overhearing.

"Now," Harlen said, seating himself in the high-backed chair behind the desk. "I'm sure you're wondering the real reason I've called you here."

"I was beginning to, my lord," Bash admitted.

"Your man did well. I'm quite impressed."

"Thank you, sir."

"I need him to continue following Kaelyn Renolds."

Bash shifted uncomfortably.

"I want to know when she's in the city, when she sleeps—every move she makes. Can it be done?"

Bash gave a slow nod. "Of course. I only hire the best."

"Excellent. I'll leave you to it, then."

Nothing more was said. Harlen turned to the multitude of papers atop his workspace—all things relating to the Order and their nefarious plans. Bash took his leave, a sense of dread filling his soul. He knew Harlen was mad, but to go against the Order? If their plans failed, they'd be burned at the stake for sure.

Battle of Wits

KAELYN AMBLED SLOWLY THROUGH THE COBBLESTONED streets of town, gripping a basket loosely in her hands, a few vegetables and necessities inside it. Without Casper around to hunt, food was harder to come by. Kaelyn had always helped her brother in the fields and in the gristmill as much as possible, but Casper was far stronger and had more stamina for such a thing. She couldn't hope to work the mill on her own and make ends meet. Gran was hardly able to hang the wash, let alone cut down wheat and grind it into flour. With Lord Harlen's impending dues hanging over their heads, Kaelyn worried for their home.

In her mindless state, she nearly collided with Lord Harlen himself. He gently gripped each of her shoulders to steady her, gray eyes almost staring into her soul. When she'd recovered from the shock, she found her voice.

"Lord Harlen. You gave me a fright."

Harlen released her, aware of the many disapproving eyes turned his way. Fending off an entire town wouldn't be easy, so he had to win Kaelyn by their customs as much as he possibly could. That didn't mean he wouldn't cheat a little.

"Apologies, madam," he replied, inclining his head minutely. "I notice you are about town without an escort. Perhaps you'd allow me the honor of accompanying you?"

"I'm perfectly capable of walking through town on my own, thank you," she returned, pushing past him and continuing on.

There was an acidity to her tone. It wasn't lost on Harlen, but neither did it deter him. He followed after her.

"Really, I must insist," he pressed.

Kaelyn stopped and whirled to face him. "And really, I must decline," she snapped. "It would be improper, and I cannot allow it."

Her raised voice had drawn the attention of many stall keepers and shoppers, clearly a denial of the want of Harlen's company. The villainous lord lowered his voice. "You cannot hide behind our customs forever, madam. Were I you, I'd consider less resistance."

With that, Lord Harlen continued on his way, rather aroused by her stubborn nature. She was like a horse begging to be broken, and break her he would.

NOT FAR FROM THE SCENE, A YOUNG BLACKSMITH'S apprentice stopped hammering a burning hot sword within the shop. His eyes fell on Kaelyn through the open door with a sense of familiarity, and he nearly dropped his hammer to rush after her. "Josiah!" the master blacksmith's voice chastised. "Get back to work!"

"Aye, sir," he uttered, watching Kaelyn disappear down the road.

KAELYN RETURNED HOME BY THE DIRT ROAD, ANGER flushing her cheeks. Harlen was right, though she was loath to admit it. By the laws of the land, she'd have to marry soon. It was improper for a young lady to remain without a male guardian past the age of twenty. Kaelyn thought it a ridiculous custom. Women were perfectly capable of taking care of themselves. Unfortunately, Harlen all but owned the sheriff. Eventually she'd be branded an old maid, disgraced forever. She had to conform, or her very future might be destroyed.

Gran was seated near the hearth mending some of Casper's trousers when Kaelyn entered. The older woman looked up as Kaelyn set the basket on the table. Gran always knew when something was wrong.

"What is it, child?" She signaled for her granddaughter to sit beside her.

Kaelyn moved slowly to Gran's side and took the hand her grandmother offered. She gave a small shake of her head. Tears welled in her eyes—tears of fear and anger. She didn't let them spill over.

"Lord Harlen is relentless," she uttered, voice wavering with emotion.

Gran's eyes glossed over with sympathy. She squeezed Kaelyn's hand. "He will not win, my love," the old woman tried to assure her.

"But if Casper doesn't come back—"

"Then I'll deal with Lord Harlen myself," Gran cut her off. "As long as I'm alive, you won't be a ward of the city. We have time, child. We have time."

Kaelyn nodded, hoping and praying Gran was right. The older woman patted Kaelyn's hand affectionately. "Good girl," she murmured. "Now, let's put the pot on before it gets much later."

CASPER SAT ON THE HILL, BROWN EYES SURVEYING THE dilemma before him. If the desert went on and on in an endless canyon circle, how was he ever to get out? The canyon walls were too high to climb now, and he couldn't see over them. The place he'd navigated down into the canyon had all but disappeared. He was certain he'd seen a river when he'd exited the passage. Where had it gone? Over and over, he tumbled the facts in his mind. He recalled how the tunnel had been a void and then, suddenly, the light materialized and he was in the desert. Perhaps the landscape constantly changed? If so, could it change again and offer a way out?

A sudden movement in the valley caught his eye. A man ran for his life, a great beast at his heels. It was large with gnarled, leathery skin, sharp-clawed fingers, a squared head, and a mouth that was nothing but jagged teeth. Its forearms were longer than its hindlegs. Though it ran on all fours, its anatomy suggested it could also stand on two legs, leaving its large forearms free to rip a man in half. Casper rose fleetly, looking about for something to help. He quickly realized it was no good. The hill was steep and difficult to travel. By the time he made it down, he wouldn't be able to reach the man in time. Besides that, he had no weapons and the creature looked fast. For the safety of his soul, he elected to stay put.

Casper watched in horror as the beast pounced on the man, biting and ripping him in half with its strong jaws and clawed hands. The miller's heart pounded in his chest, eyes transfixed in shock. The beast gave a high-pitched shriek. Casper crouched instinctively, hiding among the stinging brush but not touching it—he wouldn't make that mistake again.

The beast sniffed the gory mess spread across the desert floor but didn't eat it. Instead it huffed and melted into the sand. Casper stared at what used to be a fellow Waylander, now a bloody pile of meat on the desert floor. The buzzards descended quickly on the feast. Casper's heart hammered, and his mind raced. To die in the Netherworld was to be lost forever. That poor man had just been erased from existence eternally.

Shaken, Casper pushed himself back to his feet, grimacing at the pain in his hands. The situation was hopeless. How could he survive a place that didn't seem to have any rules? He knew if he stayed on the hilltop much longer, he'd regret it. Either the Keeper would mistakenly think he'd given up, or that terrible creature or something far worse would find him. It was best to keep moving.

Casper slid down the incline, careful not to touch the stinging brush unless he absolutely had to. Going down was far easier than climbing up, gravity aiding in his descent. He soon reached the bottom and glanced in either direction. Since the canyon was essentially a large ring around the hills in the middle, both would lead him back to the same spot, but he had to go somewhere. He chose left. It was the opposite of the direction he'd been traveling. Perhaps it would make a difference, though he had his doubts.

Like before, he walked for ages until he came to the same boulder. He didn't even blink. He simply kept going. What else could he do? To sit down would be to surrender. He couldn't give up. Not on Kaelyn. Not on Gran.

The buzzards had abandoned their circling for a while, distracted by the mess the creature left behind. That suited Casper just fine, though he pitied the man. After what he judged to be an entire day's time of wandering the cursed land, a sound caught his ear from somewhere up ahead. He stopped in his tracks. Impossible.

Casper craned his ear, praying he wasn't imagining it—the sound of roaring water. It was definitely real, tantalizing his parched throat with the promise of a cool drink. He broke into a run despite his weary body. Louder and louder the sound became until he finally noticed a split in the rocks between two plateaus. It was impossible to see walking in the other direction, disguised carefully by the twist in the rocks. At least, that was how Casper rationalized it. It simply hadn't been there before. But it was there now, and that was all that mattered. Casper raced for the narrow passage, the thought of water fueling his exhausted muscles.

The screech of another beast echoed through the canyon. Horrified, Casper glanced behind him to see it hot on his heels. He willed himself to go faster, bursting for the narrow passage ahead. Casper wedged into the tight space just as the creature jumped. *Crash!* The beast slammed into the rocky plateau, far too big to fit through the narrow opening. It swiped one of its large claws at Casper, barely missing the lad's shoulder. Angrily it tried again and again, but Casper was already out of reach. The monster gave an ear-shattering shriek.

The path rounded a corner, taking Casper out of the beast's line of sight. It was so narrow a walkway, he had to walk sideways. Even then, he was still wedged between the two towering walls. He nearly got stuck a few times, but with a little effort, Casper managed to push himself through. The sound of rushing water grew louder and louder as he maneuvered the twisting passage. He could almost smell the refreshing scent of a river.

Finally, he squeezed out of the narrow crevice. He stood on a small ledge beside a roaring waterfall that fell from the plateau high above. It descended another half mile below the small ledge he stood on, feeding a river below—the one he'd seen before!

Casper held his hands aloft, allowing the water to ease the pain of his burns. He cupped his hands and gathered water in them. Just as he was about to sip the sweet life force, something caught his eye on the opposite ledge. There was a basket of bread sitting there. Not far from it, a crossbow.

Casper dropped the water and surveyed the land. His mind pondered. Yes, he was hungry and thirsty—all the things he should be after nearly twenty-four hours trapped beneath the blazing sun. But he remembered the void, how there'd been nothing and something all at once. It wasn't until he'd ignored his logic that he'd found a way out. Casper's tawny eyes took in the waterfall, so tempting and beautiful. It looked real enough, felt real enough, but something in him was suddenly wary.

All at once he realized he felt tired and hungry, but he *wasn't* tired and hungry. Somehow he knew the water and bread would do nothing to sustain him. He didn't *need* them.

"I'm already dead," he whispered aloud to himself.

The earth tremored. Casper gripped the cliff face, nearly tumbling into the chasm. The breadbasket faded away, as did the crossbow. The waterfall remained. A searing pain cut through Casper's wrist. He clutched it tightly, trying to remain upright through the quake. In the twinkling of an eye, everything calmed. Casper leaned against the jagged, rocky wall and held his arm before his eyes. There, tattooed freshly inside the black circle on his wrist, was a clockwise spiral: the first etching of the Netherworld triad. He'd passed the first trial.

A New Alliance

THE DAYS PASSED SLOWLY IN WAYLAND. KAELYN WORKED the gristmill in the early morning and tended to matters of the house in the afternoon. Gran never left the cottage except to hang the wash or feed the few chickens they had left. Winter's chill was setting in and growing more miserable by the day. Gran's aching bones protested the weather.

Come evening, Kaelyn could always be found at Casper's bedside, smoothing his hair and whispering silent prayers to the Maker. She often fell asleep there, head lolled on her arm and hand atop her brother's. No matter how Gran coaxed, Kaelyn couldn't be persuaded to her bed.

Time was different in the world of the living. What might feel like days in the Netherworld had been weeks for Kaelyn. Her vibrant blonde hair had dulled, and dark circles constantly lined her eyes. The townspeople whispered whenever she walked through town—things like "Poor girl" and "Glad it's not me."

Most of the town sympathized with the Renolds family. George and

Marta Renolds were once well-respected members of society. George had always been fair in his dealings at the mill, and Marta was the kindest healer to ever grace the streets of Wayland. Many often noted how Kaelyn favored her mother. Since the death of their parents, the Renolds siblings had become ghosts, mingling with few save for the business dealings they had to make. Kaelyn considered Casper her closest friend, and she was far too busy helping Gran to bother with socializing.

Though most of Wayland would gladly aid Kaelyn and Gran, fear kept their hands tied—fear of Lord Harlen. He owned most of the city, and his brutish thugs on the law force were well-trained dogs. If he snapped his fingers, the sheriff would burn an innocent man at the stake—the only way to ensure a soul couldn't return from the Netherworld.

Again, Kaelyn wandered through the city market district, unescorted, for supplies, and again Lord Harlen wasn't far behind.

"How are you faring, madam?" he questioned in a gentle tone.

Kaelyn didn't bother to look up from the fabric she was perusing. Gran needed a new winter dress, and Kaelyn wanted a few more blankets before the frost settled in.

"Ignoring me is a clever tactic, but it changes things very little," Harlen warned.

"As do your continued advances," she mused, pointing out a blue fabric to the shopkeeper. The man nodded and began measuring it out for her.

Harlen stepped closer, near enough to smell the soap in her hair. "You know, I could buy you much finer things—silks and furs from the farthest corners of Wayland. Diamonds from the Civilization Across the Sea."

"Your mistake is in thinking I care about those things," she said sharply.

The shopkeeper placed the simple fabrics in Kaelyn's basket, and she pulled the necessary coin from her leather pouch.

"Then pray tell me what you do care about, and I shall make it yours."

Kaelyn's crystal-blue eyes finally landed on the lord, an icy hint to them. "My brother," she answered plainly and walked off.

Lord Harlen's eyes followed her, determination in their cold depths. His jaw tightened. He went after her as he always did, but just as he caught up to her, so did another man—a much younger man.

"There you are," Josiah said with a smile to Kaelyn, placing a loaf of bread in her basket. "You had me worried, love. I thought we'd agreed to meet by the fountain in the square."

Kaelyn looked into the man's playful green eyes. His eyebrows quirked upward, urging her to play along, and she smiled gently.

"Yes, we did," she confirmed as he took her basket. "I'm sorry. I got distracted by the fabrics and lost track of time."

"Aye, you would," he chuckled. The blacksmith's apprentice turned to Lord Harlen. "Thank you, my lord, for walking with her thus far. There are many unsavory characters about in so big a city."

Harlen gave a tight-lipped smile. "Of course."

Josiah set a strong and protective hand on the small of Kaelyn's back. "Come on, darling. We'll be late."

She smiled and gave a curt nod to Harlen. "My lord."

With that she walked on, the apprentice close beside her. Lord Harlen watched them go, malice in his eyes. Once they were out of earshot, Kaelyn's smile faded.

"You're a fool," she muttered under her breath.

Josiah grinned. "A simple 'thank you' will suffice."

"I can take care of myself," she spat stubbornly.

He nearly laughed. "Yes, I can see that, milady."

Kaelyn shot him a look, instantly struck by how handsome he was. He couldn't be much older than Casper. The thought scared her. She reached for the basket.

"Right, well . . . thank you. But I should go."

His eyes softened, and Kaelyn felt a strange glow in her heart. "At least allow me to see you safely home," he requested. "I've watched Harlen pester you for far too long. I'd feel better if I did."

Kaelyn couldn't deny the offer pleased her, but fear overtook her momentary joy. "You'd be signing your own death warrant. I can't allow that."

She tried to tug the basket from his strong grip, but his hold remained, eyes playful. "Do you really think I care? Someone has to look out for you with Cas gone." His eyes became serious, almost nostalgic.

"Consider it the duty of an old friend."

Kaelyn looked him over curiously. "Old friend?"

"Don't tell me you don't remember me," he teased, grinning. "I guess you were pint-sized last time we met."

"What was your name again?" Kaelyn asked.

"Josiah Grimm," he replied, bowing in an overly animated fashion. "At your service, milady."

Her mouth fell open a little, and a smile soon followed. "You used to dip my hair in the inkwell at Primary Academy." She punched his shoulder playfully as if in revenge.

He laughed. "Aye, that I did. And terrorized you in the wheat fields with your brother. I was sorry to hear what happened."

They both fell silent at that.

"So," he finally said, playful nature returning, "at the risk of being turned down twice, might I walk with you, milady?"

Memories flooded Kaelyn's mind of a happier time. How had she forgotten about him? He and Casper had been the best of friends as children. Her brother had retreated so far into himself in the last three years that he had no friends to speak of anymore. Kaelyn thought of the long walk to the countryside and of Josiah's offer. Suddenly she felt far safer with a familiar face by her side.

"All right." She smiled, gesturing to the basket. "But only if you carry that."

"I wouldn't have it any other way, milady," he replied, a sparkle in his eye.

Over the course of their five-mile journey, Kaelyn learned that Josiah too had been orphaned. A house fire had claimed his parents' lives, leaving no possibility of return from the Netherworld if they'd chosen to fight. He'd been fourteen at the time, old enough to pick up an apprenticeship at Stark's blacksmith shop in the city. He was training to one day own and run the shop, as Stark had no heirs. Nothing seemed to faze him, not even Lord Harlen. It was as if he had no fears at all. Kaelyn almost envied him.

He wore a faded black longcoat over his simple clothing. All the fineries in the world couldn't make Lord Harlen half as appealing as Josiah. He made her laugh and feel alive again.

"Then there was the time we built a fort in the woods," Josiah recalled.

Kaelyn beamed. It'd been so long since she'd smiled this much. "I remember that!"

"And you were so mad we wouldn't let you in without a password." He chuckled.

"You never did tell me what it was," she mused.

He grinned. "There wasn't one."

Kaelyn playfully smacked his arm, but she couldn't wipe the smile from her lips. "You're terrible!"

Josiah laughed warmly and brushed a strand of ebony hair from his forehead. Kaelyn noted the leather cuff he wore.

"That's lovely," she commented of the design.

"What? This?" He smiled, holding up his wrist. "Something I made when I was a lad. Wanted to try my hand at leatherworking. It's just my family crest."

"You made it?" she smiled, reaching to touch it. "It's beautiful."

"Perhaps I'll make you one," he mused, adjusting the basket in his hands.

They emerged from the trees, the Renolds family cottage in sight down the road. Gran raced out the cottage door, moving faster than Kaelyn had ever seen. Initially, Kaelyn panicked, moving swiftly to meet her grandmother, Josiah close behind. Gran spoke, aflutter with excitement.

"He's done it!" she exclaimed. "He's done it!"

Gran took Kaelyn's hand, all but ignoring Josiah's presence. Kaelyn's heart leapt as her grandmother pulled her inside. She flew up the ladder and dashed to Casper's side. Sure enough, the first spiral of the Netherworld triad was tattooed on his wrist. Happy tears filled her eyes.

Josiah left the basket on the table and ascended the ladder at top speed. A creak sounded on the floorboards as he stepped onto the landing. Kaelyn turned, tear-stained eyes glad to see him. "He's going to make it," she said hopefully.

Overcome with emotion, she threw her arms around him. Josiah smiled, eyes alighting on his old friend's limp form. He thought of their school days—a time when the world was rosy and all that mattered was fun. Josiah felt a sudden protective urge and held Kaelyn closer. She was still that little girl who used to tag along behind them, protesting they had to let her play too. A hardness came over his eyes. If Lord Harlen thought he was going to touch one golden hair on Kaelyn's head, the bastard was sorely mistaken.

CASPER SAT AGAINST THE ROCK WALL IN RELIEF, BREATHING heavily. Only two more trials to go. The first one hadn't been so bad . . . aside from the stinging brush and never-ending thirst. He was certain his fair skin was sunburned in every place it could be. Would resting be considered giving up? He sorely wanted to sit there for hours.

The miller's eyes looked directly across the chasm the waterfall fell between. It was only twenty, perhaps thirty feet across. He strained his eyes. It looked as though there might be another passage on the other side. His heart rate sped. Just at the edge of it, a pair of eyes was watching him.

Slowly, Casper stood, keeping his eyes glued to what he was certain was another person. The harder he looked, the more his eyes adjusted, seeing a nose, rosy cheeks, and deep red hair—a woman. She realized she'd been spotted and gasped, tearing off into the dark void behind her.

"Wait!" he shouted.

Casper judged the distance across the chasm and took a running start. He vaulted over the rift, barely landing on the other side. He nearly tumbled backward but quickly righted himself, far too interested in the presence of another person to listen to fear. Fleetly he ran, bursting into the tunnel ahead. He was in a void like the one before. "I just want to talk," he called, voice echoing in the dark space. How in the world was she navigating? He couldn't see a bloody thing. "Hullo?"

Logically, he should hear her footsteps or at least heavy breathing. He heard neither. Suddenly cold steel pressed to the back of his neck. He froze.

"Make one wrong move and you're dead," the woman's voice echoed.

Casper glanced over his shoulder just enough to see her sharp features and fair face. She had to be near Kaelyn's age, but her eyes looked much older. This was a woman who'd seen and done too much.

"I'd appreciate it if you didn't," he mused. "Death is final here."

"Then you won't mind answering a few questions."

"The sword is unnecessary, but ask away."

"Who are you? Where are you from?"

"Casper Renolds. I live on the Outer Edge. Satisfied?"

She pressed the sword tip harder against his skin. "Not remotely."

"Ow," he uttered sarcastically.

"How did you do it?" she demanded.

"Do what?"

"Pass the trial. I saw you clutch your arm. You passed the first trial. How?"

Casper sighed. "I don't know. I just did." He grew agitated. Was she another trifle the Keeper spoke of? "What the bloody hell do you want?"

She said nothing at first, deliberating. Finally, she withdrew her sword and slid it back into its sheath.

"Hmm . . . you're very brave, Renolds," she mused.

He faced her. She had a tough way about her, but she was no less beautiful for it.

"I like to think so," he quipped.

"But you're also foolish."

Casper's eyebrow quirked. "And why's that?"

"You shouldn't have followed me."

She turned away and walked on. Casper fell into step behind her, able to see her and nothing else around him. "Why not?"

"You could have gotten lost in the caves," she explained.

"Caves?"

"Aye, the bloody caves or . . . whatever it looks like to you. What do you see?"

Casper didn't want to sound crazy if she really did see something, but he answered anyway. "I don't see anything."

The woman shook her head as if he were unbelievably ignorant. "You're looking with your eyes," she said. "This isn't Wayland. You must see with your heart."

Casper's brow creased. "How do I do that?"

"Believe and it will be there," she replied patiently, not bothering to slow in her walk.

Caves, she'd said. He thought on her words, allowing himself to believe her. They were inside a cave. And then, all at once, the void shifted and the darkness was replaced by a large cavern. Casper looked on in wonder.

"Incredible," he whispered.

The woman smiled to herself, leading on. She seemed to know her way around the many passages.

"Where are we going?" he questioned.

"I have a camp not far from here," she explained. "These passages run between all the layers of the Netherworld. It's the only place the shriekers won't go."

"Shriekers?" He skirted a large stalagmite, processing her words.

"Aye," she replied. "Huge, vicious Netherbeasts that hunt lost souls."

"I saw one of those," Casper uttered, remembering what had torn apart that poor man back in the desert.

"I'm not surprised," she uttered. "They're bloody everywhere. Thus why I keep to the caves as much as possible."

They walked in silence for a while, Casper pondering her words and filing away the information. He studied her in the meantime. The way she carried herself. Her unwavering confidence. There was an air in her accent of being higher born. "Who are you?" he finally pried. "If you don't mind my asking."

"Depends on who you ask," she answered, unfazed. "You can call me Iris."

"Iris," he repeated. "Are you from the City, the Edge, or the Civilization Across the Sea?"

"The City. But I doubt we've met. I've been here a long while."

It was then that Casper noticed her wrist—a complete Netherworld triad. "Why are you still here?" he asked, fear creeping into his soul. Would he get trapped here as well?

Iris ducked below a row of long stalactites. He followed suit.

"Because something is wrong with my body *out there*," she explained. "I'm in some sort of death-like sleep, and not the same as you might be thinking. My soul is very much in my body, and it's very much here. I'm stuck between life and death."

"A comatose state," he thought aloud. "That's a bad business."

"Aye, but now that you're here, that's all about to change." A smile crossed her lips, one he didn't very much like.

"And why is that?" he pressed. He had a feeling he wouldn't favor the answer.

Iris's bright green eyes gave him a once-over. "Because you're going to survive," she answered. "And then you're going to save me."

Casper was silent. Of course she'd want something of him. He liked the idea of surviving and returning to Kaelyn, but he wasn't sure he could trust Iris. "How can you be so sure I'll make it out?"

"Because I'm going to help you," she clarified. "I've been here a year, or at least I lost count at a year. I know all the ins and outs. All the rules. You need my help."

Casper had to admit, it sounded a fair deal. She aids him in return for his help. Iris was truly taking more of a risk than he was.

"Do we have an accord?" she asked.

"You barely know me," he pointed out. "How do you know I'll follow through on my promise?"

Iris grinned. "Because you've an honest face," she teased. "And really what choice have I? Is it a deal?" She offered her hand.

Casper hesitated, looking from her hand to her fair face. It could be another test. Maybe she wasn't really there. But what if she was? What if she really could do as she said?

Iris seemed to understand his hesitation.

"You won't see another human being in the Netherworld, mate," she clarified. "We're all souls here."

Casper took a deep breath and scratched his neck nervously. What did he really have to lose? "Aye. Deal," he decided, shaking her hand with a wince—he'd forgotten they were still burned.

"Excellent." She beamed. "Now, let's get those hands taken care of."

They rounded a corner into a wider passage. A roaring campfire burned despite the lack of need for one. Crates of supplies and weapons were stacked in a neat semicircle around the camp. Iris began digging around in one of the boxes while Casper stood idly by, feeling out of place. She withdrew a container crafted from a large palm leaf, molded into a jar and tied by some sort of grass-like string.

"Sit," she ordered, gesturing to the smaller crates near the fire.

Casper did as he was told. "Where'd you find all this?"

Iris shrugged. "All over the Netherworld. It's constantly changing. You never know what you'll face when you exit the passages. For some reason, the caves are unaffected by Death's power. Something to do with the Keeper, I expect."

She used her fingers to dig a paste out of the leaf jar and carefully applied it to his sore hands. He winced, nearly pulling away.

"Sorry," she murmured.

He shook his head, signaling it didn't matter. She continued her task.

"Tell me about Wayland," she requested gently, her tough manner gone. "Is the mayor still feuding with Lord Harlen?"

Casper shook his head. "More like Harlen is the ruler and Farrel is the figurehead."

"I thought as much," she muttered.

Silence abounded after that. Casper let his eyes wander the camp, trying to imagine living there alone for so long. He'd rather face death than an eternity trapped in the Netherworld. Living alone wasn't a problem for him—alone was something he did well. But after seeing those beasts—shriekers, Iris had called them—he wasn't sure he wanted to stay in the Netherworld much longer.

"You must be highly intelligent to have passed the first trial as quickly as you did," Iris commented. She glanced up at him.

Casper shrugged. "I'm not certain of that. It simply didn't make sense to me. I had the same sensation I get when hunting—the feeling you get when all the forest goes quiet and you know something is wrong. I merely listened to it."

Iris humphed. "Most thirsty men would have guzzled the food and water and thought on it later. Rule number one in the Netherworld: eat nothing offered you."

"But—"

"Nothing," she repeated sharply. "This isn't Wayland. You're no longer bound to your mortal body and its limitations. Stop thinking as a Waylander if you want to survive."

"How should I think?"

Iris finished applying the salve to his hands and bound them carefully with cloth gauze. "You're a spirit with no true body here. You can still feel pain, still bleed, but you won't die quite as easily. You don't need food. Sleep is a thing of the past. Only a Netherworld creature or another soul can end you here. You could jump of a cliff if you wanted and still survive—Death's way of making sure we don't try to off ourselves."

This piqued Casper's curiosity. "What if you pushed me off said cliff?"

Iris smirked. "Then, maybe. Suppose it would depend on how hard you fell."

Suddenly she paused, eyes far off. Her smirk morphed into a more genuine, soft smile.

"What is it?" Casper asked.

"My father is visiting me," she replied softly. "He's talking about Mother and the house."

"You can hear him?"

Iris nodded, green eyes meeting his gentle ochre. "I'm trapped between both worlds, so I hear both." She looked down, trying to hide the sadness in her eyes. He felt a sudden surge of sympathy and set a bandaged hand atop hers.

"Thank you."

Iris met his gaze once more, regaining herself. "We should get started. You have a lot to learn before your second trial."

Killer Instinct

THE CITY OF WAYLAND WAS DIVIDED INTO TEN DISTRICTS, each of which had its own jail and a deputy to oversee the law in that section. Every deputy answered to Bash as the sheriff, and as such, they were all of questionable character and equally in Harlen's back pocket. Normally the sheriff was appointed by the mayor. The job came with a generous stipend and a home, which was attached to the jail. Bash hardly spent time in the little cottage. It was far too homey. He preferred the brothels in the Red Lantern District and the pubs in the Slums to the niceties Harlen often enjoyed. It was for this reason he could usually be found sitting in the jail pestering its occupants rather than reading by the fire.

This was where Lord Harlen found him when he pushed open the jail door the day after Josiah's interference in the matter of Kaelyn Renolds. Bash sat behind his desk with his feet propped atop it. He picked his teeth lazily with a sort of toothpick. A vile grin spread across his face at Harlen's entrance. "I wondered when you might pay me another visit," he mused in a deep voice. "Trouble in paradise, mate?"

"Something like that," Harlen answered with an ill-amused smile.

The sheriff removed his feet from the desk and sat up, leaning against the desk with interest. The three spirals of the Netherworld triad were visible on his wrist. "What can I do for you now, Charles?"

Harlen sat in the wooden chair across from Bash. "Renolds passed his first trial," he said bitterly.

"So the town whispers," Bash replied, smirking. "He's a far braver lad than you give him credit for."

"This isn't a joke, Sebastian," Harlen warned.

The sheriff stiffened. "It's Bash."

Harlen merely stared quietly at the man, waiting. The lord was used to getting his way.

Bash sighed. "What do you want me to do about it? My hands are bloody tied."

"Nothing yet," Harlen said, a dangerous glint in his eyes. "He may not pass his second trial. There is another . . . *problem* I need dealt with."

Bash waited patiently for explanation.

"Kaelyn has another possible suitor. I need you to make him disappear."

"Won't it be a bit obvious who made him disappear? First Casper, then this poor bloke."

Harlen's gaze hardened. "Don't forget who is responsible for your surviving the Netherworld. When I say jump, you say . . ."

"How high," Bash muttered, resisting the urge to roll his eyes. He leaned back in his chair. "Any particular way you'd like it done?"

"No. Your contact did a wonderful job last time. I trust you won't fail. I don't even care if it looks like an accident. Just get it bloody done."

"Who's the unlucky bastard?"

A vile grin crossed Harlen's lips. "The blacksmith's apprentice, Josiah Grimm."

IT WAS LATE, WELL PAST MIDNIGHT, AND YET THE FIRES of the blacksmith shop still roared. Josiah had spent so much time with Kaelyn of late, he'd fallen behind in his work. His master didn't mind once he'd discovered where Josiah was disappearing to. So long as he finished his work, Stark allowed the lad to do as he pleased. The apprentice often found himself working into the wee hours of the morning, only to sleep a few hours and wake at sunrise.

On this particular night, he was working on a pair of horseshoes due to be picked up the following morning. His body glistened with sweat as he worked close to the flames, sleeves rolled up and shirt untucked beneath a dingy blacksmith's apron. The leather cuff on his wrist caught the fire's light.

Josiah stoked the flames a little more and held a burning horseshoe in the fire with a pair of tongs. It glowed brighter. He moved it quickly to an anvil and hammered away at the pliable metal. For a while, the clanging was all he heard. Suddenly he paused mid-swing, eyes alert and body stiff. He thought he'd heard a creak on the stair. The noise didn't present itself again, so he shrugged it off, blaming it on his exhaustion.

The apprentice went back to hammering the red-hot horseshoe. It was the last of the set, and he desperately wanted to finish and get to bed. Without warning, a leather cord wrapped around his neck from behind. His tools thudded across the dirt floor. Josiah tried to yank the cord away, but his attacker tightened it, cutting off Josiah's air supply almost completely. The apprentice's eyes changed from panic to rage all at once. With a growl, he jammed his elbow into the assassin's stomach. As the attacker doubled, Josiah threw the man over his head.

The assailant was dressed all in black with a skeletal mask over his face. Josiah had little time to catch his breath before the assassin lunged at him again. The apprentice dodged with surprising speed, diving for a nearby water bucket. He swung the wooden pail hard. A resounding crack sounded on contact, but the attacker was only momentarily stunned.

The assassin produced a thick metal chain, spinning it tauntingly. He made to swing it at Josiah. The apprentice fleetly chucked the now-empty bucket at him. It did no damage, but it was enough to catch the assailant off guard. It gave Josiah the split second he needed to whirl and grab the nearby shovel. The assassin swung the chain wide with an angry growl. Josiah blocked with the shovel, a nasty clang ringing loudly near his ear. They struggled for a while, both throwing hits that never landed. The assassin grew frustrated. Bash had never mentioned the boy knew how to fight.

Josiah eventually knocked the chain from the killer's hand and took a swing at him with the shovel. The man gripped the tool and used the apprentice's motion to throw him away. The shovel thudded in the dirt, forgotten as the assassin dove atop Josiah from behind. The apprentice toppled to the ground. Josiah's heart raced, eyes mad with the intent to kill. He reached for the tongs and the glowing horseshoe he'd dropped. They were just out of reach. The assassin produced a knife. Josiah's fingers barely gripped the tongs. As the killer moved to stab him, Josiah flung the horseshoe behind him. A scream erupted from his attacker as the metal seared his flesh.

Josiah threw the man off and went for the hammer. The killer stopped Josiah's arm mid-swing, hand on the leather cuff the apprentice wore.

They struggled back and forth, muscles rippling. Josiah finally ripped his arm out of the assassin's grasp. The cuff tore loose, and the killer's eyes went wide behind the mask. There, tattooed on Josiah's wrist, were three perfect spirals in a triangle set within a circle—the Netherworld triad.

Before the assassin could say or do anything more, Josiah bludgeoned him with the sharp end of the hammer, the force cracking the skeletal mask, revealing a handsome but well-scarred face. The assassin fell in a heap at Josiah's feet, killed instantly by the heavy blow. Josiah breathed heavily, the darkness in his eyes fading as the danger passed.

"Well . . . that could have gone better," Stark mused from the staircase.

Josiah looked apologetically to his mentor.

Stark smiled in sympathy and descended the rest of the stairs. He knew the lad couldn't help it. He grunted. "Look at this mess."

"I'm sorry, master," Josiah said tiredly. "I'll clean it up straight away."

"No." Stark shook his head. "No, you've had a rough night, lad. Leave it till morning."

The master blacksmith bent down and picked up the leather cuff. He passed it to Josiah. "Don't lose this, boy."

Josiah replaced the cuff to his wrist with a tired nod and surveyed the dead man at his feet. "We should at least dispose of the body."

Stark nodded in agreement. With weary looks, as if dead bodies in the middle of the shop were a normal occurrence, the two men dragged the assassin's body out back and burned it.

"SO, WE DON'T EAT," CASPER SAID, TICKING THINGS OFF on his fingers. "We don't sleep. What exactly do we do?"

"Survive," Iris answered simply. "Most people don't make it past their first trial. They think with their heads, not their hearts. Normal logic won't help you here. You have to think outside the proverbial box."

"Then . . . the first trial was a test of wit?"

"Essentially." Iris moved toward a simple wooden trunk and opened the curved lid.

"And what's the second?"

Iris pulled a double-edged broadsword from the chest and tossed it at him. Casper barely caught it.

"Strength," she said, a smile on her lips.

Casper looked down at the sword in his hands. He'd never handled one in his life. "I'm doomed," he said, half-joking.

Iris pulled a second identical sword from the trunk and faced him. "Afraid you might lose to a woman?" she teased, holding her sword aloft.

Casper looked on her in disbelief. "You can't be serious."

"Quite serious."

Iris lunged without warning, and Casper barely blocked. She easily knocked the sword from his grasp.

Iris sighed. "We have a lot of work to do." She gestured to the fallen sword. "Pick it up. Let's try this again."

Casper did as he was bidden, this time ready for her advance. Steel clashed with steel a little longer, but again she knocked the sword from his grip. Over and over they did this, Iris giving him lessons and tips along the way. He had no idea how much time had passed. The longer he spent in the Netherworld, the more inconsequential time seemed to be. It could have been days, weeks. Iris put him through so many rigorous tests, he almost wondered if she wasn't merely another trial herself.

Casper wasn't in terrible shape after all the work he'd done at the gristmill, but Iris still had him running about the caves and lifting heavy stones. Sweat glistened on his body, making his shirt stick to him. Though there was no actual light in the cavern, somehow it was bright as day. It was as if the walls themselves glowed to light the path.

Iris ran ahead of him in trousers and a tunic she'd ripped the sleeves from. She was incredibly agile. Most women in Wayland weren't trained in the ways of combat, but she was far more knowledgeable in it than he was. Casper wondered if she'd always been like this or if it was the result of living in the Netherworld for too long.

They raced on toward a ravine so deep, the bottom wasn't visible. Casper slowed, but Iris kept running at full speed. His heart clenched in terror, certain she'd fall to her death. He watched in shock as she vaulted over the nearly impossible gap and landed unscathed on the other side. Her blood-red braid whipped over her shoulder as she looked back at him, beaming.

"Stop thinking with your head, Waylander," she called. Her voice echoed through the cavern.

Casper considered the drop with a wary eye. Logic told him he wouldn't make it. He tried to quiet that little voice, but it was extremely loud. His gaze shifted from the challenge to Iris. She stood, hands on her hips and a daring grin on her mouth. He took a breath and backed slowly away from the edge until he met the cave wall. His hands rested on the jagged stone behind him. He steeled his mind. If his head was the thing getting in his way, then his head game was what he needed to change. Casper took another breath and plunged forward.

Just do it, he told himself. *Don't think. Just do.*

As he neared the edge, his logic screamed danger, all laws of physics and gravity calculating that he'd fall. He moved his gaze away from the problem and focused on Iris. The edge approached. He leapt.

The world seemed to move in slow motion as he sailed over the ravine, arms flailing and legs kicking. It almost felt like flying. Gravity didn't pull him down, and the distance mattered little. He landed on the other side, rolling on impact to soften the blow. Not quite as graceful as Iris's landing, but it would do.

Her green eyes looked him up and down in appraisal. "Not bad," she mused, offering him a hand. She hoisted him to his feet. "We might make a survivor of you yet."

Casper breathed heavily, smiling. He liked the sound of that. Iris led the way back toward camp at a normal pace. It was odd how they sweated from exertion, yet he wasn't exhausted—not in the way he should be. It felt different, strange. Almost like a mental or emotional drain rather than physical.

Iris took a different route back to camp, time mattering little. It felt like days since they'd met, but it could easily have been weeks or months. Casper was simply glad of the company.

"So, who are you . . . back in Wayland?" he asked. "Our paths have yet to cross that I recall."

Iris laughed. "I'm sure you saw me once or twice. You've at least heard of me, I'm certain."

"I won't know unless you tell me, will I?"

Her eyes met his, glittering with amusement. "Does the surname Farrel ring any bells?"

Casper stopped in his tracks. Iris kept walking.

"As in the mayor's family?" he said, floored.

"That's the one," she replied with a grin.

Casper took wider strides to catch up. "You're the mayor's daughter," he realized aloud. "The one who fell ill. They couldn't find a cure."

"Clever man," she teased.

The sound of falling water grew louder and louder as the path descended. The news slowly sank in, and he suddenly felt as though he had to be on his best behavior. "No wonder the mayor has been so distracted," he said quietly.

"He may not be the mayor much longer."

"What do you mean?" Casper wondered.

"How are things back home?" she asked. "I mean, *really*."

"Well," Casper began, "to tell you the truth, it's a right mess. I don't go into the City often, but I pick up scraps of news on the few Market Days I manage to make the journey. Harlen has been squeezing many of his tenants dry, and a lot of people have started disappearing. Your father stays behind locked doors. Even the Watch is out of his control. They've passed new Netherworlder Registration Acts, trying to keep tabs on every individual who manages to make it back. There aren't many, but the rumors say Bash is keeping a list of people to blackmail into working for Harlen. Truthfully, I don't know what to believe. So much of it is sensationalized gossip and hearsay."

Iris hummed thoughtfully in reply, her eyes far off and distant.

Casper had a feeling she was keeping something from him, and he was about to pry when they rounded a corner into a larger cavern. Jewels encrusted the rocks, glittering in the iridescent light. A waterfall fell from a hole overhead, creating a pool beneath it.

"Whoa," he uttered in wonder.

"Beautiful, isn't it?" Iris smiled. "They're called Netherstones. Each one is filled with extraordinary power."

"What kind of power?" Casper wondered.

"Depends on the stone," she answered. "I'm not sure which does what, but Netherworld survivors have been obsessed with them for centuries."

"Why?"

"Imagine what life would be like with a little more magic," Iris said.

"We don't just come to the Netherworld. Things from the Netherworld can leave with us."

That spurred a whole new string of thoughts in Casper's mind. There were tales back home of sorcerers and mysterious objects, but he'd always thought they were stories told to frighten children.

"If they're that powerful, how come you don't take one for yourself?" he wondered. "Maybe something like that could wake you?"

Iris stifled a bitter laugh.

"What?"

"Nothing. I just . . ."

Casper fixed her with a sincere gaze. "You can tell me."

Iris turned her brilliant green eyes to his face. All the fun had gone out of them, replaced with a sadness he wished he could erase. "A Netherstone is what got me into this mess in the first place, so . . ."

Casper's curiosity wouldn't relinquish his tongue. "I thought you were sick?"

Iris shrugged indifferently. "Sick . . . poisoned. I suppose it's all the same thing now."

She sped up, clearly not wishing to say another word on the matter. Casper let the conversation drop, but he stared after her with growing respect. If what she said was true, then Iris Farrel had been murdered and someone on the other side didn't want her to return.

A Thief's Promise

A NEAR BRUSH WITH DEATH WOULD LEAVE MOST SHAKEN, but not Josiah. Instead he was angry and filled with more questions than answers, a place he never liked to be. He had no doubt the assassin was acting at Lord Harlen's behest. If so, it wasn't a difficult leap to assume Harlen had Casper killed. Casper's death was far too convenient, and with Bash in Lord Harlen's pocket, Josiah knew there would never be justice.

Throughout the night, the quandary never left Josiah's mind. He tossed and turned until the wee hours of the morning, finally giving up and crawling out of his cot. He pulled on his boots and reached lazily for his longcoat. If Casper had been murdered as Josiah suspected, then Harlen would have to be dealt with. For now, Josiah needed facts. With that in mind, he left the blacksmith shop and headed through the cobblestoned streets of the city, nodding now and then to the few Watchmen he passed. The Night Watch was in the process of switching out with the Day Watch.

Josiah's feet carried him toward Prior Street. His green eyes landed on the marble monstrosity at the far end: Harlen Manor. It was gated with a spiked fence and watched night and day by Harlen's lackeys. They were mostly just muscle. Josiah could take them down easily if he really wanted to, but he knew better than to draw attention to himself. Even if he managed to fend off the whole of Harlen's army on his own, he was certain the tyrant had other Netherworlders in his pocket. Against a Netherworlder, Josiah was evenly matched. He needed a few allies first.

His eyes raked over the homes, recalling darker days. His body had been rescued from the fire that killed his family by a passing thief with a rare heart of gold. Dante wasn't much older than Josiah, but it was enough of a difference to make him the older brother Josiah never had. Josiah spent a few years at Dante's side learning the tricks of the trade. Going straight was almost a betrayal, but Stark had promised Josiah a better way. In exchange for an apprenticeship, Josiah had to promise he'd leave thieving behind, and to a degree, he had. The time had come to break that promise.

Josiah took a deep breath to steel himself. A quick look left and right. The streets were mostly empty. He took a running start. It'd been a few years since Josiah truly looked at the city with a thief's eyes, but as he vaulted over a low wall, it all came rushing back. He saw handholds and hiding places. An in here and an exit there. It was all too easy to scale the side of the first house. It was older, made of wood that had aged. From windowsill to drainpipe, he climbed like a spider, and in no time at all, he was crouched on the roof.

Josiah felt a sudden wave of guilt as he saw the street from a bird's-eye view. Stark trusted him, and Josiah was breaking that trust. Worse—he was *enjoying* breaking that trust. Surely his master could forgive him if it was all to protect Kaelyn. After all, Josiah wasn't *really* stealing anything;

he was simply spying. He quickly shook off his doubts. Kaelyn was too important, and he owed Casper this much.

The early morning hour gave Josiah the advantage of few onlookers, and the lone Watchman patrolling the street seemed half asleep. All Josiah needed was to get to Harlen Manor undetected. Unlike much of the city, the buildings on Prior Street were spread out. Each estate had its own gardens and fences or walls. There were only two ways to get to the end: the main street, or through the rear gardens of the homes. Even though there was only one Watchman, Josiah knew his presence, especially in his simple and slightly sooty attire, would draw unwanted attention. It was best to traverse the gardens and inspect Harlen Manor from the shadows. What exactly he expected to find, Josiah wasn't sure, but he had to do something.

Resolved, he raced to the edge of the roof and leapt easily into the thick branches of the back garden tree. It was large with great limbs, one of which hung over the tall wall. He maneuvered through the maze of branches and dropped quietly into the next garden. This home was made of aged brick. It must have taken the workers years to complete the intricate designs. Josiah stole quietly through the yard, ducking behind the white garden shed as the back door opened.

"Be quick about it," a woman's voice said.

Josiah peeked around the corner. One of the maids had let a dog into the back garden—a large wolfhound. Josiah silently cursed. Thankfully the maid retreated inside, as the dog was in no way fooled. Someone was in his territory. The hackles on the back of his neck stood up, and a low growl rumbled in his throat.

Josiah panicked, looking for an out. The garden shed was in the back corner of the yard, not terribly far from the wall. It'd be quite a jump, but Josiah had little option. The dog was already sniffing him out. Carefully as he could, Josiah stepped atop a stack of empty flowerpots. The shed's design wasn't ideal for his purposes. Glass panes were set in all four walls akin to a greenhouse design. One wrong move, and he might break the glass.

The dog growled again, this time far closer. Josiah stepped on the wooden pane of one window and grabbed the tin roof. As he put a little weight on it, there was a resounding *crack!*

"Shit," he whispered.

Bark! Bark! Bark!

The large animal's intruder alarm sounded as the beast rounded the corner, catching Josiah red-handed. The former thief shoved off the breaking pane and hoisted himself onto the roof; all the while the dog barked madly. Josiah raced to the edge of the shed's roof and leapt just as the back door burst open.

"What the devil are you barking at?" the maid demanded.

But Josiah had already landed in the next garden. He ducked behind a large statue of a lady and paused to catch his breath. Perhaps this wasn't the best idea he'd ever come up with. He touched a hand to the bruise forming on his neck where the killer had tried to strangle him. No. He had to do this.

Recalling the attempted murder from the previous night reignited Josiah's Netherworld rage. He steadied his breathing, long since in control of the power that turned most Netherworlders into monsters. A peek around the statue showed a well-groomed garden with tall hedges. The manor on this lot was built in the same traditional stone, stucco, and decorative half-timbering as the rest of the city, but it was evidently made of more expensive materials. A gabled roof and crosshatched stained-glass windows gave the house a noble appearance. The wall surrounding the yard was topped with spikes to discourage people from climbing it.

Josiah crept around the hedges, remaining crouched. They weren't very tall, but they did the job. He traveled the circumference of the garden in this fashion. The hedges acted as a makeshift wall for the graveled circle at the center of the garden. A fountain sang a quiet melody from there, and stone benches sat around it. Josiah studied the wall from his position. Another stone bench rested against it with a gravel path, cherub guardians and a multitude of fading flowers. Though the bench wasn't very high, if he played his cards right, Josiah might *barely* make it over the spikes.

He chanced one last glance at the quiet house, deliberating. The gravel might slow him down, and it'd been ages since he'd tried anything like this. He wasn't the acrobat he used to be. Josiah shook his head to throw such thoughts away.

"Don't think so much," his old mentor's voice rang in his mind.

With renewed determination, he took off at a run, keeping to the grass as much as he could. He jumped over the gravel, propelled off the bench, gripped the spikes, and used his momentum to swing his body over the wall. He landed in a grassy no-man's-land on the other side, grimacing at a small cut in his hand. The spikes weren't very sharp, but they sure were pesky. He'd have to come up with a better way to do this.

Not far from where he stood was one side of Harlen's massive estate. A tall, black wrought-iron fence ran the circumference of it. There'd be no climbing *that* fence. The grass in this far corner of the street was taller and unkempt, mostly hidden from the road by the tall wall of the former home. It was a good place to hide. Josiah made note of it.

The side door of the house opened, and he quickly dropped, using the grass as cover. Anna-Rose exited, basket in hand, and walked down the small stone path to the herb garden. Josiah studied her carefully. She was scared, that much he was sure of. If she was scared of Harlen, she probably wasn't loyal to him. An idea struck.

"Psst," he whispered.

Anna-Rose paused, unsure if she'd heard anything. Josiah tried again.

"Psst."

She turned.

Josiah stood slowly from the grass. The maid was about to call out, but he cut her off.

"Don't scream," he said quietly. "I'm a friend."

It was enough to calm the poor girl's frightened nerves. Working for Harlen would make anyone jumpy. Josiah almost pitied her.

He approached the fence slowly. "What's your name?"

"Anna-Rose," she answered, swallowing hard.

"Anna-Rose," he repeated, flashing his kindest smile. According to the faint blush on her cheek, it did the trick. "I'm Josiah."

"Pleasure," she said, glancing nervously toward the front yard. "You really shouldn't be here, sir. If you're caught, Lord Harlen might have you killed."

"He's already tried," Josiah murmured, pointing to the bruise forming around his neck

Anna-Rose was shocked by those words. Her eyes alighted on the bruise. It was enough to prove his story true. "But how—"

"Don't worry about it," he cut her off. "The truth is, Anna, I need your help."

"My help? I don't even know you."

"No, but we have a common enemy. And you, love . . . you're behind enemy lines."

Anna-Rose didn't have to guess to know what the handsome stranger wanted. She suddenly felt sick. "Oh . . . I can't, sir. No, sir . . . I just can't. He'd have my head for sure."

"And what about all the other innocent lives he'll ruin?" Josiah pressed, glancing to the front garden. The guards seemed to be staying near the front of the house.

"But—"

"He murdered my friend, Anna," Josiah said sharply. "And he tried to kill me. Someone has to stop him, but I can't do it alone."

Anna-Rose's stomach twisted in knots until she thought she might retch. "I'm not made of anything strong, sir," she said. "I'm not sure how much good I'll do you."

"All I need is for you to report anything suspicious to me. Just send a bird. That's all," he promised. "You're the only one who can do this."

"How do I know I can trust you?" she whispered.

"Because I'm one of the good guys." He flashed her another charming smile. "Can I count on you, Anna?"

A faint blush tinged her cheeks, and she tried to hide a smile. He had her in his pocket, and he knew it.

Anna-Rose's smile faded, pondering the stranger's words. She thought on all the odd and terrible things that had happened in that house. The way Lord Harlen's eyes raked over her like she was a piece of meat. A sudden fear struck her, and she shuddered.

"I'll help you, sir," she answered somberly, "but on one condition."

Josiah didn't hesitate. "Name it."

"You have to get me out of here when it's done. I've seen enough horror to last a lifetime. He never lets me leave. Please."

Josiah's visage morphed to one of humble sincerity.

"You have my word, love," he promised. "I'll get you out."

Anna-Rose gave a short nod at that. "I'll do it."

"Excellent." He smiled, backing slowly into the shadows. "Just send the birds to Stark's. I'll take care of the rest. You really are a gem."

With that, he disappeared, leaving Anna-Rose to question her own sanity. Could she really trick Lord Harlen? She shuddered to think what would happen if he caught her betraying him. She was even more terrified of what might happen if he wasn't stopped at all.

"WHAT THE BLOODY HELL HAPPENED TO YOU?" KAELYN demanded as she answered the cottage door.

Josiah must have looked worse than he thought, or perhaps Kaelyn was merely more observant than he realized. "What?" he fumbled. "Oh . . . nothing. I . . . got into a tavern brawl. That's all."

Kaelyn raised an accusatory eyebrow. Tavern brawl indeed. Josiah was a playful soul, but she knew he didn't frequent the ale houses. "Fine. Don't tell me," she bristled, turning away from the door.

Josiah stepped across the threshold and closed the door behind him. The clouds outside threatened snow, and from the lack of the wood by the fireplace, the Renolds women weren't prepared for the coming storm. Kaelyn sat in the rocking chair by the fire and picked up the dress she'd been mending.

"Oh, hullo, Josiah," Gran greeted, a knowing sparkle in her eyes. It was no secret Gran adored him.

"Hullo, Gran," he returned.

The aged woman pulled him into a warm hug, truly happy to see him again. He was a great help around the mill with Casper gone. And moreover, she secretly hoped Kaelyn might take a shine to him.

"I wondered when we might be seeing you again," Gran said, pulling back to look him over. "Oh dear, but you have gotten yourself into a mess, haven't you?"

"Says it was a tavern brawl," Kaelyn chimed in bitterly. Josiah cast her a look.

"Well, we'll get you fixed up in no time," Gran promised. "Are you hungry, dear?" She pinched his shoulders. "You're practically wasting away," she joked. His well-toned blacksmith's muscles said otherwise.

He grinned. "Starved. But I wouldn't dream of eating for free. If you've an axe, I'd be happy to chop some more wood for you. The winter frost is on its way." He glanced at Kaelyn and added undertone, "Besides, something tells me it's colder in here."

"On the side of the house, dear," Gran told him. "It would be much appreciated, lad. These old bones do ache so when the cold sets in."

"I'll get to it, then." Josiah gave Gran a warm smile.

With that, he departed out the door. No sooner had it shut when Gran whirled on Kaelyn and set a hand on her aged hip. "What in the Maker's name has gotten into you, lass?" she asked sternly.

"I've no idea what you mean," Kaelyn replied, not daring to look up from her sewing.

"No idea?" Gran repeated, flabbergasted. "Kaelyn Mary Renolds, as I live and breathe, you will be the death of me!"

Gran moved to the hearth and stirred the contents stewing in the cauldron over the flames.

"He lied, Gran!" Kaelyn said sharply, finally daring to look up. "He lied right to my face!"

Gran fixed her with a look that could silence even Lord Harlen. "Perhaps he doesn't want to worry you," she said. "Have you considered that?"

"Well, too bloody late!"

Kaelyn turned back to her sewing, realizing what she'd said. A faint blush hued her cheek, and she suddenly wanted to kick herself.

Gran pursed her lips to keep from smiling, but it did little good. The smile broke across her lips regardless. "Why do you fight it so? It's not a crime, you know. Feeling something for the lad."

Kaelyn studied her sewing more intently, as if that would throw Gran off the scent.

"What is it, love?" Gran ceased her stirring and stepped closer, tucking a fair hair behind Kaelyn's ear. "What's troubling you?"

Kaelyn wanted to ignore the question and go on sewing, but Gran gently took Kaelyn's chin and tilted her head up.

"What is it, dearie?"

Kaelyn sighed and dropped her sewing in her lap. "It's just . . . Casper's death was too much of a coincidence, and now that Josiah has been around me, he ends up hurt too. I can't help but—"

"Don't you even think it, love," Gran said tenderly. "It's not your fault."

"But—"

"It's *not* your fault," Gran repeated, cupping Kaelyn's cheek in her hand. "Casper's death does certainly work in Lord Harlen's favor, but you cannot hold yourself accountable for that vile man's actions."

"But Josiah—"

"Can take care of himself." Gran soothed her granddaughter's cheek with a thumb and smiled. "I remember when you used to chase him around the yard. Your little legs could barely keep up with him and your brother. But he always spoke up for you when Casper was too cruel. He's still looking out for you, my dear. It's in his nature. Would you really deny him that?"

Kaelyn looked down at her hands, feeling a little guilty. "No . . . I suppose not."

"Good." Gran smiled. "Why don't you go apologize while I dish up some food? Go on."

Apology was the last thing on Kaelyn's stubborn mind, but she knew Gran would continue to pester until she'd done so. She set her sewing aside with a sigh, grabbed her shawl from a peg by the door, and went outside. It was far colder away from the warmth of the fire. Kaelyn hugged the light-blue shawl around her shoulders and looked around the yard for Josiah. Every so often a loud thud rang through the air. She followed the sound to the rear of the cottage.

Kaelyn paused as Josiah set another piece of wood on an old tree stump. With the greatest ease, he swung the axe and split the wood with one blow. She studied him, the way he moved as he picked up another piece of wood and swung the axe again. The log split easily. Perhaps Gran was right. Josiah was strong. He could take care of himself. And maybe, just maybe, he could take care of her too.

Kaelyn immediately wanted to smack herself for thinking it. Casper had only been gone a few weeks, and already she was thinking of moving on. Wasn't there a ritual to this sort of thing? The older brother was supposed to get mad at his friend for looking at his sister the wrong way. The boys bicker for a while until finally everyone sees reason. But they didn't have the luxury of time, and Casper was gone, possibly forever.

Truthfully, Kaelyn was terrified. She was a strong, stubborn woman, but Lord Harlen was a Netherworlder with strength beyond anything Kaelyn could hope to escape from. She wanted to feel safe again—to know that she had someone else to turn to. Surely she could at least allow Josiah to be a friend. It'd been so long since she had one.

"Are you going to stand there all day?" Josiah said, not bothering to face her.

Kaelyn jumped. She'd barely made a sound, and he hadn't looked up from his work even once. "How did you know I was here?"

Josiah shrugged. "Call it instinct." He finally glanced up, noting the way she hugged the shawl around her thinning frame. "You shouldn't be out here, love."

Kaelyn rolled her eyes, finally approaching him. "I'm fine. Stop worrying so much."

He smiled, and Kaelyn suddenly felt warm all over. "Perhaps you should take your own advice," he mused, setting another log on the stump. He split it and set the two pieces in the nearby basket.

"Perhaps," she said, trying not to smile. She failed.

"Did you come out here for a reason?"

Kaelyn thought on it. She could lie, but something told her he'd see right through it. She'd been spending so much time around him lately, it was as though they moved in tandem with one another.

"I . . . wanted to apologize," she started.

"Oh dear," he teased, grinning. "Has someone cracked your impenetrable armor?"

She smacked his shoulder, surprised at how hard it felt. If she hit it with true force, she might bruise her hand. "Shut it," she muttered, unable to keep the color from her cheeks.

He chuckled as he went through the motions of splitting another chunk of wood.

"Anyway . . . sorry. So, there. Now I've said it."

Josiah paused his work to quirk an eyebrow at her. "You're not very good at this, are you?"

"No," she admitted, averting her gaze.

Josiah grinned wider and turned back to his work. "Mediocre apology accepted, darling."

Kaelyn tried not to laugh, the sound she emitted almost a snort. She covered her mouth with a hand and pursed her lips. Once more, Josiah split a log and set it in the basket. He'd nearly filled it by now. His playful demeanor slowly faded.

"I don't blame you. You've every right to be cross with me," he said. "Besides, I find your temper refreshing."

"Refreshing?" Kaelyn wondered. "How so?"

Josiah stood tall and rested the axe in the dirt near his foot. He shrugged. "Most girls are so refined and placid. They're very boring."

Kaelyn laughed. "Well, I'm glad to know I'm not a bore."

"You could never be a bore," he said sincerely.

Again, Kaelyn had to look away. She wished the blush would leave her cheek, but Josiah was glad to see it there. A thief's best ally was good looks and a silver tongue, his old mentor used to say. To a degree, it was true. Josiah's pretty face bought him a lot, but with Kaelyn it was different. He didn't have ulterior motives for being kind to her. Nearly being killed by Harlen's goon merely strengthened his resolve to protect her all the more.

Josiah went back to chopping, letting the silence go on. There was a certain beauty to it, the way they could be near one another and say nothing. He knew his protective nature was stemming into something more. Some part of him almost felt guilty. He and Casper hadn't spoken in years, not since a certain accident they all still refused to speak of. And then Josiah had died alongside his parents and went through horrors he didn't wish on anyone. Now Casper was in the same boat, and what was Josiah doing about it? Flirting with his best mate's little sister. It almost felt like a betrayal.

Kaelyn allowed her mind to wander in the quiet lull, thinking on more concerning matters. She finally broke the silence. "Can I say something without sounding like a complete lunatic?"

Josiah split another log and turned his eyes on her. "Aye . . . unless you are a lunatic." He smirked.

"I'm serious," she said. This time she didn't smile or blush.

Josiah straightened and rested his axe once more. "What is it?"

Kaelyn knew she had his undivided attention, and suddenly her mouth felt dry. When she tried to say things to Gran, her grandmother kissed her head and told her not to worry. Josiah could do the same, or he could become enraged. He could brush it off as nothing. She took a breath.

"I don't think my brother's death was an accident," she said. "I think he was killed, and I'm worried that you . . ."

Kaelyn couldn't even finish that sentence. She didn't want to think it.

"I agree," he said.

Kaelyn perked up, a little shocked. "Really?"

Josiah nodded and rested his axe against the stump. "Aye. That's why I've been doing a little digging of my own."

"Is that how you got the . . . *that*?" She pointed to the bruise around his neck.

He shrugged. "Yes and no."

His words didn't make her feel any better. If anything, they made her worry more. Josiah could see it written plainly on her face. He stepped closer and set his hands gently on her shoulders.

"I'll be fine, love," he promised. "Nothing is going to happen to me."

Josiah's green eyes searched her cerulean blues.

"You don't know Lord Harlen like I do," she said. Her voice was quieter with him so close. It was like resisting a strong magnetic pull. She just wanted to sink into his arms, bury her head in his chest, and ignore the chaos going on around her.

"Actually, I know him better than you think," Josiah replied. He let his hands drop, looking anywhere but at her.

Kaelyn studied his face. He was a good deal taller than she was, and she had to look up to do so. "What are you hiding from me?"

He said nothing.

Kaelyn set a hand on his cheek and turned his face back to her. "I know you want to protect me, but secrets won't help. We used to tell each other everything."

"We were children then," he said quietly.

"Does that have to matter?" she murmured.

"I don't want you to think less of me. I'd rather you remember the boy I was."

Kaelyn gave him a warm smile. "I don't want the boy. I want to know the man he's become."

Josiah set his hand on hers, thinking. She had a valid point, but he'd been hiding his true self for so long. He mulled it over in his mind. If he told her the truth, she could hate him as much as Harlen. But there was a chance, a small chance that she would understand and worry a little less. Her brother was, after all, facing the very trials he'd gone through. Didn't he at least owe her honesty?

"If I tell you, you have to swear to never breathe a word of it to another soul," he said.

"I so swear," she answered.

Josiah removed his hand, and Kaelyn retracted her own, watching him with curiosity. Only two people knew the truth about him: Stark and the thief who'd rescued him from the fire. It was a dark truth he didn't want Kaelyn to know, but it was inevitable. She'd find out sooner or later, and he'd rather he be the one to tell her. Slowly, he pulled back the sleeve of his longcoat and removed the leather cuff. The Netherworld triad stared up at Kaelyn, black and horrific as the truth it spoke.

Kaelyn's eyes grew wide. She snatched up his wrist so fast, it might have hurt had he been normal. Her fingers traced the spirals as if to test that they weren't drawn on. They were as real as the hand she held in her own. Her eyes looked up to his face. There was shame there—shame and regret. All at once, Kaelyn understood. This was why he wasn't afraid of Harlen, why he wasn't afraid of anything.

"But," she began, "you're so . . . normal. I mean . . ."

"You mean I'm not a monster like *them*," he said.

Kaelyn nodded.

"I choose not to be," he explained. "And if your brother makes it through, I want to teach him to do the same."

Kaelyn looked on Josiah with new eyes. The Netherworld offered great temptation and power to the victors, and here he was, fighting it with every fiber of his being, trying with all his might to be the better person. He had somehow survived the Netherworld as the Maker had intended, with honor and humility. It gave her hope that Casper could too. Josiah hadn't denied the suggestion that Harlen had tried to kill him. She looked at the bruise on his neck and the tattoo on his wrist. Suddenly it all made sense.

"Say something," he uttered, worried by her silence.

But she couldn't find the words, so she did the only thing that could convey what she was thinking. She stood on her tiptoes, gripped his coat in her hands, and pressed her lips to his. Josiah was taken aback at first. He certainly wasn't expecting *that*. But the shock quickly wore off, and he wound his arms around her waist. Snow began to fall as he kissed her back in earnest. The chill of snowflakes on their cheeks brought them back to the present. They pulled apart, both grinning, and Kaelyn very, very red.

"I was hoping you'd say that," he'd whispered, leaning his forehead on hers.

She smacked his chest, drawing a chuckle from his lips. Neither one of them noticed Gran watching from the window with a knowing smile.

Iris's Tale

THERE WAS NO WAY OF KNOWING HOW MUCH TIME HAD passed since Casper's first trial. It felt like an eternity to the lad. Since then, he'd learned the art of swordplay, knives, and various tactics in hand-to-hand combat. Iris, it seemed, was as deadly as she was beautiful. The more they trained together, the more in tandem they moved. Soon Iris had to work to hold her own against him.

Steel clanged against steel as they sparred throughout the caverns. Casper parried her blows with precision, so used to a sword in his hands now, he moved subconsciously.

"Good," Iris praised as he ducked a vicious swipe from her sword. It nearly took off his head.

"Is your intention to kill me?" he joked.

"Do you imagine the Netherworld will take it easy on you?" she asked.

Their swords clanged as they exchanged blows once more.

"No," he replied.

Iris grinned. "Then I'm simply giving you a challenge."

Again she aimed for a mortal blow, but Casper blocked it. *Clang! Clang! Clang!* Their swords banged away. It almost seemed a stalemate until Casper dodged another slash, dropped to the floor, and swiped Iris's legs out from beneath her. In the same motion, he knocked her sword from her hand and set the tip of his under her chin.

"You were saying, milady?" he asked.

They both breathed heavily from the exertion. A smile broke across her face.

"I think you're ready," she said as he helped her to her feet.

Casper grinned in return and scooped her sword up, holding it out to her. "Good."

She took it and placed it back in its sheath.

Over the immeasurable time he'd spent with Iris, Casper had changed a great deal. When he'd first arrived in the Netherworld, he was but a miller stumbling blindly along. Now, thanks to her tutoring, he was a fighter. He hoped it would be enough to get him past the horrors that waited outside the caves.

Iris led the way back toward camp, ambling along. They had all the time in the world. In the heavy silence, Casper once again felt the pull of curiosity. Ever since she mentioned being poisoned, he wondered what she'd meant. It seemed so personal a question, and despite the time they'd spent together, he hardly knew her.

"Why don't the shriekers come in here?" he queried, figuring it best to start small.

Iris shrugged. "These passageways are the halls between layers of the Netherworld. From what I gather, the Keeper's presence holds them off. It's where we all begin when we die, but most never find their way back to the caves. The landscape is constantly changing."

And there it was. An opening. "How exactly *did* you die?" he asked.

Iris stiffened at the question, and he half expected her to lose that fiery temper he'd come to be wary of.

"It's just a question," he reasoned. "I know almost nothing about you. If I'm going to save your life when I get back, I think I deserve to know who I'm saving."

It was a stab in the dark, but it seemed to work.

Iris's face twisted in thought. It'd been so long since she had contact with anyone. Most souls she ran into were too busy trying to kill her. But not him. Instead, he'd simply wondered who she was. There was kindness in him, the likes of which Iris had never seen. A heart so strong, that even in the bowels of the darkest place in the world, he still seemed capable of being gentle.

Iris tried not to think of her death or the horrors that led to it. After so long trapped between life and death, it was easy to shut off her emotions. To choose not to feel. Being around Casper made her miss all it meant to be alive.

"Aye," she finally spoke. "I suppose you do."

Casper felt at ease when she didn't explode. "Well?"

The caverns suddenly seemed so large, and Iris felt so small. Being the center of attention felt odd after so long perfecting the art of being invisible. "Lord Harlen is more than a mere Netherworlder," she began. "He's obsessed with the black arts. When he died and faced his trials, he met Death himself."

"As in . . . *the* Death?" Casper interjected.

Iris nodded. "Death made a deal with Harlen. If he promised to free Death from the Netherworld, Death would grant him unimaginable power. Harlen agreed. Death gave him a Netherstone, one of the rarest and most dangerous of them all."

"What does it do?"

"If wielded properly, it would make Harlen immortal and give him power akin to the Maker himself."

Iris gave Casper no reason to doubt her words, but the whole idea seemed rather farfetched. "How exactly do *you* know all this?"

Iris twisted the end of her fiery braid betwixt her fingers. She couldn't meet his eye, dreading the words she had to say next, but if he was to wake her, he had the right to know why. "Because I was part of the deal."

Casper's face etched in confusion, and Iris could already see where his mind would leap.

"Not intentionally," she said quickly.

He nodded for her to continue.

"The black arts are a vile and horrendous form of magic. They go against the very will of the Maker, so they require rituals of the worst kind: the slaughter of innocence, the corruption of the unstained."

"What was your part?" Casper pressed, trying to keep her on track.

"The power of the stone given to Harlen was taken from the Maker himself—a drop of magic left behind when he created the world. It can only be harnessed by purity."

"You."

"Exactly. Netherstones cannot be wielded on their own. They must be fashioned into something they enchant. Harlen's stone was fashioned into a ring. In order to siphon the power from the ring, he needed a virgin. He would present her with the ring during a full moon, wed her, and consummate their marriage. The power would consume them both."

The wheels in Casper's head started turning. It all sounded so familiar.

"And what would happen to the virgin?" he wondered.

"He would take her life force, and she would die."

"So that's how you came to be here?"

Iris smiled wanly. "No."

"Then how?"

Iris gave a shrug. "Harlen needed a virgin, so . . . I conveniently wasn't one anymore, and—"

"And he poisoned you," Casper interjected.

She nodded.

"Is that why you faced the trials?"

"Aye. I was the only one who knew the truth, the only one who could stop him, but . . . I can't wake."

"That's why you needed me," he mused, the gears in his mind whirring away. And then, all at once, something clicked.

Casper stopped in his tracks. Lord Harlen pretended to be ever the gentleman, but it was a known fact he couldn't keep away from the brothels. He'd ruined enough innocent girls who were sentenced to that life because of his lust. But Kaelyn—he didn't dare touch Kaelyn. He kept to the laws of Wayland. He attempted to court her. How could Casper be so stupid?

Iris turned to look at him. "What's wrong?"

Casper couldn't bring himself to utter the words aloud.

Iris walked closer, concerned by the shell-shocked look on his face. "Cas?" She searched his eyes. "What's wrong?"

"My sister," he uttered in sheer disbelief. A quiet rage built slowly inside of him.

"What about her?" Iris pressed.

"Harlen has been after my sister," he said, voice shaking. "I wouldn't let him romance her, and now I'm dead."

Iris's worry dissipated, replaced with a horrible dread. "He's going to try again," she realized. "I mean, I knew he bloody would, but I hoped . . ."

She exhaled in aggravation and rubbed her forehead.

Casper's entire world felt like it was crumbling around him. He was dead, and Kaelyn was unprotected. He was dead while Harlen roamed free. A sudden, inconsolable rage built inside of him. An anger so strong, it almost felt sinful. Iris could see it in his eyes, a look so unlike him she feared for the sake of his soul.

"Casper," she said gently, hoping to pull him from the trance. He didn't respond, so she set a hand on his cheek. "Cas!"

The glazed look in his eyes faded as they focused on her face.

Iris breathed easier. "It's going to be all right," she promised. "I'm going to help you get out of here, and we're going to stop him, aye?"

Casper suddenly became aware of her hand on his cheek. He gave a nod, simmering down. His cheek burned where her hand rested, and the sensation didn't leave when she withdrew it. Iris didn't know what else to say, so she fell silent and turned back toward camp. Casper trailed quietly behind her. He didn't have long to wallow in thought before they neared their destination. Both froze in their tracks. The sound of rustling and hushed voices echoed down the passage.

". . . before they get back."

"I'm going as fast as I can."

Iris shared a look with Casper and held a finger to her lips. He nodded. They inched forward and took cover behind a row of tall stalagmites that edged the camp. Iris had chosen this spot specifically because of its tactical advantage. Stalactites and stalagmites formed a hedge around the never-ending fire, almost making an alcove around it. Unfortunately, Iris and Casper were now on the outside.

They peered carefully through the gaps in the limestone formations. Two other souls had invaded their camp—a man about three times Casper's size and a woman with a mean look in her eyes. They were digging through the crates and boxes Iris had so carefully stored. Casper was already on edge after realizing Harlen's true intentions for his sister. That rage only mounted as he watched them steal from Iris's personal store.

He moved, and Iris gripped his wrist in an iron vice. "Don't," she warned. "You're not yourself."

"Someone has to bloody well do something," he whispered angrily. Her grip was so tight, he started to lose feeling in his hand.

Slowly, she released him. "Let me. Don't step in unless you have to."

If her eyes were fire, he'd be scorched. Casper nodded with a tight jaw. He didn't like it, but he knew she could hold her own if things went south.

Iris stood to her full height, hand resting on her sword and a strong look in her green eyes. She looked like some sort of warrior princess as she strode around the stalagmites and into the firelight. The man was the first to notice. He let out a whistle at the sight of her.

"'Ello, 'ello," he said, a thick Slums accent on his tongue. "What 'ave we 'ere?"

Iris didn't bat an eyelash. She simply stood a little taller, an ill-amused look on her face.

The woman turned and gave Iris a once-over. "Definitely a high-born lass, she is," the woman noted.

Casper fidgeted uncomfortably. He didn't like where this was heading.

"I take it the two of you are new to the games we play here," Iris said. There was no doubting the authority in her voice.

The strange couple shared a look. Unease filled Casper at the smile they shared. Part of him didn't want this to end badly. The other part of him was dying to whip out his sword and take out his frustration on someone. He took a deep breath. Iris was right. He wasn't himself.

"I wouldn't say that," the woman mused. Both pulled back the sleeves on their tunics. Two Netherworld spirals were marked on their wrists. They'd already passed two of their trials. Iris had seen it all before. Waylanders got through the test of wit, and they thought themselves so intelligent. They pass strength, and they feel unstoppable. No one expects the third trial. No one can ever truly be prepared for it. They had no idea what was coming.

Iris smiled, and despite her beauty, she appeared quite sinister. "How quaint," she patronized. "You think you're so close, don't you? That the end is nigh?" She laughed. "How bloody wrong you are."

The man didn't seem to like being talked down to. "'O the bloody 'ell d'ya fink you are, missy?"

Iris showed her own completed Netherworld triad. "The woman who's already beaten this place. I will only ask you once—return what you've stolen, and I'll let you live."

The two souls seemed a little unnerved at the sight of her finished triad.

"Why d'you need it, dearie?" the woman said, hand on her hip. "Yeh've finished yer bloody trials."

"Come tah fink of it, why're ya still bloody 'ere?" the man wondered. "Unless yer a trick."

Casper shook his head but kept his lips tightly closed. This was going downhill fast.

"I says we kills ya and takes what's rightfully ours," the brutish man figured.

His woman grinned, revealing a row of stained teeth. "Aye, that's a grand idea, my angel."

They each took up a sword, and Iris drew hers. Casper couldn't watch with good conscience. He stood and strode into camp.

"So that's it then," he said.

All eyes turned to him. Iris looked none too pleased.

"You're just going to kill one another for this?" he continued, temper fading the more he spoke. "Need I remind you, we're *all* already dead. We're *all* souls. This is bloody pointless."

Iris didn't loosen the grip on her sword, watching the intruders' every move. It was a tense game of cat and mouse, only which was which she couldn't tell.

The tall, brutish man rolled his shoulders, cracking all the muscles and joints. "A lad with morals," he mused. "Those won't getcha anywheres down 'ere. We wants this loot . . . and we wants this camp."

"No deal," Iris said quickly.

The woman grinned, her rotting teeth so putrid, Casper could smell them from where he stood. "Then I guess we'll 'ave to fight ya for it," she said.

Iris was more than ready when the woman rushed at her. Casper, on the other hand, felt an immense sense of dread as the woman's gargantuan partner came barreling toward him. He ducked fleetly aside as the man tried to take his head off, drawing his sword. Speed and agility were on Casper's side. His attacker was large indeed, but it slowed his movements, giving Casper an edge. *Clang!* He blocked the man's next attempted blow. *Clang! Clang!*

"Yer a sprightly fella, ain't ya," the man said, cracking his neck.

Casper made no answer, far too focused on the man's heavy blows. He may have been slow, but the giant was nonetheless strong. Each blow made Casper fear he'd lose his grip on his sword.

Iris was more certain of her weapon. This game wasn't new to her, nor was the crazed look in the two intruders' eyes. They'd been tainted like most everyone who passed through the cursed landscapes. She felt no conflict in landing blows with the intention of ending her enemy, knowing her attacker would do the same.

The female intruder wasn't a bad fighter, but Iris had been trapped there longer. She'd fought off multitudes of souls and Netherworld dangers. Iris attacked with finesse and a cool head whilst her assailant landed blows with fervent anger. It was all too easy for Iris to conserve her energy while her attacker wasted her own. Soon enough, the woman made a mistake, sending a strong downward cleave for Iris's head. Iris dodged, and the woman's momentum sent the sword plunging into one of the crates instead.

The woman tried to pull it out, but it was stuck tight. Panic etched on her face. Iris seized the opportunity and ran the woman through.

"NO!" Casper shouted in protest at Iris's actions.

The light slowly faded from the woman's eyes. Her partner stopped whaling on Casper long enough to watch her disintegrate into dust.

A fury the likes of which Casper had never seen crossed the man's face. He lashed out with his sword, the blow so strong it struck Iris and sent her flying across the cavern. She slammed into the stone wall and sunk in a heap to the ground, dazed. The gargantuan had forgotten all about Casper, heading instead for the stunned redhead.

Desperately, Casper searched for an answer. His sword did him little good, and time was short. *Think, Casper, think,* he chastised himself. His eyes frantically searched the camp. Chucked carelessly beside a nearby crate was a loaded crossbow. Casper flung his sword aside and scooped it up, rounding on the massive man so dangerously close to Iris. Her eyes locked on Casper. She gave an infinitesimal nod.

Casper took a breath, imagining the man to be a great bear closing in on an innocent human life. "Oi!" he called in an attempt at distraction.

It worked. The giant turned. He barely had time to blink before

Casper aimed and fired. The crossbow bolt buried itself in the man's eye. Everything stood still. The intruder's sword clattered to the floor, and shortly after, gravity claimed him. His massive body hardly thudded to the ground before he too disintegrated into dust, leaving the crossbow bolt behind.

Casper breathed heavily and slowly lowered his weapon. He'd killed a man. He'd *killed* a man. The realization hit him like a ton of bricks. He dropped the crossbow as if it'd burned him and raced to Iris's side.

"That was a bloody good shot," she mused, still in a daze.

"I'm a hunter," he answered simply, eyes looking her over worriedly. Other than a cut bleeding profusely on her arm and a possible concussion, she seemed all right. Casper had to remind himself they weren't bound by normal laws here. The burns on his hands had healed rather quickly once tended to. He imagined this would too.

"Come on," he said, carefully pulling her to her feet. "Let's get you cleaned up."

"Don't be ridiculous," she said stubbornly. "It's just a scratch."

"Shut it and do what I say!" he ordered in a very un-Casper-like tone.

Shocked by his sudden show of dominance, Iris quieted and allowed him to help her back toward the fire. He made her sit on one of the overturned crates while he dug in the larger ones. Iris studied him as he worked, the rigid frame and sudden set to his jaw.

"You're angry with me," she realized.

"Aye," was all he uttered. He pulled out some cloth, a leaf jar of ointment, bandages, and a needle and thread.

This was all new to Iris. She'd been alone for so long, making decisions for only herself. She wasn't used to having another person's approval or disapproval. It felt strange.

"Why?" she wondered as he knelt in front of her.

Casper used the cloth to put pressure on her sliced skin. The wound was deep, but the clean cut would make it an easy heal.

"Answer me," she pleaded.

Casper sighed, keeping his tawny eyes on his work. "We didn't have to kill them," he said quietly.

Iris nearly laughed. "They were going to kill *us*. We—"

"No, they weren't," he cut her off, turning his gaze to hers. "You instigated them."

"Says the man who was about to storm into camp half-bloody-cocked," she retorted.

"To talk to them!"

Iris shook her head. "No, you weren't. I saw the look in your eyes. You would have done the same."

"No . . . I wouldn't have," he replied quietly, turning back to the wound on her arm. The bleeding had finally slowed enough for him to clean the wound.

Iris tried not to flinch as he worked. Her mind slowly puzzled through his words. She didn't understand. They were intruders. They'd invaded the camp. She'd eliminated a threat.

"Let me ask you something," he said as he threaded the needle. "If you didn't need me, would you have done the same when we first met?"

He caught her eye, and Iris suddenly felt at a loss for words. Her silence was the only answer he needed.

"As I thought," he uttered.

Casper moved to start stitching, but Iris placed a hand on his to stop him.

"I'm sorry," she whispered.

Once again, he turned his captivating gaze upward and met her eye. Apology wasn't usually Iris's style, but it felt like the right thing to do. A hint of a smile crossed Casper's lips. Nothing more was said. Nothing else had to be. He forgave her.

Iris removed her hand, and Casper returned to stitching her wound. She quietly wished they had some sort of hard liquor to numb the pain. Instead, she clenched her fist and tried to keep her mind on other things.

"You seem to know what you're doing," she mused after a lengthy silence.

"My mother was a healer," he explained. "We live on the Outer Edge in the forest near the mountains. My sister and I came home often with scrapes and bruises, and Mum was there to make them better. You learn a thing or two when you're as clumsy as I was."

Iris nearly laughed at the image of a smaller Casper tripping over twigs and stones in the woods. "She sounds wonderful."

"She was."

Iris didn't miss the inflection in his tone. Her smile faded. "What happened to her?"

"My parents were killed by bandits on the road home from the city," he said quietly. "I was eleven."

"That's terrible," she murmured.

"Aye," he agreed. "But we manage."

Iris fell silent after that, wincing now and then as Casper pulled the needle through her skin. When he'd finished stitching, he cut the thread with his teeth, put some salve on the irritated skin around it, and wrapped the wound in a bandage.

"Good as new," Casper said when it was done.

"Thank you," Iris murmured.

Again, he gave the smallest smile and nodded. Iris watched him mindlessly pack things away. She replayed the instance in her mind. Casper was so against killing the intruders, but the moment she'd been in peril, he didn't hesitate to take a life. The thought left a strange taste in her mouth and an odd sense in her gut. He'd *chosen* to save her. Even if she hadn't promised to help him with his trials, if she'd been another soul he'd never met, she knew he still would have intervened. Iris suddenly felt guilty knowing she wouldn't have done the same. The thought gnawed at her insides for ages before she understood why: Casper reminded her what it meant to be human.

The Second Trial

SWOOSH! HARLEN CLEANLY TOOK THE HEAD OFF A practice dummy with the edge of his rapier. Bash jumped at the sudden outburst, and Anna-Rose nearly dropped the tray she'd just entered the back garden with. The straw head thudded dully against the snow-covered lawn.

"Your best man," Harlen seethed, turning his steely gaze to his henchman. "You said he was your best man!"

"He was!" Bash tried to defend himself. "I dunno how the bloody hell it happened, but it did!"

Anna-Rose carefully set the tray of wine atop the stone table on the terrace, purposefully moving at a glacial pace. Lord Harlen pointed his rapier in Bash's face.

"You are treading on dangerous ground," he warned.

Bash eyed the blade, sharp to a point and in the hands of the one man who could successfully run him through. The sheriff had no intention of dying again anytime soon.

"What would you have me do, Charles?" Bash asked tensely.

Lord Harlen whirled and stabbed his rapier through the heart of the straw dummy. Bash flinched. Harlen left the weapon there, signaling for Bash to follow. Snow crunched beneath their boots as they made their way across the back lawn and up the terrace steps. Anna-Rose had just poured out two goblets of wine. She curtsied to Harlen as he approached.

"Ah, thank you, milady," he mused, eyes wandering her up and down as they always did. "But where's George?"

Anna-Rose nearly fumbled, but she managed to produce a reply without stuttering. "He was indisposed, my lord. Asked me to bring out your libations."

"Ah. Excellent," Harlen replied, not at all disappointed to see her pleasing figure. "Well, I thank you, madam. You are free to go about your duties. We can manage from here."

Anna-Rose curtsied again and headed back toward the house. When she was certain both men weren't looking, the maid ducked covertly into the bushes. She regretted the idea once crouched among the shrubbery. The snow immediately soaked the hem of her skirts and froze her hands. She took a careful breath, reminding herself the freedom that awaited if Josiah could indeed be rid of Harlen as he'd promised.

Thinking Anna-Rose had returned to the house, the gentlemen continued their conversation.

"Your man is missing, you say," Harlen spoke. The wheels of vile trickery turned behind his cold, gray eyes. "And this *blacksmith* is still alive."

"Indeed I do, sir," Bash replied regretfully. He was rather astounded himself. This assassin was the best in the guild. No one knew his name. Few knew his face. Even other assassins had feared him. How could a simple blacksmith's apprentice defeat him, if that was indeed what had happened?

Lord Harlen took a sip from his goblet as fresh flakes of snow began to fall. "I don't suppose we could press charges? Call it murder and arrest the lad?"

Bash shook his head. "Afraid not, my lord. For one thing, there's no body. If he was killed, which we don't know for certain, then they must have disposed of him. And secondly, how would you know the man was bloody well missing if you didn't order Mr. Grimm killed?"

Harlen sighed and drained his goblet. "Damn," he uttered, setting it back on the tray. He refilled it.

Bash wiped some gathering snow from his bald head. He owed Harlen for aiding him through the Netherworld trials, but these games were growing tiresome. Though he wouldn't say it aloud, Bash thought Harlen was fighting a losing battle.

Lord Harlen took another sip of wine, mulling over the facts.

"We have another problem," Bash said, setting his untouched goblet down.

"Pray tell what that would be," Harlen replied.

"The council is making a motion to have you removed," Bash explained.

Lord Harlen seemed to find this news more amusing than serious. "They can try, Sebastian, but believe me, they will fail. I am beyond even the council now."

"Of course." But Bash was far less convinced. If the Order of Nex was so easily tossed aside, it wouldn't still stand as the greatest power in all of Wayland.

An evil smile crossed Lord Harlen's lips as an idea came into his head. "The Renolds lad has yet to pass his second trial, correct?"

"Indeed, sir."

"Then we must ensure he doesn't make it to the third."

"How? Anything you do would only further point the fingers in your direction."

"That no longer matters," Harlen said, more determined. "If the council indeed seeks to overthrow me, and the blacksmith runs about unchecked, then it's time to take matters into my own hands. Kaelyn Renolds *will* wear the ring before the next full moon." He slammed his goblet on the table as if it made his point. "Once night falls, take some of your best men to the mill. Burn it to the ground and bring her to me."

Anna-Rose had to cover her mouth to hide the gasp she almost released. It took all of her strength not to race from the bushes to the pigeon coop.

Bash nodded. "Yes, my lord."

Harlen jerked his head for the sheriff to leave. Anna-Rose held her breath as he walked by, certain she'd be heard. Bash didn't slow as he passed. She let her breath out in relief, but Harlen was still on the snow-covered patio. As the white flakes fell harder, she struggled not to shiver.

George, the butler, suddenly walked out on the patio. He bowed respectfully to his master. Harlen gave the usual nod—consent to speak.

"Apologies, my lord," George spoke, his voice one of refinement. "Have you seen Miss Anna-Rose?"

Harlen gave a slow nod. "Indeed I have. She was out here not a moment ago. I sent her back inside."

George bowed and returned to the house, leaving Lord Harlen on his own. Harlen sighed and cast a weary gaze around the yard. Struggling for power was a tiresome affair, but he enjoyed every moment of the great game. Soon enough, Death would be free and Harlen would take his place where he belonged—a god amongst men.

Lord Harlen started to head inside, but something caught his eye and stopped him short—a set of small footprints in the snow. They headed for the house, then veered into the bushes. Harlen stepped closer. Snow crunched beneath his feet. He paused, contemplating. All at once, he ripped the edge of the bushes back. No one was there. Harlen grunted and continued inside the manor.

THE NETHERWORLD CAVES HAD BOUGHT CASPER SOME time, but he knew the longer he waited, the harder it would be to face what waited outside the safety of the passages. Unsure of what they would encounter, Iris packed a satchel with essentials. She never left the caves without supplies. If the landscape decided to change, it would take them longer to find their way back to the tunnels. It was always best to be prepared.

Casper changed into some lightweight armor Iris had been saving, still in awe at the objects she'd managed to find lying about the Netherworld. Iris's armor seemed to fit a little better.

"Am I supposed to be able to move?" he joked.

Iris smiled as she tucked some rope into her satchel. "No. But you look dashing, if that's any consolation."

The breastplate was adorned with the mark of the Maker, Lumen—a Netherworld spiral set in the rays of the sun. Souls traveled to the Netherworld in whatever they were wearing at the time of death. Some made it back to the land of the living. The others were erased, oftentimes leaving things behind—weapons, armor, supplies. If it could be dropped, Iris had probably found it. She had a knack for finding useful things.

Once they'd gathered all they needed, they made their way through the tunnels for one of the openings. Neither spoke. Casper had a well of nerves swirling in his stomach. The first trial was easy because he hadn't realized what it was. He'd simply known something was off. This trial would be a great deal harder.

As the cave exit loomed ahead of them, Casper felt as if he were walking into the jaws of some great beast. Fear threatened to stall his feet, but then he remembered his conversation with Iris and what Harlen was really after. Kaelyn was in danger, greater danger than she'd ever been in before, and Casper wasn't about to let death get in his way. That strange sense of rage filled him once more, only this time he embraced it and stepped outside the safety of the tunnels.

It was darker here. Some sort of amber cloud cover blocked out the light. The ground was molten rock, jagged and uneven. Steam filtered through fissures that zig-zagged across the terrain, and an overwhelming humidity pressed down upon them. A massive volcano loomed in the distance.

"Remember," Iris instructed, "our swords can harm other souls, but Netherbeasts are more resilient. Don't do anything foolish."

Casper nodded in understanding, though he wondered what she might consider foolish.

Iris took the lead and carefully descended the small incline they stood on. Casper followed behind her. He studied the new environment carefully, taking in every detail with a hunter's eye. They reached the expansive valley below, and a sudden instinct shot down his spine. He grabbed Iris's arm. "Wait."

"What?" she uttered, studying his face.

Casper gently released her. "The ground," he replied. "It's brittle."

Iris gave him a questioning look.

"The rock feels like ice on a lightly frozen lake," he explained. "One misstep and we may fall through."

Iris nodded and surveyed their surroundings thoughtfully. "It covers the terrain," she observed. "We'll simply have to be cautious. There's no way around it."

She continued forward, stepping on tiptoe. Casper followed suit. The brittle rock beneath their feet cracked and bowed with their weight. They headed slowly for the volcano. A small black mountain range surrounded it, but nothing so impressive as the steaming monstrosity. Casper silently puzzled over how he'd know what the trial was. The first trial had him wandering in a desert for what he'd imagined to be days. Would this trial too take ages to show itself?

"Help!" A voice broke through his thoughts. "Please, help me!"

Both Iris and Casper turned. It was a lad no more than twelve years of age, gangly and thin as if a decent meal were rare. He raced across the thinning rock, causing steam to shoot angrily from the fissures he passed. He ran straight for them. At his heels, a massive shrieker.

"He'll collapse the surface," Casper uttered fearfully. The fissures widened. He could feel the pressure of the rock beneath him shifting.

Iris chewed on her lip, debating.

"We have to help him," Casper said.

Iris turned away. "We have to survive. He could be a trifle."

"And if he's not?" Casper challenged.

The two of them shared a heated look.

"You said souls were the only human things here," he continued. "If he looks human, he's a soul. And right now he needs help."

"Aye, but the Netherworld lies. You told me yourself you saw your sister."

"Are you willing to risk the lad's life on it?"

Iris looked between Casper and the fleeing boy, recalling how upset Casper was about the instance with the intruders. Again, she felt a tug on what little humanity she had left. She groaned, pulling a dagger from her belt. "Damn you."

Without hesitation, she sliced the dagger across her palm, drawing blood. The shrieker skidded to a stop and sniffed the air. The young boy paused, watching the creature in fear. Would it continue after him? The smell of fresh blood seemed more enticing than the scrawny lad. A high-pitched shriek emitted from the beast's throat as it caught the scent, causing the lad to clap his hands over his ears. Suddenly, the shrieker bounded straight for Iris. Somehow its heavy steps didn't affect the terrain.

Casper drew his sword, eyes sweeping rapidly over the cracking rock. He stepped in front of Iris, a gentle hand pushing her back. She silently obeyed, gripping her injured hand as she stepped with care. Casper analyzed the fracturing rock. The shrieker was almost upon them, its high-pitched squeal deafening. Closer and closer it came until, finally, Casper slammed his sword into the flimsy rock. There was a loud crackling as the sword pierced the brittle ground straight through to the hilt. Then, all was still. The shrieker stopped and observed Casper, head quirking to the side. All at once, the rock shattered and the beast fell through the gap into nothing. Its screams echoed in the void, soon fading to silence.

Casper breathed heavily and backed away from the dark ravine he'd created. The crackling and popping of the rocks continued. Casper froze, eyes following the collapsing fissures. The lad made his way toward his rescuers.

"Don't move!" Casper shouted.

The boy stopped. Iris froze. The cracks continued in zigzag patterns across the valley. Fissures exploded as the ground fell out. There was no deciphering where solid ground would remain and where it was brittle enough to fall.

Suddenly the ground beneath Iris collapsed.

"Iris!" Casper cried as he dove for the edge. He caught his breath at the sight of her clinging to the rock that remained.

"Take your bloody time," she grumbled. "I'll just hang here for a while, shall I?"

Casper nearly laughed in relief.

With the monster gone, the young lad jumped across the newly created gaps in their direction. Casper scooted farther over the edge and stretched out a hand. It was no use. Iris was too far down. "You'll have to let go," he said as calmly as he could.

"And lose my grip?" Iris retorted. "I can't!"

"Don't think with your head, Waylander," he repeated her words, smirking.

She grinned.

Determination painted her face, and she released a hand, swinging up to grab his. She breathed in relief when he barely caught it, and she chuckled nervously. The other lad finally approached them and graciously bent down, reaching for Iris's other hand. Together he and Casper pulled Iris back onto solid ground.

Casper immediately embraced Iris. It was instinctual, natural. He almost hadn't meant to do it. Iris froze in shock.

"I'm fine . . . really," she stammered.

Iris didn't know how to react. It'd been a long time since she'd been around people. Something in her felt warm again, and she wished he'd let go, fearful of it.

"Careful, Cas," she mused sarcastically. "I might start to think you actually care."

He released her suddenly. "Right . . . sorry."

What was wrong with him? He cleared his throat and helped her stand. He was about to say something else when the world around them shuddered. They could hardly stay upright through the tremor, eventually giving up and falling to their knees. The lad trembled in terror, whispering broken prayers to the Maker. Casper wondered why so young a boy had chosen to fight.

An earsplitting cannonade ripped through the air. All eyes turned to the volcano. For a moment, Casper thought it might erupt. To his horror, the sides of the volcano unfurled, revealed as enormous, stony wings. A head followed, then a body, a tail—a dragon! Casper had only heard of such creatures. They'd long since been purged from Wayland. Clearly a few of them had found a new home.

The beast was the size of a mountain. Lava ran through its scales like blood in veins. It gave a loud, ear-shattering roar. All three Waylanders clapped hands over their ears.

"Bloody hell," Casper muttered.

He stood shakily to his feet, picking up his sword. He tugged the boy up as gently as he could. "Stay close," he ordered.

The lad nodded vigorously, not about to stand anywhere else. Each beat of the dragon's massive wings vibrated the very air around them. It growled and swooped low. All three of them ducked, barely escaping a vicious blow from the dragon's clubbed tail.

"Any ideas?" Iris uttered.

Casper shook his head, brown eyes fixed on the flying monstrosity. "Not one."

He scanned the landscape around them. All the brittle rock formations had fallen through, leaving large ravine-like gaps across the terrain. As the dragon made to dive again, Casper signaled for the other two to follow his lead.

The dragon opened its large jaws. The lava-veins in its scales glowed as if charging, and it unleashed a hot jet of fire. They jumped the first ravine, the flames right behind them. Casper's brain sought dizzyingly for a solution. There was no level ground to fight on, and he knew their swords would do little good. Maybe if they could get it to land . . .

"We need to force it down!" Casper shouted above the beast's roar.

"Aye, and how's that?" Iris leapt over the next gap, looking back at the monster. Some of her fiery red hair fell loose from her braid.

"Got anything in your satchel?"

Iris thought on it, diving aside as the dragon swirled toward them. Its talons scraped the ground where she'd been standing moments before. "May have a bit of rope," she thought aloud.

Casper distracted the beast, swiping his sword tauntingly at it. It knocked him back with its large tail. He sailed a few ravines over, landing with a sickening crunch on the rocky ground. He rolled on impact, nearly sailing off the edge into the void. Casper winced, feeling as though the wind had been knocked out of him. The dragon assessed the situation, seeing Casper as the immediate threat.

Iris dug madly through her satchel. The young boy stood by, feeling utterly useless.

"Any day now, love!" Casper chided, pushing himself to his feet.

"I'm working on it!" she snapped.

Casper tested his limits, keeping Iris's teaching in the forefront of his mind. He could run faster and jump farther so long as he didn't let logic stand in his way. It was like living in a bad dream. He had the power to do almost anything until he remembered it was a dream; then it seemed he couldn't run fast enough.

"I got it!" Iris shouted across the battlefield.

The dragon swooped away again. Casper could have sworn it laughed. It was toying with them.

"Do you know how to tie a honda knot?" he called back.

Iris's face mirrored her befuddlement. "A what?"

"I do!" the boy piped up, eager to help.

Iris shared a look with Casper, silently asking what he wanted her to do.

"Give it to the lad!" Casper shouted, sheathing his sword. He jumped across the gaps, heading back in their direction.

Iris shoved the rope into the boy's hands. "Hurry!"

The lad didn't need telling twice. As he fumbled with the length of rope, Casper rejoined them.

Iris turned her emerald gaze back to the creature.

"Why isn't it attacking us properly? We should be dead already."

Casper's eyes followed the dragon's progress across the sky. Every time it attacked, it looped back toward the indentation in the earth where it'd been nesting. *Nesting.* The idea struck a chord in Casper's mind.

"It's guarding something," he realized. "The dragon isn't the trial. It's a trifle."

"We have to get what it's guarding," Iris said, not at all liking the idea.

"Exactly."

"I got it!" the lad exclaimed, showing the looped rope proudly.

Casper grinned and ruffled the boy's hair as he took the rope. He couldn't have tied the knots better himself. "Head for the nest between the mountains," he instructed. "Whatever happens, don't stop."

All three of them took off at a run. The dragon gave an irritated growl when it noticed their change of course. It whirled in the sky and barreled toward them. The terrain, so uneven and full of collapsed fissures, worked against the Waylanders. Casper skidded to a stop as the dragon neared. "Keep going!" he shouted to the others.

He turned to face the beast, lasso in hand. The dragon whirled angrily in the sky. Iris raced for the mountains, jumping the ravines with superhuman precision. The boy could barely keep up. A vicious roar tore from the dragon's throat. The creature looked between the three morsels, sizing them up. It made a snap decision and swooped toward the redhead.

Casper swung the lasso in his hand, grounding his feet. He kept his eyes trained on the beast. It swooped low over his head, low enough for Casper to feel the wind from the creature's wings. He seized the opportunity, throwing the rope. The loop caught the dragon's talon, and Casper pulled it tight. For a moment, all was still. And then the rope went taut, and Casper was yanked into the air. He grunted at the strain on his muscles. Iris skidded to a stop, looking on in wonder.

"He's mad," she uttered to herself.

The boy kept running toward the large indentation ahead.

Casper inched up the rope. "Keep going!" he shouted down to Iris.

She nodded and raced on with no clue what she was searching for. The dragon turned its scaly head, finally realizing it had an unwanted passenger. It arched in the sky and shook its leg viciously. Casper held tight. He made the mistake of looking down.

"Bugger," he muttered.

He took a breath to steel himself. Iris neared the mountain where the beast had been dormant, not far behind the younger lad. The dragon's eyes narrowed on Iris's fiery red hair. The lava-like veins in its skin glowed, and it shot a stream of flames. Casper's heart stopped. When the smoke cleared, Iris and the boy poked their heads out from behind a boulder, and Casper found his breath again.

"Stay put," Iris ordered the lad. She tore off running for the next rock. The boy nodded and crouched farther behind the boulder.

"You are going to land," Casper growled to the beast, climbing farther up the rope.

His muscles seared. He didn't know how much longer he could hold on. The dragon seemed to have the same idea. It looped in the sky, making

Casper sick to his stomach. He lost his grip on the rope and fell toward the rocks below with a shout. The dragon completed its loop beneath him, and he latched on to its rocky scales in desperation. The beast huffed in annoyance.

Iris skidded and tripped up the steep incline of the creature's nest. There was a mountain-sized indent where the creature had once been part of the landscape. Iris searched frantically for whatever the dragon was guarding, feeling the weight of time on her shoulders.

Casper climbed the dragon's back, scale by scale, each one warm and pulsing beneath his hands. He reached its neck and hung on for dear life. The dragon snapped its mighty jaws, trying everything to reach the lad, but to no avail. In annoyance, the beast finally landed, shaking the ground.

Iris lost her balance at the tremor and fell to her knees. With every step, the dragon shook the earth. Casper could barely keep himself atop the creature.

"The rope!" he shouted. "Use the rope!"

Iris's eyes flashed to the rope, still tightly around the dragon's thick talon. She swallowed hard. Iris wasn't dead. She was alive and trapped in the world of the dead. What would happen if she died here? Iris pushed back her fear. The dragon lashed out, its powerful jaws nearly catching the redhead. Iris rolled out of the way and scrambled to her feet.

Casper was nearly thrown from the beast at the movement. He dug his fingers into its scales. His skin split and blood trickled down his arms, but he didn't let go. Iris ran between the beast's legs, heart beating madly. One step of the dragon's foot was all it would take to squash her like an insect. The creature bent low, snapping at the redhead angrily, but Iris was too quick. She snatched the rope and dodged the creature's jaws again, running beneath its massive body. Round and round she went, tangling the rope around the beast's legs. Casper hung on for dear life, his hands screaming in protest. Soon, the mountainous creature began to stumble. Iris pulled the rope tighter, nearly reaching its end.

Tears of pain stung Casper's eyes. He scoured ahead, looking for any sign of the object the beast was guarding. Something stuck out of the flat terrain ahead—a handle of sorts. As the dragon fell toward the ground, Casper leapt from its neck. Iris dove for cover, nearly clobbered by the beast's massive tail. The moment Casper's feet hit the ground, he rolled and took off running. The dragon slammed into the rocky terrain, quaking the earth. Casper stumbled but didn't fall. He raced for the odd black handle, something in him knowing it was why he was there.

The dragon growled, a burning anger in its eyes. Iris hid behind a jagged, black rock, breathing heavily and praying to the Maker it wouldn't find her. The beast closed its teeth around the rope and snapped it. Iris was forgotten, the dragon's interest fixed on Casper. The fair-haired Waylander was nearly to his prize.

The creature stood, each step of its clawed feet shaking the ground. The glowing veins in its scales brightened, and it dug its talons into the stony earth. With a mighty roar, it spewed fire in Casper's direction. Casper was nearly to the handle, but the beast's attack forced him to dodge away from his quest. He was slightly singed in the process. Sweat ran down Casper's face in beads. He and the dragon locked eyes, fiercely staring one another down.

Casper took one look at the black handle and something in him snapped. A sudden fearlessness etched his features. The dragon's veins began to glow. Casper bolted. The dragon released its fire. Casper dropped and skidded across the ground, barely under the scorching flames. His bleeding fingers closed around the handle. The fire stopped when the beast ran out of breath. Casper stood and tugged the handle. The object popped out of the earth so forcefully, Casper was thrown to the ground. It clanged across the rocks—a sword! A long, black sword!

"Pick it up, Cas!" Iris screamed. She covered her mouth regretfully. The dragon's eyes snapped angrily in her direction. Time crawled as Casper dove for the sword. His fingers closed around the ebony hilt as the beast prepared to obliterate Iris. A great power surged through Casper's veins as if the sword itself were now a part of him. The dragon snorted and backed down slowly.

Casper stood in a daze, eyes transfixed on the blade in his hand.

"Casper," Iris said, coming to stand beside him. "I think it's afraid of the sword."

The hunter looked up. The dragon was indeed keeping its distance, but he wasn't convinced it was in fear. The dragon's eyes showed respect. Casper held the sword aloft and moved it side to side. The dragon's eyes followed.

"I don't think it's afraid," he uttered. "I think I just became its master."

He studied the sword. It seemed ordinary in every way aside from the strange black metal. His eyes finally caught the glowing ruby housed on the hilt. "Is that—"

"A Netherstone," Iris uttered in disbelief.

A searing pain burned on Casper's forearm, so strong he nearly dropped the sword. The wince on his face worried Iris at first, but then the truth dawned on her. She swiftly pulled the armor off his arm and tugged back the fabric of his shirt. Sure enough, the second circle of the Netherworld triad burned red-hot into his skin.

"You did it," she said, beaming.

A pathetic and tired voice called from one of the boulders farther down the way. "Can I come out now?"

Iris and Casper shared a look, then broke into much-needed laughter.

Trial by Fire

JOSIAH WORKED TIRELESSLY AT THE BLACKSMITH SHOP. There were horseshoes to make, sword orders to fill, and new locks to fashion. With the frigid weather outside, he kept the large doors to the shop closed, allowing the heat from the fire to warm the large space. The downside? It made the interior of the shop twice as hot, and Josiah was sweating profusely. He kept a red bandana tied around his neck to catch most of it as it dripped from his face, but it could only do so much. Even with his shirt sleeves rolled up and the first few buttons undone, he was boiling.

The methodic banging of Josiah's hammer drowned out a soft tapping at the window. Mid-swing, he finally heard it and paused in his work. A small pigeon sat on the snowy sill outside, pecking incessantly to be let in. Josiah wiped his brow and abandoned his work. Stark was upstairs tending to the parchments for the day's orders, so the apprentice had little worry about reprimands for taking a break. He went to the window and opened it a crack. The small burst of cooler air was a great relief to Josiah, but as soon as the bird hopped inside, he had to close the window again. It wouldn't do to get sick.

"What have you got there, love?" Josiah cooed to the bird.

He carefully scooped it up, pulling a small note from its leg. He set the bird aside and unfurled it to find Anna-Rose's hasty scrawl:

Harlen to burn mill. Hurry.

It felt as if Josiah had been sucker punched in the gut. He had to remind himself to breathe. The stairs creaked as Stark ambled down them, uttering something Josiah didn't hear. He stopped in his tracks when he caught sight of the look on Josiah's face.

"Everything all right, lad?" he asked.

Josiah dashed for his beat-up longcoat in response and threw it on haphazardly.

"Josiah?" Stark called after him, but the lad was already gone, leaving the door to swing in the wind.

Through the snowy streets he raced, heart pumping madly. He'd never make it there on foot. Josiah's eyes alighted on the stables not far from the blacksmith's shop. Given the circumstances, surely a small act of theft could be overlooked. He didn't give it a second thought, nabbing the first horse he came to: a great black steed. With little time to waste, he rode bareback, spurring the horse through the streets with all his might. Around this turn and that, the horse galloped at full speed, hooves pounding loudly against the snowy cobblestones. The sun dipped lower in the sky, and Josiah prayed to the Maker he wasn't too late.

Soon the city wall came into view. At the sound of rapidly approaching hooves, the two Watchmen guarding the gate perked up. Before they could say a word, Josiah was upon them. All they could do was dive out of the way. The clopping of the horse's shoes changed to a duller thud as the cobblestones were exchanged for snow-covered dirt. Josiah didn't slow.

Into the trees they rode, as if Death himself were after them. The forest blocked out the fading sunlight, darkening the already-dim path. With a whinny of protest, the horse leapt over a fallen log. Five miles—that was the distance from the city to the Outer Edge. Walking with Kaelyn, the time almost flew by, but the more he spurred the horse on, the farther away the mill seemed to be.

The sun finished its arc in the sky, leaving the world to the mercy of a moonless night. Josiah was almost as tired as the horse when they finally broke through the trees. His heart froze as he pulled the creature to a stop. The windmill was already engulfed in flames, and the cottage wasn't far behind. A heart-shattering scream ripped through the air. Kaelyn.

Try as she might, the younger Renolds couldn't tear free of the bastard who dragged her away from the burning house.

"Gran!" she screamed. "No!"

Josiah's heart tore. Bash's thug pulled her onto a horse and rode off, leaving his men to finish the job. Josiah looked between Kaelyn and the burning house and cursed.

"Yah!" he cried, spurring the animal forward.

He barreled toward the home. One of the black-clad goons held a torch to the thatched roof, adding more fire to the blaze. Josiah neared and dove off his steed, tackling the man to the ground. The torch fell into a deep pile of snow, quickly extinguished by the moisture. It took little effort for Josiah to snap the man's neck.

All at once, the cottage's glass windows exploded. Josiah dropped, covering his head as small bits of glass rained down on him. Gran was still in there . . . and so was Casper.

Josiah made for the door as quickly as he could. It wouldn't budge, and the handle was piping hot. The fire was right on the other side. His eyes landed on the window, now devoid of glass save for the sharp edges around the frame. It was his best way in. Josiah pulled the bandana from his neck and tied it around his nose and mouth.

"Hey!" One of Bash's other thugs caught sight of him, but Josiah dove through the window before anything could be done.

Smoke quickly stung Josiah's eyes and nearly choked him. If he weren't a Netherworlder, it would have crippled him quickly. "Gran!" he called over the roar of the flames.

The ceiling had already collapsed, making a sort of ramp to the second floor. Fire leapt out of the window Josiah had come through. There wasn't much time. Sweat dripped down his face. The sheer heat from the flames was almost unbearable.

"Gran!" he tried again, coughing. Tears stung his eyes from the smoke. "Gran!"

A weak moan sounded from beneath the rubble. Josiah's heart bottomed out.

"No, no, no," he uttered, rushing toward it. He shoved chunks of wood aside and charred remains of furniture. Buried deep in the chaos, he found a barely conscious Gran. Blood dribbled from her mouth. Tears stung his eyes for a different reason then.

"Wake up, Gran," he uttered, placing a hand on her cheek. "Come on."

He looked her over, hoping and praying she could be moved. His heart sunk. A piece of the rafters had pierced her straight through. She was pinned. Gran had showed him every kindness over the months, as if time had never passed and he was still the little boy who came to play with her grandchildren.

Gran's eyes fluttered open. Josiah pulled the bandana down so she could see his face. The kind smile that crossed her lips made him tear up all the more, but he didn't let them fall.

"I will get her back, Gran," he promised. "You have my word."

Gran set her hand atop his. "I know," she wheezed.

The breath left her lungs, and the kind light faded from her eyes. Her hand was the last thing to fall, and Josiah couldn't hold back the well of tears. They fell in a stream as anger, shock, and grief commingled inside of him. Was there no boundary Harlen wouldn't cross? Was anyone safe from his wicked schemes? Gran didn't deserve this. Casper and Kaelyn didn't deserve this. Josiah felt it then, that Netherworld rage that slept inside of him. It spread through his body until he shook with it, shoving back his shock and grief to let it through. His hand balled into a fist as he stood. Giving in to the quick temper that often came with Netherworld strength could be disastrous, but this was different. This was a righteous anger. A slow burning, mighty flame that Lord Harlen could never hope to counter. He had to get Casper out. And then . . . then Harlen would pay.

Josiah dodged effortlessly aside as more debris rained down on him. The only way to the second floor was the caved-in bit of ceiling. Flaming debris was just beneath it, like some sort of evil stairway. With renewed determination, he replaced the bandana over his face and scaled the pile. It lurched and creaked beneath him, already unstable. All at once, it collapsed. Josiah barely caught the edge of the floor above. Flames licked the new kindling under him, tendrils reaching for his feet like demented hands. The rage inside him turned to adrenaline, which in turn fueled his strength. He hoisted himself onto the second floor like it was nothing, never losing himself to the rage but letting it bubble just under the surface.

Fire consumed much of the second floor as well, but not quite as much as the first. Casper was thankfully still in one piece, though not for long. The flames snaked quickly toward the bed, almost taking on a life of their own. Josiah studied the floor, quickly mapping where it was weakest. One step at a time, he crossed the room, dodging a bit of flame here and skirting weakened floorboards there. His Netherworlder constitution had gotten him this far, but his skin was starting to burn. If he didn't get out soon, he'd have permanent damage.

Josiah's heart clenched as the edge of the bed caught fire. If Casper's body was destroyed, he'd be erased. A wall of flames sprung up in front of him, almost as if the fire had a mind of its own with the task of keeping him back. Casper's leg caught fire, and Josiah felt his rage surge. He jumped though the flames, ignoring the sting. Josiah tore off his coat and smothered the flames on the bed as best he could. It wasn't easy with the entire room ablaze, but Josiah finally managed. The floor gave a shudder. Time was up.

Josiah left his singed longcoat and hoisted Casper overshoulder. The fire had completely blocked the way he'd entered, leaving them trapped on Casper's side of the room. Josiah looked frantically for an exit as the floor gave another lurch. The window! Better to break a few bones than be burned alive. Josiah barreled toward it as the floor fell out behind him, food for the fiery beast below.

The window was latched shut when he reached it, but a well-placed kick and some applied Netherworld strength shot it open easily.

"Sorry, mate," he uttered, dumping Casper out the window.

Josiah jumped out after him. To his immense relief, the snow in the rear of the house had been left untouched, creating a dense pile to land in. It was like falling on a soft pillow. Harlen's men were gone by the looks of things. Josiah pulled himself out of the snowy bank and dragged Casper away from the burning house. Once at a safe distance, he dropped his old friend and viewed the mess Lord Harlen had made. That rage threatened to surface again, but Josiah took a measured breath and pushed it down.

He didn't need it now.

A horse snorted nearby. Josiah turned and pulled the bandana from his face, relieved—the black steed was still there.

"Come on, mate," Josiah spoke to the lifeless Casper, dragging him toward the horse. "We're getting your sister back."

THE LANDSCAPE IN THE NETHERWORLD HAD CHANGED on them as Iris predicted it would. It wasn't a drastic change, but rather gradual like it had been in Casper's first trial. The cave entrance disappeared, and the dragon too faded. The sword, however, remained in Casper's possession. He gave his other sword to the boy and proudly sheathed the black Nethersword. Injured and lost, the threesome made their way for the nearby mountains that remained.

Soon they traded the humid landscape for the cooler air of a forest. The volcanic scenery all but melted away behind them, never to be found again even if they tried. Iris tended to her cut as they walked, binding her hand with a simple bandage.

"Sit," she ordered Casper when she'd finished.

"What?" he returned, pulled from his thoughts.

"Sit," she said sharply.

Casper absentmindedly took a seat on a nearby stone. Iris started pulling all manner of things from her bag—bandages, a leaf jar of salve, and a canteen of water. She uncorked the canteen first and dumped water over his bleeding hands. He winced.

"Sorry," she murmured.

Casper's attention shifted to the boy standing awkwardly by.

"What's your name, lad?"

"Thomas, sir," he answered. "Thomas Frye."

A gentle smile crossed Casper's lips, and he nearly laughed. "You don't have to call me 'sir,' Thomas. Casper will do."

Thomas smiled and nodded. "Casper."

"And this is Iris," he added.

The redhead didn't bother to look up from cleaning Casper's wounds. "Pleasure," she uttered half-heartedly.

"Her bark's worse than her bite; I promise you that," Casper mused.

The glare in Iris's eyes could give the dragon's fire a run for its gold.

Casper chuckled, and Thomas's smile widened.

"You were pretty good back there," Casper said. "Where'd you learn to tie knots like that?"

"Dad's a fisherman," Thomas replied. "Taught me all manner of things like that. I was to take up his work . . . before I fell ill, that is."

"Is that why you chose to fight?" Casper wondered. "For your dad?"

"Aye," Thomas nodded. "And Mum. She's with child, you see, and Dad's not very well. If I don't get back, I don't know how they'll make do."

Iris applied salve to the cuts on Casper's hands and bound them in bandages for the second time since he'd entered that cursed land.

"You can stick with us if you like," Casper offered. "Better chance of making it that way."

Iris all but chucked things back in her satchel before standing haughtily. "Casper, a word," she snapped. Before he could even roll his eyes, she'd dragged him away, lowering her voice to a heated whisper. "What are you doing?"

"Being a good person," he snapped back. "Something you've obviously forgotten how to do."

Iris bristled. It wasn't an untrue statement, but she loathed the thought. "He hasn't passed his first trial yet. The trials *find you*. If he stays with us, they'll find *us* too."

Casper shrugged. "What's your bloody point?"

Iris rolled her eyes. "You're not going to listen to me anyway, are you?"

"No." An irritating itch began in his leg, but he ignored it and folded his arms indignantly. "People change in the Netherworld. You said so yourself. But what if there's another way?"

"There *isn't*."

"But what if there was?" The itching worsened, but Casper still ignored it, digging his fingernails into his arm.

Iris had to admit, if there was another way, Casper would be the one to find it. Him with all his good intentions and bloody good looks. Before she could say another word about it, Casper suddenly collapsed, screaming in pain.

"Cas!" Iris exclaimed, the argument forgotten.

Thomas came rushing over at the noise, eyes widening at the sight. Casper writhed and screamed, clutching his leg. Iris knelt beside him, looking in vain for a solution.

"The burning," he uttered, gnashing his teeth. "Stop the burning."

Iris examined his leg. It was perfectly fine. "There's nothing there," she insisted, trying and failing to hide the panic in her voice.

"What's happening to him?" Thomas asked, feeling helpless.

"I . . . I don't know," she admitted.

Tears stung Casper's eyes at the pain. All Iris could do was run her fingers through his blond hair and try to soothe him. The truth suddenly dawned on her, only worsening her panic.

"Something must be happening to his body on the other side," she reasoned.

"That can happen?" Thomas panicked.

Iris nodded but said nothing further. She was at a complete loss. As Casper writhed and groaned, all the others could do was watch. Sweat gathered on his brow and his cries died down, too tired to keep fighting. Casper was prepared to meet his fate, certain that Harlen had caught up and he was done for, when all of a sudden, it stopped. His breathing evened out, his heart rate slowed down—everything seemed normal.

Iris breathed a heavy sigh of relief and let her head fall on his chest. If she lost him, she lost all hope. Loath though she was to admit it, she needed him.

"Careful," Casper uttered, exhausted. "I might start to think you care."

"Shut up," she grumbled.

The Scaths

IT WAS A TERRIBLE THING, REALIZING HER OWN WEAKNESS. No matter how kaelyn kicked and screamed, no matter how hard she struggled, she couldn't seem to escape the brute who'd slung her over his horse like a prized pelt he'd won on a good hunting day. If anyone saw the six horses riding through town or heard her cries, they didn't try to stop it. All six men wore Watchmen's longcoats, and no one dared disagree with the Watch. Especially not when they knew who the Watch really reported to these days. Kaelyn eventually gave up her fruitless struggle, choosing to save her energy.

Gran had still been in the cottage . . . so had Casper.

Agonizing pain stabbed her chest, welling tears in her eyes. She was alone. The last Renolds standing. Who would save her now?

She presently realized it wasn't up to anyone else. She had to save herself. She might not have the physical strength to throw the guard off, but she could make him miserable. She could make them all miserable. Whatever Harlen wanted of her, Kaelyn wouldn't let him have it.

Whatever scheme he'd hatched, Kaelyn would ruin it. Somehow.

By the time they dismounted outside Harlen Manor, Kaelyn was bruised all over from the ride. She didn't let her discomfort show on the outside. No matter her fate, she would get her revenge.

She didn't struggle as the guard led her through the ornate entryway with its split marbled staircase. Up the stairs, past tapestries and suits of rusting armor, they went, Kaelyn saying nothing, steel in her eyes. Her sudden silence seemed to unnerve the guard, who kept an unnecessarily tight grip on her arm despite the five other men walking with them. Something had snapped in Kaelyn, something Harlen was going to wish he'd never awoken.

Lord Harlen stood waiting in his study, the fire blazing behind him. Kaelyn was thrown at his feet. She didn't cry out or complain. She waited, calmly and coolly, for Harlen to show his hand. An evil smile curled on Harlen's lips.

"Welcome home, milady," he said darkly.

The guards left at a signal from Harlen, leaving the two of them alone. Kaelyn rubbed her sore arm and stood carefully, a defiance on her porcelain face.

"I am not home," she spat.

Harlen took a step closer and fingered a loose strand of her golden hair. "I'd get used to the idea, my dear. We're going to be spending a lot of time together."

"Don't touch me," she warned, fire in her eyes.

Suddenly, Harlen's hand gripped her throat, and he slammed her angrily into the bookcase. She struggled to breathe, his face inches from hers.

"You are officially my ward by the laws of the city," he spat. "I can do what I please."

He threw her away and straightened his longcoat. Kaelyn caught herself on the desk, gasping for air as rage billowed inside her. She spotted the letter opener so carelessly left within her reach. Her fingers coiled around it as she pretended to sob, sensing him inching up behind her. When she felt his hand on her waist, she whirled and slashed his cheek with a cry of fury. Harlen staggered back in shock, clutching his now-bleeding face.

"You may do as you please," she seethed, "but I will fight you every step of the way. You murdered my brother, my gran; you tried to murder Josiah. If you think for one bloody moment I will cower in fear of you, you are sorely mistaken, my lord. It is you who should cower in fear of me. I will never yield to the likes of you!"

The look of pure loathing in Harlen's eyes gave Kaelyn satisfaction. She no longer cared about propriety or manners. He didn't deserve them.

Harlen pulled a handkerchief from his pocket and flicked it angrily open. He pressed it to his bleeding cheek. "I have plans for you, my dear," he fumed. "And none of them require you to be in one piece."

Kaelyn opened her mouth to retort, but he backhanded her so swiftly and forcefully, she was thrown to the floor, unconscious. Harlen swore, kneeling to check her pulse, breathing easily when it thrummed against his fingers—he hadn't snapped her neck. After a breath to calm himself, he shouted for the guards and ordered them to take her away. His cheek smarted as her limp form was dragged from the study. Of all the sacrifices he could have chosen, why did he always find the ones who wanted to fight back?

IT DIDN'T TAKE LONG FOR CASPER TO PULL HIMSELF

together again. There were no marks on his leg to speak of, not even a rash. Iris said he was lucky, but Casper wasn't so sure. If her theory was correct and his body had been attacked, then something back home was wrong.

Regardless, Casper quickly threw that notion aside. He seemed fine for now, and there were more pressing matters at hand, such as finding the caves again. Thomas was a regular chatterbox as they walked. He talked about the Slums where he lived, painting them a wonderful place. Casper had only ventured that far into the lower city once, and he vowed never to do so again. The streets there were filthy and the people more so. Gang violence and murder were rampant there, and the Watch rarely did anything about it.

"My, aren't you cheery?" Iris commented.

Thomas shrugged. "Well, we've got to be, haven't we? I mean, how can we make the world better if we don't stop mopin'. That's what my dad always says."

Casper grinned. "Sounds like a brilliant man, your dad."

"Oh, he is!" Thomas insisted.

Iris walked a little ahead of the group. Though she tried her best to be patient, Casper could tell she was getting irked by the younger lad. Thomas didn't seem to notice.

"My mum's pretty grand too, but then I suppose most mothers are," Thomas continued.

"Yes, indeed," Casper mused.

And then came the inevitable. "I'm getting frightfully hungry," the lad said. "Have we anything to eat?"

"No!" Iris and Casper shouted in unison.

Thomas jumped at the sudden outburst, looking as if he'd been stung and might break down crying at any moment. Iris didn't seem to care, but Casper had been an older brother long enough to have at least a little compassion. He set a hand on the lad's shoulder as they meandered through the trees.

"What we mean to say is," he began. "Well . . ."

"Oh, for heaven's sake," Iris groaned, rounding on the both of them. "The rules are simple here, pint-size. Don't eat anything. Don't drink anything. And above all, don't get killed."

She whipped back around as quickly as she whirled on them, walking on without a care in the world.

Thomas grinned. "Pint-size . . . I sort of like that!"

He all but jogged to catch up to Iris. Casper pursed his lips in an effort to conceal a smirk. It seemed Iris had herself an admirer.

The farther into the forest they walked, the denser the trees became until the sunlight was almost completely extinguished. Thomas soon fell silent, and Casper didn't have to guess why. The very air itself was colder as if warning something sinister lurked nearby. The hair on the back of Casper's neck stood up. He stopped suddenly.

"Casper?" Iris whispered.

"I feel it too," he told her.

They were being watched. He couldn't say from where or by what, but something was definitely there. Thomas moved closer to Casper's side. The ruby in the hilt of Casper's sword began to glow. Curious, Casper pulled it from its sheath and studied it. Nothing seemed out of place. For all he could tell, the jewel just decided to come alive. And then he heard it. The whispers. They were unintelligible, more gibberish than actual words, but the very sound of it sent a chill down Casper's spine. Thomas gripped Casper's arm in an iron vice.

"Do you hear that?" he breathed.

Casper nodded. "Aye . . . I bloody well hear it," he murmured, turning to Iris. They exchanged worried looks.

"Casper," Thomas whispered, tugging on Casper's arm.

When the lad had Casper's full attention, he pointed a shaking finger at the reflection in Casper's sword. Gradually, Casper and Iris turned their eyes to the reflective surface. It took all of Casper's strength not to panic. There, standing right behind them, was a ten-foot-tall, slender creature with clawed hands and wrinkled, dark skin that seemed to billow and reform like smoke. Its mouth was sewn together as if to keep it silent, but it did nothing to stop the whispers now growing louder. Black eyes stared at Casper's reflection, and Casper was mesmerized . . . until a clawed hand reached for his head.

"Run!" he shouted, whirling on the creature, arching his sword in one great slash. But when he turned, the creature was no longer there.

The others had already torn off. Casper turned to do the same. Before he could take a step, something slammed into his chest and he was thrown into the air, dropping his sword. He crashed into a tree and thudded to the ground. A distant scream split the air—Iris.

Casper struggled to get up. The whispers were louder now, multiplied and excited. There were more of those things, whatever they were. Something moved in the corner of his eye. He whirled to face it, but again the horrific beast was gone. Another scream. This one sounded like Thomas. Casper couldn't see them through the thick trees.

A gathering of the creatures seemed visible in the corner of his eye. Every time he faced them, they disappeared. As far as he could tell, they seemed to have made a circle around him, cutting him off from the rest. But why him? Was this his next trial? Iris hadn't even explained the third trial to him. He had no idea what to expect of it. He heard Iris cry out again, and something in him snapped. All the fear these creatures stirred up was pushed aside, replaced with a new resolve—he had to get to Iris.

Casper's eyes frantically searched for the sword he'd lost. The creatures' whispers grew irritated. They seemed to be moving closer, but he couldn't get a clear look at the edge of his vision. What were they waiting for?

Suddenly, he spotted the sword, its jeweled hilt barely peeking out of a patch of tall grass. If it weren't for the glowing ruby, he may never have seen it through the gloom. He took a step. Giant, invisible claws ripped through his breastplate.

Before Casper could begin to contemplate the sheer strength of these creatures, he was yanked off his feet and dragged away from the sword. He clawed at the earth, pulling up grass and dirt in an effort to anchor himself. His fingers finally clamped onto a tree root jutting out of the soil, and he kicked with all his might at something he couldn't see. The creature let him go with a howl of rage.

Why weren't they dogpiling him and ripping him to shreds? A pack of shriekers would surely have ripped him in half by now, but that didn't seem to be the motivation of these things. Despite their strength, they only seemed interested in keeping him from the sword. He wondered if the gem in its hilt had anything to do with it. It hadn't been alight all this time, and now that they were near, it burned bright as a fire.

Casper pushed himself to his feet. The creatures seemed to be watching, waiting. Every time he moved for the sword, they attacked, but if he stood there, they were immobile. He turned in a slow circle. The terrifying beasts were visible at the corner of his eye, though not as clearly as they had been in the reflection of his sword. Another cry in the distance. If he didn't get that weapon, they were done for.

Movement caught his eye, only this one didn't disappear when he looked at it. *Thomas.* The lad quietly crept through the trees toward him, holding his sword in front of him like a mirror. Casper smiled to himself. *Clever lad,* he thought.

Thomas locked eyes with Casper, and the latter made a gesture for the silver sword. Ordinary though it was, Thomas seemed to have the right idea. The lad gave a single nod. Somehow he looked far different from the boy who'd been chattering incessantly mere moments ago. If the creatures noticed the interaction, they didn't show it. In a fluid motion, Thomas threw his sword. It whooshed through the air, thankfully landing within Casper's reach. He dove for it, heart clenching in terror as he scooped it up. Near twenty or more of the horrifying creatures stood around him, all with their hands outstretched.

Suddenly, the whispers changed, morphing into intelligible words.

"Weak," they hissed. *"A disgrace to your family. Can't even protect your sister."*

Casper's heart beat faster.

"Left them all alone."

"Don't listen to them," Thomas called. "Whatever they're saying, don't listen!"

The creatures closed in, tightening their circle. The Nethersword was forgotten where it lay.

"Let Iris down too," they whispered in unison. *"She died without a protector."*

The more they talked, the more terror and despair Casper felt. It was like being caught in a trance. As the creatures formed a tighter circle around Casper, Thomas's eyes wandered to the Nethersword. The ruby still glowed like a thousand suns. Silently, he slipped through the trees and toward the black weapon.

"Useless. A mistake. Unfit to hold a sword."

Casper sank to his knees. The weapon in his hand thudded on the damp earth.

"Not strong enough."

Suddenly, Casper jolted. A stream of silvery energy was pulled from his chest, floating like a fluid, glowing smoke. It split into separate streams, each drawn into the hands of the monsters standing over him. He jolted again, and a cry left his lips. A daunting chill overtook Casper, sinking into his very bones. It was like everything that wound him up, everything that made him *Casper* was being taken. Screams echoed in his mind—screams of his loved ones being slain, of innocent people getting hurt. It was like facing all the little things he feared or worried about. The more he felt panic, the more they fed on it, and the weaker he became.

"Hey!" Thomas's voice interrupted. He stood on a fallen log, brandishing the Nethersword with two hands. It looked overly large in the smaller lad's grip. "Leave my friend alone!"

The lad's distraction was enough to loosen the creatures' hold on Casper. The silver essence faded away, and Casper broke free. He was weak, but not down for the count. "The sword," he uttered with difficulty, getting clumsily to his feet. "Give me the sword, Thomas."

Thomas suddenly found himself rooted to the spot.

"They're afraid of it, lad. They won't touch you while you have it." It was a stretch, Casper knew. He couldn't even see the creatures to tell where they'd gone.

"Aye. That's why I think I'll keep hold of it," Thomas said, jumping at all the shapes moving at the edge of his vision.

There was a roar, and the log broke in half, sending Thomas tumbling to the ground. His panic and fear doubled, but he managed to keep his hold on the weapon. "Give me the sword!" Casper shouted, really wishing he hadn't. It made him feel sick.

Thomas stumbled to his feet and broke into a run, thrusting the mighty weapon into Casper's hands. Instantly, Thomas was swept off his feet and pinned to a tree by an invisible source. The silvery light was painfully pulled from him, wrapping like tendrils around an invisible hand at the lad's throat. He screamed.

With the sword in his hands, Casper felt some of his strength returning. Warmth spread throughout his body, and Thomas's cries ignited a hidden rage. Though the creature wasn't visible, Casper could see the light around the creature's clawed hand well enough. He slashed with a feral snarl, slicing the beast's arm clean off. Thomas fell in a heap on the ground as the creature shrieked and moaned. The sword seemed to know what it wanted, thrusting forward and burying itself deep in the monster's chest. As it died, it became visible, slowly shriveling up on the end of Casper's sword. Casper yanked his weapon from the beast and kicked it to the ground.

"Who's next?" he said angrily.

The whispers, unintelligible again, became agitated. As the beasts swiped and clawed at Casper, the sword acted almost of its own accord. The creatures fell one at a time to the blade until a pile of visible beasts lay at his feet. One monster's claws came dangerously close to Casper's head, trimming some of his fair hair off the top. It too fell to the Nethersword.

Soon the sword's jewel ceased to glow, and Casper's sudden rage slowly faded. He breathed heavily, looking down at all the bodies he'd piled up. Had he really done that? Thomas poked his head out from his hiding place behind a tree. His eyes grew wide as ripe tomatoes.

"Whoa," the lad uttered. "That was bloody brilliant!"

Casper sheathed his weapon with a tired smile, but it quickly faded. "Iris. Where is she?"

Thomas waved for Casper to follow him and darted through the trees. Sticks crackled underfoot as they ran. Rocks and tree roots made the ground uneven. Thomas nearly tripped, but Casper quickly caught him by the back of his shirt and pulled the lad up. Iris was sprawled on the ground, trembling and muttering to herself. She was barely conscious, never a good thing in the Netherworld. Falling asleep only meant one thing: the ultimate death.

The ruby on Casper's sword glowed once more, and he swiftly drew it. The whispers were so faint he hadn't heard them at first, but the reflection in his sword showed one last creature that had stayed to finish her off. It slowly turned its emaciated head. This time Casper wasn't afraid of the cold, black eyes, but rather infuriated. He raised his sword and swung at the beast. He didn't land a blow. He tilted his sword and glanced at the black reflective surface. The creature was nowhere to be seen, yet the ruby still shone.

"Stay close," Casper uttered.

Thomas nodded and took a step nearer. The forest around them was still. Casper's tawny eyes scoured every inch of the wooded area, checking now and then in the sword's reflection. With Iris fading by the second, Casper didn't have much time to waste.

Suddenly something shifted in the reflection of his weapon. The creature's head was sticking partway out of a tree, looking right at Thomas. "Look out!" Casper yelled, pushing the lad aside. He swiped the sword, trusting the weapon's lead. There was a *snick* and a dull thud. Casper breathed heavily as a decapitated body melted into view. It fell to the ground not far from the severed head.

"Bloody hell," Thomas whispered.

But Casper hardly heard. He was already sheathing his sword and racing for Iris. She moaned weakly when he shook her, still trembling and uttering nonsense. "Come on. Don't do this to me," Casper murmured.

Thomas came over, a sullen look on his face. "How is she?"

"Not good," Casper answered. He scooped her up in his arms, not really sure what to do. If they could find their way back to camp, he might be able to find something in one of those crates to help her. Just as soon as the thought crossed his mind, he saw it—the entrance to the caves. It was hidden beneath a rock outcropping, barely visible.

"Looks like she found it," he said. "Come on."

As Casper walked toward the cave mouth, Thomas looked down and studied his arm. A fresh black spiral was tattooed there, and an overwhelming guilt slammed into him like a boulder. The creatures had been his first trial. Iris was hurt, and it was all his fault.

An Old Friend

STARK HAD BEEN NONE TOO HAPPY TO FIND JOSIAH AT the back door, disheveled and with a body overshoulder, but once the young apprentice had a chance to explain, the blacksmith admitted him entrance. Josiah dumped Casper's body on the cot in the workshop, and Stark immediately tended to the burns on Casper's leg.

Days passed with little change. Casper remained dead, Anna-Rose sent no messages, and the absence of Kaelyn had Josiah in a foul mood. He needed a plan, and he needed one fast. He fiddled with a large door lock he'd made the day before, examining the inner mechanism. To achieve his aims, he had to break his vows to Stark. Sneaking down Prior Street hadn't exactly been underhanded. Certainly he'd skulked, but his next plan would involve actual thieving.

His previous mentor had been an avid lock pick and had taught Josiah the art well. Now that Josiah was a blacksmith's apprentice, he made locks and keys daily. He knew the internal workings like a child's primer book, and moreover, he knew exactly what kind of locks were on many of the major city buildings, having crafted them himself.

His eyes wandered to the cot where Casper's lifeless body lay. Part of Josiah felt as though he'd let Casper down. Even though they hadn't spoken in years, he still felt a strong kinship with Casper. Josiah had been selfish to stay away, to hide, but after becoming a Netherworlder, he'd felt more like a monster than a man. He was in control of the strange power now—"the rage" as they called it. It wasn't really anger, though it certainly burned like it. It was power. Harlen had lost himself to it, as had Bash. Josiah refused to give in to such darkness.

There was a danger that Casper wouldn't be so lucky. The Netherworld was a horrible place, unkind to all. It would put temptation in his path, test his good nature, and do all it could to break him. Even good people didn't survive unscathed. If Casper survived and he hadn't succumbed to the darkness that slept in them all, Josiah could teach him a better way.

The floorboards overhead creaked, the signal that Stark was meandering off to bed. Josiah set the unfinished lock aside and glanced at the candle clock on the far wall. It was nearly ten at night, give or take a few minutes. Stark often forgot to replace the candle at the twelfth hour and had to reset it by the church bells. The Archive staff should have cleared out by now.

Josiah stole one last look at Casper, then set the lock aside and extinguished the nearby oil lamp. There once was a time when this sort of thing had been easy, when it'd been a way of life. Now, despite its necessity, it felt wrong. If he were caught, he'd lose a hand . . . or worse. He shoved the thought aside. Sometimes good people had to break the law, and in spite of his good nature, Josiah was rather gifted at it.

He shrugged on a faded dark longcoat and tied the red bandana around his face. Did it look silly? Perhaps, but he'd rather not risk identification. After one last pause to listen for movement from Stark, Josiah slipped out the door and into the cobblestoned streets of the city. Though the snow from the week before had melted away, the air was still frigid with winter's breath. The moon hid behind cloud cover, creating even more shadow to hide in. It was as if the Maker himself approved this plan. The thought was encouraging, and Josiah pressed on.

Wayland was a strange city with many laws, one of them being a curfew imposed for the supposed safety of the land. Past ten, all business should be done for the day, and anyone caught on the street was subject to inquiry. The only real exception to the law was the Slums in the lower town. The Watch rarely traveled there, caring little for the depraved souls who lived in the crumbling ruins.

Of course, curfew didn't keep everyone indoors. The officers in Bash's Watch weren't always the sharpest swords in the armory. Josiah had seen the odd young man or two climbing into a young lady's bedroom window. Some stayed for ale at the alehouses well past curfew, and once the church bells rang out ten o'clock, it was time for the city's best thieves to go to work.

Josiah moved silently, keeping to the shadows along the building's edge. Wayland was like a maze with all its twists and turns, but he knew where he was going. He slipped beneath an arch between buildings and stole quickly down a narrow alley. The Watch would comb them from time to time, but more often than not, they could be found sharing a smoke around one of the street lanterns or keeping to the well-lit areas. Bash didn't hire the most stout-hearted of men.

Josiah soon reached the center of town, with its glorious fountain and colorful banners. It was like a ghost town now, littered with runaway papers and the occasional trash from the bustling day at the market. There were four street lanterns, one on every corner of the square. Each had three different lamps on the iron post. Flames flickered behind the glass casing, making the shadows dance. It was one of the most well-lit areas of the city and also the only way to get to the Archive.

One of the Watchmen lazily patrolled the square, eventually sitting on the fountain's edge. From the glazed look in his eye, Josiah deduced the man was intoxicated. Sure enough, the guard pulled a flask from his coat pocket and took a swig.

"Don't let the captain sees ya," another guard said as he entered the square. He must have been patrolling the street amid the few shops farther down.

The inebriated guard offered a drink to the new one. The man shrugged and said, "Why not?"

As the newcomer took a seat beside his colleague, Josiah scanned the square. Down the way the guard had come from were more permanent shops: the silver smith, the dressmakers, the pawn shop. Vendors from other sections of town would bring their carts to the square once a week for Market Day—the day Kaelyn usually came to town. For the farmers and hunters who lived on the Outer Edge, Market Day was a great help. Otherwise they'd have to traipse all over the vast city to find what they needed. Wayland was so large, there were some sections of town people never saw in their lifetime. Even Josiah wasn't sure if he'd seen it all.

In the other direction, past the fountain the two men sat on, the connected buildings housed law offices, the printers, the book binder, and a doctor's office. Nestled at the end of the square was a six-room tavern called The Dreary Dragon. It was one of very few inns throughout Wayland, and by far the most expensive. Beyond the tavern, the street split in two directions. One snaked to the right of the building, and the other meandered off to the left. The next alley Josiah needed was off the latter path, which meant crossing the square entirely.

The two guards seemed more than content in their drinks and pointless conversation. Josiah was barely paying attention to their chitchat, though he did pick up a few words such as "fat maiden" and "good time." Shadows were limited in the square, and other than the fountain, there was nothing in the square to hide behind. Josiah turned his eyes skyward. If he could just find a way onto the roof . . .

He jumped up, anchoring his hands and feet on both sides of the narrow alley walls. Quietly as he could, he crabbed his way up to the rooftop, out of breath by the time he reached it but nonetheless exhilarated. It'd been a long time since he'd seen the city like this, spread out around him like a great tapestry of flickering lights. His childhood came rushing back. Nights spent trying to keep up with Dante on the rooftops. Days spent dodging the Watch. It was peaceful up there. Quiet. He almost forgot he had a job to do.

The wheezing laughter of the two guards below brought Josiah back to the present. He peered over the edge of the roof. The sober guard was steadily becoming less so. Good. That would make it easier for Josiah to get back. He skulked across the rooftops, taking his time. Though all the buildings shared a wall, some of the roofs were more slanted than others, requiring extreme caution. The last thing he needed was to stumble and alert the guards.

He made it to the end of the square without incident. The distance from his position to the tavern roof was much too far to jump. With the guards sitting on the fountain facing away from the tavern, he decided to risk the lit street. He slid cautiously down a nearby drainpipe, pausing to ensure the small bit of noise hadn't been heard. The guards didn't move.

Josiah kept his eyes trained on the two chattering Watchmen. They were so absorbed in their story, they weren't bothering to watch the square. He decided to chance it. One step at a time, Josiah crossed the street in front of the tavern. His feet barely made a sound on the cobblestones. Every so often, he glanced back at the guards to ensure they were still oblivious. Josiah almost wondered if *anyone* got caught out past curfew. The Watch was clearly ineffective. As he neared the corner of the tavern, eyes glued to the idiotic guards, he missed a cat sleeping in the shadows against the building. He stepped on its tail, and it gave an ear-shattering screech.

Josiah dove around the corner as the two men jumped to their feet, both pulling swords from their belts. They looked about with crazy eyes. The cat scurried off, hissing. Josiah kept his back pressed firmly to the wall, keeping to the shadows on the other side of the tavern. He hoped liquor and distance would keep him invisible. The last thing he needed was a full-out chase. The two Watchmen scoured the square with squinty eyes.

"Just a bloody cat," the second guard said to the least sober one.

"Stupid animal!" the drunkard called.

Josiah breathed in relief. He hated cats, and this didn't help their case any.

While the guards went back to drinking and shirking their duties, Josiah continued on down the dimly lit side street. Every so often, there would be a patch of light from a lantern lodged in the side of a building. Josiah skirted these as best he could, even with no one present. The street here slanted up and curved around to the left. Soon he found the narrow alley he needed and slipped inside. The darkness swallowed him whole, which was almost comforting. He breathed more easily once the light was far behind him.

Wayland's back alleys were even more tangled than the city streets. They were so narrow, Josiah brushed against the brick on either side with each step. Some passages opened into wider courtyards with back entrances to shops or city dwellings. Josiah didn't venture down any of these. He turned down a few side passages, eventually coming out on another street. It was larger than the market square, set up in a sort of triangle. A raised platform of brick and stone was the centerpiece of this massive section. A wooden pole was set in the middle of it. This was where the executions happened—death by burning.

This large courtyard too was lit by several tri-lantern lamps. At least six guards patrolled here, walking back and forth like mindless creatures. Josiah observed their patterns. They stayed mostly to the edges of the triangular street. His eyes wandered next to the point of the triangle. There, teetering dangerously on its three-story design, was the Archive. The front of the building was narrow and curved like the point of a second triangle, flaring wider on each side as the building followed the two wider roads on either side of it. Josiah wouldn't exactly call it prime real estate, but lately Waylanders weren't so thirsty for knowledge. He doubted the Archive turned much of a profit anymore.

One of the guards stopped to lean against a lamppost. He pulled a small leather pouch from his belt, extracted a purple cigarette, and lit it. The man drew from it and blew smoke skyward—even the smoke was purple. Josiah shook his head in disapproval. It was a new type of Euphoria, a drug that brought on pleasure and a state of transcendence. Euphoria took many forms, each as volatile as the next—injection, inhalation, ingestion. Over time, it affected the mind and body, eventually leading to insanity and even death. But Euphoria users never thought of that. They all said the same thing: "That will never happen to me." On the bright side, the guard would be too distracted to notice Josiah, leaving the other five to contend with.

Around the square, bits of lumber had been stacked, along with barrels and tools. The city was in the process of redesigning the burning post for multiple burnings to speed things along. There were murderers and evildoers among the sentenced, but some who faced the death penalty were innocent souls. Lord Harlen was vindictive, and despite the mayor's protests, he always found a way around the law.

Josiah stole one last glance at the Archive. The front stoop was dimly lit by two smaller lanterns set in the wall on either side of the door. One of the guards would surely see him. Josiah's eyes alighted on some cloth, a smaller piece of lumber, and the smoking guard. He smiled beneath the red bandana. All he needed was a distraction.

The other Watchmen continued their bored patrol of the cobblestoned street. Josiah watched them each carefully, leaving the shadows of the alley once their eyes were safely elsewhere. He slipped carefully behind a large pile of lumber and pulled a small, spring-loaded blade from his inner pocket. He used it to cut a piece of the cloth covering the wood. Despite his best efforts, there was still a modest tearing sound. Every second that passed, Josiah held his breath. It echoed like the clanging of bells to Josiah, but not one guard seemed to notice. He breathed more easily once the fabric had ripped clean away from the whole.

With careful movements, he stowed his knife and reached for a minuscule piece of lumber, no bigger than a small tree branch. Two items down—now for the third. He stuffed the cloth in his pocket and peered around the lumber pile. The smoking guard wasn't terribly far from Josiah, but the area beneath the lamp was well lit. If any of the other guards saw him, it was game over. Suddenly Josiah had second thoughts. Maybe it wasn't the best plan. He glanced toward the Archive, thoughts turning to Kaelyn. Not the best plan at all, but it was worth the risk. He needed to get inside that building, whatever the cost.

The smoking guard seemed less and less attentive, and his comrades hardly bothered to notice. Pride of the Watch they were. Josiah waited until the others were a good distance away from his side of the street. He studied the smoking Watchman, the way his eyes glazed over and the purple smoke curled toward the sky. Josiah's gaze traveled to the guard's belt, where the man kept his small pouch. As long as the other Watchmen didn't call attention to Josiah, he should easily be able to pick the man's pocket.

The wind picked up in the square, blowing the sickly sweet smoke in Josiah's direction. He held his breath and crept closer, crouching to keep out of sight. As he slipped into the brighter lights, he felt exposed. The sensation tingled down his spine and to the tips of his fingers as his heart beat rapidly inside his chest. The guard was in his own little world, so far from the square Josiah wondered how he was still standing. Euphoria was fast acting no matter how you took it. Smoking it was supposedly a new sort of transcendence, and it clearly worked.

Josiah tried his best not to catch a whiff of it when the Watchman exhaled. Even secondhand Euphoria was effective, so much so that the brothels in the Red Lantern District had their dancers smoke it to intoxicate the clients. The air in the dens of sin was so thick with purple smoke from every direction, it was impossible not to get high. Josiah experienced it once as a lad when attempting to steal from the distracted clients. He didn't remember much about that night aside from Dante hauling him outside. He'd been as disoriented as a child spinning in endless circles. Never again would he go near the stuff.

Josiah paused right behind the guard, letting one of his knees rest on the cobblestones for balance. His eyes swept over the square. The other Watchmen had split up on the other side to check the shadows. Some of them were competent, it seemed. The former thief turned back to his mission and carefully reached for the small pouch on the man's belt. He didn't have the luxury of time at the rate the other guards moved, so he cautiously lifted the entire pouch from the man's belt.

"Hey!" one of the men shouted.

Josiah dove for cover as the smoking guard whipped around. He held his breath.

"Come 'ere. Look at dis," the guard continued.

Josiah breathed, and the smoking guard turned back to his escape as one of the other guards joined the first. Whatever it was they were looking at, Josiah didn't find out. Their voices became hushed. It didn't concern him.

Josiah peered over the top of the lumber pile he'd dived behind. At least three of the other guards were still patrolling actively, making Josiah's distraction of the utmost importance. The hay cart used for the burnings was a good distance away, but with a careful hand, he might just be able to get it alight. He quickly took the cloth from his pocket, wrapped it thickly around one end of the wood, tied it off, and set it aside. The guard's voice echoed from the other side of the square.

"Should we call for the cart?"

"Nah. Just a dog. They can bury it in the morning."

They went back to their rounds.

Josiah dug in the stolen pouch for matches, finding them quickly in the small space. He struck one against the side of the cheap box. It sparked but did nothing. He tried again, this time setting the match ablaze. He held it to the dry cloth, hoping for success. A breeze blew out the flame before it caught. Cursing, he lit another, this time cupping it more carefully with his hand. The cloth caught, and he tucked the matchbox in his pocket to take up his makeshift torch. It wouldn't burn long, but with any luck, it'd burn long enough to catch fire to the cart and divert attention from the Archive door.

Josiah slowly rose above the lumber pile, took careful aim, and tossed the torch. Thanks be to the Maker, it didn't get snuffed out as it sailed through the air. He crouched again, watching hopefully. Gradually the fire discovered a new source of food in the dry, yellow hay, and it was certainly hungry. In no time at all, a decent crackling fire emerged, enough to catch the attention of one of the guards.

"Fire!"

As the men scrambled toward the burning cart, Josiah slipped in the other direction, moving from lumber pile to crates, to barrels, and finally to the Archive door.

"This is all *your* bloody fault," one of the men shouted at the smoking guard.

He didn't seem to care, too far lost in Euphoria. His glazed-over eyes landed on the orange and yellow flames that steadily grew, and a dopey smile crossed his face.

While chaos abounded in the square behind him, Josiah crouched in the dimmer light in front of the door. The Archive lock was a big iron square like all doors in Wayland, but it had a more complicated pattern inside the mechanism. Josiah had designed and made his own lock picks to help him with just such a thing. He slipped the two slim picks from his inner pocket and inserted them into the large keyhole. Shouts of "Fire!" and "You stupid bloody idiots!" rang in the background, but Josiah paid little attention to them. With a few twists and turns, he caught the latch and slid it aside. There was a *click*, and the door opened with ease. Josiah slipped into the dark confines of the building, shutting out the noise from the square as he closed the door.

The interior of the Archive was almost pitch-black. Josiah could just make out the shadowed edges of pillars and a sort of reception desk. He made his way over and felt along the desk for a candle, thankful he'd stolen the matches. He discovered a solitary candlestick. Without hesitation, he lit it.

The area around him came alive in the orange glow. Fifteen-foot ceilings were held up by marble pillars. The desk sat beneath a rotunda that went all the way to the third floor, allowing diminished moonlight into the space through four small windows. Beyond the desk, the Archive opened up like the books it held, expanding to the left and right with two-story shelves perched precariously. Rolling ladders sat on tracks to aid the archivists in shelving and un-shelving books. Josiah might have been impressed if he actually enjoyed reading.

One careful step at a time, he ventured forward, glancing at the plaques on the end of the shelves. He passed histories, biographies, and bard tales. None were what he sought. He needed the city records. A regal, grand staircase stood at the end of the aisle. Josiah took the steps carefully.

Upstairs he met another locked door. He made short work of it and stepped inside. The smaller room had a ten-foot ceiling and rows of shelves with cubbyholes. Inside these were scrolls, loose parchment, and the occasional book. This was the city record. Row by row he went, holding the candle up to the silver plaques until he finally found one marked City Designs. He set the candlestick down on the small table built into the shelving and started pulling drawings and documents from the slot. He laid them out across the table within the candle's flickering glow. There was no order to the documents, making the search a bit like looking for a needle in a haystack.

After several long minutes of digging, he finally found blueprints of the city layout. Every inch of the crazy streets had been mapped as the city was built. He riffled through these with renewed excitement until he found a page with Prior Street laid out like an exposed skeleton—everything above the street . . . and everything below.

"I've got you now, you bastard," he whispered to the spirit of Lord

Harlen.

A tingle of Netherworld rage pricked in his gut, but he shoved it aside, well-practiced at controlling the power that slept within. He gingerly rolled up the blueprint he needed and returned the rest to their cubbyhole as haphazardly as they'd been stored before. The blueprint was far too large to fit in his pocket, so he simply carried it back toward the staircase. He was halfway down when voices echoed in the supposedly empty space.

"I'm tellin' ya, mate. I saw that door bloody open."

"Quiet, you. If'n ya did, ya'd be given away our bloody position now, wouldn't ya?"

Josiah froze. This was not part of the plan. He snuffed out the candle and set it aside, taking the stairs more quietly than before. It took his eyes a moment to adjust to the dark, but once they did, the Archive was like a whole new world of shadow and light. He skulked forward, heading for the door while simultaneously listening to the footsteps of the guards. He heard a dull thud and paused. Moments later there was another. He clutched the blueprints tighter in his hand as he weaved a maze through the bookshelves. He'd use them as a weapon if he had to.

At the end of the row, Josiah stopped and pressed his back to the bookcase. He peered cautiously around it to see the third and final guard. The man was trembling, looking this way and that in terror. Josiah's brow furrowed. What was he afraid of? Something quietly exploded at the man's feet, and he collapsed not a breath later. Josiah waited for the dust to settle before he rushed forward and felt for a pulse. He sighed in relief—still alive. But who had done it?

Josiah turned slowly, his green eyes traveling up one of the tall bookcases. There, perched on the top of the bookshelf with black hood drawn, was The Raven—the man Josiah knew as Dante Black.

"Yer gettin' sloppy," Dante said. In the shadows of the dark room, he looked every bit like the majestic bird he was named for.

Dante stood in a fluid motion and slid down one of the ladders, far more athletic and lither than Josiah, even without Netherworld strength. He was dressed for the art of thieving in black boots, black trousers, black fingerless gloves, and a black vest with a white tunic shirt beneath it. Over it all, he wore a black, hooded longcoat. Two daggers were at his sides, along with various pouches, and an array of throwing knives crossed his chest on an ornate leather strap. The Raven pulled back his hood. Even in the dimly lit space, Josiah still recognized the wavy ebony hair and piercing blue eyes. Dante Black was five years older than Josiah's twenty, and far cockier. He had a selfish greedy streak that made him the perfect thief, but a few lucky souls such as Josiah knew that underneath his cold, heartless exterior beat the heart of a do-gooder.

"Aren't yeh gonna say somethin'?" Dante pressed playfully as he stepped closer. "I dunno, maybe a bloody 'Thank you.'" Dante tugged the red bandana down, exposing Josiah's face. "Yeh look ridiculous, mate."

Josiah couldn't find his voice. It was like running into his older sibling after ages of separation. Dante had to get in all the quips he could before serious conversation ensued, and Josiah simply bore it with the good nature of a younger brother.

Dante crossed his arms, looking from Josiah's face to the blueprints and back. "If yeh needed somethin' stolen, why didn't yeh jest tell me? I'd have done it fer yeh."

Josiah shrugged, finally finding his mouth. "Didn't think you'd want to see me."

The master thief had a chuckle at that. "Why? Because yeh bloody left? Don't be daft. We both knew thievin' wasn't in yer blood. Yeh can pick pockets and locks, aye, but yer heart's not in it. Yeh needed a better life."

It wasn't entirely the truth. Dante had felt a sting when Josiah left, and he'd vowed to never take on an apprentice again. He'd grown a bit colder and more sinister since their youth, but it didn't show in the moment. He pulled the ex-thief into a headlock and ruffled Josiah's dark hair before he released the lad. Josiah couldn't help but chuckle. His eyes landed on the unconscious guard.

"What the bloody hell did you do to him?" he asked curiously.

Dante reached into one of the pouches on his belt and pulled out a small brown sack so tightly tied it made a perfect round ball around the contents. "Knockout bomb," he explained proudly. "I make it meself from the poppies that grow on the Edge. Learned a thing or two from the apothecary."

Josiah had to admit, he was impressed. His friend had come a long way since he'd seen him last. "I take it you're a full-time thief now," he said.

"*Master* thief," Dante corrected. "There's a grand difference, lad. We do more than jest pick pockets."

"Right," Josiah replied, trying and failing to hide a smirk.

Dante smiled as well.

"How did you find me?" Josiah finally asked.

"I was doin' me rounds on the rooftops fer the night, heard the commotion in the square, and came to investigate. Imagine my bloody surprise when I find yeh breakin' into the Archive. Thought I'd stick around fer a bit and watch."

"And?"

Dante clapped his old friend on the shoulder. "Stick teh yer day job, boyo," he teased.

Both got a laugh out of that. Dante pulled his hood back up, casting the majority of his face in shadow once more. "Come on. I'll give yeh an escort home."

With that, the two men disappeared back into the night like two shadows that had never been there at all.

Lost and Found

THOUGH THE CAVES DIDN'T CHANGE LIKE THE Netherworld beyond them, where Casper and the others entered the maze of tunnels was never certain. At first Casper didn't recognize anything inside the crazy caverns, but he soon found his way, Thomas trailing behind him. Thomas's eyes were gigantic as he looked around in wonder. He didn't seem to have any trouble seeing the caves. Casper wagered it was because he was still a child. Children were always more receptive to imagination and believing than adults.

Thomas's marvel didn't end when they reached camp. He poked around in all the boxes, warmed his hands by the fire, and drooled over the multitude of weapons. The crossbow still lay where Casper had dropped it.

"Fetch some blankets, would ya, lad?" Casper requested.

Thomas went back to one of the larger crates where he'd seen a few such fabrics and plucked some of the softest out of the jumble. He brought them to Casper, wonder suddenly fading to concern as Casper set Iris down near the fire. She was awake but barely, and still uttering gibberish. Casper made a sort of pallet out of the blankets, folding one up like a pillow to rest beneath her head. He pulled the warmest blanket over her. Iris twitched and fidgeted. Casper had no idea what to do. Iris was the one who'd been here longest. She was the one who knew everything about the Netherworld and its strange afflictions. He'd no doubt she'd known exactly what those creatures were.

"Is she goin' to be all right?" Thomas murmured.

Casper tucked a lock of loose scarlet hair behind Iris's ear. "I dunno, lad . . . I dunno."

With a sigh, Casper rose and set to poking about the supplies. There had to be something in all that mess to help. Thomas sat himself beside Iris, looking on her fondly. It wasn't a child's crush, as most would call it, but rather the fondness of a child looking on their mother or older sister. As Casper dug aimlessly through the crates, Thomas happened to look up and catch sight of the black sword—the jewel was glowing again.

"Casper," Thomas said nervously.

Casper turned at the sound of his name. On seeing the lad's gaze, he looked down at his weapon. So far, the sword had only glowed when there was danger nearby, and Casper knew well enough that even the caves weren't completely safe. He dropped the leaf jar he'd been holding back into the crate.

"Stay here," he ordered, scooping up the crossbow. He retrieved another bolt and loaded it for the lad, passing it off. "Watch over her. Shoot anything that isn't me. Do you understand?"

Thomas looked like a deer caught in a hunter's sights. He nodded tentatively.

"I'll be back. I promise."

Casper squeezed Thomas's shoulder affectionately, feeling a strange sense of protectiveness for the lad. He hated to put such a burden on Thomas, but after dealing with the strange creatures in the woods, he had a feeling the boy could hold his own.

The caves seemed quiet enough as Casper left the safety of their little camp. Though he saw nothing in the vicinity, the jewel in his sword hilt still shone brightly. Something was nearby. It had to be. Casper ventured on around the stalactites and stalagmites surrounding their base. He followed the passage around the corner, hoping he hadn't made a mistake leaving Thomas alone to guard Iris. He didn't get far before he found the source of the jewel's awakening. What he saw stopped him in his tracks and shattered his heart. There, standing not ten feet away, was the Keeper, and beside him stood a smiling Gran.

"No," Casper uttered in disbelief. "No . . . it can't be."

If Gran was here, then . . .

"Oh, thank the Maker!" Gran exclaimed, rushing forward and embracing her shell-shocked grandson.

Casper was so floored by the unexpected scene, he didn't even hug her in return. He stood still as a statue, finding his limbs unresponsive and a sudden ache in his chest. Gran pulled back and looked up into Casper's face. At six feet, he was much taller than she, taking after his father. Gran's eyes were glossy as she set a hand fondly on his cheek.

"I knew he'd pull you out. I just knew it," she murmured, happiness bubbling in her chest.

Casper finally found his voice. "Pull me out? Of what? Who?"

"Josiah Grimm," she answered tenderly. She dropped her hand, wringing her shawl betwixt her fingers and studying the floor. "After you died, he found us . . . protected us."

Casper set his hands on Gran's frail shoulders, the pain in his chest growing worse. "Gran . . . what's happened?"

He didn't want to know. He wanted to pretend this wasn't real, but if Gran was here, then Kaelyn . . .

"The mill is gone," Gran said somberly.

"Gone?" Casper repeated in exasperation. "What do you mean gone? How—"

"Harlen burned it to the ground," she cut him off gently, her kind gray eyes full of tears. "I didn't make it, lad."

"No," Casper said, shaking his head.

"Josiah tried to save me," she explained, "but he was too late."

Gran's words slowly sank in. Fire. Death. Gran's body. It would have been destroyed. Suddenly a crushing weight pushed on Casper's shoulders, and he sank to his knees. "Then you're . . ."

She knelt beside him and draped a loving arm around him like she'd always done when he was upset. "I'm not coming back," she whispered. "The Keeper was kind enough to let me stay . . . long enough to say goodbye."

The pain in Casper's chest ripped open like an ugly wound, and he felt as if he couldn't breathe. He shook his head, willing it to be untrue. It couldn't be true. Salty tears stung his eyes. "You can't leave me," he said, his voice cracking. "You can't leave us. Kaelyn—"

"Has a wonderful older brother to look after her," Gran interrupted. She stood in front of him and lifted his head to see his eyes. "You will win, Casper. I *know* it." She stroked his fluffy blond hair. "And when you do, you and Josiah will stop this monster once and for all. Promise me that."

A tear escaped despite Casper's best efforts to hold them back. "I promise," he murmured.

"Good lad," she breathed.

"It is time," the Keeper's regal voice echoed above them both.

Gran kissed his forehead and slowly backed away.

A knife stabbed through Casper's heart, and his head ached from holding back tears. "Please don't go," he begged.

"I must," she said, smiling. "We'll see each other again, my love. My time is done, but you have so much more still to do. I believe in you, Casper. Leave this place. Survive and bring Harlen to his knees, and when you see Kaelyn again, tell her how much I love her; how much I love you both."

"I will," he stammered.

Gran stood at the Keeper's side again, and Casper watched in torment as a bright light encompassed her.

"Oh my," she marveled. "It's . . . it's so beautiful."

And then, all at once, she was gone. Casper couldn't breathe. Every inch of him felt the pain of his heartbreak in ways his mortal body could not. His very soul was in agony. Tears poured, warm and fresh down his cheeks. He'd failed. He'd failed, and now Gran paid the price.

"I am sorry, Casper Renolds," the Keeper's voice spoke above him. "You have endured much for the sins of another."

The Keeper held out a kind hand. Casper stared at it for a moment before he pulled himself together and accepted it. The Keeper pulled him to his feet.

"Come," the Keeper said. "Let us talk."

Before Casper could even argue, there was a bright light, and the tunnel around them disappeared. Casper was suddenly standing in lavishly decorated study. The walls and stalactites hanging from the ceiling told him they were still somewhere in the caves, somewhere Casper had never been. His pain slowly dulled, wonder taking its place.

"Where are we?" he murmured.

"My home," the Keeper said.

Casper looked around in awe. Large, hand-woven rugs of the brightest colors covered the cavern floor. Couches of the finest quality sat across from one another with an expensively stained wooden table between them. A bookshelf was built into the far wall, lined with beautiful mahogany and stacked with so many books, some of them had to be stacked on top of one another just to fit. Beautiful columns stretched from floor to ceiling along the expansive room. Beyond the sitting area, a small set of steps led up to an alcove with more stuffed bookshelves and a desk.

"Sit," the Keeper instructed.

Casper all but fell onto one of the couches, brown eyes still looking around in shock. It took a moment for him to remember himself. With a deep sigh, he ran his hands over his face and tangled them in his hair. His heart still throbbed every so often no matter how he tried not to feel it. It was different being nothing but a soul. He couldn't shut out his emotions or build a wall against them. He had no choice but to feel them all in their entirety—his rage, his heartbreak, his compassion.

"Would you like some tea?" the Keeper offered, holding up an ornate teapot.

Casper dropped his hands, looking puffy eyed at the strange demigod. He recalled Iris's warning. *Don't eat or drink anything.* "No," he uttered. "Thank you."

"You are safe in here, Casper Renolds. My job is not to test you, but rather to protect you," the Keeper explained. "It will ease your pain."

Casper shook his head.

With a wave of the Keepers hand, the teapot disappeared. "Suit yourself."

The jewel still glowed in Casper's sword. Was it because of the Keeper? Casper's agony was forgotten, replaced by a sudden wariness.

"Ah," the Keeper spoke, brown robes swishing as the portly man glided forward. "I see you have found the Nethersword. May I?"

He held out a large hand for the sword. Casper looked between the glowing weapon and the outstretched hand. If there was danger, he'd be handing over his only means of protection.

"It is good to be wary, Casper Renolds," the Keeper said. "But I am a servant of Lumen. I mean you no harm."

Reluctantly, Casper pulled the sword from its banged-up sheath. He was starting to despise the stupid armor he wore. It was falling apart and made movement clumsy and difficult. He passed the sword, hilt first, to the Keeper. The jewel pulsed as the Keeper's hand touched it.

"Ah, yes. So it is you," the Keeper marveled.

Casper's brow furrowed. The Keeper's eyes were completely black: no iris or pupil, and no white. It was hard to determine what he was thinking or where he was looking. "What do you mean?"

The Keeper held the sword aloft at both ends, treating it as a treasured item. "You are the one we have been waiting for."

"We?" Casper questioned. "Who's we?"

"Me," the Keeper began, a smile breaking across his lips—it was almost frightening. "And the Maker."

Questions flooded Casper's mind, followed incessantly by doubt and fear. "Is this some kind of joke?"

The Keeper's unseeing eyes seemed to be on the lad's face. "Only one who would wield the sword for good and not evil could have pulled it from the ground. Only he would the dragon obey. Many pass through these lands, Casper Renolds, and each has given in to temptation and hatred . . . but not you. You are compassionate where others are spiteful. You are kind where others would be wicked. Thomas is proof enough of that."

"That's brilliant," Casper said unenthusiastically, "but I still don't understand."

"You have tipped the balance," the Keeper went on. "Because of you, the Netherworld has seen a rare kind of magic it has not witnessed in centuries: *hope*. Things have already begun to change. You must be cautious, Casper Renolds. Nex will not be happy with you."

"Nex?"

The Keeper nodded. "The god you know as Death."

"Fantastic," Casper uttered, not sure he wanted to incur the wrath of a god.

The Keeper held out the sword, and Casper took it, once again feeling that strange warmth spread up his arm as he held it.

"The jewel on the sword glows when a Netherbeast or being is near," the Keeper explained. "This weapon has great power, strong enough to harm even Death himself. It will help you on your quest to defeat Charles Harlen."

Casper studied the sword in his hands. Was it really that simple? Could he simply run Lord Harlen through and be done with it?

"Why me?" Casper wondered. "Why now?"

"Even I do not have all the answers," the Keeper replied. "But I will say this: You must defeat Charles Harlen. He must not harvest the stone he possesses. Only you can stop him. Beyond that, I am given no further instruction."

Casper suddenly felt as though the weight of the world rested on his shoulders. All he wanted was to keep his sister safe, and now the both of them were caught in some whirlwind of evil.

"I'm no hero," Casper murmured, looking at the sword.

"Thomas Frye would disagree with you," the Keeper said. "As, I am sure, would your friend Iris Farrel."

Iris. Casper was suddenly reminded of her dire situation and the reason he'd left camp in the first place. He stood swiftly, sheathing the sword decidedly. "My friend," he uttered. "I have to go. She's hurt."

The Keeper gave a single, slow nod. "I will take you to her."

He held out his arm, and Casper took it. A bright light flashed, and the two of them appeared not far from the campfire. Thomas shrieked and discharged his weapon, burying a crossbow bolt in the Keeper's shoulder. The Keeper shared a glance with Casper, who shrugged innocently and scratched his fingers nervously through his hair.

"S-sorry," Thomas stuttered. "I panicked!"

The Keeper pulled the bolt from his shoulder and tossed it aside like it was a nuisance. "You are forgiven," he said in his peculiar monotone.

Casper was at Iris's side in an instant. She still stared blankly ahead, uttering nonsense. "Has she done anything in the last few minutes?" he asked, turning to Thomas.

The lad shook his head sadly. "No . . . she did call for you once."

"It would seem," the Keeper interjected, "that you have run afoul of the scaths."

"Of what?" Thomas asked, his face twisting in confusion.

Both Casper and Thomas turned their eyes on the Keeper, who went on to explain. "The scaths are Netherbeasts who feed on fear. They can only be seen at the corner of one's eye or in a reflective surface. Once they get a hold on you, they prey on your fears until you've little of your sanity left. Your friend is very lucky to still be alive."

Casper recalled the silvery light and how it was painfully yanked from his very soul. He felt all the worse for letting the beasts separate them. The Keeper knelt beside Iris and placed his fingers to each of her temples. She didn't even flinch at a foreign touch, too far gone to notice. It wasn't clear what the Keeper did, but soon Iris glowed as if she were made of light herself. Casper's heart clenched in fear, remembering how his grandmother had passed on. Was the Keeper taking Iris from him too?

Thomas moved closer to Casper, and the older lad in turn wrapped an arm around Thomas's shoulder. Neither of them moved an inch as the Keeper worked. Soon the light faded. Iris was still there.

"Iris?" Casper said, leaning closer. Thomas stayed back.

She blinked her eyes, recognition crossing her face as Casper's fair hair and brown eyes came into view. "Cas," she said gently, setting a hand on his cheek.

Casper held it there, not caring that anyone was watching or that she might pull away. He finally released the breath he was holding, sweet relief flooding his already-damaged soul.

"Don't do that to me again," he uttered. "Don't you bloody dare do that to me again."

"Yes, Mum," she mused, half-joking.

She took her hand back, and Casper helped her into a sitting position. Her eyes found Thomas, and she smiled. "Hey, pint-size."

Thomas didn't hesitate. In one swift move, he threw his arms around her neck, nearly bowling her over. Casper kept her upright, disguising a smirk. Iris gingerly patted Thomas on the back. "Good to see you too, lad."

"It would have been me," he gave a muffled reply. "You saved me."

"Aye . . . I did, didn't I?"

Casper and Iris shared a glance, and he quirked an eyebrow at her. She tried to look innocent, but Casper knew better—Iris was starting to like the lad.

He turned to thank the Keeper, but the demigod was already gone.

A Gilded Cage

WHEN KAELYN FINALLY AWOKE IN HER ROOM AT HARLEN Manor, her first sensation was that of pain. She winced and brushed careful fingers over her cheek, where a bruise had bloomed from Harlen's vicious backhand. She didn't regret what she'd done. If anything, the bruise only served to strengthen her resolve. Indignance was her only weapon, and she intended to continue wielding it. She sat up carefully on her elbows, surprised to find herself lying in a feather bed with an expensive red half canopy. She was even more surprised to find herself wearing a nightdress of the finest silk. Kaelyn tried not to think about who might have put her in it, hoping it hadn't been Harlen himself. The thought made her shiver.

The rest of the room was as lavish as her bed and new clothes. She'd been supplied with a whole wall of books, a small settee and coffee table, and a wardrobe brimming with clothes that would make any woman envious. It made her sick to her stomach to think it all came from *him*. She slid out of bed and tiptoed on bare feet to the window. *Bars*, she noted ruefully. There would be no escaping through that window. Next she tiptoed to the door and pressed her ear to the red-stained frame. Breathing came from the other side, slow and steady as though someone were napping.

A guard, she thought.

She grasped the doorknob and gave it a turn. Locked. She huffed in annoyance. There was no way out of this ridiculous prison. Kaelyn almost preferred a proper dungeon to this exceedingly lavish comfort, but she didn't want to end up there either. She wanted to get out. To go home.

And then it hit her, and she sank onto the settee in despair.

She had no home. Harlen had burned it to the ground, along with Casper and Gran. And Casper was still in the Netherworld. If he didn't have a body to return to . . . he was erased.

The sobs finally hit, hard and uncontrollable. Every gasping breath was wrenched from her lungs as though she'd forgotten how to breathe. She cried until she couldn't cry anymore, curling into a ball on the settee and trembling until she fell asleep. She had no idea how much time had passed when the door opened. She startled awake, peering anxiously at the entryway. Anna-Rose entered, and Kaelyn released the breath she was holding.

"Beggin' your pardon, miss," said Anna-Rose as the door was locked behind her. "I was instructed to bring you supper."

"I'm not hungry," Kaelyn sniffed, lying back down. She stared numbly at the ceiling. Did anything matter anymore? Did Josiah know what had happened? Surely he'd gone to the mill by now and found it in ruins. Would he think her dead?

"I'll just put it here if you change your mind," Anna-Rose murmured. She set the tray on the coffee table and returned to the door, giving a gentle knock. Kaelyn heard the door open, then close and lock again.

Anna-Rose felt sorry for her. Kaelyn could tell by her tone. That alone made Kaelyn like her a little better. Perhaps she was as much a prisoner as Kaelyn. With a heavy sigh, Kaelyn let these thoughts fall out of her head, returning to her numb state of being. She wanted to regain her fire again, but the weight of loss kept dragging her further down into the depths of grief. Once she hit the bottom, it was almost impossible to find her way out.

The days ran together as time wore on. Kaelyn remained locked in her room. She barely slept or ate. Her usually vibrant blond tresses dulled to a lifeless hue, and dark circles lined her eyes. Anna-Rose brought Kaelyn's daily meals and tended to whatever Harlen ordered her do. Each time the maid entered, the door was firmly locked behind her until she knocked to be let out again. Kaelyn ignored Anna-Rose on these encounters, pretending she didn't exist or giving only a grunt in response to the maid's questions. Kaelyn knew she had to claw her way out of this state, but at present, she felt too heavy to try. Every day was more of the same. Books brought her no comfort. Food was tasteless in her mouth. She sat in the window seat most days, staring out at the snow-covered hedge maze in the back garden. She memorized the various paths from her bird's-eye view and imagined herself taking flight and finding refuge in those towering walls. If only she could sprout wings and fly away. If she wished hard enough, would the Maker make it so?

Nothing seemed to break the spell Kaelyn found herself under until, one day, Anna-Rose said something unexpected.

"I've a message for you, miss," Anna-Rose whispered.

It wasn't the words but the tone, as if the maid didn't wish to be overheard, that made Kaelyn turn her head away from the barred window where she sat.

"A message?" Kaelyn wondered. "From whom?"

Anna-Rose set the tray of food aside and pulled a small piece of parchment from her apron. She passed it to Kaelyn. Josiah's haphazard scrawl covered the front. It read:

Give to Kaelyn.

With anxious fingers, Kaelyn unfurled the note to read:

Don't fret, my darling. I'm coming for you.

Kaelyn's heart leapt, every pen stroke injecting her with much-needed hope.

"It's from a bloke named Josiah," the maid explained. "I've been watching Harlen for him. He can get us both out, milady. I'm sure of it."

"Oh, I've no doubt," Kaelyn replied, overjoyed. She threw her arms around Anna-Rose, feeling more alive than she had in days.

Anna-Rose was surprised after days of being ignored, but she smiled all the same, happy to help.

"He's coming," Kaelyn said aloud, letting the truth sink in.

"He means a great deal to you, doesn't he, miss?" Anna-Rose realized.

Kaelyn nodded. "That he does."

"Oh, I see," the maid uttered. "You're a lucky woman then, miss. He seems a right fine gentleman."

Kaelyn could see a bit of disappointment in Anna-Rose's eyes. Josiah was a very charismatic man, and he was certainly handsome. It wasn't a difficult leap to think others could adore him too. But Kaelyn didn't grow territorial. Instead a piece of her heart bled for Anna-Rose. She knew all too well the sting of unrequited love. Kaelyn reached out and took Anna-Rose's hand. A gentle smile painted her rosy lips. "We will get you out of here," Kaelyn promised, feeling that fire inside her rekindle.

The maid suddenly took on a whole new persona to Kaelyn. Up until that moment, Anna-Rose was just another of Harlen's pawns, but to know Anna-Rose was truly on her side and that Josiah trusted her—that changed everything.

One of the guards opened the door. "What's taking so bloody long?"

Anna-Rose stiffened, but before she could even think of a word, Kaelyn spoke for her.

"We're having a conversation, you buffoon," she replied saucily. "I've been locked in here for days with no one to speak with. You will tell Lord Harlen that I require Anna-Rose's company . . ."

"But—"

"*. . . or I will not behave myself at all.*"

If Kaelyn's blue eyes could look any harder, the guard might have been struck down by her gaze. It was clear she was serious, and after the fight she'd put up, the man knew she could be more stubborn than their resolve. He sighed.

"All right, lass," he muttered, eyes falling on Anna-Rose. "But you best see to your chores first, missy. Harlen's in a right foul mood today."

Anna-Rose curtsied, trying to disguise a smile through tight lips. The thought of spending time with Kaelyn was a welcome one, and it'd be a lovely change from the day-to-day monotony of cleaning and maintaining the house. She was the youngest servant at the age of twenty-three, finding herself constantly on the outside in the social matters of the house and locked behind the iron gates to keep her from seeing the world beyond them.

"I'll see you later," Kaelyn said kindly, giving such a warm smile that Anna-Rose thought her heart would melt.

"Of course, miss," she replied, beaming herself.

Anna-Rose departed, and the guard closed and locked the door behind her. Kaelyn pulled the note out of her clenched fist, where she'd hidden it. "My darling," Josiah had written. Imagining the way his hand had curved over every word made Kaelyn's stomach twist with butterflies and her heart sing with joy. He was coming for her, and Lord Harlen didn't stand a chance. The thought of Harlen pulled her from her reverie. He had yet to visit her in this glittering prison he'd made, but if that changed, this parchment would incriminate her and Josiah. Though it went against her desire to keep Josiah's note close, she approached the nearest candle and promptly set it ablaze, tossing it into the empty fireplace where it curled in on itself until it was nothing but ash.

Fear

AFTER IRIS'S NEAR MISS, CASPER DECIDED TO WAIT A WHILE before they ventured back into the Netherworld. In the meantime, he found some comfortable but sturdy clothes in one of the larger crates and happily discarded his clunky armor. Casper was a hunter, not a warrior. He felt armor made him a target. He found something for both Iris and Thomas to change into. The shirt was a little big on the younger lad, but at least the trousers fit. At the bottom of the box, Casper found a slew of coats in a tangled heap.

"Where the bloody hell do you find all this?" he asked, not for the first time.

Iris smiled. "There's more than wilderness around here if you know where to look," she gave the same amused reply.

Casper took a beat-up, dusty brown longcoat for himself, tossed a dirty green medium longcoat with a hood to Iris, and handed an ash-blue jacket to Thomas.

"Going all out this time, I see," Iris mused, pulling the coat on over her tunic shirt. It fell to her mid-thigh and was loose enough to allow a good range of motion.

"Last time we lost sight of the caves, and it took us a while to find them," Casper pointed out. He dug through the ammo crate, pulling out all the crossbow bolts he could find. "I want to be prepared. I've been clumsily doing things since I got here, but the Keeper reminded me of one very important thing."

Iris came to stand beside him, her long red braid standing out against the earthy green of her coat. Casper locked eyes with her, more aware than usual of how close she stood.

"And what's that?" she asked, curiously meeting his gaze. Did her eyes always sparkle so? Or was he imagining it?

"Being myself is what changes things here," he answered. "So that's what I'm going to do."

Casper didn't want to tear his eyes away from her face, but he did, turning back to pulling any bolts he could find from the crate. Ever since nearly losing Iris, Casper found he had an overwhelming desire to kiss her, but every time the moment seemed to present itself, he couldn't do it. Iris might not feel the same way, and he still had a long way to go with her before they'd have to part ways.

Thomas watched the two of them from his seat near the campfire and rolled his eyes. Grown-ups could be so stupid at times. Their chemistry was obvious to anyone on the outside looking in, but both of them fought it as if it were a terrible beast that would kill them the moment they admitted it. "Do I get anything fun this time?" he asked, changing the subject before the awkward tension in the air got any worse.

Iris and Casper both shared a glance, silently talking with their eyes. Iris quirked her mouth and gave a little nod.

Let the lad have a chance.

Casper turned to Thomas, viewing the lad up and down. He was small for twelve, but Casper knew better than to judge him by size. Thomas had proved that with his bravery against the scaths. "What are you good with?" he inquired, leaning casually against the crate.

"I'm not bloody bad with knives," Thomas answered, perking up excitedly.

"Knives," Casper uttered thoughtfully. He returned his attention to the ammo crate and dug around a bit. He pulled out a shoulder strap with little niches and threw it to the lad. With a little more digging, he extracted six throwing knives. He wanted to be sure of the lad's proficiencies before he handed weapons over, so he only passed Thomas one blade. "Show me," he instructed.

Thomas tested the weight of the blade in his hand as he stood. It was about as heavy as his knife back home. "What do you want me to hit?"

Casper surveyed the camp, spotting a tall wooden spear on the rack across the way. "The wood of that spear. Go on. Give it a try."

Again, Thomas tested the weight of the blade in his hand. He loosened his muscles, eyes trained on the staff of the spear. It wasn't a large target, but Thomas was determined to prove himself. He wouldn't be the one they had to babysit. With a careful breath, he held the blade properly betwixt his fingers, took aim, and let it fly. In the blink of an eye, it buried itself in the wood just beneath the spearhead. Both Iris and Casper were left speechless. Thomas grinned.

"See? Not bad with a blade."

"Where'd you learn to do that?" Casper asked, impressed.

Thomas shrugged innocently. "I help Dad clean the fish sometimes, and I get bored. The wood beams at home have taken quite a beating."

Casper and Iris shared another look, both breaking into a smile. Casper chuckled and handed the rest of the blades to the lad. "All right, then, but keep your sword close too. You don't want to use all of these at once, aye?"

Thomas nodded, grinning proudly. He finally had a job, a purpose. He slotted the knives into the leather strap and draped it across his body over the waist-length jacket. Casper smiled, again feeling that protective nature for the boy. He found another slotted leather strap and inserted all the crossbow bolts he could fit into it, sliding it diagonally over his body. He attached the crossbow itself to the part of the strap on his back. Iris added a dagger to her belt, content with her sword.

The three of them gathered around the fire, each sitting on a smaller wooden crate. Casper stared into the flames. He hadn't told them about Gran or of the Keeper's prophesied words to him. It was his burden and his alone to carry. Even so, nothing he did eradicated the ache in his chest. Iris's voice pulled him from his silent wallowing.

"The last trial is the hardest," she said. "It's the hardest to find and the longest to complete, and most go mad before they see the end."

"You survived," Thomas said. "It's not impossible."

Iris smiled a little at that. Though she hated to admit it, the lad truly was growing on her. Between he and Casper, she was steadily finding the human bits of herself she'd long since discarded.

"What *is* the last trial?" Casper asked.

Iris locked onto his brown eyes over the fire's dancing flames. "Fear," she answered.

Casper felt a chill traverse his spine. He didn't know what he was expecting. Sunshine and roses? A bloody beach with ale and good company? This was the Netherworld, not a picnic.

"Not mine, aye?" Thomas threw in, suddenly looking a bit nervous.

Iris shook her head. "Not yet, lad. You've yet to pass your second trial. I'm sure we'll run into that too."

"Which is?" Thomas pressed.

"Strength," Casper answered.

"I'm not sure which will come first or how this will work," Iris admitted. "I've never traveled in a group before, and I've already passed my trials. They're not looking for me."

"Don't worry, lad," Casper said tenderly. "We'll get you out of here. I promise."

Iris wanted to say he shouldn't promise anything, but she kept her mouth shut. It was Casper's way, she'd learned. He gave others hope, even if the situation seemed hopeless. There were times when it annoyed Iris to no end, but deep down some part of her almost envied it, the ability to see the good in things. Her temper usually got the better of her first.

"I know it's not an easy thing to do," Iris began, "but we need to make a list of your fears. I've no doubt Nex will throw them at you and more."

Fears, Casper thought. What did he fear? It was indeed a difficult question to ask himself. There was one for certain, but it seemed silly to him to admit as a hunter.

"We won't judge you," Iris promised. "We need to know before we leave the caves . . . because you will confront them, Casper . . . your worst fears. The ones you know of, and the ones you didn't even realize you had."

He sighed and rubbed a hand over his face. "I'm not overly fond of bears," he answered.

"Bears," Iris repeated with a nod. It was a start.

"Why bears?" Thomas wondered. He'd never really been to the Outer Edge himself.

Casper's chestnut gaze found the fire more interesting than either of their faces.

"The more we know, the better prepared we are," Iris said gently.

"The Netherworld will throw the book at you in ways you can't possibly imagine."

Casper sighed. He hadn't thought about it in years. He and Kaelyn never spoke of it, though it was typically there, in the back of their minds like a ghost weighing them both with guilt. Even Gran never mentioned it.

"It wasn't always . . . me and Kaelyn," he said quietly. "We had a younger brother . . . Calvin."

Both Iris and Thomas fell silent as a tomb. It was the first time Iris had really seen Casper so somber.

"Cal was four years younger than I, and two from Kaelyn," Casper continued. "He followed me everywhere like a lost pup. Wanted to be big and strong like me, he said. Back then, Kaelyn and I went to Primary Academy in the city. Cal wasn't quite old enough to go yet, so he got left at home. Most days my best mate, Josiah, would walk home with us, and we'd venture into the woods to play. Cal followed us. Mum made Kaelyn stay behind that day to help with supper; told us to be safe and stay away from the mountains . . . but we didn't listen."

Dread crept into Iris's soul. She almost didn't want to hear the rest of the story, having a bad feeling about its direction. Thomas's eyes were wide.

"It was all a grand adventure to us, breaking the rules," Casper continued. "We followed the stream up to the mountain's edge. Josiah found a cave entrance, declaring it to be the home of a fearsome dragon. We didn't think anything of the danger. We just went inside. It was dark and cold. Cal immediately confessed he was scared, but I held him close and kept going. That was when we heard it: a low grunt. A hulking black shape moved somewhere ahead of us, and a terrifying roar echoed through the cave. We ran. It wasn't until we got out of the cave that I realized Cal was no longer beside me. I heard him scream. Josiah tried to stop me. I yanked out of his grip and raced back inside . . . but I was too late." He paused, reliving it as he told the tale. He could see everything, smell everything. It was like he was there. "Cal's blood was all over the place . . . I didn't have to see him to know how mangled his body was. I could hear the bear . . . ripping him apart . . ."

Iris's eyes glistened, and Thomas was slack-jawed.

"How did you get away?" Thomas wondered, enraptured.

"Josiah," Casper replied. "He came into the cave after me. I'd retched all over the floor, rooted to the spot by the shock. Josiah dragged me outside while the bear was distracted, and we ran like hell." He paused. "It was my bloody fault. I should have left the moment Cal said he was scared . . ."

Casper didn't even realize Iris had moved until her arms wrapped around him. She understood now why he'd been so insistent on saving Thomas and why he looked after the lad so tenderly. She worried it wouldn't bode well for Thomas once they left the caves.

"It was an accident," she said quietly. "And you were just a boy."

"But I was still the eldest . . . and I did nothing."

Iris knew there was no changing his mind. She hated that she'd made him talk about it. *Best to be prepared,* she reminded herself. Iris wanted to stroke his hair and make him feel better but instead found herself patting him awkwardly on the back and moving across the room. Casper watched her go. Thomas fell quiet across the way, eyes fixated somberly on the flickering fire. Of all the questions on their minds, one thing was certain—the next time they left the caves, they wouldn't be coming back.

The Bear

DANTE DISAPPEARED AGAIN ONCE JOSIAH WAS SAFELY back to his corner of Wayland. It'd been just like old times on the way back—Dante flying across the rooftops like a fearless bird and Josiah navigating the streets below. The Raven had given little more than a salute before taking his exit. Josiah doubted they'd run into each other again. Wayland was big, and they were part of different worlds within it. The thought made him sad. In a way, Dante was the only family Josiah had left. Now that he knew Dante didn't despise him for going straight, Josiah had almost hoped Dante would stick around. But he was fooling himself if he thought they would get along now. Josiah walked the straight and narrow as much as possible. Dante danced on the wild side, skulking in shadowy places where honorable men should never dare go. It was better to let the past stay in the past.

Though Casper had passed his second trial before the mill's burning, he showed no signs of progression when Josiah checked the following day. He grew restless, leaving the city for the roadways of the Outer Edge.

He couldn't storm Harlen Manor on his own. All of his planning and sneaking about would be worthless if Casper failed. Josiah didn't need another man; he needed another Netherworlder, and those were hard to come by in Wayland—at least the ones who weren't sick and sadistic bastards. Casper was his only hope. He was Kaelyn's only hope.

A sick feeling wormed its way into the pit of Josiah's stomach at the thought of Kaelyn. This wasn't the first time he and Casper had been between a younger Renolds and danger. *Calvin.* Had Josiah really forgotten the poor lad so easily? It was Calvin's death that had driven a wedge between Casper and Josiah in the first place. So much had happened since then, Josiah almost felt as though he'd lived several different lives.

He kicked a rock down the dirt path, mind lost in the memory now that it'd been recalled. Finding the cave, venturing inside, and Calvin's screams. Oh, Maker, the screams. It was all Josiah's fault. He'd found the cave. He'd gone in first. If he'd just stopped being his reckless self for five minutes . . . but no. It wouldn't have helped. Josiah made a mess wherever he went.

Rapaxion bears weren't known for being forgiving. They were giant, vicious, and carnivorous. Calvin wasn't the first Waylander to meet Death by mauling. Though Casper's father had taken a hunting party to kill and skin the beast, Josiah was left with overwhelming guilt, unable to face the family he'd come to love so dearly. With his body mangled beyond belief, Calvin had no way to return from the Netherworld and had been forced to pass on. It was for the best, Josiah supposed. He highly doubted the lad would have survived the trials.

The trees finally gave way to what was left of the Renolds family mill, and Josiah's heart tore. A few patches of snow still clung to the grass here and there, but most of it had melted. Both the windmill and the cottage were left in ruins. The thick snow that day had kept the fire from spreading, but the elemental beast had swallowed everything else. Josiah doubted he could even find Gran's body to give her a proper burial.

He sank to his knees on the muddy front lawn. It was still cold enough for his breath to fog the air, spiraling toward the sky like a misty incarnation of his sorrow. His green eyes surveyed the damage as a feeling of utter despair took hold of him. *Gran.* Her last moments haunted him. The look in her eyes as she faded. He'd been too late, and yet she viewed him tenderly, like a part of the family. He realized now what he hadn't then: She forgave him. Josiah prayed it wouldn't be in vain. If he was responsible for the death of another Renolds, he wouldn't be able to live with himself. As if to mock his pain, a rapaxion bear appeared at the tree line. It stared at Josiah with curious eyes, decided he wasn't worth its time, and wandered off.

THE MOMENT FINALLY CAME TO LEAVE THE CAVES. CASPER made Iris quietly promise she would guide Thomas once Casper was gone, whether Casper faced erasure or returning to life. She agreed with a heavy heart. Unlike Casper, Iris didn't always see the best in things. The way he guarded Thomas and encouraged the lad was not unlike an older brother. The Netherworld would prey on that, she was certain, but she kept it to herself. To say so would only scare Thomas and enrage Casper. Both would need level heads.

Casper led the way through the caves, Iris and Thomas in tow. He felt more at home in a longcoat, more like himself. Bright light shone ahead as they neared the tunnel mouth. Thomas stuck close to Iris's side, and for once she didn't mind. As soon as they stepped outside, it would be a very different game indeed; they could all feel it. Thomas swallowed hard.

Casper was the first to step into the sunlight. His foot sank into deep snow, and a chilling wind tousled his fair hair. Thomas and Iris stepped out just behind him, hit with the same burst of cold.

"Well, the jackets were a good plan," Iris mused.

A rumble sounded behind them, and all three turned in unison. The cave mouth was gone, replaced with a thick, rising cliff face.

"No turning back now," Casper said, venturing forth. The other two followed closely behind.

They'd exited the tunnels in the midst of a snowy mountain forest. The ground sloped away from the former cave entrance, littered with tall pines. In some places, the snow was knee-deep, slowing their progress. Every direction they turned seemed the same: trees, snow, and uneven ground. For a while the wind and the crunch of snow were the only sounds. None of them spoke, all on high alert for something, anything, to go wrong.

A chilling howl echoed in the distance. They stopped in their tracks.

"What was that?" Thomas asked, fearful.

Casper's breath curled in the air as he surveyed the area in the direction of the noise. "A wolf," he said.

A second howl answered the first.

"Definitely a wolf," Casper added.

Thomas's mouth was suddenly dry. He'd never encountered wolves before. In fact, he'd never really been in the woods before. He kept to the city, mostly near the docks and the Slums. The dangers of the forest were a new threat, and not knowing what to expect made him nervous.

"Are they bad?" he wondered.

"Just territorial," Casper replied.

That didn't make Thomas feel any better.

Casper led on, following the ridge of the mountain. Every so often, another wolf would howl. Each was far enough away that Casper didn't let it trouble him, but he certainly remained wary. Thomas kept himself equidistant from Casper and Iris. For a time, nothing happened. They trudged aimlessly along, breaths swirling in the frigid air. Their boots and coats could only do so much against the cold. Thomas's teeth started to chatter despite his attempts to silence them. At one point, he stopped moving completely.

"Come on, mate," Casper said gently. "We have to keep moving."

Thomas gave a halfhearted nod and trudged on.

Iris grew nervous the more they wandered. She knew well the last trial would drag out the longest. Other than the wolves howling to one another, they hadn't run into any danger. She feared what might happen if they all became complacent.

Soon the wind picked up, and snow began to fall. It only served to make them more miserable. A sudden sharp sting burned Casper's arm. He looked down, slapping at it. A fresh singe mark marred his coat sleeve. His brow wrinkled. He watched as another snowflake landed on the fabric of his coat. It too burned through the fabric, this time leaving a hole. Thomas cried out as a fleck of snow burned his skin. Iris fleetly pulled her hood over her red tresses.

"Acid snow!" she cried above the heavy wind. "We need to find shelter! Now!"

The wind blew furiously as the storm moved closer. Casper broke into a run, at least as best he could on the snow-covered terrain. Iris stayed behind Thomas to keep him from falling behind. Snowflakes singed skin and fabric wherever they landed. If the storm picked up any more, they'd be done for.

"There!" Casper cried. "Up ahead. Another cave entrance!"

Going back into the caves hadn't been his intention, but they had to escape the storm somehow, lest they perish. The incline toward the wide opening was steep and laden with roots and rocks that jutted out of the snow. They used these to stumble and climb their way up, finally diving into the shelter. Iris accidentally landed on Casper's back in the gloom.

"Sorry," she whispered, quickly pushing herself up. She pulled her hood down.

"It's all right," Casper uttered. He shoved aside the thought of how much warmer he'd been for those few precious seconds.

Iris helped Thomas to his feet as Casper stood, looking about in confusion. The cave tunnels had always been mysteriously bright, but this place was almost pitch-black.

"It's not the tunnels," Iris answered his unspoken question as she dusted Thomas off. The poor lad had a few minor burns on his neck and hands from the snowfall. She knelt in front of him and set her satchel down, digging inside of it for the leaf jar of ointment.

"I'm gathering that," Casper said quietly.

Iris carefully dabbed the ointment over Thomas's burns. The lad flinched now and then.

"I know," she murmured, an almost motherly tone to her voice. "But I've got to."

Casper's eyes slowly adjusted to the dark. Where they stood was bathed in light from the cave opening, but the further into the passage he looked, the darker it became. "Do you have a light somewhere in that satchel?"

Iris thought on it. "I think so."

She shoved the bag his way, preoccupied with tending to Thomas's burns. Casper knelt and riffled through the bag's contents. He was surprised at how much fit inside, and even more impressed by how light it seemed.

"How did you get all this in here?" he asked.

Iris replied in singsong, "You're thinking with your head."

And then he remembered what she always told him: *Don't think with your head, Waylander.* If she wanted the bag to be infinite, it could be. She simply couldn't let logic stand in the way of her imagination. Casper tossed the thought aside and went back to digging. There were loads of odd things in there: bandages, leaf jars of unknown contents, a book *(Why the hell does she have a book?)*, twine, spare clothes, a random key, strips of cloth—the list was endless. Casper extracted some matches, hoping to at least find a torch to go with them. If all they had were matches, they'd be done for. With a little more digging, he was surprised and relieved to find an old oil lantern with glass casing.

"You really do think of everything," he said, smiling.

Iris smiled in response, touching up one last burn on Thomas's neck. "Not really. I just see something that looks useful, and I shove it in the bag."

"He's right," Thomas said. "You're bloody brilliant."

Iris's cheeks turned a bright shade of scarlet, not used to getting positive attention. Perhaps she should have befriended other Netherworlders long ago. "All done," she assured Thomas, turning to tend to any burns she had. Thankfully her hood had protected her neck and hair, leaving a few on her hands and only one that had made it through her coat sleeve.

Casper was too preoccupied to care about his own burns. He found a small canteen marked Whale Oil and took it out as well, then set the satchel aside. The lantern was empty, but after uncorking the canteen, Casper soon fixed that, pouring oil into the housing until it was full. He opened the glass case, carefully struck a match, and lit the blackened wick.

Warm yellow light bathed the tunnel walls. All three of them turned their gazes down the passage as far as the lamplight allowed. The rock was brown in hue and lacked the phosphorescent glow of the other caves. Nothing but gloom lay beyond the lantern's reach. Casper turned back to the tunnel mouth, a sigh escaping him. Snow fell in full force, swirling angrily as if to say it had them cornered. They certainly wouldn't be leaving the cave for a while, if at all.

A sense of déjà vu struck Casper when he looked down the foreboding passage yet again. It was similar to the cave his brother had died in. A pang of fear captured his heart and worked its way down his spine. Iris didn't miss the look on his face.

"You know what's in here," she said gently, moving to stand beside him. "You can do this."

Her words were of some comfort at least, but Casper found himself rooted to the spot, staring at the darkness beyond the lamp's yellow glow. He wasn't a fool. The Netherworld would no doubt take his fear and magnify it tenfold. Whatever waited in the darkness would be a nightmare.

Something nudged Casper, and he looked down to find Thomas smiling up at him. "We've got your back, mate," the lad said earnestly.

The words brought a smile to Casper's lips, and he ruffled Thomas's hair. "Thanks, lad."

Iris scooped up the satchel, fixing her gaze on Casper's tentative expression. Fear made him wary, but he seemed nonetheless resolute. He held the lantern aloft and ventured forward, Iris and Thomas right behind him.

The steady *drip, drip* of water echoed through the cave, telling Casper it was vast and deep. He scanned the rocky ground in search of tracks or signs of a creature living in the vicinity. To his horror, the lamplight came across one that made his stomach lurch.

"Bloody hell," Thomas uttered in shock.

There, splayed on the floor, was a mottled human skeleton—a Waylander who'd gone before them. Dark blood stains covered the rocks around the bones. Casper knelt and examined what was left of the body. No flesh remained to speak of, and the limbs were scattered—a rib here, a tibia there. The Waylander had been torn apart postmortem.

"The poor sod was picked clean," Casper uttered. Why were the bones still here? Was this merely a scare tactic of the trial?

Thomas had to look away, finally feeling a sense of fear mixed with a terrible urge to be sick. Iris placed a reassuring hand on the lad's shoulder—a silent promise she wouldn't let the same happen to him. The sight of a horrifically mangled corpse didn't faze Iris in the least.

"Not a Netherbeast, then," she stated.

Casper rose fluidly. "How so?"

"Netherbeasts don't need to eat," she explained. "I'm certain you've seen a shrieker tear someone apart and leave the corpse to rot."

"I thought everything here was a Netherbeast."

Iris shook her head. "Netherbeasts serve Death. They defy the natural world."

Casper pondered on it, making the connections. The shriekers melted in and out of the world, and the scaths were invisible except for reflections or the corner of one's eye. They all had some sort of supernatural traits.

"If it's not a Netherbeast, then it should be easier to kill," he said.

Iris met his gaze, trying and failing to hide her doubt. "Don't count on it," she murmured.

Almost as if answering her statement, a low grunt and growl echoed down the passage. Casper's blood ran cold as it was answered from the other direction.

"There's more than one," he uttered, mouth suddenly dry.

They followed the path in the direction of the noise, coming to a sort of overlook into a larger cavern below. Light filtered in through a small fissure in the ceiling, accompanied by flurries of acid snow. Casper looked on both with fear and a hunter's curiosity. Sure enough, there were two bears, the likes of which Casper had never seen. Both were massive, the biggest at least fifteen feet tall when on its hind legs. Thick black fur covered their bodies, and two glowing red eyes were set in each of their heads. One bear was smaller than the other. Every time the larger bear got too close, the smaller would slap its snout and growl. Then they'd circle each other and do it all again.

"What are they doing?" Thomas whispered.

"I think it's a mating ritual," Casper whispered back.

Iris rolled her eyes. "Brilliant. Shall I get snacks?" she uttered sarcastically. "We need to find a way past them."

Casper nodded, surveying the room below. A side passage led off the cavern. It could be an exit or another dead end. There was only one way to find out, and that was to get through the bears.

"Thomas." Casper rounded on the boy and held out the lantern. "I need you to stay out of sight. Can you do that?"

"But—"

"I mean it, lad. I won't make the same mistake twice."

Thomas conceded begrudgingly, accepting the lantern and backing away from the ledge. From their position, Casper had the upper hand and a hunter's precision. If he could land a shot to the head, the beasts would fall with ease . . . or so he hoped. He pulled his crossbow from his back and loaded it.

"Are you sure that's a good idea?" Iris whispered. Admittedly, she was a little nervous. If Casper didn't succeed in returning to Wayland, she would suffer the consequences as well. And perhaps she cared, if only a little.

"No," he replied. "But they'll spot us either way. Better to attack first."

Casper took careful aim, setting the smaller, presumably female bear in his sights. Again the larger male approached, and again the female swatted him away. Casper waited until the female was farther from the male in their odd little mating circle. For someone as wary of bears as he, Casper felt strangely calm. Perhaps it was the notion he'd seen the bears before they saw him, or maybe it was the female's head caught in his sights that made him feel brave. He tracked the female with his crossbow, finger tensing on the trigger, awaiting the right moment. And . . .

Suddenly the ledge crumbled beneath him and he misfired, smashing and tumbling down the rocky incline. The female roared, enraged as the bolt pierced her side instead. Casper lost his grip on the crossbow in the chaos, rolling across the floor until he came to a stop right between the animals, slamming his head on the ground. His ears rang, and the world seemed to move more slowly. Every inch of his body ached. The larger bear reared up on his hind legs with an angry roar, spewing saliva. Casper's blurred vision made the image twice as terrifying. He was going to die. He was going to die just like his younger brother, erased from existence forever.

"Casper, get up!" Thomas's voice echoed, hazy through Casper's spinning head.

To Casper's horror, both bears looked up, eyes turning toward the noise, turning toward Thomas. Calvin's anguished screams echoed in Casper's mind, and he realized too late it was never the bears he feared—it was his failure as the eldest brother, the failure he'd never forgiven himself for. As the gargantuan demon bear turned for Thomas, Casper found new strength, pushing himself, disoriented, to his feet. Iris had run down the sloping path into the cave below, and now stood guard in front of it, sword drawn.

A vicious roar sounded behind Casper, and he whirled just in time to see the female charge. He dove aside when she lunged, unsheathing his sword as he rolled to his feet. The bear skidded on the stone flooring, claws scraping against the jagged edges and a furious look in her gleaming red eyes. The bolt still protruded from her side, dripping sticky, warm blood through her fur. Now and then, a drop or two would fall to the floor and leave a trail behind her. Casper looked from the bolt to the bear's jaws. The bolt was her weak point, but it required close quarters. One wrong move, and those teeth would rip into his flesh.

Across the way, Iris was having problems of her own. The male bear was larger and twice as vicious. It seemed his only aim was to get to Thomas, as she'd feared. But Iris was no greenhorn when it came to fighting the beasts of the realm. Armed with a sword and a strange, almost motherly urge to protect the boy, Iris charged the animal with a rebel yell. The bear was taken aback at first, despite its size. Most cowered at its presence, but this smaller creature showed no fear. It made the bear wary and curious. Iris swung wide at the creature, striking its forelimb. Her sword barely made a dent, vibrating as if she'd struck stone. Her brow creased, and the bear made a noise almost akin to laughter. With a bored expression, he swatted her with a paw as if flicking a fly out of his way. Iris sailed across the room and slammed into the jagged wall with a sickening crunch. All the air was knocked out of her.

"T-Thomas," she tried to call out, searching the overlook for the lad. Their eyes locked. "R-run," she wheezed.

Thomas's heart gripped in terror. He could barely hear Iris, but he knew what she meant. He tore off into the darkened passageways, clutching the lantern tightly in hand. The light bobbed and weaved against the cavern walls as he ran. A heart-stopping roar bellowed behind him. He didn't dare to look back. He didn't have to. The quaking ground beneath his feet was enough to tell him the bear was right on his tail.

Back in the cavern, Casper and the female bear were having a sort of stare-off. His head throbbed dully, pounding with each heartbeat, and a small cut on his cheek burned. Locked in the bear's luminous gaze, Casper felt much like a deer caught in a hunter's sights. Thomas screamed somewhere down the passage, and Casper's heart dropped.

"Come and get me, ugly," he spat at the bear. He turned and ran, sheathing his sword. The female bear bounded after him.

Iris's breath returned. Gasping, she propped herself up on her arms, allowing sweet oxygen to fill her previously devoid lungs. Her eyes landed on Casper's empty crossbow lying on the ground not far away. She had extra bolts somewhere in her bag. Thomas's screams for help echoed again.

As Casper neared the other cavern wall, he ran swiftly up it and backflipped, landing on the approaching bear's back. He didn't hesitate to reach for the bolt sticking out of the beast's side. It wasn't easy to get to, especially once the beast started bucking and running into things in an attempt to throw him off. Pain erupted in Casper's side when she slammed into the wall. He'd almost had the bolt.

That strange rage filled Casper's gut, a determination that radiated through his fingertips and fueled his very strength. He gripped the beast's fur tightly in one hand and leaned over so far he was nearly hanging off the giant creature. Though the bear bucked and attempted to snap at him, Casper's hand firmly closed over the shaft of the bolt. He twisted it maliciously, forcing it farther into the cavity behind the bear's forelimb. Her roar turned to a whine of pain. He twisted again, and the elephantine beast toppled forward, crashing snout-first into the ground. Casper sailed over her head.

Stinging sensations prickled all over his exposed skin, and he realized all too late he'd rolled beneath the opening where acid snow still filtered in. It hurt far worse in full force. He scrambled for the edge of the torrent, brushing the snow madly from this hair and coat, too late to save his skin from the singes. Thankfully the thick material of his coat held up against the burns, though it was terribly blackened.

In his momentary panic, he'd almost forgotten the bear. Her angry paw connected with his side and he went sailing, slamming into the ground for the second time. His head was positively screaming from all the abuse, but the bear limped terribly now. It was working. Iris seized her moment.

"Casper!"

His head snapped toward his name to see her holding his now-loaded crossbow. He fought through the foggy sensation and forced himself to his feet. Thomas's cries for help still echoed down the passages, filling Casper's heart with hope. He wasn't too late. Not yet. Iris threw the crossbow, and Casper caught it effortlessly, rounding on the bear. The beast stopped suddenly, realizing she was no longer the hunter, but the hunted. Casper fired. *Schick!* The arrow lodged itself in the bear's gleaming red eye. She swayed for a moment, all her functions shutting down. Like a candle that'd been snuffed out, the glowing light faded from her eyes, and she collapsed, never to terrorize another soul again.

Casper breathed heavily. Everything ached, and the spinning in his head worsened. He was certain he had a concussion. Iris was beside him in an instant, sore but certainly far less damaged than Casper. He swayed on the spot, but she steadied him, hands on his shoulders, looking him squarely in the eyes.

"Stay with me, Cas," she said carefully. "Can you manage?"

He nodded, despite being speculative of the answer. Thomas

needed them.

Iris was unconvinced of his reply, but she took his hand and led on anyway. They raced up the sloping passage, soon swallowed in darkness. Both stopped in their stride, maintaining their hold on one another lest they get lost in the gloom.

"Which way?" she whispered.

Without the lantern, it was pitch-black. Casper smelled the air. The massive bears carried a rancid smell of death and decay. It seemed the strongest in a particular direction. Casper followed it, Iris keeping hold of his hand as he took the lead. It was suicide, really. Neither could see a bloody thing. They might just as easily walk off the edge of a cliff as get killed by the bear. Thomas screamed for help again, and Casper picked up the pace, heart pounding wildly.

Warm light emanated from somewhere ahead. Casper dropped Iris's hand, positive they could both find their way toward it. His fingers fumbled for another crossbow bolt as he moved, determined not to fail this time. Clumsily, he loaded the mechanism. When they finally approached the edge of the lamplight, it was easy to see how Thomas had managed to last so long. The lad had found a small nook behind several limestone columns with an opening just big enough for him to fit. The hiding place made a sort of natural cage around him, protecting Thomas from the angry bear swiping and pawing at all the openings in an attempt to get to the boy. Thomas could just make out Casper's silhouette at the edge of the light.

"Help!" he shouted.

Casper aimed his crossbow and shouted at the monstrosity. "Oi!"

The beast turned, and Casper fired. Everyone held their breath. One moment, the bolt was true to its mark, and the next it clattered to the floor. It took Casper a tick to comprehend the bear had swatted it aside.

A few choice curses came to mind as the bear rounded on him, standing a little taller on its four legs. Even on all fours, it towered over Casper.

Iris drew her sword, recalling the bear's tough resilience. She needed a softer entry point. The creature lunged. Both Iris and Casper dodged aside, Casper unsteadily. Iris pushed off the wall and buried her sword in the meaty flesh of the beast's side. It growled in pain, rounding on her. She barely dodged its powerful claws, rolling to the end of the passage at the bear's backside. Her sword clattered to the ground beneath the beast. The bear was so large, it could barely turn itself around in the tight space, leaving Casper the only one in its sights. Head spinning and balance questionable, Casper unsheathed his sword.

Screams echoed in Casper's mind once again, ghosts of his younger brother's agony haunting the darkest corners of his mind. As he stared into the horrifying red eyes of the beast, doubt rooted itself in Casper's heart. He couldn't even save Calvin. How could he possibly save Thomas? The bear noted Casper's hesitance. With a fierce bellow, it charged. Casper didn't stand a chance. He swiped with the sword as the gigantic beast bowled him over. The Nethersword skidded across the floor.

Terror seized Casper like a shock of cold water. The bear's heavy paw rested on his chest, pushing him into the ground. He was pinned. Thick slobber dribbled from the monster's bared teeth, slathering over Casper's face. He was too paralyzed to be disgusted. *Thwumpa, thwumpa, thwumpa.* Casper's heart hammered in his chest. All he could hear was his brother's screams and the sound of a bear ripping Calvin's flesh from his bones.

Iris's eyes flicked from the beast to the Nethersword, calculating the distance between both and whether she could reach it in time. As she pushed herself to her feet, her heart stopped. Thomas had left his little hidey-hole and was skittering to a stop in front of the creature. He clawed at his chest for a throwing knife. Iris's mouth went dry. Trapped behind the bear, there was little she could do to stop him.

All Casper could see was teeth and spittle as the bear prepared to rip him apart. He braced himself for the end. Suddenly the bear growled in rage, and the pressure on Casper's chest disappeared. A knife protruded from the monster's eye, too shallow to pierce the brain but deep enough to cause pain and blind the beast. The bear backed off Casper, pawing at the knife in an attempt to get it out. It only made it worse. Angrily, it turned for Thomas.

This was the moment Casper feared. The one he was afraid he couldn't stop. Thomas swallowed hard. The bear leapt over Casper's limp body. Try as he might, Casper couldn't push himself up. The world spun like a kaleidoscope, blurring the nightmare unfolding before him. He stumbled for the sword only to see it snatched from the ground before he reached it.

Iris raced for the monster. She jumped and propelled from the cave wall, sailing through the air with the Nethersword raised. Thomas braced for impact. The bear lunged. Iris landed on its back, screaming with rage. The beast hardly had time to register Iris's presence before she plunged the Nethersword into the monster's head, buried so deeply the tip protruded from the bottom of the creature's jaw. The glow in its ruby eyes went out and it toppled over, throwing Iris to the ground.

Thomas peeked out from behind his arms, slack-jawed. He'd thought he was done for. "Whoa," he uttered.

Exhausted and adrenaline fueled, Iris simply lay there on the ground, breathing heavily and praying to the Maker there wasn't another bloody creature hiding somewhere in those caves. Casper remained slumped against the cave wall, finally giving in to his spinning head. They'd done it. Thomas was safe, and both bears were dealt with, but Casper still couldn't shake one thing from his mind: it was Iris who'd delivered the killing blow, not him. How could he possibly be the hero the Keeper suspected him to be if he couldn't even protect his loved ones?

Anna-Rose

LORD HARLEN WAS NONE TOO PLEASED WITH KAELYN'S request for Anna-Rose's company, but after much arguing with Kaelyn and the timid guard at the door, he realized it would be best in the long run. He needed Kaelyn healthy and somewhat happy if his plan was to succeed. In order for the ritual to work, she must willingly wear the ring. With the full moon fast approaching, he had little time to see that done.

And so it was that Anna-Rose paid Kaelyn frequent visits. She often brought with her spare cakes from the kitchen or an extra book from the vast library. Kaelyn found her imprisonment far brighter in Anna-Rose's company. There was something to be said for the sharing of a secret between women. It strengthened their bond and made them the most unlikely of friends. On one of the maid's highly anticipated appearances, Kaelyn found herself most curious.

"How exactly did you come to work for such an awful man?" she wondered from her place on the window seat.

Anna-Rose sat comfortably in a simple chair across from Kaelyn. "Oh, you don't wish to hear about that, miss. It's not a pretty story."

Kaelyn's eyes glossed over with sincerity and kindness. "I'd like to hear it all the same."

The maid studied her hands tightly clasped in her lap. No one ever seemed to care about her woes. It was all work and little play in Harlen Manor. The cook, Mrs. Rogers, would sometimes lend a sympathetic ear, but in the end she'd always tell Anna-Rose to buck up and get used to it. They were all of them prisoners, and there was naught to be done about it. But Kaelyn, she was different. In those eyes, Anna-Rose saw the kindness of the world epitomized. Perhaps for once her woes and fears would not fall upon deaf ears.

"I grew up on the West End with my parents," she began. "I was an only child. Father was a bookkeeper for the general store on that side of town, and Mum usually stayed home with me. I went to Primary Academy at age six as everyone does. Life was normal. I like to think I had a happy childhood."

Kaelyn wrapped her arms around her knees and listened with rapt attention.

"As I neared my eighteenth year, business went very bad for Father," Anna-Rose continued. "He'd made a miscalculation that set the store back several months and cost them a significant sum. Naturally, they released him from their service, refusing to pay him a penny owed. Father tried to get the law involved for a breach of contract, but the law found favor with Mr. Grist, the store owner. They said my father owed Grist the money he'd cost him."

"How cruel," Kaelyn said quietly.

"Cruel indeed," Anna-Rose agreed. "To make matters worse, Lord Harlen owned the building we lodged in. When our payments were late, he came to investigate. My father begged and pleaded, but Harlen was determined to throw us out on the streets." She paused. "But then . . . he saw me hiding behind a bookcase in the corner. Once an idea forms in his hideous head, it doesn't relent. He told my father he'd go easy on one condition: I was to come and work as a maid in his home. My parents were reluctant, of course, but I agreed if only to save them. Harlen sends them money from my pay. It's worth it in the long run . . . so long as they're looked after."

Kaelyn felt as though her heart had torn. How awful a thing to be sold into service like that, and Anna-Rose had willingly gone for her family's sake. Kaelyn's hatred for Lord Harlen tripled. He really did destroy all he touched with his vile and cruel hands.

"I'm so sorry," Kaelyn uttered, and she really, truly meant it.

Anna-Rose smiled, but the glow of it was dimmed by the sorrow in her eyes. "S'all right, miss. I've survived."

A knock at the door made them both jump. Without acknowledgment, the door creaked open and George stood in the frame.

"Anna, when you've quite finished, Lord Harlen requires your presence in his study," the butler said, an incredibly bored look on his lined face.

The maid's heart suddenly stopped. "Me, sir?"

"Aye, you," George replied. "If I were you, I shouldn't keep him waiting too long. He's not in very good spirits this afternoon."

With that, George closed the door and the lock clicked back into place. Anna-Rose shivered despite the lack of cold in the room.

"Perhaps he just has a task for you," Kaelyn said, trying to help.

"Perhaps." Anna-Rose sighed, meeting Kaelyn's kind gaze "I'm not fond of being alone with him."

Kaelyn empathized with the poor girl. The way Harlen undressed Kaelyn with his eyes was most unsavory. She was certain he likely did worse to her. "I'll be here when you get back," she promised, wishing there was more she could do. She too was at Harlen's mercy.

Anna-Rose nodded shortly, her stomach twisting in knots as if she might be sick. More than anything, she wanted to stay in the safety of that room behind the locked door—to be where Harlen couldn't do any of the things Anna-Rose was sure he did in his wildest fantasies. So far, he'd been content to make her cringe, but one day he would get bored of that, and when he did, Anna-Rose would be ruined.

Mouth dry and sick to her stomach, Anna-Rose left the confines of Kaelyn's gilded cage. The closer she came to Harlen's second-floor study, the harder her heart pounded in her chest. There were a million reasons he could have summoned her there at this time of day, and none of them were good. She knocked timidly on the door when she'd reached it.

"Enter," came Harlen's monotonous reply.

The door creaked as Anna-Rose pushed it open. "You . . . you wanted to see me, sir?"

Harlen glanced up from the papers on his desk, a smile curling on his lips. "Ah, yes. Do come in, my dear," he said as he rose. "Close the door behind you."

Anna-Rose swallowed hard as she came in and shut the polished door. Harlen had her by the arm in an instant, dragging her across the room. "Have a"—he pushed her roughly into one of the chairs by the fire—"*seat.*"

Anna-Rose would have given anything to have some sort of power right then. Strength, magic—anything to combat the man she'd grown to fear. "Is everything all right, my lord?" she said, voice laced with uncertainty.

Harlen was pleased to see the maid frightened and subservient. Perhaps he could work this to his advantage. "I'm not sure, Anna," he said, walking behind her chair.

She didn't dare look up. She hardly dared to breathe.

"Why don't you tell me?" Something fell into her lap. Her blood ran cold when she recognized it—a dead pigeon with a note on its leg. The bird thudded to the floor as she jumped to her feet, but Harlen gripped both of her shoulders from behind and yanked her down forcefully. His hands didn't leave her shoulders, though she was seated once more. He leaned forward, cheek pressing against the side of her ear. "Oh, yes," he whispered, breath tickling against her skin. She cringed, and he reveled in it. "I know what you've been up to, Anna-Rose. And I'm not happy."

Bile rose in the back of Anna-Rose's throat. She couldn't find words to respond, rooted to the spot by terror and his strong grip.

"I've been good to you, haven't I?" he said, stroking her cheek with a finger. "Kept my distance."

She shuddered in disgust at his touch, and a repugnant smile crossed his lips.

"The birds must stop, of course," he murmured, "but I am willing to overlook your insubordination . . . in exchange for something else I desire."

Panic flooded through her veins, charging every inch of her with want of flight, but his grip on her shoulder was too strong. She was trapped. Harlen was certain the ambivalent maid would give him exactly what he wanted—so much so, he'd already begun to kiss her neck.

A new defiance settled within Anna-Rose as she thought of Kaelyn and Josiah and the many more lives Harlen would wreck. She shrank away from his lips.

"I'd rather die," she spat.

Harlen stopped mid-kiss, all the fun suddenly taken out of it. He wanted her to cower, to quiver beneath him, timid and powerless. To be submissive out of fear, all the while loathing every minute. Anger surged within him. Kaelyn had tainted this too.

"Fine," Harlen growled.

Suddenly Anna-Rose couldn't breathe. Harlen's large, strong hand gripped her throat in a vice, crushing her airway with all the strength his Netherworld rage allowed. She writhed and fought against him for a different reason then, clawing at his hand with all her might. It was fruitless. With one final, virulent squeeze, Anna-Rose's airway was completely crushed and she fell limp in the chair, eyes staring blankly ahead.

Lord Harlen stood back to his full height, absolutely seething. This was not the ending he'd hoped for, but he couldn't very well let her live, defiant and free to disobey him yet again. He went into the hall and called for his guards to gather the body. Instead of heading for the yard to dispose of her, he headed for Kaelyn's room, not even bothering to knock. She sat on the end of her bed, lovely as ever, her bold nature shining in her forget-me-not blues.

"In here, gentlemen," Harlen said, standing aside for the men to pass.

The guards trailed in behind him and dropped Anna-Rose's lifeless body on the floor like a sack of flour. A horrified shriek left Kaelyn's lips at the sight, a sound that brought Lord Harlen immense pleasure.

"I gave her a choice, and she chose death," Harlen said innocently. "Pity."

Kaelyn dropped to the floor beside the maid's body. The eyes were still open, blank and staring, cold gray in the place of brown—Anna-Rose had chosen to pass on.

"What have you done?" Kaelyn wailed.

"I did nothing, madam," Harlen replied. "It was you and your precious Josiah Grimm."

Kaelyn turned her teary eyes up to the man she'd come to loathe most in the world.

"Oh, I know all about that," he continued maliciously. "And in time, I'll kill him too."

"You won't win," Kaelyn glowered. "So long as there is breath in my lungs left to pray, you will *never* win!"

Harlen had a laugh at that. "Don't waste your energy, darling. I already have."

He departed then, leaving Anna-Rose's lifeless body on Kaelyn's floor for her to contend with. The Renolds girl needed a dose of what happened to those who defied him.

The door slammed shut, and Kaelyn burst into tears. Sobs choked her every breath, painful and body-wrenching. She'd promised Anna-Rose they'd save her. She'd promised to set her free. This wasn't at all what Kaelyn had meant. With a trembling hand, Kaelyn closed Anna-Rose's staring eyes.

"I'm so sorry," she sobbed, a whole new wave of tears spilling over until Kaelyn was so overcome with shock and grief, she couldn't pull herself from the floor.

Have hope, Casper would say. But where had that gotten her brother? He was dead. Dead and erased. Everyone she ever loved was gone, all except for Josiah. Lord Harlen's mania would certainly end him too. She was helpless, cornered by a man who had little respect for human life. Prostrate on the floor, she cried until she could cry no more, finally giving in to sleep beside the corpse of the only ally she'd had within the walls of Harlen Manor.

The Anaradix

CASPER AND THE OTHERS HAD LEFT THE CAVERN FAR behind, taking their exit by the secondary passage Casper spotted earlier. Iris helped him along most of the way, insisting he rest, but Casper would hear none of it. The fight with the bears had been too close a call, and what was worse, the third Netherworld spiral hadn't appeared on his wrist—he didn't pass the trial. Was it because he didn't deliver the killing blow? Or were the bears a trifle?

The passage let out in the lower mountain valley, and with the malicious blizzard gone, it was once again safe to travel. The ground was even here with a sharp drop off to one side. A frozen lake, regal and dangerous, covered the expanse between the two snowcapped mountains. On and on they trudged with no real direction, now and then pausing for a rest. It seemed they were going nowhere. In some places the snow was so deep, they were practically wading through it.

Eventually Casper's foggy head cleared and the slice on his cheek closed over, becoming nothing but a faint red line. The acid burns on all three of them were now nothing more than little red specks against their skin. It was curious the way things defied logic in the Netherworld. Casper often wondered if injury to the soul would carry over to the body should they be reunited.

Time didn't exist in the Netherworld, but it certainly felt to them as if hours had gone by. Their clothes were damp in some places from deeper snow, and the lack of direction waned their patience. It could just as easily be Casper's trial as Thomas's that came next. They'd wandered aimlessly for so long, Casper became complacent and lost in thought, much to Thomas's detriment. One moment they marched solemnly along, and the next, Thomas shrieked and fell through the snow.

"Thomas!" Iris cried.

Casper's heart clenched, still terror ridden he'd fail the lad somehow. He scrambled through the snow, cursing the way it slowed him down, and reached the spot at the same moment as Iris. Both peered down into the hole, and sweet relief flooded their spirits. Thomas was at the bottom of a deep snow pit, safe and uninjured other than a few bruises. Casper could hardly wipe the grin from his face.

"Snow trap," he said, elated. "Nothing too serious."

"Aside from how the bloody hell you intend to get him out," Iris mused. It was far too deep a hole for either of them to bend down and reach him, and Thomas could hardly climb out; the walls were made of iced-over snow.

"Have you still got that rope?" Casper asked.

"Your pet dragon snapped it, remember?" Iris replied waspishly.

"All right," he said, a hint of annoyance in his tone. "No need to be so bloody snippy."

Iris knew he had a point, but she was cold and aggravated, and now Thomas was yet again in peril, albeit safer peril than previously. Casper looked high and low for a solution. There was a single tree among the tall pines a little different than the rest. It wasn't uncommon in the forest for smaller trees to take seed among the more bountiful, larger trees, so Casper thought nothing of it. An idea formed in his mind, and he carefully made his way to it, keeping an eye out for more possible traps. Iris froze as Casper drew his sword.

"Casper, don't," she warned as he raised it.

"Do you want to get him out or not?" Casper replied, still a little aggravated with her. "It's just a bloody tree."

"No! Don't!" she cried.

But he'd already put his full force behind the swing. The branch came clean off. Blood gushed from the tree like a wound, and Casper stared in horror. Trees didn't bleed. A horrible, agitated clicking noise emanated from the tree, and the ground shook.

"You idiot!" Iris chastised, coming to stand beside him, weapon drawn and ready. "You've awoken an anaradix!"

Casper watched, terrified, and feeling equally foolish, as the tree's roots ripped up from the ground one at a time. The branches morphed into five long, spindly arms with sharp-edged fingers (one of them had been cut off by Casper). The top of the trunk elongated and rounded into a gruesome head with leaves for hair, sharp wooden teeth, and angry yellow eyes. Casper glanced down at the sword to find the jewel glowing—a Netherbeast. Why hadn't it glowed before?

"What's going on up there?" Thomas called, fearful. He couldn't see anything, but he could certainly hear the hair-raising clicks and groans of the beast.

"Just stay down there and keep quiet," Casper called back. At least Thomas was safe and out of the way. One less thing for Casper to worry about.

The anaradix fixed its yellow gaze on the fallen limb and the bloody sword in Casper's hand. Casper smiled sheepishly. "Come on, mate. We can talk about this."

An angry flurry of clicks replied, and the beast smashed one of its remaining limbs into Casper's chest. Casper sailed into the air, smashed into one of the pines, and face-planted in the snow. "Or not," he uttered with a wince.

The creature moved on its roots like spidery tentacles, ignoring Iris completely. Her eyes wandered to the branch laying in the blood-colored snow. Casper's sword could slice through the anaradix with ease, but her own would require a lot of hacking to achieve the same. As the hideous creature reached out with one of its many arms, Iris studied it, watching in horror as the anaradix slowly regrew its missing sixth limb.

"Shit," she whispered under her breath.

Casper clambered to his feet as the monster swiped for him again, suddenly at a loss. How could he kill something that could heal itself?

"Any bright ideas?" he called to Iris.

"Me?" she bristled. "Why does it always have to be me?"

He hacked off the anaradix's hand as it swiped at him, causing the beast to hiss and click angrily. "Because you've been here longest, and you seem to know bloody everything!"

"I read about it in a book!" she cried, instantly regretting it.

"A book?" he spat back, annoyed. He remembered the book he'd found back in the bear cave. "You got everything from a bloody book? Where the hell did you even—"

"The Keeper's library," she cut him off. "I was trapped here, so he loaned me whatever I wanted! That's how I've survived this long! I've never fought a bloody anaradix before!"

Casper dodged another swipe. "Brilliant," he muttered. "Absolutely, bloody brilliant."

"I told you not to touch it!" she shouted angrily.

Casper fell silent at that. There wasn't a single argument in his favor he could make. He used to be the more easygoing Renolds sibling. Lately he found his stubborn streak coming out. It was odd to think he'd become more alive in death.

"What did your book have to say about this horrendous thing, then?" Casper asked. The anaradix still seemed interested only in Casper. Educated though Iris was as a wealthy-born child, her memory wasn't perfect. She dug madly in her satchel and pulled out the book, chagrined that she'd told him her secret. Iris enjoyed seeming the tough woman who wasn't fazed by anything; to admit much of her survival was due in part to her own personal research almost diminished her hard-as-nails facade—at least, she thought it did.

"Gotcha," she uttered, finally pulling the faded volume from the boundless satchel. "Keep it busy!"

"What the bloody hell do you think I'm doing?" he said under his breath.

Iris flipped madly through the book. Luckily she didn't have far to go since the creature was in the A section. Speed reading was a particular talent of Iris's, and she soon had an answer.

"You have to cut off all its limbs before they grow back!" she shouted to Casper. "It'll get angry and shoot poison spores from its chest! Stab the exposed core!"

Sounded easy enough, or so Casper lied to himself. The anaradix was particularly angry and far stronger than it looked. "I'll take care of it! Help Thomas!"

Iris nodded and took up the long, fallen branch, retreating to the pit where Thomas was trapped. "Don't worry, lad," she said. "I'll get you out."

Thomas was much relieved to see Iris above him. It was frightfully cold down there. Iris studied the pit and found, to her dismay, that it'd be impossible to pull Thomas out on her own. Though the lad was small, the depth of the pit and the weight of Thomas would surely send her toppling headfirst into the snow trap. An idea sparked. There was enough snow around them to bury Wayland ten times over.

"I'm going to start dumping snow down there," she called to Thomas. "I need you to pack it down. We need to get you as close to the top as we can so I can pull you up. Think you can do that?"

Thomas nodded vigorously. "Aye."

Iris set the tree branch aside and set to work rigorously pushing snow into the hole. Thomas was dusted uncomfortably with the frozen flecks, brushing them frantically from his hair and neck. Once a small mound of snow stood to one side of the pit, he stomped it down and packed it tighter. Iris moved to the other side and repeated her actions, moving as fleetly as she could.

Behind her, Casper found himself in a bit of a predicament. The anaradix had grown back its severed hand and was more furious than ever. Two of its tentacle-like roots dove beneath the snow-covered earth. Casper's brow creased. A loud explosion thundered behind him, and snow rained down like a fresh storm. He whirled. Before he could comprehend the roots towering over him, they coiled around Casper and lifted him from the ground. Tighter and tighter they squeezed until Casper thought his bones might crack. Luckily the harder the beast squeezed, the more it also pressed against the Nethersword. Casper struggled to move at first, but with a little applied determination, he finally managed to turn the sword with the side of the blade facing out. Unfortunately, that also meant one side was turned on him. He gritted his teeth against the pain, crying out.

Iris looked up, and her heart stopped. Casper had told her to help Thomas, but it was evident he couldn't do this on his own. "Stay here," she called down to the lad.

Thomas sighed. Where else would he bloody go?

Iris was in the process of racing toward the fight when the anaradix suddenly shrieked and dropped Casper. He thudded atop the snow, turning it red from the fresh wound in his leg. Iris rushed over.

"I thought I told you to help Thomas," he said, wincing.

Iris pulled him to his feet. "You did," she replied. "But you evidently need my help more. He's fine. Are you?"

Casper nodded despite the pain in his leg. All the falls he'd taken since arriving in the Netherworld had taught him to shake it off. "Did you learn to fight from a book too?" he wondered.

"Is now really the time?" she said with agitation.

Adamantly she turned for the beast, now moving toward them as fast as an arachnid on its tentacle roots. Casper watched her draw her sword and suddenly felt a newfound admiration for Iris. Where she thought her intelligence demeaned her, he saw it as highly attractive and equally stalwart.

"You take one side, I'll take the other?" he offered as the anaradix swiped with a strong arm and reached for Casper with yet another.

Iris replied with a nod, certain she could do little but distract the beast. While she rushed for the creature's backside, Casper took on the front. Six arms to four was quite an unfair advantage. It took a lot of dodging and acrobatics to keep from being completely leveled by the anaradix's strong, branch-like arms. The roots, all except for the two Casper injured, presented another problem entirely, snaking about and doing all they could to trip up the two attackers. Casper hacked at the creature left and right, swiping at anything that moved while simultaneously jumping or ducking another. He soon managed to completely hack off a limb, putting the number back down to five arms once again.

The anaradix shrieked and clicked furiously, grabbing at Casper with another hand. Momentarily elated by his success, Casper missed the movement and the beast caught hold of his injured leg, hoisting him into the air. He cried out, nearly dropping the sword, eyes watering in pain. Iris hacked and kicked at all she could reach, mostly contending with the spider web of tree roots snaking this way and that. If she hindered its movement, they might have an advantage. The beast reached for Iris with one of its free branch-like hands, grasping for Casper's sword with another. Despite its many limbs, it only had one head and one mind. Focusing entirely on two enemies wasn't an easy feat. As it tossed Iris headfirst into the snow, Casper finally managed to swing up and slice off the hand holding him. He landed on his injured leg, once again painting the snow red. Willfully he pushed himself up and chopped off what remained of the limb. Two down, four to go.

Iris stumbled to her feet, bruised but none too worse for the wear. She charged the anaradix and jumped determinedly over its tentaclesque roots, now snaking far beyond it, in and out of the earth in an attempt to brace itself. Her sword targeted the arm to the rear of the beast, hacking away with a charged fury. Already angered and pained by the loss of a second arm, the anaradix was shocked to feel agony in a third. Its horrifying clicks and groans became enraged. One of the roots snapped out of the ground and wound around Iris's neck, lifting her off the ground. Her sword fell beneath the snow as she instinctively clawed at the vines.

Panic shot through Casper like adrenaline, spurring him forward as fast as the snow and his injured leg would allow. Iris's face rapidly turned purple. Desperately Casper swung the Nethersword, slicing the root in half as if it were nothing. *Smack!* Iris landed on the ground, gasping fiercely for air. Casper fleetly turned and cleaved off the arm Iris had nearly cut loose. Three to go.

The anaradix was daunted now atop being nettled. Little shoots began to grow where each of its limbs had been chopped off. Time was running out. Iris scrambled for her sword as Casper dodged another attempt by the roots to scoop him up. The most difficult branch to reach would be the one nearest the giant creature's head. Casper had to get that one next, and quickly.

"Distract it!" he shouted to Iris.

All she gave was a nod in reply, finally closing her hands around the silver broadsword. She pushed herself up and swung away at the creature's backside, ignoring the throbbing in her head from lack of air. The anaradix grumbled in an odd sort of way and swiped at her as though trying to smack away a gnat. Casper chose that moment to run at the beast. He jumped on the lower arm and leapt to the next highest, putting himself within easy reach of the tallest branch. When the anaradix realized what Casper was doing, it shook its arm in an attempt to throw him off. Casper held on firmly. Finally the beast held its center branch still in the hopes of using the tallest and lowest to grab Casper. Unfortunately for the anaradix, in doing so, it brought both closer to the Nethersword. Casper swung with ease, first chopping off the tallest, then slicing through the lowest. One to go.

The Netherbeast was livid. It let loose an ear-piercing shriek followed by angry clicks. Casper was thrown to the ground. The anaradix whirled, smashing its remaining limb into Iris. She sailed through the air and crunched into deep snow far from the creature. Casper clambered to his feet, and with one last vicious swipe he cut the final branch from the anaradix's trunk. The creature's survival measures were triggered, causing a hatch to open in its chest. Yellow spores were released, poison to all they touched. Casper ducked to avoid the first batch. The wind carried most of them up and away. Once the stream had stopped, Casper lunged, plunging the black sword into the exposed glowing core of the anaradix. The beast wailed, coiling its roots into itself like a spider dying. Casper yanked out the sword. Back and forth the anaradix teetered, until, at last, it crumpled into a heap in the snow, dead.

Casper breathed heavily, eyes searching madly for Iris. He finally spotted her far off, climbing out of a deep snow pile. "I'm fine," she called across the way. Casper nodded and returned to the pit that had started the whole mess.

"All right, lad?" Casper asked.

Thomas was sitting with his arms curled around his knees trying not to shiver. "I've been worse," he answered.

Casper smiled at that. The lad was ever the optimist. Iris soon joined Casper, and together they pushed snow down into the pit until Thomas was close enough for them to use the branch. Iris bent over and held the limb out to the lad. Casper kept hold of her from behind. Once the lad had a firm hold, they hoisted him up together. Thomas instantly threw his arms around both of them, drawing laughter from the older Waylanders. Casper met Iris's eye, and something passed between them. Protecting Thomas was no longer only Casper's aim—it was a responsibility they shared together.

Nex

HARLEN MANOR WAS COLDER WITHOUT THE USUAL MAID to go about cleaning and lighting all the fireplaces. The staff had been told of her insubordination and was warned against any further betrayals. George was ordered to keep an especially close eye on the household staff, to which the butler delightedly accepted. George was oddly loyal to Lord Harlen, a fact that some of the staff despised. Now under closer scrutiny, conversation stopped almost completely as they went about their day-to-day chores.

The note Harlen had uncovered was another matter of concern. Josiah, it seemed, was planning a rescue of sorts. The note didn't say how or when, but Lord Harlen was certain to double the watch. For all his security measures, one would think *he* was the mayor instead of John Farrel.

Back in his secret chamber behind the bookcase, Harlen lounged in his high-backed chair pondering the issue before him. He twirled a lovely ring between his fingers, the stone akin to an opal. It was easy to see upon first glance there was something different about this stone. It had an almost ethereal sheen to it, one that Harlen stared at hungrily. He wanted the power that slept within that stone, and his patience was running thin.

Bash watched his superior in silence, awaiting some sort of instruction. He'd come for his daily reports, and the news of Josiah Grimm was disconcerting. Harlen continued to call Josiah's survival against the assassin a fluke, but Bash wasn't willing to take that chance.

"Do you want I should get rid of him, my lord?" Bash asked quietly.

Harlen remained silent, pondering the inquest. In his mind, it would be all too easy to sweep Josiah aside like ashes, but the time it would take . . .

"No. He's just a boy," Harlen said, finally bothering to look at the sheriff. "Now that his confidante is gone, I daresay all his plans are foiled. From what I gather, he knows nothing of our intentions, only that he wishes to rescue the Renolds girl."

"But sir—"

"Did I stutter, Sebastian?" Harlen said icily.

"No, my lord," Bash sighed.

"The full moon is in five days' time. We have much to do before then. I will not let another pass us by. Now go." Harlen gave a bored wave of his hand and turned his attention back to the ring. Bash bowed respectfully, withdrawing from the room. Alone once again, Harlen ogled the ring as if it would somehow come to life in his very hand. The council was steadily turning against him, making time no longer a luxury the tyrant could afford.

THE WINTRY LANDSCAPE WAS A FAR DIFFERENT BACKDROP for Casper's final trial than the others had been. He, Iris, and Thomas were constantly cold, so much so they were almost numb to it. The weather changed from calm to a blizzard at random intervals, and the sun, usually fixed in the sky, moved across the heavens despite the lack of time in the Netherworld. With dusk fast closing in, Casper decided it best to make camp. They scouted out a flat area amid a cluster of trees. Iris stayed behind with Thomas while Casper searched for firewood.

The glow of the oil lantern was the only light, save for the setting sun. Thomas hugged his knees to his chest while Iris dug through her satchel for supplies. "I know I bloody put one in here," she muttered to herself as she reached impossibly far into the bag.

Thomas rocked back and forth in an attempt to keep warm. "Do you think he can do it? Leave here?"

"I know he can," Iris replied, finally closing her hand around a wool blanket. She yanked it out of the satchel and wrapped it tenderly around Thomas's shoulders. "There we go. Better?"

Thomas nodded, clutching the warm fabric tightly around him. His shivers slowly ceased.

The lower in the sky the sun sank, the colder it became. Iris pulled up her hood for warmth and wrapped her arms around herself as she sat against a tree trunk. It felt like Casper had been gone for ages. She knew he'd be fine. He'd come a long way since they'd first met, and even then he hadn't been completely hopeless. He'd passed the first trial on his own, after all. Why, then, was she so worried?

"I think you'll make it out of here too," Thomas murmured.

Iris turned her gaze to the boy, and a gentle smile crossed her lips. "We all will, lad," she promised. She wished she had a way to be certain, but other than making a deal with Death, there was little that could be done.

Every so often, Thomas would shiver again. Iris couldn't help the strange maternal instinct that took her over. She scooted closer and wrapped her arms around his tiny frame. "Try to think warm thoughts," she murmured.

"Hot cider . . . wouldn't be so bad," he stuttered through chattering teeth.

Iris chuckled at that. "Aye. And hot cakes with cream and chocolate filling."

"What will you do when you get back home?" Thomas wondered.

"Me? I'm going to eat all the pies in Wayland," she replied, grinning.

Thomas laughed. "That's going to take a long time."

"Precisely," she said. "Not one strawberry pie shall be safe from me."

He laughed even more, and Iris couldn't keep the smile from her lips. It was hard to believe what she'd been willing to do to Thomas when they'd first run across him. That shrieker would have gotten the kill it desired, and she and Casper would be traveling on their own. Iris subconsciously hugged Thomas closer.

When his laughter died down, Thomas peered up at Iris, a curiosity in his sparkling brown eyes. "Do you fancy Casper?" he asked innocently.

Iris was taken by surprise. She met his gaze with a confused, almost defensive expression. "What kind of silly question is that?"

"It's all right if you do," Thomas said. "I think he's nice. You need someone nice."

"Oh, do I?" she replied, unable to believe they were having such a conversation.

"Aye, because you're nice," he answered. "Even though you pretend not to be."

"Do you have to notice everything?"

Thomas shrugged innocently, and Iris sighed. Maybe she did fancy Casper, if only a smidgen. He was handsome and kind, and he never gave up hope even when things seemed hopeless. Iris had needed a bit of that in her miserable purgatory. But soon he would leave her, and it wouldn't matter. He could go back on their deal, or Lord Harlen could end him. There were so many things that could go wrong. Getting attached was a risk she simply could not take. Even as she thought this, she realized she was making the same fatal mistake at that very moment with Thomas.

A howl sounded in the distance, and Iris jolted, eyes looking about in concern. The sun had completely set by now, leaving the two of them in the glow of the flickering lantern. Crunching in the snow grew closer—footsteps. Someone with two feet. Was it Casper? Or another soul who'd spotted their light?

"You two look comfortable," Casper's voice came from the dark. He crossed into the lantern's glow, arms laden with firewood.

Iris released the breath she was holding and took her hand off the dagger on her belt. "Where the bloody hell have you been?" she scoffed.

"Lovely to see you too," he answered, dropping the wood.

Casper set about starting a fire while the others looked on. Iris studied him as he worked. He'd been different since the incident with the scaths. Sometimes he couldn't meet her gaze, and others he seemed unusually quiet. Was it something the scaths had whispered to him? They never seemed to slow down long enough for her to ask.

Soon Casper had a blazing fire going, and the lamp was extinguished. Iris set Thomas closer to the flames where the lad gratefully held his hands out to warm them. Casper remained at the edge of the firelight, staring out at the wilderness. Thomas nudged Iris's shoulder and pointed at Casper. Iris rolled her eyes, and mouthed, "No."

Thomas gave her an innocent but scathing look.

Iris sighed. "Fine," she breathed.

She pushed herself up, mentally cursing the lad. Casper was always hopeful, and Thomas was meddlesome. Some lot she'd fallen in with. The snow crunched beneath her boots. Casper glanced aside once she stood next to him. Iris pulled her hood down, exposing her brilliantly red hair to the glimmering firelight. It made every crimson strand seem ten times brighter and more vibrant. Iris didn't know what to say, and likewise Casper couldn't find words, so they both defaulted to staring into the dark landscape around them.

"I've never seen this before," she commented.

"Seen what?"

"A landscape where the time of day changes," she answered. "It's always one or the other."

"First time for everything, I suppose," he mused.

Iris nodded at that. The space between them seemed heavy with the things Casper hadn't said and didn't want to say. He fought a good fight, but Iris could see the changes in his perfect brown eyes. He was carrying a lot of weight on his own.

"You know you can talk to me," she uttered, "about anything."

Silence followed her offer, and after a long enough pause, she assumed he didn't want to trust her.

"Just a thought," she murmured, and turned to leave him be.

"Gran died," he said.

Iris stopped in her tracks, face twisting in puzzlement. Slowly, she turned back, eyes full of sympathy. "What?"

"While you were under the scaths' spell," he continued. "I found her . . . talking with the Keeper."

Iris moved closer, feeling sadness in her every bone. "I'm so sorry."

"Everything's gone," he said. "The mill, Gran—all gone."

"And your sister?"

Casper finally turned his eyes toward her, full of pain and an anger he tried to keep at bay. "I don't know," he murmured.

Iris's heart bled for him, no longer hating that he made her care. The poor man had lost everything to the same vile tyrant who'd stolen her life. Without stopping to think about what she was doing, Iris wrapped her arms around him and buried her head in his chest. "We will solve this," she promised. "You'll get home, and you'll make him pay."

Casper rested his chin atop her head and held her close, exhaling with trepidation. "I hope you're bloody right," he whispered.

Iris smirked. "I'm always right."

The smallest of smiles crossed Casper's lips. He didn't say anything else. He simply enjoyed holding her, truly feeling that he wasn't alone amidst the chaos. The Netherworld had given him the sword as if it wanted him to defeat Harlen. That things would line up in such a manner seemed a strange thing to Casper, almost as if another supernatural hand were at work. Prophesies and gods had never been Casper's main interest aside from the weekly sabbath. He'd said his prayers as a boy and did all that he was always told he should do, but he'd never imagined how much more there was to the story, how much they all missed behind the veil.

Their small moment of bliss was fleetly interrupted by yet another howl. Iris perked up in Casper's hold, head whipping around. Both were suddenly alert, eyes scanning the terrain. Thomas went rigid by the fire, terror gripping his heart. The howls had never been so close. A bright red glimmer added its own light to the night. All eyes turned to the sword— the ruby glowed.

"Netherbeasts," Casper said urgently. He released Iris, and she immediately went for her sword.

Thomas threw off his blanket and moved behind them. Casper drew the Nethersword with determination. Several pairs of purple eyes burned in the darkness, coming nearer to the edge of the light. Casper's mouth went dry as one of the beasts crossed into the lantern's glow. A giant black wolf with carnivorous, strong jaws stared him down.

"Lucytes," Iris uttered fearfully. "Death's dearest pets."

"I take it you've seen these before," Casper mused.

"Oh, yes," she replied, readying her sword. "Whatever you do, don't get bitten."

Casper didn't like the sound of that. Steadily the lucytes surrounded them on all sides, growling and snapping at the Waylanders, almost taunting them. As if by an invisible snap of someone's fingers, they attacked. It quickly became evident they were faster and stronger than the average wolf, biting and snapping at any bit of the humans they could reach. The Nethersword sliced through them like tissue paper. With a few swings, Casper had already felled three beasts.

Behind him, Iris was having a more difficult time keeping the beasts at bay. Her sword did damage just fine, but not quite as smoothly as Casper's. She had to move twice as fast to keep away from their jaws, wounding the animals as she went. Thomas was doing all right for one so small, using his knives when he could. Despite their tough skins, the lucytes fell pretty quickly when a projectile hit them square in the eye.

The fight didn't last much longer. As quickly as they'd attacked, the remaining beasts quickly retreated. Casper's brow wrinkled, watching them go. It wasn't fear that made them leave. It was an order. A condescending, slow clap sounded from the darkness. All eyes turned toward it. A man walked into the light, handsomely fashioned with a chiseled jaw, prominent cheek bones, dark eyes, sandy hair, and a stubble beard. He wore all black and stood with an air befitting royalty. Casper knew at once he was looking at a god.

"Ah, Casper Renolds," the man spoke, an archaic accent on his every word. "The man I've heard so much about. You know, you really are as handsome as they say."

The man circled the three souls. Iris pulled Thomas close, keeping a protective arm around him.

"Who are you?" Casper demanded.

The stranger smiled sinisterly. "I would have thought you'd worked that one out," he said.

Casper's eyes followed the man's movements. "Death," he uttered.

"Ah." The god stopped his motion, standing in front of Casper once more. "See, now that wasn't so hard was it? No, no. Don't bow," he patronized, grinning. "That'd be awkward since I'm the one who's been single-handedly ruining your life. Please, call me Nex."

"What do you want?" Casper asked evenly.

Nex chuckled. "I want what I always want. To make a deal."

"Don't listen to him, Cas," Iris warned.

"Quiet," Nex ordered, snapping his fingers. Iris fell unconscious in the snow.

"Iris!" Thomas squeaked, dropping at her side and trying to shake her awake.

"Relax, lad," Nex assured. "She's just sleeping. I can do that." He fixed his dark gaze on Casper once more. "I can do quite a lot."

Casper worked his jaw. The Keeper had warned Casper of this, and yet he still hadn't expected Nex to approach him directly. "What kind of deal?"

The god spread his arms and took a step back. "You see, I've been working very hard to escape from this hell my brother has trapped me in, and you are getting dreadfully close to mucking it all up."

"Your brother?"

"Oh, you know . . . Lumen. The one you all affectionately call Maker. He's a right git, I can tell you that. Punishing me for all eternity just for having a bit of fun."

This was all news to Casper. The story of the Maker and Death painted them as old friends, never brothers. "So you want to stop me, then," Casper said.

"No," Nex half laughed, moving closer once again. He set a hand on Casper's shoulder. "I want to help you, mate. We can be pals, can't we? Imagine what we could do *together*."

Casper thought about Kaelyn and all that would happen if he didn't get home.

"You miss your sister, don't you, lad?" Nex said, pretending to sympathize. "I can get you home to her. All you have to do . . . is hand over that sword."

Casper's eyes wandered down to the weapon in his hand. The gem still glowed at Nex's presence.

"This weapon has great power," the Keeper's words echoed in Casper's mind, *"strong enough to harm even Death himself."*

Casper lunged with the sword, but Nex disappeared, suddenly behind him. A dark, amused laugh rumbled in the god's chest. "Did you really think that would work? I'm a *god*, Casper. One of the many reasons you even exist. If you want to kill me, you'll have to do better than that."

Casper swiped once and twice more, but Nex easily dodged the weapon, laughing. "That sword does no good in the hands of a mere mortal, lad. You're wasting your time."

Angrily, Casper lowered his weapon, eyes glowering. Amusement painted Nex's heavenly face. "Hand it over," he said with hand outstretched.

Casper looked from the sword to Nex's hand.

"Now," the god demanded sharply.

"You can't take it from me," Casper realized, a slight smile playing on his lips.

"Don't be a fool," Nex warned.

With a triumphant grin, Casper slid the sword back into its sheath. "I think I'll hold on to it."

Nex lowered his hand, dark eyes livid. "Don't underestimate me, Casper. My reach extends far beyond the boundaries of the Netherworld. I've been trying to stop you for a *very* long time."

The god's words wiped the smile from Casper's face. "What do you mean?"

"Did you really think your life was so littered with horrid circumstances because you had rotten luck?" Nex grinned vilely. "Your younger brother in the rapaxion bear cave? Me." He circled Casper, enjoying every look of pain on his face. "The slaughter of your parents by a band of thieves on the roadside? Me," he whispered in Casper's ear. "Isn't it funny what a little touch of darkness can do?"

Casper shook both with rage and shock.

"Did you really think Harlen would have noticed your sister if I hadn't first pointed her out?" Nex mused, standing in front of Casper once more. "I may be trapped here, lad, but I assure you, I still have ways of influencing the other side. So unless you want to lose everything else, I suggest you hand over that sword."

Casper glared at the god before him. The Keeper had been right to warn Casper of Nex, but as he stood face to face with the man responsible for all his pain, he wasn't afraid. He was driven.

"Never," Casper stated boldly.

Nex nearly laughed in shock. "Bloody unbelievable," he uttered. "No matter how many times I knock you down, you still have the nerve to keep fighting back." The god shook his head, chuckling. "We'll see how that fares for you in the very near future."

Suddenly, Thomas collapsed in the snow. Casper's heart plummeted. He was instantly at the lad's side. Thomas trembled in pain, and a sweat broke on his brow.

"What did you do?" Casper demanded, his accusing gaze boring into the god like fire.

Nex shrugged innocently. "I've done nothing. You might want to ask my precious lucytes which one of them *bit* your poor little friend."

Desperately, Casper searched Thomas's body, soon finding a tear in his jacket where a bloody wound frothed.

"I'm sorry," Thomas uttered. "I didn't mean to. . . ."

"Shh," Casper soothed.

"I can save him, Casper," Nex said. "All you have to do is agree to my terms."

Casper's jaw went rigid. He worked it back and forth, seething.

"You have until first light to make a decision," Nex continued. "Or your friend *dies*."

There was a rustle of wind, and Nex was gone. Iris suddenly took in a gulp of air and snapped upright. It took her a moment to get her bearings. When her vision righted itself, Casper's fair hair and strong physique came into view hunched over a very ill Thomas.

"No," she whispered, clambering toward them. She examined the bite, tearing Thomas's jacket a little more to see how much damage had been done.

"Can you do anything?" Casper asked, desperate for an answer. He couldn't let Thomas die.

Iris smoothed Thomas's hair away from his forehead and gave a minuscule shake of her head. "All we can do now is make him comfortable."

Furious, Casper shoved himself to his feet, trying and failing to keep his temper under control. He scooped up a spare bit of firewood and lobbed it as far as he could with a cry of rage. It smashed into a tree a good distance away, breaking into pieces. This was all his fault. He should have watched the lad more carefully.

Iris gently moved Thomas closer to the fire and propped him against a tree, draping the blanket over the boy's trembling form. Tears stung her eyes, tears of anger and regret. It wasn't right. Thomas was just a lad. As the poison spread, Thomas's temperature steadily spiked. Iris continually brushed his hair from his forehead, desperately wishing she could take his place. He deserved to live more than she. It was only now that she realized how selfish she'd been. Even helping Casper was only in service to herself. All the souls she'd killed without question, all the darkness she'd given herself to, it was all in the name of self-preservation. But Thomas, he fought to return to his family so they could put bread on the table. He maintained his innocence despite the evil around him. Where Iris had once seen weakness, she now saw strength, and it pained every part of her body to know it would no longer exist—Thomas would no longer exist.

Casper stared into the darkness of the forest beyond the fire's reach, everything inside him twisting in anger and heartbreak. It seemed as if everyone around him died. He pretended it didn't affect him, but every time he lost someone, he could feel a little piece of his soul chip away. Thomas's pained breaths tore through Casper's soul every time they shuddered through the air. Nex would stop this if Casper would hand over the one thing the Keeper had told him to wield.

"Don't," Thomas wheezed, eyes fixed on Casper's rigid form.

Casper whirled, face morphed in confusion. "What?"

"I h-heard . . . him," Thomas answered. "Don't . . . give it to him."

Iris looked accusingly at Casper. "What's he going on about?"

With a deep sigh, Casper folded his arms over his chest. "Nex wants the sword. He said he would cure Thomas if I handed it over."

"Then bloody well hand it over!" she snapped.

"I can't."

"Why not? Is your friend's life not more important than a stupid bloody sword?"

Casper worked his jaw, averting his gaze. He'd told her about Gran, but he'd neglected the part about the Keeper's words.

"Answer me!" Iris demanded.

The weight of two worlds seemed to be on Casper's shoulders. He didn't know why Nex wanted the sword, but no good would come of handing it over. "Because," he sighed, "I'm meant to use it to stop Harlen."

"Then we'll find another way," she spat.

"There is no other way!"

Iris fell silent. Casper had never yelled at her before. Not like that.

"Believe me, I want to hand it over, Iris," he went on, his voice one of forced calm. "I don't want any of this, but the Keeper said I was meant to find it, and Nex said he's been trying to stop me since I was born."

"Stop you from what?" Iris questioned.

"I don't know." He ran a hand stressfully through his blond tresses, torn between two decisions.

"It's okay," Thomas wheezed.

Casper's angry expression softened toward the lad. "No, it's not," he murmured. "This is all my fault."

Thomas shook his head. "You can't . . . give him the sword."

"You don't know what you're saying," Iris countered.

"Yes . . . I do," Thomas uttered.

Iris knew she was fighting a losing battle, but she couldn't give up—she wouldn't. "What exactly did the Keeper say to you?"

Casper turned his thoughts back to the conversation in the Keeper's study. "He said I was the one they'd been waiting for, that I was different. Only someone with good intentions could get the sword and only that person would the dragon obey . . . or something like that. He said the sword was so powerful it could kill Nex himself."

Iris felt a heavy weight of despair. "That's why he wants it," she murmured in understanding. "In the right hands, it would mean his end."

Casper nodded solemnly, unable to meet her gaze. More than anything, he wanted to save Thomas, but if he made a deal with Nex, he'd be no better than Lord Harlen. A pink tinge began on the horizon, steadily growing brighter. Thomas's time was running out. Casper knelt beside the lad and took his hand. Thomas was ashen and trembling with fever. His every breath rattled in his chest. "I am *so sorry*," Casper murmured, voice cracking.

Thomas weakly shook his head. "Don't be," he said, voice barely above a whisper. "It's not . . . your fault."

Hot tears stung Casper's eyes, and his throat burned. "Yes, it is," he said shakily. "I should have been faster. I should have protected you." A tear escaped despite his best efforts. His entire body ached with the weight of his grief.

The sky grew steadily brighter, dawn almost upon them. Thomas's breaths grew more ragged and pained. He clung tightly to Casper's hand, wheezing with every exhale. "Do me . . . a favor," he rasped.

"Anything you want, lad," Casper promised.

"Can you . . . find my parents?" he whispered.
"Tell them . . . I love them . . . and . . . I'm sorry."

A lump formed in Casper's throat. Iris tried to hold back her sobs beside him, smoothing Thomas's hair with a shaky hand. All Casper could do was nod. A tired smile crossed Thomas's lips. He reached for one of

Iris's hands and joined it with Casper's. "Take care . . . of each other."

Iris nodded, her face wet with tears. "We will," she vowed.

The sun peeked over the horizon, and Thomas jolted at a sudden pain in his chest. His mouth hung open in silent pain. He took a few short breaths, and then suddenly, he stopped.

"Thomas?" Casper uttered in despair, agony stabbing through his soul. He shook the lad's limp form. "Thomas!"

But it was no good. He was gone.

Casper sobbed in earnest, unable to combat the pain in his soul. It flooded his every nerve ending, threatening to overcome him. Iris covered her mouth as silent tears streamed down her face. Thomas's body slowly dissipated, leaving nothing behind but a memory. A heart-wrenching cry left Casper as he buried his face in the snow where Thomas's body had been. Calvin, his parents, Gran, and now Thomas. Why did everyone he loved have to die?

Iris wrapped her arms around Casper's trembling form, her tears staining his jacket. Her soul tore twice more seeing him like this. She wished she could take his pain away, to bear it herself so his soul could breathe, but nothing could heal this hurt. All she could do was soothe it.

Once his sobs died down, Casper pushed himself to his feet. His grief morphed horribly inside of him, changing into rage until the look on his face frightened even Iris. "NEX, YOU BASTARD!" he screamed to the wind. "I'LL KILL YOU FOR THIS! MARK MY WORDS! I'LL KILL YOU!"

Casper's voice echoed through mountains, chilling and livid. Atop the highest peak far from the two souls, Nex smiled. "We shall see," he said to himself. In the blink of an eye, he was gone.

Across the Lake

THE BURDEN OF THOMAS'S DEATH WAS A DIFFICULT CROSS to bear. Both Casper and Iris felt it was their own fault, and no matter how much they tried to forget it, the lad's absence was heavy around them. Trudging aimlessly through the deep snow seemed pointless now. All-consuming agony flowed through every nerve ending in their bodies. Casper desperately wished he could make himself numb to it, but in the Netherworld he was a soul, cursed to feel every emotion in its entirety.

On and on they went, never speaking a word. Another night came and went with little incident. Iris spent it curled up in Casper's arms near the fire, head resting on his chest. They still said little to one another, finding solace in simply being. By the time the sun rose, their grief had faded to a dull throb and Casper felt as though he could almost breathe again. He surveyed the terrain around them with folded arms, the rising sun sparkling off freshly fallen snow. His expression was far from happy.

"What is it?" Iris asked.

"We've been going in circles," he replied monotonously. "Still no trial, and now I've pissed off Death."

"The trial will find you," she said with certainty. "It has to."

Casper nodded, remaining stoic. "I know," he sighed, dropping his arms.

Iris took his hand and gave it a gentle squeeze. "We'll get through this," she promised.

The ghost of a smile crossed his lips, there barely a moment and gone. He squeezed her hand back, a silent agreement. Before he could scarcely think of a new plan, a high-pitched shriek rang through the air. Casper and Iris whirled in unison, a new emotion suddenly overtaking them—fear.

"A shrieker," Iris said quietly.

Another sounded, and another.

"Aye," Casper murmured, "and it's not alone." He shoved her toward the steep incline they'd been avoiding. "Go. Go!"

The sound of at least a dozen shriekers echoed in the thick mountain air, growing closer. Soon the beasts raced into view, gargantuan and running on all fours, long forearms and claws itching to tear Casper and Iris apart. Jagged mouths wrenched open in their squared heads as they shrieked in excitement at nearing their prey. Hand in hand, Casper and Iris raced down the steep hillside as fast as they could, the first few creatures gaining on them at a dangerous pace. Casper yanked Iris forward as a shrieker lunged. It missed and sailed into a tree, shattering the trunk.

Running downhill was complicated enough, but the snow made it harder still. Iris slipped and toppled into Casper. He stumbled. The two of them fell, rolling head over heels down the mountainside. The shriekers attempted to follow, soon losing their footing as well. The Waylanders fell so rapidly, it was almost impossible to miss the trees. They slammed into the tall trunks and into each other all the way down.

Iris groaned when they finally tumbled into a heap at the bottom. "If we weren't already dead, I'd kill you," she complained.

Casper winced. "Perhaps later, aye?"

The shriekers screeched loudly through the trees. Casper pushed himself up and tugged Iris to her feet. The beasts drew ever nearer, causing the ruby in the Nethersword to glow a deep crimson. Casper made a mad dash for the frozen lake. Iris followed closely behind. Back in Wayland, running across ice was improbable. Casper banished the thought, remembering what Iris had taught him. Soon they reached the lake's edge. Casper raced across the ice as if it were solid ground. Iris ran just as easily behind him.

"Casper!" Iris shouted. A shrieker dove over her head, missing her by inches.

Casper drew his weapon and whirled. The blade cut the shrieker's head clean off—something any other sword would never manage on a Netherbeast. Dozens more raced across the frozen water, teeth bared with the intent to kill.

"I've never seen them in packs like this," Iris observed.

Casper stared at the beasts, mouth suddenly dry. "It's the sword," he realized. "Nex sent them for the sword."

"To hell with that!" Iris shouted above the screeches. "Thomas died to keep that sword away from the bastard. He's a nutter if he thinks he's getting it now."

Casper looked about desperately for a solution. They were nearly halfway across the lake with shriekers bearing down on them. The opposite shore was too far to make it safely, but one sword was hardly enough to fight off the multitude of monsters. *Monsters.* An idea struck.

Casper held the sword toward the heavens.

"What are you doing?" Iris demanded, tugging on his arm in an attempt to make him follow her.

"Dragon, I summon thee!" he called. It looked silly. He felt silly. But Casper was out of plans.

"Oh, please." Iris rolled her eyes. "That's not going to—"

A vicious roar came from the clouds. The oncoming shriekers skidded to a stop. Iris's jaw dropped. The dragon burst through the cloud cover, great wings flapping like mighty thunder. It soared for the shriekers. The vile beasts scattered as the dragon swooped low, spewing fire and molten rock. A grin spread across Casper's lips. Some of the shriekers managed to skirt the blaze, but the dragon kept them busy.

Iris tapped his arm. "Uh . . . Cas?"

He followed her horrified gaze. The dragon's fire was scattering and scorching the shriekers all right, but it was also melting the ice, causing steam to rise and obscuring visibility along the path created by the dragon's breath.

"Not good," he muttered.

Casper tugged Iris toward the other bank. They sprinted desperately across the frozen landscape, two shriekers nipping at their heels. The cracks in the ice reached for the Waylanders like evil hands, shifting and turning, hell-bent on drowning them in the water's frigid grasp. The other shore seemed to get farther away the harder they ran. The larger of the two shriekers was nearly upon them. It screeched as it dove for Casper. The lake crackled beneath them.

"Casper!" Iris screamed.

The shrieker slammed into Casper, and they crashed through the ice. The black sword fell from the miller's grasp, skidding across the ice toward Iris. She fleetly scooped it up, whirling as the other creature lunged. The sword cleaved through one of the shrieker's forearms. Blood stained the ice a deep scarlet as the beast crashed onto it. The lake between them split apart, separating Iris from the wounded shrieker.

Patches of ice floated apart across the entire body of water. Iris scanned the lake's surface frantically, searching for any sign of her friend.

"Casper!" she yelled.

Helplessness ripped her heart in two. If he died, she'd never wake, but that wasn't what terrified her most. If he perished here, she would never see him again.

Suddenly Casper's head broke the surface far from Iris's position. Blood oozed down the side of his face, and his clothes were ripped almost to shreds. He clawed at one of the floating pieces of ice, barely hanging on. Iris's heart leapt. She scrambled toward him, jumping from ice patch to ice patch.

"Hang on!" she cried.

The ice bobbed and swayed beneath her, making it difficult to move swiftly. It threatened to throw her headfirst into the glacial waters. The dragon roared as a wave of shriekers attacked it, ripping into its flesh. It batted them away with its tail and set others aflame. More and more of the nasty creatures poured out of the forest, but the dragon never faulted in its quest to protect its master, setting half the forest ablaze in its pursuit.

Iris was nearly to Casper when his grip slipped. Fear pushed her faster. She dove onto Casper's patch of ice just as he slipped back into the water.

"No!" she exclaimed, plunging her arm into the freezing lake. It tore at her skin like knives. She barely caught the fabric of Casper's torn coat. Iris pulled with all her strength. His head came back above water, but his lips were blue and he wasn't breathing.

"No, no, no!" Iris tugged him partway onto the ice. He was heavier than he looked, especially when drenched and half-frozen.

The dragon gave a feral snarl as it devoured the last shrieker. Wounded but still in one piece, it sought its master. Iris struggled to pull Casper from the lake. The sword slid dangerously toward the edge of the ice. Iris gasped, barely catching it with her foot. The dragon beat its thunderous wings, taking off into the sky. Iris couldn't let the sword fall, nor could she lose Casper. The dragon hovered overhead. Iris met the beast's gaze imploringly.

"Help me! Please!"

Unable to disobey the sword wielder, the dragon scooped Casper up in its talons. Iris dove for the sword as it fell over the edge. A shrieker jumped from the water like a deformed shark, nearly taking her arm off. She screamed and rolled aside, clambering to her feet. The beast tried to climb onto the bobbing ice patch. Iris growled and came at it with the sword. With a rebel yell, she impaled the creature's hideous head with the blade. The shrieker shuddered, then fell dead. Iris ripped the sword from its body and kicked the beast into the water.

The dragon landed on the opposite bank and laid Casper's limp body in the snow. Iris hopped between ice patches and dropped to her knees beside her unconscious friend. She tried to shake him awake. "Cas," she uttered. "Come on, love. Wake up."

He didn't move.

"Damn it, Casper! Don't do this to me!"

She pounded on his chest with her fists and shook him furiously, terrified that he would turn into dust at any moment. He didn't stir. Frantic sobs racked her body as she banged on his chest again. She didn't know what else to do. He couldn't leave her. He simply couldn't leave her.

All at once, he spit up water and gasped for air. Iris yanked him up and threw her arms around him. He grimaced, still catching his breath.

"Don't ever do that to me again," she cried, almost shocked at her own behavior. "Don't you *ever*!"

Casper nodded, shivering. Iris could almost kiss him, she was so relieved. His trembling frame called more immediate needs to attention. "Come on. We need to get you dry," she said, returning the sword to the sheath at Casper's side.

She carefully helped him up and draped his arm around her shoulders. The dragon followed their progress with its large, yellow eyes. Iris moved Casper as far inland as she could. He was weak, and regardless of how strong she may be, dead weight was never easy to carry. Casper shivered, doing all he could to keep one foot in front of the other. His head spun, and he could barely see a thing through the spots.

Iris found shelter from the biting wind behind a large rock outcropping. She sat Casper carefully against it. "I'll get a fire going," she said. "And then we can get you out of those wet clothes."

"You'd like that . . . wouldn't you?" he joked, teeth chattering.

Iris smiled wanly. "Perhaps," she teased. "I'll be back. Try to stay out of trouble."

Casper nodded stiffly, finding it difficult to move. The dragon lay down nearby, curling its massive tail around the camp like a protective wall. He glanced up at it, not sure he liked the look it gave him. "What?" he uttered.

The dragon huffed in response.

Soon Iris returned with firewood in hand and set up everything. Her hands were numb from the cold. She hated the Netherworld. Things such as hunger and sleep couldn't affect them, but the environment could. Inquisitively, she met the dragon's yellow gaze.

"Would you mind?" She gestured at the wood.

The dragon looked to Casper.

"It's all right," he uttered through clicking teeth.

The dragon's scales glowed and it breathed gently, spewing a soft fire that engulfed the wood with a warm blaze.

Iris smiled in wonder. "Thank you."

She took only a moment to warm her hands over the flames. Casper didn't look well at all. His lips were still blue, and his skin was discolored. She had revived him well enough, but if they didn't play their cards right, he could still catch his death.

A part of Casper almost wanted to die, if only to end his pain. The gash in his head throbbed, and he was certain he had a much larger one along his back. Kaelyn's face appeared in his mind's eye. He remembered her voice, her kindness, and her goodness so far away. And then there was Iris. Stubborn, tough, and headstrong Iris. He'd spent nigh on three months in close quarters with her. They'd saved each other's lives many times, but in the end he'd have to leave her here. Casper had come to rely on her almost as an extension of himself—another sword working in conjunction with his. He never would have survived if she hadn't taught him how to. She was in Wayland somewhere too, waiting for him to return and wake her. They needed him to survive this. He couldn't possibly let them down.

Iris dug through her satchel and pulled out some spare clothes and medical supplies.

"You t-think of everything . . . don't you?" he mused, teeth chattering.

Iris smiled.

Delicately she helped him out of his tattered longcoat and shirt to examine his wounds. The majority of the damage was on his back, though the head wound was certainly a concern. Iris winced at the sight of his shredded skin. "He really got you, didn't he?"

"Aye." Casper winced. "Thankfully he wasn't a good swimmer."

He tried in vain to keep from shivering as she worked. The fire helped a little, but he was so cold it mostly just seared his nerve endings. He fought to stay awake, knowing sleep would mean something different for him—erasure.

Once Iris finished patching him up, she carefully helped him into some dry clothes and curled up in his arms to warm him. Casper rested his head atop her strawberry tresses, still trembling from the cold. The fire, new clothes, and her body all worked in correlation with one another, slowly warming him. Casper wished they could fall asleep in such a fashion—escape the Netherworld for a while. He hoped they'd leave the nightmare behind soon.

Time passed, and eventually his shaking ceased. The dragon's heavy breathing was almost like a cat's purr as it slept. Casper soothed Iris's arm with his hand, his gaze lost in the flames. "What do you miss most about being alive?" she murmured into his shirt.

Casper took a deep breath, allowing her question to roll around in his mind before he answered. "I dunno," he said quietly. "The normalcy of it all, I suppose. No monsters or magic, just ordinary, mundane things."

"I miss dreaming," Iris said. "Escaping in sleep to something else, something better."

"Aye," Casper agreed, smiling slightly at their shared thought. "I miss that too."

As Iris snuggled closer, he wondered what passing the trials would mean for the two of them. It was impossible to deny his feelings now, and despite his prior concerns of her indifference, she obviously shared them. Even holding her made his soul lighter than air. He dreaded what would happen if he failed to wake her, or worse—if he lost her between now and passing his final trial. No doubt, Nex had thought the same. Casper's eyes wandered to the gigantic dragon sleeping at the edge of the tree line, and a mad, inspired idea crossed his mind. He smirked. A mad idea indeed.

The Bayou

"YOU CAN'T BE SERIOUS," IRIS COMPLAINED WHEN, AGES later and back on his feet, Casper explained his genius plan. "It'll never work! It's like . . . cheating."

"Do you think Nex plays fair?" Casper asked as he kicked snow and dirt over the fire.

"We can't fly a dragon!"

Iris had been making the same arguments over and over for a while now, and Casper was reaching his wits' end. Counterarguments clearly weren't working. He fixed her with an incredulous look, eyebrow quirked. It drew a groan of annoyance from her lips.

"This is insanity," she grumbled, stomping closer to the dragon. She'd once thought it enormous, but it was a hill compared to the mountains around them. The creature's yellow eyes bored through Iris mistrustfully. The redhead stopped in her tracks. "I don't think it likes me very much."

It became apparent to Casper that any excuse would do. Iris was determined to avoid flying. The very thought seemed to make her frantic.

"You're afraid of heights," he realized aloud, amused for the first time since Thomas had died.

Iris whirled. "Rubbish."

He chuckled. "It's obvious."

"Don't make me impale you," she warned, fire in her perfect green eyes.

"That would solve all of our problems," he mused sarcastically.

Casper considered the possibility of leaving her behind. It was a ludicrous thought, born of desperation and determination. Regardless of her feelings, they had to get on that dragon.

"Well, I'm going," he decided, looking to the dragon as if asking for permission. The dragon bowed its head, granting it. He climbed up the creature's massive stony leg and sat in the space just below its neck. The dragon's scales provided a heated seat, a lovely buffer against the cold. "You can either come with me or stay here."

Iris glared up at him with an indignant huff. It was meant to be *his* fears they were facing, not hers. She'd already passed her trials, for goodness' sake. Still, the threat of being alone in that frozen wasteland was just as daunting. In spite of her strong desire to keep two feet firmly planted on the ground, she approached the dragon. Casper leaned down and offered a hand to help her up. Iris stared at it as if it were a venomous beast.

"Sometimes I truly loathe you," she muttered, taking his hand.

"I know," he said.

He tugged her onto the dragon's scaly side. Once safely astride the creature, Iris wrapped her arms around Casper's waist. His tattered longcoat reeked of smoke and the wild, plus something else that was so uniquely Casper. The dragon stood to its full height. Iris panicked, tightening her grip. This was madness. Sheer and utter madness.

"Let's go," Casper said to the dragon.

It snorted with an affirmative nod and unfurled its great wings. Iris buried her head in Casper's coat, eyes squinched shut as if it would somehow keep the dragon from taking off. The creature pumped its wings in a steady rhythm. Each *swoosh* brought them ten feet higher until the ground below was so far away, it looked like a toy landscape. Soon they were level with the peaks. Casper looked across the mountain valley in wonder. The lake had refrozen as if nothing had happened, and all the trees scorched by dragon's fire not a sunrise ago had already regrown. Every fingerprint they'd left, every small detail they'd destroyed—it was all wiped clean.

The dragon continued its vertical ascent until they were nearly level with the clouds. Casper finally ordered it to halt, and there they hovered, rising and falling a little with each flap of the dragon's wings. The view took Casper's breath away.

"Whoa," he uttered.

Below them the Netherworld unfurled like a giant, constantly changing map sewn together by various mountain ranges, rivers, and lakes. Every so often a piece of the landscape would change. A mountain moved. A river gone. Sudden clouds. It was spectacular.

"Iris, you have to see this," Casper said.

She shook her head, still buried face-first in Casper's coat.

"Really," he insisted, "it's not that bad. Give it a go."

For someone who'd defeated the Netherworld already, she looked rather ridiculous cowering at the thought of how high up they were.

"Come on," he encouraged.

She sighed. He wasn't going to give up, and the sooner they got back on solid ground, the better. Reluctantly she turned her head and peeked at the landscape below. Her initial reaction was panic, but it was swiftly replaced with awe at the sight below them. For all the time she'd spent in that horrid place, she'd never seen the Netherworld like this. It was almost beautiful.

"It's all one huge landscape," she said, enraptured. From the way it changed every time she'd entered the caves, Iris had always imagined they'd entered smaller arenas to fight.

"This must be how Nex keeps an eye on everything," Casper reasoned. He could see specks like ants moving below, some creatures and others wayward souls fighting for their lives. It was difficult to decipher one from the other at such a height, but Casper imagined a god was little challenged in knowing.

As Iris took in the ever-changing landscape, her fear forgotten, Casper's daring plan suddenly didn't seem so mad. "Do you feel pulled in any certain direction?" she asked.

Casper looked over the massacred quilt of the Netherworld, paying closer attention to the way each corner of the world affected him. "There," he said, pointing to a region buried in storm clouds several mountain ranges over.

He scarcely had to give an order before the dragon swooped lower and glided in the desired direction. Iris clung to Casper for dear life. Wind tousled Casper's hair and whipped Iris's long braid behind her. The freezing air of the snowy mountain region disappeared behind them, replaced by a warmer, humid climate. The dragon presently began its descent. The trees in this region were so thick, the beast couldn't land, choosing instead to hover near the topmost branch of the tallest tree. Casper held out a hand to aid Iris in dismounting, waiting until she was safely perched on the branch before he slid from the beast's back. The dragon remained hovering, looking at Casper for instruction.

"Thank you," he said. "You can go."

The dragon bowed its regal head and ascended with a heavy thrust of its wings, disappearing above the overcast sky. Casper looked out over the new landscape. The trees here were far different from the pines of the snowcapped mountain. The branches were huge on the willow they'd landed in. Hanging moss draped over the limbs like nature's shawl, and an intense humidity pressed down on them. Sweat already clung to Casper's brow. He navigated the way safely below the greenery, Iris just behind him.

"Well, this is potentially problematic," Iris mused.

All around them, the trees were submerged in murky water, leaving not a speck of dry land to walk on. Thunder rumbled in the distance warning of a coming storm, frogs croaked an off-key melody, and fireflies dotted the trees here and there like beacons of hope in the dark bayou.

"Aye," Casper agreed.

Climbing into the water would be suicide. Anything could be lurking beneath the muddy surface.

Iris tugged on his coat sleeve. "Look."

He followed her pointing finger. Below the large roots of the tree was a raft fashioned of reeds. It was convenient—almost too convenient—but they had little option lest they swim, risking leeches and far worse. One at a time, they slid down the tree trunk and jumped over the large roots. The raft was moored by a single rope, held to the tree with a dagger embedded in the bark. Had a wayward soul left it there? Or was Nex playing games? Casper studied the raft warily. Nothing seemed amiss to the eye.

"What are you waiting for?" Iris chided. "An invitation?"

There was no way but forward, he knew, but Nex could still take Iris from him as easily as a queen could knock down a pawn on a chessboard. Casper had no doubt Nex would stop at nothing to get the Nethersword.

Casper leapt from the tree to the raft. It bobbed under his weight but seemed sturdy enough. He nodded for Iris to come aboard. She landed like a cat beside him, lithe and unfazed. With a graceful turn, she yanked the knife from the tree. Casper picked up the long stick that acted as a makeshift oar and pushed off the tree. The current was stagnant, leaving him to do all the work. He did so vigilantly, keeping watch on the trees. Some were misshapen and bent at odd angles, while others stood tall and proud as if they thought themselves the most regal trees in the forest.

Iris kept watch at their flank. The waterway remained still like a giant puddle, which only served to grate on Iris's nerves. Quiet meant complacency, and complacency in the Netherworld meant mistakes. They moved at a glacial pace, following the natural path left by the moss-covered trees. Soon the approaching storm dumped rain in torrents, soaking the two souls to the bone almost instantly and reducing their field of vision to within a few feet of the raft. Lightning cracked overhead, and in the momentary brightness Iris caught sight of a dark shape swimming behind them.

"There's something following us," she called above the wind.

Casper looked over his shoulder in search of the mysterious shape. He saw nothing. "Are you sure?"

Suddenly the raft jolted, nearly toppling them into the murky water. Both looked about in fear. Without dry land, they were at a terrible disadvantage.

"Maybe we hit a log," Casper said hopefully.

"Fat chance," Iris replied.

Casper withdrew the pole from the water, eyes studiously searching for a cause. Again something slammed into the raft, sending them both stumbling. A third attack almost immediately after had Iris on her knees, dangerously close to the edge. A pair of jaws narrowly missed her face. She gasped and clambered back.

"Alligators!" she cried. And they were not the normal kind. One beast was roughly the size of two average reptiles put together.

"Aye," Casper said, "and they look bloody hungry."

With the rain blinding them and the raft bobbing uncontrollably, it was almost impossible to fight the beasts. There was no way to decipher how many creatures swam in the gloom around them. Over and over, the alligators pounded their massive tails into the raft, trying to knock the human morsels into the water. By now the raft bobbed so much, trying to stand was futile. Another crack of lightning revealed over a dozen alligators, all colossal in size with row upon row of sharp, jagged teeth. Some attacked the raft while others swam around it, creating a current that spun the makeshift boat in circles. The constant banging and new current had them tilting and whirling so much, the edges of the raft dipped into the water.

Lightning and thunder clashed together as one of the largest beasts lunged. It landed on the partially submerged corner of the raft. Both Waylanders cried out as the transport tilted, sliding them toward the alligator's monstrous jaws. Thinking apace, Casper held the pole ready and jammed it into the beast's gaping maw. The alligator growled angrily and slipped back into the water, trying and failing to get the pole out of its jaws. The raft fell flat once again, tossing Casper and Iris in a heap at the center.

"Well done," Iris said, trying to catch her breath.

"There are too many of them."

Lightning once again revealed the creatures. They swam so violently, there wasn't a segment of calm water. With two swords and no steady ground, cutting the alligators down was a fool's errand.

A resounding *snap* split the air—the large beast had broken the pole.

Still bobbing like a cork in the choppy water, it was only a matter of time before the reptiles nearly flipped them again.

"How much whale oil is left?" Casper wondered.

"A bit. Why?"

"I've got an idea."

Teeth snapped at them and tails pushed the raft to and fro, sloshing water onto the already-soaked souls. Casper dug through the satchel, rainwater cascading from his nose and chin. It was ruddy hard to see. Iris pulled out her sword and hacked at the reptiles that came too close.

"Tell me you aren't going to do what I think you are," she said.

"How would I know?" he replied. "I can't read your bloody mind!"

"It's pouring!" she cried. "You can't set them alight!"

Apparently she could read his mind. "Not indefinitely, but we can damn well scare them off!"

The raft lurched alarmingly, and he almost lost the canteen.

"You better hurry, then," Iris said, scooting away from the edge to avoid the jaws of another beast.

What Casper hoped to achieve wasn't an exact science, but Iris had drilled into him since day one that he couldn't think with his head. If he believed this would work, it would . . . he hoped.

Hastily he unscrewed the cap and sloshed flammable oil at any alligator that came too close. He imagined the canteen to be bottomless, and the thought seemed to work—the oil never ran out. Satisfied that all the reptiles were coated, Casper dug for matches. This was the hard part. Matches were stubborn at the best of times. He didn't expect them to behave at the worst. True to their nature, he broke two and lost a third before he finally got one lit. He cupped a hand around the feeble flame, protecting it as best he could from the wind and rain. Lightning briefly illuminated the swarming alligators. Casper aimed and tossed the match. As it sailed through the air, he and Iris held their breaths. Nothing.

Then . . .

Foom! The oil caught fire and, in a magnificent burst, spread from alligator to alligator. The reptiles made noises of protest, diving beneath the surface of the water in hopes of alleviating their pain. Some weren't so lucky to escape death. The rest, seeing their fallen brothers, decided to flee. No meal was worth this. Relieved, Iris and Casper collapsed side by side on the raft, staring up at the relentless rain.

"I admit . . . it was a good plan," Iris said.

Casper grinned. "Was that a compliment?"

"Shut up."

The rain continued to pour, leaving them both sopping wet and shivering. Without the pole, they had little choice but to float aimlessly. Thankfully the torrential downpour had swelled the waterway, pushing them on. There seemed to be no end to the bayou, but Casper still felt drawn as if by some unforeseen magnet. The true test of his final trial was near. He could feel it.

Eventually the storm passed. Iris dug in her satchel for some spare clothes, and the two of them changed clumsily, backs to one another. They discarded their coats, choosing to wear lighter shirts with the sleeves rolled up. The waterway moved steadily after the heavy rain, giving Casper hope they might find land soon.

Frogs started their singing once again, and the fireflies came out of hiding. An annoying buzzing accompanied this—gnats and mosquitoes. With the rain gone, they swarmed the river in droves. Casper slapped his neck as a mosquito nipped into it.

"Pesky buggers," he mused.

Iris nodded in agreement, swatting a few away and slapping another off her arm. "Almost makes me miss city life," she said.

It wasn't long after that Casper spotted something in the trees.

CHAPTER TWENTY-ONE

"Kaelyn?" he wondered aloud.

His sister was jumping across the wider roots of the trees, laughing. Calvin was just behind her. The raft rocked as Casper rose suddenly to his feet.

"Cas?" Iris called out, but he didn't hear her.

He squinted through the dimly lit forest. The water changed to dry land and the trees to tall pines. Young Kaelyn and Calvin were running from him.

"You can't catch us!" Kaelyn jeered, laughing her musical laugh.

Casper moved to step off the raft, but Iris swiftly drew him back.

"But she's right there," he said, trying to yank free of Iris's hold.

"Who is?"

"My sister!"

Iris waved a hand in front of Casper's face. He didn't even notice. "You're hallucinating," she realized, shaking him. "Snap out of it!"

If either one of them fell in the water, there was no telling what might happen. Iris highly doubted alligators were their only problem. For his own safety, Iris pulled strips of cloth from her bag and tied him down. Visions of his siblings haunted his mind.

Iris had barely tied his arms behind his back when she heard her name, crystal clear and loud as it echoed through the bayou. At first, she thought it might be a visitor back in Wayland, but then she saw him standing at the base of a tree.

"Father?" she uttered.

John Farrel merely grinned and nodded. Her first instinct was to clamber from the raft and race into his arms, but after watching Casper succumb to what she assumed was a toxic mosquito bite, she remained on the transport, arms hugged around herself for stability.

"You're not real," she whispered over and over. "Not real."

Her fingernails dug into her flesh, leaving angry red marks until she nearly drew blood. Horrified, she watched Lord Harlen slay her father, the bayou fading into the manor Iris called home back in Wayland.

"Not real. Not real," she repeated, rocking back and forth.

Her red-headed mother wept over the body, agony keeping her on her knees. With malice, Harlen struck her down too. Iris winced as the blow was delivered, the pain in her now-bleeding arms the only thing keeping her grounded. Both she and Casper were so lost in their hallucinations, they didn't notice the raft bump against the shore.

No Honor among Theives

WAYLAND COULDN'T SEEM TO DECIDE IF IT WANTED another winter snow. The previous blanket had all but melted during a warm spike, and now the temperature once again plummeted. Whether the storm clouds would bring rain or sleet, no one could guess. The weather had been very fickle that year. Changes in climate were of grand importance to Josiah Grimm's plan. Anna-Rose had sent no correspondence in days, and a worried knot kept twisting in his stomach—something was wrong. With Casper still dead as a doornail and Anna-Rose mysteriously silent, Josiah was running out of options.

It was for this reason he found himself wandering into the Slums late one evening. The narrow paths trapped a rancid smell that practically burned Josiah's nose hairs—the sort of smell that abounded when too many bodies were packed in one place. Now and then, a metal brazier lit the way. The cry of a hungry infant pierced the chilly air, accompanied by a dog's territorial bark. The very air itself seemed staler, as if Josiah had entered a whole new world. In many ways, he had. Rules were different here, as was the culture. The rough and toughs all gathered in the darkest corners of the Slums, ignored by the city because they weren't of a certain class. So low had the Slums fallen, they were below even the lower class. It was here that Josiah had begun his new life as a Netherworlder, and it was here that Dante Black still chose to live.

The strong smell of water and mildew filled the air as Josiah neared the wharf. Resting just over the water was a dingy ale house called The Drunken Cat. This was the place where deals were done, where plots were hatched, and where the lowest of humanity gathered for merriment. It was a favorite haunt of Dante's, and if The Raven was anywhere to be found, this was the first place to look.

Josiah took the rickety steps down to the dock on which the grimy building rested. He passed a man and woman locked in a furious battle with each other's tongues, not bothering to hide their private acts from public view. Josiah rolled his eyes and shoved open the door, feeling immensely out of place. Fiddle and fife music played loudly behind the raucous laughter and conversation of the patrons. Josiah went unnoticed as he meandered inside, quite to his relief. He saw a few familiar faces from bygone days, but he didn't stop to chat. He wasn't there to relive a past he'd rather leave behind.

Barmaids wandered the tables, refilling drinks and offering their best smiles. A glass broke somewhere. Josiah pushed through a large group with a muttered apology, eyes scanning to and fro for a familiar shock of black hair. There was no sign of his friend in the upstairs balcony, nor the rickety booths nearby. Not but a moment later, Josiah heard an unmistakable accent from across the room. His eyes followed the sound, spotting Dante at the bar laughing with a few other men. He seemed in the middle of some elaborate story, and his audience listened with rapt attention. Josiah navigated between the grubby wooden tables, skirting people and chairs as he went. Dante's voice grew louder and more intelligible as Josiah neared.

". . . and the bloody idjit jest stares at me," Dante said, voice laced with amusement. "I stole the paintin' and leapt out the window without another word. Poor bugger thought he'd seen a ghost."

"In a way, he did," Josiah chimed in.

All eyes turned to him, and Josiah suddenly wished he'd been subtler. Dante's face changed from shock to a wide grin.

"I wondered when yeh might turn up here," the thief said, clapping a hand on Josiah's shoulder. "Pull up a chair, laddie. Have a pint."

"Not tonight, mate," Josiah declined. "I wonder if I might have a word . . . in private."

The onlookers scrutinized Josiah with a judgmental gaze. His clothes, while still worn by common folk, were much cleaner and far newer than what most had in the Slums. Some were more fortunate, to be sure, but Josiah's mannerisms and general standoffishness were another point of interest. He was obviously not a local. It was almost as if he feared catching fleas, which in truth was a concern among some of the riffraff.

Dante gave a curt nod and slid off his barstool, indicating for Josiah to follow him. He led the way to a rickety staircase near the back, and together they climbed. Again, Josiah was hit with a sense of nostalgia. This had been his life once, his home. By the grace of the Maker, he'd gotten out, but now he found himself yet again sinking to low levels to achieve his aims.

Dante found them a small table in the back corner of the wraparound balcony. The hubbub still carried from below mixed with the noise of the patrons dining above. It was enough to mask any conversation spoken quietly enough, and the corner provided a natural barrier, an almost bubble of silence and protection against those who might overhear.

"Right, then, boyo," Dante said in his nonchalant and charismatic manner. He propped his feet up on the table and folded his hands behind his head. "What's this all about?"

Josiah decided to cut to the chase, finding no pleasure in it. "I need your help."

That drew a laugh from the master thief. Dante folded his arms as his chuckle subsided. "Yeh show up here after six bloody years, and all yeh've to say is 'I need yer help'? What happened to a 'Hullo' or a 'How are yeh?'"

Josiah rolled his eyes. Though Dante had a point, the apprentice didn't want to hear it. "I would have thought our reunion the other night counted," he mused.

"I was bored," Dante said. "Yeh had me curious."

"So, you weren't merely helping an old friend?"

Dante grinned. "I'm not the sentimental type, and yeh know it."

Josiah nodded, though he didn't believe him. Dante often acted as if he didn't care, but in truth he cared a great deal. Josiah had seen it.

"What's the job, then?" Dante asked.

This was the part Josiah had been dreading. "I need help breaking into a manor. . . ."

"Sounds easy enough."

". . . on Prior Street."

Dante nearly fell out of his chair. "Prior Street?" His raised voice caused a few heads to turn. "Are yeh barkin' mad?"

It was exactly as Josiah expected. Prior Street was the place thieves usually avoided. Dante had done the odd job or two there if the pay was good enough, but he was a master at his trade. Josiah was skilled, surely, but not for a score as big as Prior Street.

"I have a plan," Josiah promised.

CHAPTER TWENTY-TWO

"And which house are yeh thinkin' of robbin', I wonder?"

"Harlen Manor."

If the air between them got any tenser, Josiah was certain it'd explode. Dante's jaw was tight and his frame rigid. It wasn't unexpected.

"And I'm not robbing it," Josiah clarified. "It's more of a rescue."

"Why the bloody hell would someone need rescuin' from Harlen Manor?" Dante asked sharply. He was already shutting down to the whole idea. Josiah knew he had to choose his words carefully.

"Have you paid any attention to the comings and goings of the city, mate?"

"I like to think I'm the authority on it."

"Then you'll know all about Lord Harlen trying to take it over."

Dante dropped his feet and leaned against the table. "Don't tell me— he stole yer bonny lass, and now yer tryin' to win her back."

"You'd do it for Elise," Josiah said bitterly.

Anger flashed in Dante's forget-me-not blues. "Leave her out of this."

The two men had a bit of a staring contest, Dante softening as the seconds ticked by.

The thief sighed. "Look . . . I'd love to help, lad; really, I would, but I can't."

"Can't or won't?"

Dante deliberated and gave up with a shrug. "Wee bit of both, I suppose."

Josiah was equally enraged and disappointed. Of all the people he could have turned to, Dante had seemed the most likely to tackle such an adventure. Having nothing more to say, Josiah stood. "Right, then," he muttered. "Sorry I asked."

As he started to walk off, Dante grabbed his arm, eyes sincere as he looked imploringly up at his former apprentice. "Be careful, lad," he warned. "Few who tackle those great homes see the light of day again."

Josiah gave little more than a nod in reply, continuing on his way once Dante released him. It seemed he was back to square one, watching and waiting on Casper. There were two Netherworlders in Harlen Manor, and it would take two Netherworlders to take them out.

The Final Trial

CASPER WAS THE FIRST TO WAKE FROM HIS STRANGE stupor. It was like getting too close to a mirage and watching it melt away. He blinked a few times, confused. He'd been in Wayland mere moments ago; now he appeared to be on some sort of boat. The truth came to him like a rock bashed into his head. He was dead. He was in the Netherworld, and Kaelyn was in danger. On finding himself bound, he panicked, but with little effort at all, he soon freed a hand and set about untying his feet. The water lapped against the damp, grassy shore, pushing the raft repeatedly into the embankment. The trees weren't as thick here, and he wagered if they walked far enough, they'd soon come to a clearing.

"Iris," he said her name gently.

The redhead sat, clenching her teeth and practically ripping the flesh from her arms. Her form trembled.

"Iris," he tried again, this time shaking her.

She jumped and flailed frantically. It took all of Casper's strength to hold her down.

"It's not real," he said. "It's not real."

But his words were of no use. For several long minutes, she cried and fought against him. He soon realized she could no more hear his voice than stop seeing the hallucinations conjured by the bites. Even more worrisome were the cuts and scrapes her nails had made up and down her arms. They were angry and bleeding. If he didn't tend to them soon, they'd fester, but he couldn't release her to find salve either. There was no telling what she might do. There was nothing for it but to wait, and so, with a heavy heart, he kept her pinned.

Iris kicked and cried for some time, no doubt imagining him some great monster. Every whimper tore his heart in half, but there was nothing he could do. Thomas's absence was keenly felt. The lad could have searched her bag for bandages while Casper held her down. The thought made his whole body ache with sadness. He shoved it aside. Now wasn't the time to give in to grief.

There was no way of knowing how much time had elapsed. The raft had moved down the shore a ways, but they were, thankfully, still just against the embankment. Iris ceased trembling. Her glazed eyes found depth once again, and for the first time, she seemed to register the pain of her self-inflicted wounds.

"Cas?" she said quietly.

Casper sighed in relief. "Thank the Maker. I thought you'd never snap out of it."

He helped her gently into a sitting position, swiftly diving for the bag now that she was safe to release.

"I saw the most . . . awful things," she murmured.

Casper extracted salve and bandages. "I know," he said quietly.

Iris didn't dare ask what Casper had seen. Given the painful things he'd been through in life, it was no doubt dreadful. Likewise, Casper didn't seem to want to discuss it. What had begun as images of his siblings happy and healthy had ended brutally with both of them horribly disfigured. He worked in silence, patching her wounds. Save for a wince now and then, Iris showed no emotion. Thomas's death loomed between them like a monstrous elephant rocking the boat. Neither said a word about it, a sort of unspoken pact to leave the subject untouched.

The current continued pounding them into the shore. Casper finished the job and helped her stand. Iris took up the bag, and together they jumped from the raft onto the sodden, muddy grass. As if waiting for them to dismount, the raft sank beneath the murky water, glubbing and bubbling as it did. Neither made any comment on it.

Beyond the bayou was a massive field with tall, shoulder-high grass. Far in the distance stood an old mansion, teetering on its supports. Storm clouds gathered in the backdrop, threatening another ugly bout of rain.

"There," he said knowingly, dread filling his soul. "The final task is in there."

Lightning cracked in the distance as if foretelling their demise.

"Brilliant," Iris muttered. She draped her satchel overshoulder. "Come on, then."

Through the tall grass they trudged, the waving blades often impeding their view. Casper kept glancing at the ruby on his sword, expecting something to go wrong at any moment. The tall grass could be home to anything—snakes crossed his mind the most—but nothing came forth. When they finally exited the grassy field, the house loomed before them like a death trap. It was something of a nightmare, tall and rickety with broken windows and a cemetery. Two large weeping willows stood on either side of the front lawn, so gnarled and twisted they seemed to have faces. Casper had heard enough ghost stories growing up to know that none of this boded well.

"Remember," Iris said, "this test is designed to play with your head. Don't let it."

Casper nodded and swallowed hard. Despite all he'd faced, his mouth was suddenly dry. "Any idea what might be in there?"

"None," she admitted, her green eyes turning sympathetically on him. "Your fears will mold the trial, even the ones you didn't know you had. Overcome them to pass."

It sounded so easy when she talked about it. He doubted the doing would be so simple.

Carefully the duo made their way up the dying lawn. A crow cawed from the lowest branch of the left tree, causing both souls to jump. The bird did nothing but watch them with its glowing red eyes. Casper half expected the willows to come to life and attack, but they remained motionless as the Waylanders passed. The wind howled through the branches, bringing the damp smell of rain—the storm was getting closer. The wooden steps creaked as they ascended, and the aged porch felt as though it might give way beneath them at any moment. Casper tried the handle of the front door.

"Bloody locked," he uttered.

"It's an old door," Iris observed. "We could kick it in."

It was an idea, certainly. Casper moved closer and examined the hinges. He didn't know much about craftsmanship, but the bolts were clearly designed to keep such a thing from being done.

"It's no use," he sighed. "We need a key."

"Then let's find a key," Iris said resolutely.

The pair of them set about searching the porch, pulling up loose floorboards and dumping out the flowerpots—nothing.

"Buried in the yard?" Iris suggested.

But Casper wasn't listening. His mind tumbled over the problem and the irate supernatural being behind it all. He would search for hours and never find it, unless . . .

"Your bag," he spoke aloud, turning toward her.

"What?"

"Your bag," he repeated. "I pulled loads of stuff from it earlier. There was a skeleton key. Do you still have it?"

"I ought to," she replied. She rummaged in the satchel, pushing aside all manner of junk. As was per usual in a woman's bag, the key was in the hardest place to find: the very bottom of the satchel. Iris closed her hand around the silver key and pulled it out. Lightning cracked simultaneously across the ever-darkening sky.

"Comforting," Casper mused of the phenomenon.

He took the key from her and turned for the door. It loomed mockingly.

"Just do it," Iris pressed, sensing his hesitation.

Casper took a breath and inserted the key in the lock—it fit. He turned it, hardly surprised to hear the latches moving aside. The door creaked open. Beyond it stood a dark hall, barely lit with gas lamps. Casper's heart hammered in his chest. He took the skeleton key from the door and pocketed it, just in case. As he crossed the threshold, a surge of wind blasted down the hall and slammed the door shut. Casper whirled. Iris was still on the other side.

"Iris!" he panicked, twisting the handle. It wouldn't budge. He pounded on the door, shouting her name, but if she heard him she made no reply. The truth fell on Casper like a great weight. "Fear of being alone," he whispered.

Casper turned resolutely for the hall behind him. It was long and narrow, lined with rusted suits of armor, crumbling wallpaper, and very unsettling portraits. A chill hung in the air, the sort you feel when ghosts or ghouls are near. There was no staircase, no other door. The only way was forward through the narrow hall. Casper now understood why so many failed this trial. Fear was a very powerful emotion. At that moment, fear had his feet nailed to the floor.

"Come on, mate," he tried to bolster himself. "You've faced dragons. This is easy."

But it didn't feel so easy. A dragon was large, loud, and a giant target. Here he was simply waiting for things to go wrong. He took a deep breath and let it out slowly, then put one foot in front of the other. He ambled down the hall, afraid he might step on some trip wire or fall through a trap door. The suits of armor creaked, their rusty heads following his movements with dull amusement. Something moved to his right, and Casper nearly jumped out of his skin. The pictures were moving!

Every single portrait was of a human subject, very lifelike and well-painted. Not that this calmed Casper. He'd always hated paintings. Anytime he walked past one, the eyes seemed to follow him. These were no better. They banged against their canvases and frames, some rocking back and forth, others nearly jumping off the wall. Their shouts and screams were quiet, but no less terrifying—they were trying to escape.

Casper fought the fearful urge to run. Panicked flight could end in ruin. No, he had to keep a level head. He kept a hand firmly on his sword hilt. The hall stretched with every step he took toward the end. The portraits continued their banging and rocking. It was only now that Casper realized each had a nameplate below the frame. Curious, he leaned closer to one. It read:

Jonathan Perring of Cherry Street

Casper's brow furrowed. Cherry Street was a block of nice middle-class homes in the East Sector of Wayland. A horrible, sick feeling hit Casper as he stepped back and observed the angry portraits. They weren't paintings at all; they were souls. Every one of them. Souls trapped in canvases. They weren't trying to get out; they were trying to warn him.

Just then, a shadow loomed behind Casper. He felt a chill and pivoted—nothing was there. The suits of armor still followed his every move, heads creaking as if they were watching a slow game of cricket. The paintings banged more violently against the wall, every single one pointing down the hall in the direction Casper had come from. He turned glacially. The Nethersword's jewel glowed a brilliant red. A hideous figure stood at the end of the hall, not quite a monster and not quite a man. It had two legs and two arms, a head, but no face. It seemed to be made up of multicolored goop that moved constantly, dripping and falling wherever it stepped. Its movements were twitchy like a jammed windup toy, and a horrible screeching growl emanated from somewhere—Casper couldn't be sure where, as it had no mouth.

Step by step, the creature made for him. Try though he might, Casper couldn't seem to move. The beast laid two gruesome hands on suits of armor and propelled itself forward, leaving gook behind. He was going to end right there, trapped forever behind an oil canvas. The creature came closer, still clicking and screeching away. Something warmed Casper's hand, and he looked down in surprise. The sword! He'd nearly forgotten it. Once again, the creature braced itself on suits of armor, preparing to slingshot forward and bowl Casper over. As it launched, Casper unsheathed his sword and swung desperately.

For a moment, he couldn't decipher what had happened. Had he been pulverized? Had he won? Both he and the creature stood dumbfounded, seemingly asking the same questions. All at once, the creature's upper half slid away from its lower and fell in two pieces on the floor. Casper stared. It had been instinctive. A reaction. He was so overcome with relief, he almost fell to his knees. The sword held him upright, propped against the floor like a cane. It was then that he noticed the rattling of the paintings had ceased. He turned. Every canvas was wiped clean. Every nameplate, vanished. Casper had set the souls free, a reminder of the Keeper's words to him. He was changing everything.

Casper sheathed his sword and continued on. The suits of armor followed his progress down the hall. This time the hall didn't seem endless, and Casper soon reached its end. A musty, ornate staircase unfolded before him, teetering in such a way he feared one misstep would send it toppling. There was no other door, not even a window. The only way forward was up.

Casper set a careful foot on the first stair. It creaked loudly but seemed sturdy enough. He stepped on the next. Still sturdy. Gaining confidence, he ascended the staircase at a slow but steady pace. A colony of bats terrorized him briefly near the top, frightened from their perch in the rafters. They left Casper well enough alone, screeching their distaste and flying angrily by. Casper subconsciously brushed a hand through his hair as if a stray bat might have taken up residence there.

On and on he went. The staircase twisted this way and that, going up for ages until Casper could no longer see the ground floor through the gloom. It'd be a pity to fall from such a height. Casper drew away from the stair railing as though the very thought would push him over. Finally he came to the second-floor landing, if it could even be considered the second floor. There was little space. The walls were devoid of decoration—not even a window—simply peeling wallpaper and a very dim gas lamp. Straight across from the stairs stood a solitary door. It was dark and chipping with a black knob. Casper tried to open it. Locked. He pulled the skeleton key from his pocket, feeling a little more confident than he had in the entry hall. His heart hammered in his chest as he inserted the key in the lock. Before he could turn it, it shocked him. He shook the pain from his hand, the stinging forgotten in lieu of the horror he felt. The key was turning by itself!

Casper's hand went to his sword. The jewel didn't glow. A terrible, nails-on-chalkboard sort of screeching occurred as the key turned until, finally, the lock clicked. Casper inched tentatively forward. The door creaked open of its own accord. Every instinct said to bolt the other way, but to do so would cost him his trial. He stood right at the threshold, trying to get a glimpse of what lay beyond. No matter how he stared, the next room appeared a black void. Suddenly an unforeseen force shoved him through. He landed on his hands and knees amidst a cloud of low-hanging mist. The door slammed shut behind him.

The key! he thought, scrambling to his feet. He raced for the knob, but it was no use. The door was already melting away, fading into a wall of tarnished mirror. Casper's dumbstruck face stared back at him from the glass, strangely multiplied as if he were looking down a long hallway with a hundred mini-Caspers moving in unison. He'd seen the trick before in a magic show. It was achieved using multiple mirrors. He reached out and touched the glass. The multiple reflections of himself did the same. If this was only one mirror, then . . .

Casper turned, and a great sinking feeling hit him. Every wall and even the ceiling was made of mirrors. It was almost impossible to tell which way was a real turn and which was an illusion—a maze with no way out. "Fear of getting lost," Casper muttered. "Brilliant."

There was nothing to do but keep moving, he supposed, so he put one foot in front of the other with no real sense of direction. He wondered where Iris was, worry sinking into his soul. Did Nex have her? Was she facing some far viler creature? Over and over his thoughts tumbled until he thought they might make him sick. Iris was a grown woman, he reminded himself. She'd survived without him before, and she would now.

The strange rolling mist displaced with each of Casper's steps. He walked with a hand outstretched, now and then nearly colliding with a wall of glass. It wasn't so difficult to decipher direction if he took his time. Other fears rolled through his mind. What if he was stuck in here forever? What if there was no way out? He shook his head to clear them, but they wouldn't leave him be. Echoing whispers filled the air, and in his reflection, the red jewel on his sword hilt glowed. He froze in fear. Something else was reflected there. Something tall and slender with its mouth sewn over—a scath!

Casper dodged aside as the monster reached for him, or rather thought he did—instead he collided with another mirror. Thrown off balance, he stumbled forward, seeing more and more of the terrifying creatures reflected in the mirrors around him. The mirrors made it look as though they came by the hundreds. There was no way to decipher which way they came from or where they would go. For a moment, Casper was paralyzed by fear. Then some still, small voice inside of him said, *Run.*

As if propelled by an electric shock, Casper bolted, drawing his sword as he ran. Scaths seemed to come at him from all sides, clawing and swiping. It was nearly impossible to dodge them. The whispers echoed loudly. Casper ran into one wall and then another, hardly able to make out direction. He swiped desperately with the sword, taking off a hand and wounding another. Suddenly he sailed through the air and slammed into a wall so hard, the glass cracked. He crumpled to the floor, the Nethersword clattering to the ground beside him.

"Failure. Disappointment. Murderer."

The scaths' voices echoed over and over one another, twisting and morphing Casper's mind into anxiety. The mirrors showed the monsters surrounding him, so multiplied by the many reflective surfaces, it appeared they came by the thousands.

"Thomas died because of you."

"I tried," Casper uttered pathetically as they hemmed him in.

"You will die too. Alone, without a friend in the world. The last of the Renolds line to ever see the light of day."

A silvery essence pulled from Casper's chest as they fed on his anxiety and fear, his low sense of worth—all the horrid emotions that kept one up at night. Casper's resolve was slipping, blinded by the pain, but something else caught his eye—the glowing jewel of the sword. If he could just manage to reach it . . .

Another painful jolt made him cry out. Tears stung his eyes. The sword was only centimeters away. He reached fruitlessly for it, held in place by the horrid creatures siphoning every bit of emotion his soul had left. But there was one emotion they would not touch. One they couldn't. As Casper's thoughts went to Kaelyn, something swelled in his heart. The thought of her bouncing curls and musical laughter arose, bittersweet when mixed with the thought he'd never see her again.

Something warm and bright broke the monsters' hold. For a few precious seconds, Casper was free. He closed his hand around the Nethersword. Its energy flowed through his hand, up his arm, and filled his whole body. That was it—they couldn't stand love. The scaths moved in for another go at him, but Casper was too encouraged to be stopped now. He thought of Iris, her beautiful red hair and the way her green eyes sparkled when she thought he wasn't looking. The sound of her voice filled his head, and he thought about what it would be like to hold her back in Wayland after they returned.

The whispers of the scaths became unintelligible and annoyed.

"I'm going home," he said resolutely. "And I will save them!"

Another burst of light and the scaths were blown back, at least so far as he could see in the mirrors. A mad idea occurred to him, and he turned toward the cracked mirror behind him. The scaths were slowly regrouping. If he was going to escape, he had to do it now. Casper took the sword in both hands and gave it a mighty swing. It shattered the tarnished mirror, and Casper bolted through the space beyond it.

Casper ran until his lungs burned, giving no attention to his surroundings. It was only when he tripped on an upturned piece of carpet and went tumbling head over heels that he realized he was no longer being chased. He lay there motionless, taking the time to catch his breath. He was in another long hall, this one lined with doors. The musty carpet, which was haphazardly laid on the wooden floor, smelled strongly of mold and mildew. Like the cramped second-floor landing, there were no decorations here.

Casper pushed himself up, this time keeping his sword aloft. The jewel on the hilt was once again dim. The flickering gas lamps made eerie shadows on the walls as he moved down the hall. He tried each door in passing, every one of them locked, not that he was surprised. Thankfully this hall didn't stretch like the entry hall had, and he soon came to the door at the end. Something surged behind it, calling to Casper and warning him to stay away at the same time. There was no doubt in his mind this door would be unlocked. The house was like one giant maze, forcing him in the direction it wanted him to go. Apprehension churned Casper's stomach. He reached out and turned the knob.

Like any old door would do, this one creaked loudly as it opened. Casper was surprised to find a seemingly normal study beyond. Books were stacked everywhere, teetering from shelves, lining the desk, and crowding all the corners. A giant paned window barely gave a glimpse of the yard beyond the manor. Rain fell in torrents against the glass, and Casper hoped Iris wasn't stuck in it. Dust and cobwebs covered everything like a blanket of age. Nothing seemed out of order at first glance.

"I wondered when you'd turn up," a familiar voice said.

It had come from the desk chair that, Casper only now realized, was turned away from him toward the window. He glanced at the sword. It wasn't glowing. Whoever was in the chair wasn't a Netherbeast.

"Who are you?" Casper demanded.

"Are you sure you really want to know?" the voice replied. "You may not like the answer."

"Would I ask if I didn't? Show yourself!"

The chair swiveled and lightning cracked. Fear hit Casper like an icy brick. Sitting in the chair before him was a demented version of himself. A self-satisfied smirk crossed his doppelgänger's lips, a touch of cruelty there that didn't belong at all on Casper's face.

"I told you you wouldn't like it," his twin mused. "No one ever does."

He looked like Casper in every way apart from black eyes and a darker visage. Circles lined his eyes, and a sinister scowl was permanently etched on his face.

"What are you?" Casper struggled to ask.

"I thought that'd be obvious," the doppelgänger replied. "I'm you. All the worst parts of you. You when you leave this place to save our pathetic sister."

"Kaelyn isn't pathetic!" Casper snapped.

His twin laughed, rising from the chair. "Aye, she is. Why else are we always having to protect and save her? She can't even wield a sword."

The doppelgänger walked out from behind his desk, shoving his hands in his trouser pockets. Casper kept his sword trained on him. The look-alike cocked his head to the side like a curious animal observing another.

"Do you really think any of this will matter, Cas?" his twin asked. "The trials? Returning to Wayland? Kaelyn will be gone by the time you get back, and you'll have failed . . . again. Just like you did with *Calvin*."

"Don't you *dare* say his name," Casper warned.

His doppelgänger laughed. "Why? Is the guilt too much for you? Or is it the truth . . . that you were happy when he was gone? He was no longer an annoyance."

"That's a lie!"

"Is it?" the other Casper goaded. "Because I think you'll be glad when Kaelyn is gone too. No more responsibility. No more waiting around for life to happen. You can start fresh, maybe even with Iris." He walked closer as he talked until the tip of the Nethersword touched his chest. "We've always wanted to leave the mill. Now's our chance. Gran is gone, and soon our sister will be too."

"No," Casper said. His voice trembled. He'd had selfish thoughts like this before. Thoughts of leaving, of letting it all go. This corrupted version of himself was all the things he feared becoming.

"Don't worry, Cas," his doppelgänger crooned. "We'll overthrow Harlen and take his place. No one will ever hurt us again, not so long as we wield the sword."

"And how many innocent people will you hurt to achieve it?" Casper wondered.

The corrupt Casper sighed. "See, this is why we've amounted to nothing. You always get in the way with that damn good-natured heart of yours. It's a liability, Cas. The sooner you see that, the better."

"I will *never* be like you," Casper spat.

"You already are," his twin whispered darkly.

Something in Casper snapped, and he took a wild swing at the smirking look-alike. He was surprised when steel clashed against steel. Where had his doppelgänger gotten a sword? The two weapons banged away at each other, their bearers evenly matched in every way. The doppelgänger finally managed to kick Casper away, and they resolved to circling one another.

"It's not wise to fight yourself, mate," the look-alike said. "We're a team. We're in this together."

"I want no part of your cruelty," Casper replied.

All thoughts of the trial and Iris's whereabouts were forgotten in lieu of the strange threat before him. If his doppelgänger was truly a picture of what the Netherworld would do to him, perhaps it was better not to survive.

"So, you're giving up, then?" the twin asked as if he'd read Casper's mind.

"I never said that."

"You're thinking it."

Casper remained silent, moving as his look-alike did to always keep him in front.

"I'm not your enemy, Casper," the doppelgänger continued. "I'm your ticket out of here."

Still Casper remained silent, brown eyes fixed on the figure across from him. He thought about the strange rage he'd felt the longer he stayed there, a sort of sleeping power—something dangerous. He remembered how it fueled his every sinew when the two souls invaded camp, how he'd been so resolved to kill until Iris stepped in. He wouldn't have talked to them. Iris was right about that. His anger would have gotten in the way.

"Take it, and we'll go home," the demented Casper said.

He'd pulled an actual ticket from his pocket, though to what, Casper could only imagine. It shimmered as the doppelgänger twisted it skillfully through his fingers.

"Take it, and all this will be nothing but a bad dream."

It was a tempting offer. All Casper had to do was reach out and accept it, and then all this madness would end. He could go home. He could save Kaelyn and Iris. He could rebuild the mill. No more fighting. No more danger. He could go back to a boring life and pretend none of this ever happened. For a moment he almost considered it, but the offer came at a cost. Casper could see it lurking behind the cold, demented eyes of his look-alike. If he took that ticket, his doppelgänger got to come along. Casper would beat the trials at a great cost—himself.

"No," Casper spoke evenly. "I won't take the easy way out . . . not this time."

The ticket caught fire in the dark Casper's hand, forcing the look-alike to release it. It took Casper a moment to realize *he* had done it. A livid expression crossed the doppelgänger's face. It was evident he wasn't used to losing.

"Well, then," the look-alike said, "I guess we'll stay here for all eternity."

"No," Casper said again. "I'm going home. I'm simply not taking you with me."

All at once, he swung the Nethersword in a wide arc, and the doppelgänger threw up his sword to block it. The Nethersword cut through the enemy weapon like it was paper. Casper's look-alike stared in shock, fear crossing his face for the first time as Casper readied to swing again the other way.

"Wait!" the doppelgänger cried.

Against his better judgment, Casper paused.

"Take me with you," the doppelgänger pleaded. "I'm as much a prisoner here as you are. Please! I promise, you'll be in control. I'll be quiet as a mouse. I'll stay in the shadows. You won't even know I'm there. You're the boss, mate. You lead the charge. I'll just be there when you need me. If you need me. You can't do this alone, you know. Saving our sister is going to require a resolve you don't have without me. You *need* me."

It was true. Casper didn't usually face his problems head-on. He'd preferred to stay out of the way, operating under the lie that if he kept his head down long enough, the bullies and tyrants of the world would let him be. Harlen was ruthless. Casper would need to be ruthless if he was going to win.

"Yes, yes," the doppelgänger encouraged desperately. "You need me. I can stop him. I can save Kaelyn. I can make sure no one ever takes her from you again."

Again, Casper felt the pull of temptation. It sounded like a good deal. Surely he was in enough control of himself to keep this part of him in check.

"How?" Casper demanded.

The doppelgänger faltered. "What do you mean, how?"

"How will you stop him? How will you keep this from happening again?"

Evil Casper rolled his eyes. "Nex almighty, you really are a shining star, aren't you? I'm going to kill everyone in your way, of course. You really need to stop letting your compassion get in the way. You're too *good*, Cas. Don't you see? If you had even a sliver of backbone, Harlen never would have eyed Kaelyn in the first place. She would be safe, and Gran would be alive. We wouldn't even be having this conversation. You need me."

Gran. Her name brought an image of his grandmother to mind. Her twinkling eyes and knowing smile. Her aged, wise voice. Her patience even when he was stubborn. What would Gran say if she could see him now? What would Kaelyn think of her brother if she knew he'd become a murderer? And then his thoughts turned toward Thomas, who didn't beg Casper to give in to Nex to save his life but willingly accepted erasure. His doppelgänger would surely have given the sword to Nex to save Thomas.

Worse, he might even have pledged himself to the god of death. The thought struck another chord. Most in Wayland used the phrase "Lumen's shield" as an expression of extreme emotion, but his doppelgänger had invoked the name of Nex instead. He already served Nex, and if Casper accepted the deal for passage home, he himself would be serving Nex, and Nex would then have the sword.

That settled it.

"You're right," he agreed, brandishing his sword.

"Don't you dare," his doppelgänger warned, his thoughts in tune with Casper's.

"I am too good. And that's exactly why I'll be defeating Harlen *myself.*"

Casper swung his weapon in tandem with the last word. The sword cleaved a gash through the doppelgänger's middle. Instead of drawing blood, it left a ripple of light through his twin as though the demented Casper were an illusion made of light itself. The brightness poured from the wound as if all the goodness within Casper was pouring out from inside his evil twin, consuming him from the inside out.

"No!" the doppelgänger shrieked. "No!"

Casper ran him straight through, an even brighter light protruding from the imploding doppelgänger's chest. Casper felt no pity for the darkest sides of himself. The look-alike screamed and writhed, falling helplessly to the ground. The light consumed him like a parasitic beast until, all at once, he exploded in a shower of sparks. Casper dove behind the desk in the same instant, covering his head as best he could. Sparks trickled down like dying fireworks, a few flecks landing in Casper's hair. He brushed them out absentmindedly, eyes peering around the dingy study. His doppelgänger was completely gone.

The rain stopped its relentless pounding against the window. Casper rose fluidly and approached it, looking across the swampy landscape in wonder. The sun peeked out from behind the clouds, painting the once-horrid landscape in its bright glow. The trees seemed happier somehow, no longer scowling across the yard like guard dogs but rather enjoying existence. A few flowers popped out of the muddy earth, and steadily the yellow grass greened. Everything that made the bayou horrifying was displaced with something that made it good. All fear and darkness was eradicated. Casper sheathed his sword and smiled.

Suddenly the ground shook, and Casper was thrown back into the desk. He barely caught himself. A searing pain burned up his arm. He clutched it fruitlessly, holding it aloft to see a bright spiral glowing red-hot, tattooing itself to his skin—the final spiral of the Netherworld Triad. Casper stared at it in disbelief as the world around him faded away.

The Return

DAYS HAD PASSED SINCE JOSIAH SKULKED TO THE WHARF in search of Dante. A quiet rage still slept in Josiah after the encounter. He pounded it out on a glowing hot poker, embers spewing with each hammer like a whiff of dragon's breath. How could Dante be so selfish? How could he refuse? Josiah banged each question out of his mind until he realized how silly he was being. Dante was an expert in his field, but even his agility was no match for a Netherworlder. Taking Dante along would have been suicide. For the hundredth time in the last few days, Josiah's anger dissipated. He dipped his project in cool water and set it on the work bench, mopping his brow.

All at once, Casper shot up, gulping air as if he'd never breathe again. Josiah whirled, frozen. Casper's eyesight was blurred, and his breaths were pained. Josiah snapped out of his shock, registering the truth—Casper was alive at last!

"Stark!" Josiah called, rushing to his friend's side.

Casper trembled, unable to see, hardly able to hear. His heartbeat was painful, having been jolted awake after months of inactivity.

"Hey," Josiah said, grasping each of Casper's shoulders. "Easy, mate. Easy." He slowly pushed Casper back down. This wasn't the way he wanted to be reintroduced to his former friend.

Panic flooded Casper, but it felt different than before. In the Netherworld, he felt things in his entire body. Now he only felt them in his chest. "W-where . . . am I?" he asked. His voice was barely above a whisper, throat dry from lack of use.

"Stark's," Josiah answered. "You're safe."

Stark, who'd just been in the middle of a shave, came barreling down the steps with his face half done and foam still on his cheeks. "What is it? What—" He caught sight of Casper, the lad hiccupping for air and clearly in pain. "Lumen's shield," he uttered, a common expression of praise or relief. "He did it."

"Fetch some water," Josiah instructed.

Stark nodded and tottered back up the steps to do so. Casper was still very much panicked. Josiah looked like a giant blur, unrecognizable to his tired eyes. The apprentice's voice, while intelligible, was garbled beyond distinguishing its owner. If Casper's body didn't feel so heavy, he might think this another trick of the Netherworld. Stark returned, a patina cup in hand. He thrust it toward Josiah, looking on Casper with wonder. He'd never witnessed someone return from the Netherworld before.

"Will he be all right?" Stark asked.

"In time," Josiah answered. "He's been dead for months. It won't be an easy transition."

Casper heard all of this as if he were in some sort of vacuum. He imagined this must be what it was like to be terribly drunk and sucker punched in a tavern brawl. A terrible ringing started in his ears.

"Here, mate," Josiah said gently. "Drink this."

Casper inched up with Josiah's help, wary at first. He quickly realized that he actually was thirsty—a weak feeling he hadn't felt in a very long time. It was almost foreign. He guzzled the water like a malnourished pup.

"Careful," Josiah warned. "Remember to breathe."

Breathe, Casper thought. Yes, he was breathing, wasn't he? The thought nearly made him choke, and Josiah withdrew the cup before he could, carefully laying Casper back down.

"You need to rest," Josiah said.

Stark finally wiped the foam from his face, having forgotten it in his haste. As Casper registered Josiah's words, though still not fully registering Josiah, his first instinct was to negate him. He shook his head pathetically.

"Have to find . . . Kaelyn," he wheezed. "And Iris."

"Iris?" Josiah repeated. "Who's Iris?"

"Could be the mayor's daughter," Stark suggested, quite intrigued.

Casper tried to get out of bed.

"Whoa!" Josiah pushed Casper back. "No. Hey. Stop it." Casper was trying to fight against him. "Mate, it's me. I'm your friend. It's Josiah. I'm your friend."

Josiah. The name rang a distant and faint bell. Yes. The schoolmate he'd once gone on adventures with. Gran had mentioned him. Casper relaxed again once he retained that he was truly in the hands of an ally.

"Kaelyn," he uttered, unable to say more.

This was the part Josiah dreaded. If Casper had indeed given himself over to darkness, there was no telling what Josiah's words would spark.

"Harlen has her locked up," he said carefully.

It was evident the news unsettled Casper, but he didn't fly off the handle as Josiah expected. There was a heavy silence as Casper's tired mind worked it all out. The Netherstone, Harlen's dark plans for Kaelyn—the fight was far from over.

"We need to get her back," Casper said in as urgent a tone as he could muster.

"And we will," Josiah assured, "but for now you need to—"

"No, you don't understand," Casper cut him off. "He's going to kill her."

A prickle of panic made the hairs on the back of Josiah's neck stand up. "How do you know?"

"Iris," he said, struggling to talk. "There's a ritual . . . full moon."

"The moon will be full tonight," Stark said.

"We have to go . . . now," Casper insisted, trying once more to get up.

Josiah held him down, his Netherworld strength a little stronger than Casper's at the moment. A surge of anger once more threatened to ruin his good countenance. "You're in no fit state to go anywhere," he pointed out.

Casper's stomach growled like a vicious beast, and he cursed his human needs.

"I'll go whip up some stew," Stark said, once more hobbling for the staircase.

Try as he might, Casper couldn't fight against his old friend. He chalked it up to being newly returned from the dead.

"Why don't you start from the beginning," Josiah said, curiosity and worry lacing his tone. Casper needed time to adjust, and the more he talked, the more his voice would return.

Casper, on the other hand, felt like his throat was on fire. Talking seemed to do little good. "Water," he rasped.

Again, Josiah helped the revived miller sit up and sip from the patina cup. Once Casper had polished off the contents, he lay back, feeling he could at least whisper. He began with meeting Iris after his first trial, regaling Josiah with the most important of his exploits, especially the bits about the Netherstone and Iris's own unjust murder.

"So," Josiah spoke once Casper finished, "Harlen is going to use Kaelyn as his sacrifice?"

Casper nodded.

"Bloody hell," Josiah muttered. He'd always imagined the man was mad, but this was beyond any horrors Josiah had dreamed up. He'd been hoping Casper would have more time to recover, that he'd have more time to explain.

Silence weighed between them as both men tried to process. What had begun as a mere accident had spun into a plot so riddled with evil deeds, Casper could scarcely believe it was really happening. "I saw Gran," he said, "in the Netherworld . . . after she passed. She said you pulled me from the fire?"

A surge of modesty rose up in Josiah. "I did," he uttered.

"How did you manage it?"

Here Josiah paused. Admitting what he was to Casper wasn't an issue, as Casper was now the same, but telling the man who'd once been his best friend that he'd died, that was another matter. They'd drifted so far apart after Calvin's death, Josiah doubted Casper knew anything of his life over the last decade. "You're not the only one who's met Death and lived to tell the tale," he murmured.

Casper's eyesight, though still poor, had improved marginally. He could just make out the expression on Josiah's face—a far older version than he remembered. It was evident in Josiah's posture and mannerisms that he felt horrible about the things he'd done.

"You?" Casper marveled. "You've done it too?"

"Aye," Josiah said. "It wasn't easy. Almost lost myself . . . but I found my way well enough."

The realization that they now shared more than friendship weighed between them, and Casper found a new respect for his friend. He now felt guilty for letting what happened to his brother come between them. Josiah had died, and Casper hadn't been there for him. Unnerved by the silence and the sudden onset of honesty, Josiah stood suddenly. "Can you stand?" he asked.

"What happened to 'You need to rest'?" Casper wondered.

"If the full moon really is tonight and Kaelyn's life does hang in the balance, we'll have to nurse you back to health bloody quick," the apprentice said. He extended an arm to help Casper up. Casper clasped it and rose shakily to his feet. Something heavy and metallic fell from the sheets. Both men turned to look in confusion—the Nethersword.

"Where did that come from?" Josiah said.

"I must have brought it back with me," Casper realized. The Keeper and Iris had both mentioned the possibility of taking things to and from the Netherworld, but Casper couldn't help being a little surprised something hadn't held the sword back.

Josiah scooped it up with his free hand, examining the craftsmanship. "I've never seen its equal," he praised, examining every angle as best he could while still supporting Casper with his other arm.

"Aye, and it'll bring about Harlen's end," Casper said, worried his friend might get ideas about taking it for himself.

Josiah caught the inflection in Casper's tone, easing in his astonishment of the weapon. "Sorry, mate," he uttered. "Occupational hazard." He leaned it against the wall.

The sword was the least of their worries at the moment. Casper could barely make it up the stairs. Josiah all but dragged him up them, the fair-haired miller limping on his injured leg. Flesh was so much weaker than spirit. Casper felt as though his body wasn't his own, that he was trapped inside it and someone else was pulling the strings.

The two men finally made it to the top of the stairs, Casper leaning heavily on Josiah. The upper apartment only consisted of two rooms—the main, which doubled as a dining and living area, and the back room, where Stark slept. Josiah usually slept on the cot in the shop below since he often worked late, but since bringing Casper home, he slept on the floor by the fireplace to keep warm. A sparsely filled bookshelf sat on one wall, pots and pans on the other. Stark was busy cutting up sweet meats and peppering them with spices.

"You don't have to go to all this trouble," Casper rasped. Talking grew easier the more he did it, but he still sounded like he was getting over a bad cold.

"Nonsense," Stark replied as Josiah helped Casper into a chair. "Any friend of Josiah's is welcome in my home."

Josiah silently threw a blanket around Casper's shoulders, knowing the chills would soon start. "How's your leg?" he wondered.

"Twinges a bit," Casper said.

Josiah sat beside Casper, tapping nervously on the table. Nothing was going according to plan, which greatly worried him. Even if he could get Casper near normal, he wouldn't have his full strength. Against one Netherworlder, they might have a chance, but against two?

"So," Casper interrupted his friend's snowballing thoughts. "How exactly are we going to get Kaelyn back?"

Josiah's finger stopped its incessant tapping. "I've a plan, but . . . it's a bit mad."

"I just had several months of mad. Give it a go."

Josiah stood and moved to the bookshelf, very aware of Stark's eyes on him. He pulled a very plain-looking book from it, something about the origin of candle clocks from what Casper could see of the title. Josiah pulled a folded parchment from between the pages and set it on the table. Stark looked between the parchment and Josiah, an accusatory glint in his eye.

"What's that, then?" he asked as Josiah tossed the book haphazardly back on the shelf.

"Blueprints," Josiah answered cryptically. He moved back to the table and unfurled the map of Prior Street, regaining his seat.

"And where did you get them?"

There was a pause thick with so much tension, Casper feared one of them might explode at any moment.

"Borrowed them," Josiah answered. He kept his gaze on the table, unable to look up, afraid of the disappointed look he was sure was painted on Stark's face.

"I thought we agreed no more stealing," Stark said sharply.

"It was important," Josiah defended himself.

"And you didn't see fit to tell me?" the blacksmith went on. "You could have been caught, Josiah. You could have endangered us all."

"You wouldn't have let me go!" Josiah snapped, his brilliant green eyes flashing to the man who'd been like a father to him since he was fourteen. "Someone's life is at stake. I didn't have time for formalities."

The burly blacksmith folded his arms, letting his apprentice's words sift through the cogs and wheels of his mind. He knew the lad well enough. There was no darkness in his heart, no desire to go back to a life of dishonesty. He simply had a skill set that, while Stark didn't condone it, sometimes became necessary. Stark sighed, exasperated but resolved. These were mad times, and though he'd never met Kaelyn, he knew how much Josiah cared for her, how much the Renoldses both meant. He supposed he couldn't blame the lad.

"Fair enough," he consented quietly, and Josiah visibly relaxed.

A chill set in, and Casper was suddenly grateful for the blanket his friend had knowingly provided. He wrapped it tighter around himself. "What's all this, then?" he asked, turning their attention back to the task at hand.

Josiah leaned over the blueprints, a sense of anxiousness churning in his stomach. He hadn't shared this plan with anyone, and he had serious doubts about its success, but it was the only plan they had. "So," he began, "this is Prior Street, where all the well-to-dos like to congregate. Harlen Manor is here," he pointed to a large estate, "at the end of the row. Near impossible to get in without being spotted. Even the roofs are tricky."

"And I'm not as good at the rooftop ballet as you," Casper pointed out. He'd never been as coordinated or athletic as Josiah, though he wondered if that would be different now.

"Exactly," Josiah said. "But—" He folded back the top blueprint, revealing another set beneath it. "There's a network of sewer tunnels beneath the city, and they just so happen to run below Prior Street."

"Excellent for getting down the road," Casper mused, "but how will we get inside?"

"That's the fun bit." Josiah pointed to a small opening just below Harlen Manor. "All these great homes have the luxury of an indoor privy."

It wasn't difficult to connect the dots of Josiah's daring plan, and Casper couldn't keep the grimace from his face. "Charming."

Stark, who'd turned back to cooking mid-conversation, let out a mild chortle. "Up to your neck in sewage. That's your master plan?"

"Have you a better one?" Josiah demanded.

Stark shrugged in an innocent, noncommittal fashion, choosing to stay out of it. What business was it of his? He only housed two unregistered Netherworlders, which was strictly against the law.

"That takes care of getting in," Casper went on. "Where are they keeping Kaelyn?"

"In a room on the top floor. It won't be easy to get into or out of. All the windows are sealed with bars."

Silence ensued as Casper took time to process Josiah's information. The manor would likely be crawling with guards, but after dealing with Netherbeasts, Casper felt confident that part would be easy. "Rescuing Kaelyn can't be our only priority," Casper realized aloud.

"What do you mean?" Josiah asked, arms folded as he once more relaxed in his chair. Rescuing Casper's sister was the only thing on the apprentice's mind.

"The Netherstone," Casper explained. "I have to destroy it."

Josiah didn't say anything, but Casper could see the hesitation in his friend's emerald eyes.

"I've got to," he said, putting as much strength behind the words as he could. "Harlen won't be stopped otherwise. He'll find another girl, try again. Ending him and his madness, that's my mission."

"You'll get yourself killed . . . again," Josiah uttered.

"It's worth the risk if it saves more lives." Casper didn't exactly know how to go about it. Before the Netherworld, he never would have condoned taking a life, but he could see now that there were some men too evil to let roam freely. Besides, the Keeper had made it pretty clear that it was his destiny to stop Harlen and that the sword would help him do it. Casper had never been surer of anything in his life. Before the night was out, Lord Harlen would die at the tip of his sword.

Josiah said not another word about it, and Casper didn't fully explain. Talk of the Maker and prophesies was exhausting, and he didn't know how much his friend would believe him. Stark soon finished cooking, and all thoughts of their plotting were put on hold. Casper had never tasted anything so delicious in all his life, though he was certain it was only because he was starving. The rest of the afternoon was spent recuperating and trying to regain his strength. As some of his normal functions returned, Casper realized they were somehow stronger. His sight was better, his hearing sharper—even his reflexes seemed to be quicker. Josiah schooled Casper on his changes as they presented themselves. Once he was strong enough, they set about sparring. Even against Netherworlders, the sword seemed to know what it wanted, and Casper had little difficulty in disarming Josiah.

"Very good," his friend praised after he'd done it for the third time.

"I've had a bit of practice," Casper said, his voice now normal. Other than a slight limp due to the burns on his leg, Casper could stand on his own. Every sinew seemed to beg for a run like a lithe panther on a hunt, fueled by adrenaline and a desperate need to see his sister safe. He was determined. No one else would die if he had any say in it. No one.

"Again," Josiah insisted, raising his sword.

Harlen Manor

RAIN POURED LIKE TEARS OF SORROW FROM THE heavens. Casper's dark hood did little against the torrential downpour, but at least his face was hidden. He stole through the cobblestoned streets of Wayland with Josiah, ducking down back alleys and keeping out of sight from the Night Watch. As it was hastily explained to Casper, Josiah had gone through a bit of a dark streak when he'd first returned from the Netherworld. He'd used his enhanced senses to steal, and not always for the sake of survival—he'd enjoyed it. With Stark's help, Josiah found a better path. Running through the streets of Wayland like criminals, Casper couldn't help thinking his friend seemed to enjoy himself far too much.

Due to the rain, the Night Watch wasn't particularly vigilant, a fact that worked well in the two Netherworlders' favor. Most of the men hid in doorways or under overhangs. The only light in the streets came from a few oil-fueled streetlamps and torches set in the walls. Many of the torches had been put out by the rain, offering a large amount of shadow for the men to skulk through. Casper was surprised by the scale of the city. Living on the Outer Edge hardly afforded him the opportunity to explore, and he often wondered how Josiah didn't get lost.

They stopped about a block away from Prior Street. Josiah peeked around the corner of the low wall surrounding the section of the city.

"Anything?" Casper pressed.

"Four night Watchmen and two hounds," he answered. "No worries, mate. We'll get around them."

The apprentice waved a hand for Casper to follow and led the way back down the street. A grate covered the sewer entrance, locked tightly from the outside. Josiah knelt and wordlessly pulled two lock picks from a pouch at his belt. Casper kept watch as Josiah fiddled with the tumblers and adjusted the crossbow on his back. A part of him hoped he wouldn't have to use it. The other part of him wanted to kill everyone who got in his way.

There was an audible click. "Got it," Josiah whispered.

Casper helped him lift the heavy grate and push it away. The former thief jumped down the dark hole first. Casper followed suit. He was instantly overwhelmed by the stench, scrunching his nose. "Bloody hell," he muttered, covering his nostrils.

Josiah chuckled as he pulled a torch from his satchel and lit it. "Aye. Enhanced senses aren't always what they're cracked up to be. Not even the street vents can clear that smell."

The orange glow of the fire almost made the sewer seem eerier than the dark. Rats protested and scurried out of the light as the Netherworlders ambled forward. A small path lay to the side of the foul-smelling water. It was so narrow they had to walk single file, Josiah in the lead with torch held high. Casper observed the rats. At first he'd thought they were running from the light, but on closer inspection they seemed genuinely terrified.

"Rats don't like Netherworlders," Josiah answered his unspoken question.

Casper nodded in understanding. Animals were very perceptive creatures. To them he supposed he and Josiah were like wolves passing through.

Josiah led the way down one passage and another. The drip-drip of water echoed in the empty space. They finally turned down a narrow passage with small chambers leading off it. The stench was unbelievable.

"Are you sure about this?" Casper questioned warily.

"Positive," Josiah answered.

The apprentice snuffed out the torch as they entered a small chamber at the end. Feces and sewage were stuck to the small incline that carried it down to the water. Casper thought the smell might permanently burn his nose.

Josiah tucked the torch back in his satchel, green eyes carefully observing the hole in the ceiling. It wasn't very large, and it was just out of reach.

"I'll give you a boost," Josiah said. "Think you can pull me up?"

Casper nodded. "Aye."

The miller removed his crossbow so he'd fit through the narrow space. Josiah cupped his hands and hoisted Casper up. It took a bit of wiggling, but Casper managed to fit through the tight spot. He pushed up on the privy lid, tossed his crossbow through first, then pulled himself up via the seat. He was thankful the gristmill cottage didn't have a sewer outlet, as it was proving far too easy to break in. Then again, there probably weren't many mad enough to brave the stench.

Once he had his feet on solid ground, he returned his crossbow to his back and reached through the space for Josiah's hand. The apprentice propelled off the wall to slingshot himself up. Casper gritted his teeth as Josiah grabbed hold. He took a deep breath and pulled his friend up until Josiah could grip the privy sides. It was a tighter squeeze for Josiah's broader shoulders, but he managed, soon standing beside Casper.

"I'd give anything for a normal sense of smell right now," jested Casper, pinching his nose.

Josiah stifled a laugh and gestured for Casper to go to the door. "Let's work on those senses, aye? What do you hear?"

Casper crept to the wooden door and pressed his ear to it. As he closed his eyes, he could almost see the hall outside simply through the sounds he picked up.

"Footsteps," he whispered. "Two guards."

"Simple enough," Josiah breathed.

"Don't be all day about it," one guard grumbled. "We're not supposed to take privy breaks, and I won't have my head—"

"Keep yer bloody shirt on," the other cut him off.

Some sort of instinct tingled down Casper's spine in warning. He and Josiah simultaneously rolled to either side of the door as the guard opened it. The guard moved to light a candle, and Josiah clobbered him with a chop of his hand.

"Oi! What's going on?" the other guard complained, bursting through the door.

Casper took hold of the man's arm and used the guard's momentum to slam him into the wall, rendering him unconscious.

"Hide the bodies," Josiah instructed.

Casper nodded and dragged his victim to a dark corner. Josiah haphazardly threw the other guard atop his comrade. The two Netherworlders made their way into the ornate hall.

CHAPTER TWENTY-FIVE

"No matter what happens, stick to the plan," Casper whispered.

"I'll get Kaelyn out of here," Josiah promised. "But then I'm coming back for you, mate. I never leave a man behind."

A slight smile crossed Casper's lips. It was good to have his friend back. "Right, then. You get Kaelyn. I'll take care of the stone."

THE HALLWAYS OF HARLEN'S MANOR WERE ALL THE SAME: gray stone walls, colorful tapestries, artwork, and finely woven rugs. Harlen was born into money, but since returning from the Netherworld his riches had gone beyond his previous means. Casper didn't have to ask how the tyrant survived the Netherworld. He was a bloodthirsty, cruel man who'd do anything for power. Some of the trophies on display in his home proved that. Casper's face twisted in disgust as he passed a hand kept in a jar of fluid.

Footsteps echoed down the hall, and Casper fleetly ducked behind a suit of armor. Guards shuffled past, the one in the lead carrying a lantern. He hoped they'd keep their pace so he could get a move on, but the one carrying the lantern stopped.

"What now?" his partner demanded.

"Do you smell that?" the lantern bearer asked.

Casper swore in his head. The sewer stench must have clung to his clothes.

"I don't smell a thing; now come on," the other replied sharply. "I want a smoke."

Casper breathed in relief. Once they'd gone, he slipped from his hiding place, face etched with determination. He stole quietly down the hall, following the instructions Josiah had given him based on the blueprints of the house. He took a flight of stairs to the cellar.

The room glowed an eerie orange from the light of two torches. Shelves were lined with wine bottles and dried sweet meats. A tall center shelf ran the length of the room. Casper sensed another guard nearby, though he couldn't see them. He crept forward and pressed his back to the shelf, grabbing the neck of a wine bottle. He eased it from the shelf. As soon as the man's head was in view, Casper smashed the bottle over his head. The guard crumbled, out cold. Casper dropped the broken bottle neck beside the wine-soaked man and continued on.

He moved carefully across the room, looking for traps. Surprisingly he found none. At the end of the cellar stood a blank wall with two torches beside it. Casper ran a hand over the surface. There was definitely something behind it. But how did he open it? The Netherworlder spotted a latch on the floor well hidden from normal sight. He stepped on it, and the wall swung forward.

Casper took one of the burning torches and squeezed into the narrow passage. He had to shimmy sideways to make it through. It soon opened into a wide, circular room—Harlen's vault. Lockboxes lined the walls, all with keyholes. Josiah would have had a field day breaking in to each one. At the center of the room stood a glass case with a combination lock. Casper approached it tentatively, eyes combing the room for possible trip wires. Pressure plates lined the floor, but he stepped easily around them.

Finally he reached the glass case. Firelight glinted off the reflective surface, and Casper's heart dropped. The Netherstone—it wasn't in the case. A horrible, sinking feeling hit Casper. He'd assumed Harlen would wait until the moon reached its apex. Had he made a miscalculation? Panic hit him like a stone, and he raced from the vault, nearly setting off the traps. If Harlen had already taken the stone out of the vault, then someone would be on the way to fetch Kaelyn. Josiah would get caught for certain.

KAELYN HAD GONE TO BED HOURS BEFORE, BUT THE mysterious clicking of the lock made her stir. She rolled over, scratching her fingers through her blonde curls. Her brow pulled together. That didn't sound like a key. The lock clicked again. She sat bolt upright and pulled the blankets to her chest. Something was wrong.

Carefully she crept from her bed and lifted the nearby candlestick from the nightstand. Another click. She tiptoed to the entryway of her room and pressed her back to the wall. The door creaked open. Kaelyn grasped the candlestick in two hands, heart beating madly. A shadowy figure entered the room. As soon as its head was in view, she crashed the candlestick over it. The intruder collapsed to the floor with a groan.

"What the bloody hell was that for?" Josiah complained, down but not out.

Kaelyn dropped the candlestick in shock. "Josiah?" She knelt at his side and rolled him over. "Josiah!" she whispered. "Thank the Maker! I thought you were dead!"

The apprentice groaned. "Am I not?" he joked.

Kaelyn attacked him with kisses, so overjoyed she couldn't contain it. Josiah smiled against her lips. "I take it you missed me," he murmured.

"More than you know," she breathed, leaning her forehead against his. Her nose wrinkled. "What is that ghastly smell?"

"Took a detour through the sewer," he mused. As much as he wanted to revel in the moment, they didn't have much time. He tried to sit up, but his head was pounding. He winced. "Not a bad arm you've got there," he teased.

Kaelyn helped him up the rest of the way. "Sorry," she uttered sincerely. If he hadn't been a Netherworlder, a blow like that would have knocked him out cold.

"Don't be. You didn't know it was me."

Kaelyn beamed and threw her arms around him, enduring the sewer stench. He could smell the soap in her hair, a familiar scent he couldn't easily forget. Relief washed over him. He'd found her. He'd found her, and she was safe. The nightmare was almost over.

"Come on, love," he said quietly. "Let's get you out of here."

"I wouldn't count on it," a voice came from the doorway.

Both turned to see Bash standing there. Four guards accompanied him, all with crossbows aimed at Josiah's head.

CHAPTER TWENTY-SIX

The Netherstone

THE CHAPEL IN HARLEN'S MANOR WAS ONCE ORNATE, no expense spared in its construction. Now it sat in extreme disrepair. Kaelyn reasoned he didn't spend much time in prayer. Pigeons scrambled from the rafters as Bash pushed her forcefully down the center aisle. The other four guards nudged Josiah forward, each with a crossbow trained on him. His hands were bound in chains, but he was already working at the locks. Harlen was at the altar with a priest held at knifepoint by one of his goons.

"Oh, isn't this delicious," Harlen mused. "I should thank you, boy. You've finally given me the ammunition I need."

Josiah was forced to his knees near the altar, nearly dropping his lock pick. Thankfully the guards were too ignorant to notice.

Kaelyn glowered at Harlen. "I've given you my answer, you foul pig."

"And I've found a way around it, my dear," he replied, a dark glint in his eye. He waved a hand and the four guards aimed their crossbows at Josiah's head, ready to fire. Kaelyn's heart clenched.

Harlen pulled a ring from his pocket. The band was a simple silver entwined around a brilliantly colored opal gem—the Netherstone. "Agree to marry me," Harlen demanded, "or your beloved dies."

Kaelyn's eyes filled with angry tears, and her contempt nearly overwhelmed her. She'd lost everything: her brother, her gran, her home—all because of the vile man who stood before her.

"Don't do it, Kaelyn!" Josiah blurted. "It's a trick!"

Bash drove his boot into Josiah's side. "Quiet, you!"

"What's it to be, my dear?" Harlen pressed.

Panic filled Kaelyn's heart. She couldn't lose Josiah—not again. Either way she chose, she'd lose him. It wasn't fair. "Fine," she spat, disgust in her gaze. "But just know I will make every waking moment of your life a living hell." She held her left hand out, turning her eyes away so she wouldn't have to watch.

"Kaelyn, no!" Josiah objected.

Harlen took hold of her hand, an evil smile on his lips. The ring was inches from her finger. She could feel the magic of it, realizing at once that something was off.

Suddenly a crossbow bolt whizzed through the air and pierced Harlen's hand straight through. The ring clattered across the floor. Harlen gritted his teeth to stifle a cry of pain, clutching his hand as he searched angrily for the culprit.

"Let her go, or the next one is aimed at your head," Casper's masked voice echoed through the chamber.

He crouched in the shadows of the rafters, hood drawn and crossbow in hand. He reloaded the weapon as all eyes turned toward him. Josiah smiled to himself, using the distraction to finish picking the locks on his wrists.

"Show yourself," Harlen growled.

The priest, whose bonds had been loosened by a jumpy guard, slowly backed away in search of somewhere to hide. Casper slipped from the rafters, nearly denting the floor as he landed. Harlen held his breath. Bash's eyes narrowed. Only a Netherworlder could jump from a height like that unscathed. "Shoot him!" the sheriff ordered.

Crossbow bolts flew at Casper instantaneously. He dodged left, right, and suddenly flipped in the air to avoid the last two. Every single bolt missed him by inches. The others looked on in awe.

"Who are you?" Harlen demanded. Blood soaked his hand, the bolt still stuck in his palm.

Casper slowly stepped into the light and removed his hood. Audible gasps echoed through the cavernous space. Kaelyn fell to her knees, mouth agape and eyes wide with shock.

"I'm the man who's come to send you back to hell," Casper spat.

He aimed and fired. The bolt sped through the air, closer and closer to its target. Bash knocked it out of the air with his sword. "Run, my lord!"

Josiah stole a dagger from one of the guards and sprang into action. The priest rushed for cover, muttering prayers under his breath. Everything became chaos. Casper tossed his now-useless crossbow aside as Josiah skillfully took down the four men surrounding him. Something told Casper the apprentice had done this before. More guards spilled into the room, encircling the two Netherworlders at Bash's command.

"Casper!" Kaelyn screamed.

Lord Harlen was dragging her toward the back exit of the chapel. She struggled like the fighter she was, and he only had one good hand to work with, having yanked the bolt from his palm. Kaelyn sent a rather impressive punch to Harlen's jaw with her free hand. The lord muttered a few curses, but his grip remained.

Casper rushed toward Harlen, but three of the black-clad men cut him off—assassins just like the one sent to kill Josiah.

"My lord!" Bash shouted.

Harlen turned, and Bash tossed him the ring.

Casper drew the Nethersword just in time to block an attack. He whirled, fending off another, and rounded just in time to parry the third. Before his death, Casper might have thought such odds impossible, but now it was child's play.

Steel rang against steel as he parried each attack, wounding and taking down Harlen's black-clad army with ease. Josiah fought at his back. They worked in conjunction with one another, like two arms on the same body.

"Casper!" Kaelyn shrieked, struggling against Bash, who'd taken possession of her.

Lord Harlen's goon dragged Casper's sister through the door behind the altar. Casper angrily stabbed the man he fought.

"Go!" Josiah shouted above the battle. "I can handle this!"

Casper hated the thought of leaving the apprentice on his own, but Kaelyn's screams pressed him to heed his friend's words. He wouldn't put it past Harlen to consummate his affections for Kaelyn before they wed. The thought made his blood boil.

Casper slashed through the next two men. "Be careful," he urged Josiah.

"Always am, mate," his friend replied cockily. Only six men remained—hardly an army.

Casper nodded, trusting his friend could handle his own. He raced for the door, passing the priest, who cowered behind a dusty pew. The door was bolted shut. Kaelyn's cries for help echoed through the passage beyond. An insurmountable rage ignited in Casper. He channeled it into action, growling as he kicked down the door. It flew right off its hinges. Kaelyn's blonde hair disappeared around the corner ahead.

Casper sprinted after them, sword in hand. He cried out as something sharp stabbed into his arm. He yanked out a dart. His brown eyes searched for the source, soon realizing the hall was lined with traps. Kaelyn's shouts spurred him forward. He tore off down the hall as fast as he could, barely keeping apace of the darts. A few grazed his skin, but Casper barely noticed the sting. His injured leg screamed in protest. Casper embraced the pain, refusing to succumb to it. He rounded the corner. A long flight of stairs spiraled upward. Casper took them two at a time, gripping his sword tightly in case of attack.

Another door stood in his way at the top. He kicked it down easily. It let out onto a sort of patio that ran the length of the roof. All seemed quiet. The Netherworlder paused and trained his ear on every sound. The wind tousled his hair. A bat flew overhead, chasing an insect. A muffled cry sounded at the far end of the massive balcony. A long line of chimneys blocked Casper's view. Cautiously, he ventured forward. He could feel eyes on him. Though his instincts were more attuned, Bash and Harlen were both Netherworlders. Against them, Casper was evenly matched. Underestimating them could mean the loss of Kaelyn.

A thrill ran down Casper's spine, and he dove aside just in time to miss the blow of Bash's sword. The sheriff swung again. Casper blocked.

"Fancy sword you've got there, Renolds," Bash quipped. "Steal it, did you?"

Casper blocked the sheriff's next three attacks and parried. "Not quite."

The sword seemed to know exactly what Casper needed it to do. It was like an extension of him. The magic appeared to sense another Netherworlder. Perhaps it would easily cut through them as it had the shriekers.

The miller stepped carefully, forcing Bash to circle in the other direction. If he could get to the end of the balcony, he might not be too late to stop this madness. Kaelyn's muffled cries for help were carried on the wind. Casper's jaw set, his tawny gaze cold and angry. He rushed at Bash, his back now to the row of chimneys. The blows between them were less playful, each landing with the intent of bringing death. Casper carefully backed inch by inch down the long patio as he fought. Bash parried a blow and kicked Casper into one of the chimneys. Brick dust rained down on impact.

"You're too late, Renolds," Bash chided. "Nothing more than a washed-up miller who thinks he's a hero."

Casper took a sharp breath in, clutching his chest. He was certain one of his ribs was cracked. Josiah appeared behind Bash, looking a little haggard from the fight but nonetheless determined. The apprentice had been so quiet, not even Casper had heard his approach. Casper smiled. "Don't make the mistake of thinking I'm the only Netherworlder here."

Bash's face painted with confusion, but before he could ask, Josiah's sword ran through him from behind. The sheriff looked down in shock. Blood pooled in his mouth. Casper didn't stay to watch what he was certain would be a brutal and satisfying death. He scrambled for the end of the balcony, not bothering to be silent. When he rounded the last chimney, horror consumed him.

Kaelyn glowed with Netherworld magic, the ring on her finger. She was tied up, Harlen atop her in the process of ripping through her clothes. The rage that filled Casper was all-consuming, erasing the kindhearted man he was. He barreled for Harlen with a ferocious growl. The Nethersword clattered to the ground, quite forgotten in Casper's fury. Bodies collided. Casper's hands clenched around Harlen's throat, and he slammed the tyrant's head repeatedly into the stonework.

Kaelyn breathed in relief, still struggling with her bonds. Though the rain had passed, the air was still cold and the ground damp. She shivered, now in nothing but her tattered muslin underdress. She screamed when someone suddenly grabbed her.

"Hey, it's me, love," Josiah soothed. "It's just me." He removed his hooded longcoat and wrapped it around her trembling shoulders. Once he dispatched the ropes, Kaelyn hugged the coat around her, quite embarrassed to be seen so improperly.

Casper dashed Harlen's head into the stones once more. The older man fleetly stabbed a knife into the crook of the lad's arm. Casper cried out, and Harlen kicked him off.

"You can't best me, lad," Harlen chided, drawing his sword.

Casper was beginning to feel the effects of being newly awoken. His limp was back, his head ached, and he felt as if he might collapse at any moment. He ripped the knife from his strong arm, backing away slowly. If Casper crossed blades with Harlen now, he'd do it with his weak hand, a less dangerous risk if Harlen weren't also a Netherworlder.

"I'd quit while you're ahead, boy," Harlen mused. "Leave now, and perhaps I'll let you live in my new world."

Casper's eyes flitted to the black Nethersword just out of reach. "You threatened my family," Casper seethed. "And killed Gran. Don't count your chickens just yet, mate."

"Had your parents killed too," Harlen gloated.

That did it. Casper snapped. He dove for his sword, barely ducking beneath Harlen's swing. A loud clang filled the air as their swords clashed, Casper on one knee and Harlen above him.

"Josiah! Get Kaelyn out of here!" Casper yelled. He pushed Harlen's sword off and rolled to his feet.

"You're too late, Renolds," Harlen spat, kicking Casper into the stone rail.

Casper cried out as his already-fractured ribs split all the more.

"The magic already flows in her veins. And once I kill you . . . she will be mine."

Kaelyn tried in vain to remove the ring, but it wouldn't budge. "Help him!" she demanded as Josiah tried to drag her away. "I can take care of myself! Help him!"

Josiah looked between Casper and the ring on Kaelyn's finger. The Netherstone was the problem, not Harlen. "I've an idea, but you won't like it."

Kaelyn looked from the ring to Josiah's emerald eyes. She understood. Fear consumed her, but it was the only way. The stone was melded to her by magic. "Do it," she said, voice wavering a little. "If it will end this madness, do it!"

Josiah took her hand, every bit of him wishing there were another way. "I'm sorry," he whispered.

Kaelyn closed her eyes, bracing herself. A heart-wrenching scream reverberated through the air as Josiah severed her finger.

Casper hardly blocked Harlen's next swing, thrown off-kilter by the blow. It took both hands to steady his sword. His arm seared, blood now soaking his dark sleeve down to his wrist. His parents. Gran. Everything he'd lost had all been because of this man. Pure hatred fueled Casper's weapon. He gave a battle cry and went on the offensive, hacking and jabbing for any part of Harlen's body he could reach. He came rather close to taking off the bastard's ear. Harlen grew nervous, but he had the advantage of age and experience, not to mention Casper's deteriorating state. The lad hadn't rested long enough after his return. He was weak, falling apart. Harlen used Casper's weak arm to his advantage, sending a kick to the bleeding wound.

Casper cried out and staggered back.

"Casper!" Josiah shouted.

Casper turned just in time to see the ring flying in his direction. Josiah ran at Harlen, cutting into the fight. Casper caught the Netherstone, not stopping to question why it was soaked in blood. Kaelyn trembled from behind the chimney. Josiah sent a well-placed blow to Harlen's face.

"Destroy it!" he shouted to his friend.

The world seemed to slow. Harlen's attention shifted. He saw the bloody ring in Casper's hand. Casper set it on the stone railing and raised the black sword.

"No!" Harlen growled, running for Casper. In doing so, he left himself wide open.

Josiah stabbed his sword through Harlen's exposed torso, stopping the tyrant in his tracks. Casper brought the black weapon crashing down on the Netherstone. A bright light exploded from it, knocking them all back. Casper slammed into the chimney and sunk to the ground.

"Cas!" Kaelyn cried. The tall chimney had saved her from the blast. She raced to his side, no longer glowing. She looked terrible—hair a mess, bloody hand wrapped tightly in cloth ripped from her underdress.

"I'm fine," he uttered, wincing. "I'm fine."

Everything pained him more in the world of the living than it had in the Netherworld.

"You're hurt," she countered.

"Aye. So are you," he reasoned.

Josiah approached, breathing heavily, bloody sword in hand. He grinned down at Casper. "Not bad . . . for a miller." He extended a hand.

Casper smiled and allowed the apprentice to hoist him up, wincing at the pull in his fractured ribs. Adrenaline was the only thing keeping him upright, and he knew it'd soon run its course. His attention moved to the dying Lord Harlen. Josiah helped Kaelyn stand as Casper approached the vile man. Blood filled Harlen's mouth and spilled from his stomach. "Have . . . mercy, lad," the man sputtered. "Kill me."

Casper's eyes grew cold and enraged. "Like you showed Gran or my parents? Like you showed me? You deserve to suffer!"

Kaelyn's gentle touch on his arm made him soften. He met her gaze inquisitively. She held Casper's blood-soaked sword in her good hand.

"Don't sink to his level, brother," she said tenderly. "You are far better than this. The Netherworld doesn't have to change you for the worst. The choice is yours."

Kaelyn held the Nethersword out to him with a gentle smile. "Be the man I know you are."

Everything inside Casper wanted to push the sword away, to make Harlen suffer and possibly die in the Netherworld. He was beyond furious. Why should he grant even a shred of mercy?

The tightness in his jaw told Kaelyn of his thoughts. "Please, Cas," she urged. "Let it go. Finish this."

Casper's eyes turned to Harlen's quaking body. It would take Harlen hours to die if Casper let him be. Josiah stood back, knowing the pain of Casper's choice well. The Netherworld changed all who passed through, but how it changed them was solely up to the survivor.

Casper met his sister's kind eyes. He saw faith in them. An unwavering faith in him and the choice he would make. Could he really betray that trust? For his own anger and the hatred pulsing through him, would he hurt his sister?

The frigid edge to Casper's gaze softened, and he carefully took the sword from Kaelyn's grasp. Kaelyn's smile widened. Josiah gave him an encouraging pat on the back. Casper faced Harlen, every human instinct within him rebelling against mercy. Harlen choked and sputtered on his own blood, unable to give a decent wisecrack.

"Don't get comfortable in the Netherworld," Casper said evenly. "You won't be there for long."

Before another word could be spoken, Casper drove the Nethersword through Lord Harlen's heart. The man jolted and let out his final breath. Casper felt an enormous weight lift from his shoulders, and with it, his remaining strength. He backed away slowly, head spinning. The Nethersword clattered to the ground.

Worry tinged Kaelyn's face. "Cas?"

All at once, he collapsed. Josiah barely caught him before he hit the ground.

"What's happening to him?" Kaelyn asked.

Shouts came from the stairwell. "Over here!"

"He returned only this morning," Josiah said. "His body wasn't ready for this."

Josiah's face, though rather near Casper, was blurry to the miller's sight once again. His ears thrummed with his heartbeat.

"Will he be all right?" Kaelyn demanded.

"I dunno," Josiah breathed.

Multiple footsteps pounded across the rooftop balcony. The last thing Casper saw was half a dozen Watchmen running toward them before he was plunged once again into blackness.

The Farrels

CASPER FULLY EXPECTED TO HEAR THE KEEPER'S VOICE, to once again be surrounded by the caverns that ran between the layers of the Netherworld. He was prepared this time to pass on and leave life behind, so long as his sister was safe, but death never came. Instead he was met with only darkness—an immense void. Through it, he heard garbled voices whispering unintelligible words. Now and then, he'd pick up his name or something in reference to his peaky appearance, but then he would fade yet again.

There was no telling how much time had passed when his eyes finally fluttered open. He was lying in a bed in a room he didn't recognize. The sheets were the softest silk, and the bed more comfortable still. Red cloth and wallpaper decorated the room, speaking of the wealth no doubt held by the family whose house it was. Such a color was very expensive, as the beetles used to make the dye were difficult to find. Casper had barely glanced around the room when he was bowled over by Kaelyn.

"Thank the Maker!" she cried, nearly choking him she held him so tightly. "I thought you'd never wake."

He patted her back tiredly, still not quite recovered. Everything was sore. When she finally pulled back, beaming, Casper could see the damage done. She looked almost anemic, likely from refusing to eat, as he was sure Harlen had tried to feed her, and the color of her bright hair had faded to a dull gold. She had a split lip and appeared a little bruised, but otherwise she was none too worse for the wear. Her hand had been properly bandaged, and she was dressed in a gown of brilliant blue. Casper felt much relieved to see her. He took her good hand as she sat on the edge of the bed.

"Where are we?" he murmured.

"In the Farrel home," she answered. "The mayor really is quite a lovely man. Stark rushed off the moment you left to tell our plight to him. Mr. Farrel was furious. He stormed the Watch and called all who were loyal to arms. Sent them straight off to help you. Once Iris awoke, she told them the full story, and the Farrels insisted we be brought here."

Casper perked up. "Iris?"

"Aye." Kaelyn beamed. "She's downstairs."

Casper tried to get up, but his sister pushed him back down. "Easy, Cas. The doctor said you need to take it easy for a week—bed rest and no excitement."

"Doctor?" Casper uttered, confused. His mind was still a bit groggy.

Kaelyn nodded. "He was here yesterday."

"Yesterday?"

"You've been out for nearly twenty-four hours," she explained.

The news almost made him panic. "Harlen . . . Bash . . ." He tried and failed to get a coherent thought out.

"The Watch took care of them," Kaelyn promised. "They're gone. Burned. They won't be coming back again."

"So . . . it's really over?" he asked in disbelief. Kaelyn squeezed his hand and nodded. "And Iris . . . she's all right?"

"Aye."

A flood of relief washed through him, all fear and concern erased at his sister's words. It gave him a new sense of strength.

"I want to see her," he insisted, trying again to get up. This time Kaelyn didn't push him back down. He looked hastily about for something to throw on over his nightshirt. A robe was laid over the back of a nearby chair. Nothing could have stopped him from diving out of bed and throwing it on, not even his sister. He had to see Iris for himself.

"Cas," Kaelyn tried to slow him down. "Be careful. No excitement, remember!"

But he was already barreling for the door, a sense of his clumsiness coming back. He moved down the mahogany-lined hallway as swiftly as he was able, taking the steps two and three at a time. He skidded to a stop in the dimly lit foyer. Voices floated from the parlor. He edged his way toward them, weak in body but far too resolved in spirit to care. Kaelyn's footsteps sounded on the stair behind him. She could tell there was no stopping him, but she could at least make sure he didn't fall or hurt himself again. The door creaked open at his behest, and every eye in the parlor turned his way. There was only one pair of brilliant green eyes that he noticed: Iris.

She was sitting on the loveseat next to her father, dressed in a calm green gown and looking more beautiful than Casper remembered. Her ginger hair was braided over her shoulder, and her eyes seemed to sparkle when she realized he was awake. Iris rose slowly, caring little about propriety and the fact that her parents were present. To Casper and Iris, no one else was in the room. They bolted for one another in unison, embracing as if they thought the world would pull them apart again at any given moment.

"You're alive," she murmured. "Thank the Maker, you're alive!"

To the chagrin of everyone in the room, Iris pulled Casper into a passionate but tender kiss that surprised even him.

Kaelyn tinged pink and averted her gaze. Josiah came to stand beside her, an almost proud look on his face. John Farrel turned to his wife. She shrugged innocently. "Don't look at me. She's *your* daughter."

When Iris pulled back, both of them were breathless. Casper rested his forehead against hers in a stupor. A lazy smile crossed his lips, and she nearly laughed, she was so overcome with good emotions. Words were needless between them to convey what they felt—relief and an overwhelming, unspoken affection.

"You should sit down," she said, once the moment passed and she remembered where they were standing. "You're not supposed to be out of bed."

"Right," he uttered, still overrun with shock and disbelief. She was there. She was alive. He was alive. Harlen was dead. He almost expected it all to be a dream.

Iris helped him to sit on the opposite loveseat.

"It's just as well," Mr. Farrel said. "I was hoping to have a word . . . alone."

Casper shared a look with Iris. She nodded as if saying it was safe to be alone with her father.

"Come on, then," Cordelia Farrel ordered the others. "Let's vacate the room. I'll have the maid make us a spot of tea."

As the others filtered out, Casper glanced back, catching Josiah's eye. His friend winked, a silent *Well done, mate.*

Finally left alone with the mayor, Casper's hands suddenly felt clammy. They hadn't even been properly introduced, and he was already snogging Mr. Farrel's daughter in front of him. He half expected the man to be upset, but instead he seemed amused.

"Iris has told me much about you, Mr. Renolds," the mayor began. "You're a very brave young man."

"Thank you, sir," Casper replied modestly.

"It is I who should be thanking you, lad," Mr. Farrel corrected. "You saved my daughter's life . . . and perhaps the city itself. I have been so blinded to the vile deeds happening right under my nose, but you have brought them to light."

Casper didn't know what to say.

The mayor continued, "I was very sorry to hear about the mill and your grandmother."

"Nothing can be done about it now, I suppose," Casper mused.

"No," Mr. Farrel agreed. "I suppose not, but I can offer you something as repayment for what you've done."

Casper's face twisted in confusion. "Sir?"

"A job."

Casper's mind spun like a top. He hadn't really thought about what to do once Harlen was dispatched. It never dawned on him that he no longer had a home or a way to make a living. "A job, sir?"

"Aye," Mr. Farrel replied. "As it turns out, I'm in need of a new sheriff . . . one who's a little more trustworthy."

Again, Casper was at a loss for words. The post paid well and came with lodging—more than Casper could have ever hoped to achieve.

"I realize it's a bit sudden. You may, of course, have time to think it over."

It was indeed a lot of responsibility, far greater than Casper had ever been asked to take on. He was still in awe over the multitude of blessings seemingly occurring at once. "Why me?" he wondered.

Mr. Farrel's eyes were kind as he observed Casper, full of sympathy and understanding. "Because you have demonstrated a kind of bravery I have not seen in a long time, and a will to do what is right over what is easy. You are a different breed, Mr. Renolds—a rare breed. The Watch could use a goodhearted man like you at its head."

"I'll think on it," Casper promised, overwhelmed.

"Good man," the mayor said as he rose to his feet. "And now I think it's time we got you back to bed. The doctor will not react kindly to your being out of it."

He held a hand out to Casper, which the latter accepted gratefully. Iris smiled at Casper in the foyer as her father helped him back up the grand staircase. Casper smiled back. For the first time in years, Casper knew everything was going to be all right.

CHAPTER TWENTY-EIGHT

Lumen

MONTHS HAD PASSED SINCE CASPER'S RETURN AND THE defeat of Lord Harlen. As it turned out, destroying the Netherstone had broken whatever curse lay upon Iris, thus allowing her to return to the land of the living as a Netherworlder. No one could really be sure why she was tethered to the stone or how Harlen had managed it, but Casper hardly cared. He was simply glad to have her back, and he didn't intend to waste a single moment of their mortality together. Casper had accepted John Farrel's job offer and quickly took up the lodging in the city. It was nothing quite so grand as Iris's home, but with Kaelyn's touch it was grand enough for the two Renolds siblings. Both were simple people, desiring little in the ways of finery.

Josiah eventually told Casper about him and Kaelyn, which at first took the older Renolds by surprise. After much consideration, however, Casper found that he couldn't have picked a better match himself, and so he blessed their courting as the male guardian in her life. As time progressed, life took a turn toward a new normal. Casper made it his duty to weed out the corrupt in the Watch, replacing them with men who would better serve the city. He made a move with the mayor to abolish the Netherworlder Registration Act, as it only promoted fear and did nothing to keep the villainous ones at bay. This was a great relief to Josiah, who'd been hiding his status for six years. The ridiculous curfew enforced by Bash and his men was eradicated, and slowly the city began to breathe again.

Still the hardest of Casper's tasks was fulfilling his promise to little Thomas Frye. When he ventured into the Slums near the wharf, all the downtrodden souls he passed scuttled away in fear. He supposed the Watch hardly dared enter the dirtiest part of the city, but Casper was glad he did. It directed his attention to a dire need he intended to later address. Upon finding the Frye home, he discovered the father to still be very ill. Thomas's mother wept when Casper explained the reason for his visit, and the new sheriff allowed her to cry on his shoulder, a few tears of his own threatening to leak down his cheeks. He'd been very fond of the lad. As a show of his compassion, Casper later sent the doctor their way, all expenses paid, and spoke to their landlord about holding the rent, promising to take care of it until the family could get back on their feet.

As far as Casper was concerned, life couldn't get much better. People were no longer afraid to leave their homes, and the Watch was never more effective. Kaelyn was happier than he'd ever seen her. Her bright eyes and cheerful manner were contagious every morning, continuing to encourage him that he'd done the right thing. Even more thrilling was the addition of Iris in his life. Casper had never thought of marrying and settling down, but the more time he spent with her, the more it became a possibility until finally, with her father's permission, he worked up the courage to ask her the most important question he'd ever asked in all his life. She said yes and kissed him with such fervor, he went pink around the ears. It seemed to him that the Netherworld and all its terrors were far behind them. He didn't know then just how wrong he was.

The spring festival was in full swing at the center of the city. Colored streamers and bright ribbons adorned the lampposts and shop windows. Scents of lavender, honeysuckle, and rose joined the smells of various cakes and pies. Music wafted through the air, joined by laughter and the claps of bystanders, all watching couples dance to a lively tune. Casper stood at the edge of the dance floor. He looked official in the black longcoat of a Watchman, badge on his chest and a smile on his face.

"Stop fiddling with it," he whispered to Iris who was standing beside him.

She was wearing a dress of gentle violet with her red hair piled high in a beautiful ribbon. A sparkling diamond ring sat on her left hand, twinkling every time she twisted it around her finger. She dropped her hands indignantly.

"I'm not," she insisted.

"Yes, you are," Casper replied, entwining their fingers.

It was different seeing Iris in a dress. He'd seen her in armor and trousers, wielding weapons no other woman he knew would dare touch, but since their return she'd become the mayor's daughter again. This meant parties, gowns, and all the trappings her status could afford. It was a side of Iris that Casper had greatly enjoyed getting to know over the past few months.

Josiah spun Kaelyn around the dance floor, the two of them less shy about their attraction now that they had Casper's approval. Kaelyn looked radiant in a dress of bright blue, her golden hair twisted up with forget-me-not flowers. The smile on her lips seemed to light up the square, and Casper never tired of seeing it. As the music swelled and the dancers spun, something else caught Casper's eye: a bright red glow. He looked instinctively to the Nethersword, sheathed as always at his side. The jewel was alight. First bewilderment crossed his face, then concern. He shared a look with Iris. She too had stiffened.

"I'll look into it," he whispered. "Stay here and watch for anything suspicious. Are you armed?"

"What do you think?" she replied with a smirk.

That brought a half-smile to Casper's lips. He didn't dare ask *where* she was armed. Knowing full well that she could take care of herself, Casper wandered off in search of what had brought the sword to life. He kept the blade hidden beneath his longcoat so as not to draw attention to himself. The ruby in its hilt hadn't glowed since the final trial, a fact that concerned Casper. What in Wayland could possibly make it shine? It was only when well away from the party that he dared pull out the weapon. The jewel fluctuated, seeming brighter when he went in the direction of the nearby back alley. The sound of the festivities faded away as he entered, muffled by the alley's brick wall that rose high on either side. The sunlight wasn't as strong here, making the path akin to a dark maze. There were all manner of dark creatures that would enjoy hiding in such a space. He wasn't sure he wanted to discover which one had chosen to do so now.

Casper followed the jewel's glow around one turn and then another. It brought him to a dead end, where the back doors of businesses and homes let out. He paused, listening. The music and jovial laughter of the festival had completely gone.

"Looking for me?" a familiar voice broke the unnerving silence.

Casper whirled, sword aloft, to see Nex standing there dressed in royal blue fineries.

"Easy, lad," the god soothed, hands up in surrender. "I am many things, but I am not my brother."

The words took longer to process than usual. Casper kept his sword trained on the man who looked so much like Nex, it was hard to believe otherwise. They were twins in every way, but the longer he stared, the more Casper noted the differences. This man's beard was better groomed and less scraggly, his eyes were kinder, and his face lacked a certain sneer.

"But if you're not him," Casper started, "then—"

"You may call me Lumen," the god spoke, finally lowering his hands.

Casper nearly dropped his sword, staring in awe, eyes wide as saucers and mouth agape like a panting dog. Should he bow? Fall to his knees?

"You don't have to do either," Lumen answered Casper's thoughts.

"You can read my mind?"

"In a manner of speaking," he replied.

Casper merely stood there, dumbfounded. His mind tumbled over and over, filled with questions and statements, none of which he seemed able to present. Lumen stood by patiently, quite understanding Casper's shock.

"There is something you wish to ask me," the god stated, pressing Casper to speak.

Casper shook himself out of it. "Er—several things, actually," Casper uttered, finally sheathing the sword before he could make himself look more ridiculous than he was certain he already did.

"The first?"

Lumen, of course, already knew what was on the man's mind, but for the sake of politeness, he gave Casper a chance to ask.

Casper decided to start with the easiest question. "Why can I see you?"

"All who pass through the trials and return to Wayland have the ability . . . if I allow them," Lumen answered.

"Why show yourself to me?"

"Because you are different from most, Casper. You didn't give in to my brother's dark temptations."

"But Josiah—"

"Will see me in time," Lumen assured. "You are both but two of many valuable puzzle pieces in a far grander plan."

"Why me?" he asked the question that plagued him most of all.

"Because you were innocent," Lumen said. "Innocence unjustly slain leaves a mark—a power far greater than any my brother will ever understand. If he did, he wouldn't have encouraged your murder."

"Encouraged my murder?"

"Oh, yes. Nex may no longer be in this realm, but his influence, unfortunately, still extends here."

Casper mulled over the Maker's words. The thought that his death had changed anything was odd to Casper. He was nobody—just a miller trying to make his way. He didn't see how he'd made any difference.

"You've made all the difference in the world, Casper," Lumen once again answered his thoughts. "You've brought hope—the most powerful magic we have in all the realms. The tiniest drop can topple empires. You did it all by merely being yourself."

Casper remained speechless. Had he really done all that?

Lumen spoke, this time more gravely, "There is more on the horizon than Harlen, I'm afraid. My brother thinks he is winning, which means we still have a chance."

"A chance? At what?"

"To end him."

It seemed odd to Casper for anyone to talk so callously of a sibling, but he'd met Nex. The Maker's twin was vile and malicious—Thomas was proof of that.

"I'm sorry you've suffered so much at his hand," Lumen said with the greatest of sympathy.

Casper was taken by surprise. The man before him had created Wayland and even Casper himself, and he was apologizing? Casper had to admit the Maker was nothing like he'd imagined.

"Why does he hate you so much?" he asked. Nex had been very adamant about the sword and stopping whatever path Lumen had quietly set Casper on.

"It's hard to say," Lumen admitted, eyes far off in thought. "We were close in the beginning, but I'm a god of creation and he, a god of mischief. I suppose we were always meant to oppose each other in the end—the dark and the light." He turned his gaze on Casper, a seriousness in them that rocked Casper to his core. "A war is coming, one that will shake Wayland to its knees. When the times comes, I need you to be ready for the end."

Casper's mouth suddenly felt dry. "The end? The end of what?"

Lumen's words echoed on the wind like a prophesy. "The end of the Netherworld."

The Maker faded away, leaving Casper alone in the dark alley, dumbfounded. He'd thought for certain his new life would be the end of all the madness, but he now realized the madness had only just begun.

Acknowledgments

Acknowledgements are, by far, the hardest part of any book for me to write. There's a never-ending list of people to thank, and it grows exponentially with each project. I wish I had enough space at the back of this book to thank each person in my life who deserves recognition for their support, but that list could fill an entire novel. So, my first acknowledgement goes out to every person who sat next to me at the university coffee shop to ask me what I was working on, to every friend over the last few years who read rough pages I stuck under their nose, and to the MVPs who let me ramble about plot points that were driving me crazy. Your importance is not forgotten.

The publication of this novel would not be possible without the reactions of a few specific individuals. First I must thank my cousin Candi for reading the original draft of this book way back in 2015. It was an absolute mess then, and I'm embarrassed anyone ever saw that draft, but you read it and loved it enough to tell me not to give up on the story. It would still be hiding in the bottom of my trunk without you.

To my dear cousin Roxanne: Your love and excitement for this story are infectious, and your reaction upon finishing the last line in this book is still saved on my phone. This book wouldn't be in print if your encouragement hadn't spurred me to never give up on it.

Katie, my sister and biggest fan, you have read everything I've written since I was fourteen, and this was no exception. Though some of your criticisms irked me at first, they brought about much-needed changes that made the final novel even better. I'd be lost without you.

There is nothing more encouraging as a writer than to have a professor believe in you, even long after you've left school. A hearty and sincere thanks to Ron Davis. You not only read a draft of this cover to cover but also offered your help and have bought every novel I've published since. Your encouragement and belief in me kept me from giving up. Thank you!

As always, I must thank my amazing editors: Jon, Amy, and Robin. At first, I was nervous about how this book would be received, but your notes and reactions gave me hope that maybe I could do this crazy thing after all. I gave you a lump of coal, and you returned to me a diamond. This story is so dear to my heart, and your support of it means the world.

To Ashley: the Pan to my Hook and my forever friend. We've been through so much together over the years. You bring much-needed pixie dust into my life. Your support of my creative endeavors and all your hard work on this novel are worth more than I could ever put into words.

To my entire family, extended and immediate, your love and support keep me going. Not one of you called me crazy or tried to suppress my writerly habits as a child. Instead, you've supplied me with journals, ink, and pens over the years, many of which were used to pen this very novel. Writing is an extremely lonely profession, but I have never truly done it alone. Thank you for being my anchor to reality and my inspiration to keep going.

Finally, I must thank God for this story's fruition. When inspiration ran dry, You fueled my pen. When I wanted to give up, You gave me what I needed to keep going. I create because You first created. Thank you for enabling me to do the coolest job in the world.

About the Author

Ari Ryder is a mystery, science fiction, and fantasy writer who revels in the thrill of a good adventure. When she isn't writing, she can usually be found studying forensic science, traveling on research trips, and solving impossible puzzles. Ari has a master's in publishing from The George Washington University, which has forever deepened her love and appreciation of books. Ari currently lives in Virginia with her stubborn Siberian Husky, where she's working on her next novel.